What People Are Saying about *Secrets and Lies*

"Through memorable characters and a plot that keeps you turning the pages, Rhonda McKnight takes you on an emotional roller coaster ride that holds you hostage until the end! A wonderful debut!"

—**Victoria Christopher Murray**, *Essence* Bestselling Author of *Lady Jasmine and Too Little, Too Late*

"Rhonda McKnight has written an emotional but inspiring story of faith, trust and forgiveness as well as the importance of having God in our lives. *Secrets and Lies* also reminds us that just as a braid requires 3 strands—so does marriage: Husband, wife and God. I truly enjoyed this story and would recommend that not only married couples, but anyone thinking of getting married, read it."

—**Jacquelin Thomas**, *Essence* Bestselling Author of *Jezebel* and *Redemption*

"Rhonda McKnight is a fresh new voice in Christian fiction who writes with the skill and grace of a seasoned pro. Her characters seem like friends and her prose flows effortlessly. Pick up *Secrets and Lies* and prepare for a long night – you won't want to put it down until you reach the satisfying end."

—**Stacy Hawkins Adams**, National Bestselling Author of *The Someday List* and *Watercolored Pearls*

"Great debut! Rhonda McKnight is definitely an author to watch. *Secrets and Lies* was a thoroughly enjoyable read with well developed characters and lots of thought provoking lessons for all."

—**Sherri Lewis**, *Essence* Bestselling Author of *The List* and *My Soul Cries Out*

"Rhonda McKnight's debut novel doesn't disappoint. It mixes appealing and relatable characters with doses of drama and mischief that kept me hooked until the last page."

—**Tia McCollors**, *Essence* Bestselling Author of *The Truth About Love* and *A Heart of Devotion*

SECRETS AND LIES

RHONDA MCKNIGHT

www.urbanchristianonline.net

Urban Books, LLC
1199 Straight Path
West Babylon, NY 11704

ISBN- 13: 978-1-60162-940-1
ISBN- 10: 1-60162-940-0

First Printing December 2009
Printed in the United States of America

10 9 8 7 6 5 4 3 2 1

Distributed by Kensington Corp.
Submit Wholesale Orders to:
Kensington Publishing Corp.
C/O Penguin Group (USA) Inc.
Attention: Order Processing
405 Murray Hill Parkway
East Rutherford, NJ 07073-2316
Phone: 1-800-526-0275
Fax: 1-800-227-9604

Dedication

In loving memory of my Auntie, *Laura Wilson*. I know you really, really wanted to see this novel finished. I miss you.

and

Donna Mitchell, my 10th grade Honors English Teacher and advisor for the school paper, *The Megaphone*. You saw the potential a long time ago.

Acknowledgements

Wow! I can't believe I'm actually writing acknowledgements. How cool is that? First, I want to thank my Lord and Savior Jesus Christ for the gift. I feel so honored to have been trusted with something so powerful. I pray *Secrets and Lies* glorifies you in every word and on every page.

My parents, Jimmy and Bessie McKnight: Mom and Dad, thanks so much for shaping me into the person I am today and for your role in my purpose. Dad, I've always heard about the poetry you wrote for Mom when you were dating, so I'm thinking the writing was your contribution. Mom, thank you for instilling in me that spirit of excellence and supporting me in every dream I've ever shared with you. You both taught me to believe I could do anything I set my mind to.

To my sons, Aaron and Micah: I hope one day you'll understand how much this accomplishment is about you. I pray to be a living example of the legacy of purpose. Walk in your God-given talents. Aaron, thanks for keeping your little brother entertained, changing his diapers, and getting him snacks while I clicked away at the keyboard to get this story down. I couldn't have done this without you.

Cynthia and Kenny McKnight, I love you! You know that. You are the best little sister and brother a girl could have. Please continue to reach for your dreams and don't let anything get in the way. Cynthia, thanks for staying with the kids so I could go to *Faith and Fiction*. You'll never know how much that meant to me.

I have two friends that I just can't thank enough. Seriously, I had to flip a coin to figure out who went first. Margaret Brown . . . heads . . . you're first. This book would NOT have happened if it weren't for you and Caleb. Thanks so much for taking care of Micah on soooooooooo many Saturdays and Sunday afternoons while I stole away to the *Chick-Fil-A* and *Dunkin Donuts* down the street to write. Janice Ingle, second, but always first, you read every version of this story from its horrible little beginnings to the finished product it is today. How many drafts was it? Way too many, but you hung in there with a sistah. Thanks so much for believing in me.

Aaron Coleman—here's a shout out to you! Thanks for keeping me on task. You have no idea how the question, "How's the book coming?" kept me in front of the computer. Thanks for keeping my feet to the fire.

Now, for my writer friends: We all know that no one does this by themselves. First and foremost I have to give immeasurable love to my literary godmother, Victoria Christopher Murray. God chose you, so you are blessed and highly favored to be the birth-mother of the African American Christian fiction genre. You paved the way for this genre with *Temptation* in 1997. It's been ten years since you first encouraged me to write the story of my heart. I finally did it. Thanks also for taking me under your wing and showing me and so many others how to do Luke 19:13 ". . . occupy until He comes." I appreciate your leadership, mentorship, and friendship. There's nobody like you!

Jacquelin Thomas, thank you for answering every little

email I've ever sent you over the years and taking time to show love and support for aspiring writers. Patricia Haley, Angela Benson, Stacy Hawkins Adams, Marilynn Griffith, Claudia Mair Burney, Sharon Ewell Foster, Michelle Sutton, Carmen Green and Pamela Samuels Young—I love your work and really appreciate your advice and encouragement. Jacquelin and Stacy, thanks so much for reading *Secrets and Lies* and endorsing it. Tiffany Warren, thank you for the vision of the *Faith and Fiction Retreat*.

Now for the brightest, baddest writing sistah girlfriends on the planet, *Atlanta Black Christian Fiction Writers*: Y'all know I appreciate you letting me in your little group. I mean what's the number 9 without a 10 behind it? Big hugs and lots of love to Sherri Lewis for encouraging me to be excellent about the craft and for always getting a critique done in a tight. Tia McCollors, you were the first to be published, and you'll always set the standard for doing it with class, girl. Love you! Dee Stewart, you taught me everything I know, and I still haven't got all that stuff out of that head of yours. You are the ultimate story genius. I can't wait to hold your Christy Award winner in my hand. (That's prophetic—reach out and grab it.) Veronica Fields Johnson, I don't know where I'd be if you hadn't invited me to that first meeting. Thanks so much for listening to the Holy Spirit and for giving me feedback on the book. Vanessa Madden, another sharp eye that the literary world has yet to behold. Thanks for the feedback. Ashea Goldson, you know you motivated a sister like no one else. Stepped out there and sold your book while I was slackin'. LaMonica, Sharrunn, and Trina—come on now. I'm waiting and so is the world. *Visions in Print*, thanks for all your support and love. Shawneda Marks—you are so next!

To my new family at *Urban Christian Books*: I'm proud to be in the number. Kendra Norman-Bellamy, Dwan Abrams, Sharon Oliver and Monique Miller, thanks for all the tidbits of knowledge. Joylynn Jossel, thanks so much for taking my novel out of the "NO" pile. Great is your reward in heaven. My agent, Sha-Shana Crichton, thanks for taking me on and believing in me. I promise to make you some money one day! Dana Pittman of *Nia Promotions*, thanks for reading and giving me feedback. You should be on the payroll by now.

Jeannie Buffington, I appreciate your expertise on the ADR and mediation stuff. I hope I got it right. To my other *Mercer* classmates, I can't think about "purpose" without thinking of you. You'll always be a part of every journey. Desmond Miller, thanks for helping me make Jonah a real man with a real issue. Sherri Lewis, gotta give you some more love for the medical stuff. The same for all the women in my family who make a living in healthcare. See, I was listening. Donnell Kennedy, cuz, when you gonna admit you bleached that dialyzer☺.

Other people I love: Heather Miller, Travis and Chelsea Miller, Felesia Bowen, Sharon Armstead, Aunt Nell, Aunt Delores (Sis), Aunt Dot, Uncle Downing, Etta Hill. Thanks for your support. If I left you out, forgive me. There's always book two.

And last but not least, my husband, Basil Nain, thank you for buying my first computer and first comfortable chair and not complaining about why it took me 10 years to produce a book. I appreciate you believing in me. Big hug and Love Always.

To My Readers:

The doctrine of the Trinity—that God the Father, God the Son, and God the Holy Spirit are each equally and eternally the one true God—is the foundation of the Christian faith. John 14:26 says, *"But the Comforter, which is the Holy Spirit, whom the Father will send in my name, he shall teach you all things and bring all things to your remembrance, whatsoever I have said unto you."*

The Comforter, the Holy Spirit, is the small voice in our head that comes from a place in our hearts. The Holy Spirit challenges us, chastises us, comforts us, but most importantly, guides us. In *Secrets and Lies*, **bold** print is used to indicate the voice of the Holy Spirit.

I pray Jonah and Faith's story touches your heart. Thanks for your support.

SECRETS AND LIES

Chapter 1

He's cheating. Faith Morgan pushed the END button on the phone. Three hang ups in two hours. She tried to shake off the sense of foreboding she felt every time it happened, but she couldn't. Her heart pounded as she walked back to the island where she'd been chopping the ingredients for her husband's favorite meal. She looked at the piles of sausage and shrimp; the onions, and other vegetables that were next in line to be sliced and diced. She wanted to swipe everything into the trash can. Jonah didn't deserve this hard work. Not if some woman was calling their home.

Faith's shoulders dropped, she leaned her weight back against the counter and let her sneakered feet slide forward along the slick tile until they met the grout and stopped. She had ten years invested in this marriage. It had to last. She couldn't march down the aisle a third time. It was so Zsa Zsa Gabor-ish. And the truth was, she loved him. She loved the way he looked, she loved the way his scent filled her nostrils when he kissed her good-bye in the morning, she loved that husky quality his voice had just before he fell asleep at night, and she loved the way he touched her—when things were good between them.

A burst of giggles erupted from the family room, and she looked up to see Elise, her four-year-old, who remained positioned in front of the television. Elise adored her father. And at the age of ten, Eric was approaching that time in his life when he'd need a man to help him sort through the man stuff. This wasn't just about her and whether or not she loved Jonah. She was fighting for the children too.

The ringing of the phone nearly sent her heart into spasms. *Not again,* she thought. Faith pushed herself off the counter and took the few steps necessary to reach the receiver. She looked at the caller ID, let out the breath she'd been holding, and picked up the phone.

"Hey, girl," she said.

"I have a taste for Ben and Jerry's Chunky Monkey. I've been craving it for three days."

Faith's mouth fell into an easy smile. "So have it. Get some New York Chocolate Chunk for me."

"No no no," Yvette Taylor shrieked. "You're supposed to talk me out of it. Some friend you are. I need to lose five pounds to fit into the dress for the women's banquet."

"What you need to do is buy a new dress and stop trying to fit into things you wore in college," Faith teased.

"Very funny, Miss Forever A Perfect Six. This *is* a new dress. It's just the same size as the dresses I wore in college." Yvette was barely able to keep the laughter out of her voice. "You're not the only one who can maintain her girlish figure. A sistah can fight to keep the pounds down."

A small smile parted Faith's lips as she moved back to the island and began scooping the food she'd chopped into a large bowl. "You've dialed the wrong number if you're looking for someone to tell you to watch your calories. I'm making gumbo."

"Gumbo in May? You only start chopping and cutting up stuff when you're stressed. What's up?"

Faith emptied the bowl into a large pot of soup that was simmering on the stove. Then she looked to make sure Elise was still distracted by the television.

"More phone calls," she whispered.

Yvette was silent for a moment. "Are they still not saying anything?"

"Just silence and hang-ups."

"Did you call the phone company?"

"No." Faith bit her bottom lip.

"Why not?" Yvette asked. "You're torturing yourself."

Faith let her eyes fall on the four-carat diamond that weighed down her ring finger and swallowed. "I don't know. I just . . ." She took a deep breath. "Losing, I think," she whispered. "Losing everything I have."

"Faith, you're trippin'. It's probably just kids or some telemarketing company. Women don't call wives anymore. Those heifers out there just wanna have fun, not wash some man's drawers. I'm telling you, it's not what you're thinking."

Faith wanted to believe that, but she had a bad feeling—a hair-rising-on-the-back-of-her-neck kind of feeling—that it was no prank or computer glitch in a telemarketer's system. Jonah worked late all the time, or so he said. He could easily have another woman with the hours he kept. A wave of nausea swept over her. Just the thought of her husband with another woman made her sick.

"Faith . . ." Yvette's voice broke through. "Don't sit around there acting like a victim. That's not even your style. Call the phone company and have them put a trace on the calls."

Yvette was right. "I'll call. I promise. First thing in the morning."

"You have the interview in the morning. Call now."

Faith's eyes rolled upward. She'd forgotten about that. "I should cancel."

Yvette didn't say anything.

"I haven't worked in five years. I'm just going to embarrass myself."

"Girl, please. You have the bomb resume. You shouldn't be afraid to step out with it."

But Faith was afraid. She was afraid of everything. Afraid to go on the interview, afraid of how her husband would react if she found a job, and afraid someone else was stealing her man. *Jesus.* She had to get it together.

"Look, I'm about to get on the interstate, and I don't have my earpiece."

Faith nodded at the phone as if Yvette could see her. "Thanks for listening."

"What are friends for? You listen to me complain about my money problems."

"And food cravings," Faith added with a smile.

"That's right."

"Well, girlfriend, pass on the Chunky Monkey. Nothing tastes better than that dress will look on you."

"I know that's right." Yvette let out a cackle. "Later."

Faith put the phone on the counter, picked up a large spoon, and stirred her masterpiece. That's what Jonah had called it the last time she prepared her mother's gumbo recipe. He loved her cooking. He loved her. At least she thought he did. But they had been fighting about everything lately—and now the phone calls. Faith felt tears welling. She clenched her teeth. Yvette was right.

She had to be a woman about this. Let the phone company trace the calls. If he was cheating, she'd have to deal with it.

"Mommy, is the gumba soup almost done?" Elise had crept up and was now pulling the tail of her blouse.

Faith kept her back to her until she got her face together. Forcing a smile, she turned. Elise reminded Faith of sunshine standing there with her long auburn curls falling in ringlets around her small heart-shaped face.

"Mommy, why are you sad?"

Faith tried to mask her feelings by forcing another smile. She lowered her body so that she was almost eye level to her daughter. "Mommy's not sad, honey."

"You are too. Your smile is not in your eyes," Elise said. "Are you mad at Daddy?"

Faith crossed her fingers behind her back. "No, baby. I'm not mad at Daddy."

"Good. 'Cause I don't like it when you and Daddy are mad."

Elise's words stung. So much for hiding their problems from the children. Obviously she hadn't done that as well as she thought. The child knew a phony smile when she saw one, and there had been plenty of those in the past few months.

"Why don't you let me finish cooking so we can eat and go to church."

"But I wanna help you," Elise whined.

Faith needed Elise out of the room. She felt guilty about it, but her emotions were too raw to deal with her children right now. Besides, it was still possible that she could call the phone company today, and she didn't want Elise to overhear.

"Why don't you go upstairs and find your smock? I bet they'll let you paint tonight."

Elise was silent for a moment, obviously considering her mother's offer.

Faith leaned over and playfully swirled her index finger around in her daughter's bellybutton. Girlish giggles filled the kitchen as she scooped Elise up in one arm and continued to tickle her with her free hand.

"Okay, okay, Mommy." Elise was hysterical with laughter. "I'll go, I'll go."

Once Elise's feet were planted on the floor, she scampered away, clearly satisfied to have gotten some of her mother's attention.

Faith watched her leave the kitchen. *My smile's not in my eyes.* Jonah's draining the life out of me. She clucked her teeth, let out a long breath, and walked back to the sink. She had just begun wiping the counters when the shrill ring of the telephone froze her in her tracks.

The caller ID read UNAVAILABLE.

Faith pressed the talk button and brought it to her ear. "Hello."

Silence.

"Why don't you say something?"

Silence again.

"You don't have anything better—"

"You're stupid." The words cut her off just before she heard the dull drone of the dial tone.

A stun gun wouldn't have shocked her more. Her harasser had spoken, but they'd done it so quickly that she couldn't tell if it were a man or a woman. She did hear one thing though—they'd called her stupid. That didn't sound like a kid. That sounded like someone who thought she was being a fool.

The call to the telephone company had been quick and painless. After telling them about the frequency and nature of the calls, they set her up with a call trace feature. Because of the volume of the calls, it would only take a few weeks to record a sufficient number to get a good trace, and then she could block all phone calls with unavailable identification. They also suggested she take the information to the police and really stop whoever was doing this. Yvette was right; it was time for her to stop behaving like a victim.

"Mommy, Eric is home," Elise shouted from the top of the stairs. Her bedroom faced the front of the house, and as usual, she bolted out of the room to announce anyone who was approaching before they could ring the bell.

Faith went to the door and opened it. She waved to the baseball coach as he pulled his van away from the curb. Eric walked up the driveway, head down and shoulders slumped.

"What's up?" Faith closed the door once he stepped in.

"Coach says he's moving me to right field if I don't get better by the next game." Eric choked out the words. "He's going to put T.J. on first base instead of me. T.J.'s dad practices with him everyday. That's why he's better than me."

Faith felt like a knife had sliced her heart. Of course. T.J.'s dad, Rashad's dad, Ryan's dad, Ben Wilson's dad . . . all the dads spent time with their boys. They attended practices and games, but Jonah didn't. Jonah Morgan said he didn't have time.

"I don't know. Some people are gifted to play certain sports. You know basketball is your favorite."

"That's not it. Coach said I would be better if I practiced." He pounded his small fist into his baseball glove. "Do you think Dad will be at my game tomorrow?"

His eyes were searching hers. He was so desperate for her to say yes, that Jonah would come. Faith felt the knife in her heart plunge a little deeper. "I hope so, honey. I'll ask him tonight. In the meantime, go wash up and change. We're going to church after dinner."

Eric looked at her like she had delivered even worse news than the coach.

"I'll take you for ice cream afterward," she chimed to build anticipation.

He tried not to show it, but she was sure she'd just won him over. She noted a little more pep in his step as he climbed the stairs to his bedroom. Ice cream did it every time.

Faith's frustration level was rising. How many times had her son looked her in the eye and asked about his father? How many games and school activities had he had to bear the disappointment of not seeing his father amongst the attendees? Faith knew when she was growing up, fathers didn't always attend these types of events. Cheering mothers were in residence. It was their motherly duty. But times had changed; fathers played just as big a part in children's lives and activities as the mothers did. Today's woman just didn't put up with absentee fathers anymore. *So why am I tolerating it?*

The familiar noise from the rising garage door pulled Faith from her thoughts. It figures he comes home early the one night she wanted to go out. As she passed through the foyer to the kitchen she stopped and yelled up the stairs, "Kids! No church! Your dad is home!" Then she hurried into the kitchen to finish cooking.

Jonah entered the house just as she pulled the chicken out of the oven. Without a word, he walked into their home office next to the family room. Ten minutes later he appeared, distracted by the mail in his hand. Faith felt his closeness even before he kissed the back of her neck.

"How's my girl?" he asked wrapping his arms around her waist and squeezing.

"Good." Faith quivered from his touch. "How about you?"

"Not good, but I think I smell something that's about to make it all better."

She closed her eyes and melted in the melodic timbre of his voice. "I wanted to do something special for you," she said. It was a half truth. They'd fought so bitterly last night that she just wanted peace in her house, and the phone calls she'd been receiving had her thinking she'd lost him to someone else. Her mother taught her that a man with a full belly was usually a content one. She had to balance the fighting. It was her peace offering.

Jonah moved his arms from her waist and turned her to face him. He looked into her eyes for a few seconds, kissed her on both cheeks, and then the lips. Faith dropped the kitchen towel she'd been holding, wrapped her arms around his neck and squeezed tight. He pulled her closer to him and squeezed back. The sound of the mail hitting the floor was muffled by the beating of her heart.

Jonah pulled away from her, but just enough to give him access to her face again. He found her lips and attempted to kiss her deeply. Faith tried to give him the passion he wanted, but her body tensed when she caught sight of a glass of bourbon on the island. He couldn't even wait until after dinner to have a drink. She was disgusted.

Jonah released her and bent over to pick up the towel and mail and placed them on the counter. When his eyes met hers again, she could see disappointment etched in his face. He planted his hands on her hips and began massaging her lower back with his fingers.

"What's it going to take, Faith?"

She knew what he meant. What's it going to take to get the loving back into this marriage? Her answer, which was counseling, would cause a fight, and she hadn't peeled shrimp and chopped vegetables all afternoon for that. So instead, she changed the subject. "What was so bad at work?" she asked, stepping out of his embrace.

She could tell Jonah was put off by her dismissal of the subject. He hesitated, and then picked up the ladle on the stove, and with a finger, swiped some of the gumbo before replying.

"Cooper in the staff meeting. Whining about how many more pro-bono patients he sees."

Glad her back was to him, Faith rolled her eyes upward. She didn't like to talk about the problems Jonah was having with the other doctors in the practice, because usually she didn't agree with her husband.

"You know Cooper."

"I know I'm getting sick and tired of going through all this drama every time we have a meeting. If they're not careful, they'll lose me. I could probably make more money on my own anyway." He put the ladle down and picked up his drink. "Do you know they want me to see five pro-bono patients a month? I don't have time for that." He took a drink and made his way to the desk in the corner of the room.

"I thought you were seeing fifty people a day. You're never here," she mumbled under her breath.

"What was that?" Jonah asked, tossing the mail. "Did I hear disagreement from the person who spends most of the money?"

"Oh puleeze," Faith said as she poured glasses of lemonade. "I don't spend all the money around here."

"Well, somebody's spending it." He removed the newspaper from his chair where Faith had left it for him.

"Look, are we going to eat soon or are you just going to keep dressing the table?" Residual annoyance peppered a tone that was harsher than what she saw in his eyes, but it still annoyed her that he had the nerve to rush her when he rarely came home before nine o'clock.

"Like I had any idea you would be home at a decent hour," she mumbled again.

He was standing in the doorway between the kitchen and the foyer holding his drink, but her tone brought his eyes to hers, where they locked for a moment. Faith knew Jonah hated sarcasm, but he didn't say anything. He didn't have to. His stoic demeanor caused her to shrink.

"How about calling the kids," she said, backpedaling out of the contest she wouldn't win.

He pushed the button on the intercom system, and after a beep, summoned them with a deep-toned, "Kids, come on down for dinner!" Then he took a seat at the table.

Within seconds, Elise's footsteps pounded in the upstairs corridor. She descended the stairs at a rapid pace and made her way directly to the kitchen.

"Daddy!" She leapt into his arms and wrapped her arms around his neck.

Jonah pushed back tendrils of hair from her face and pulled her into a tight hug. "Hey, baby girl, now that's a greeting fit for a king."

Faith could feel his eyes burrowing into her back.

"I didn't hear you come home," Elise said.

"Well, maybe I wanted to surprise you. Where's your brother?"

"His room. He's mad." Elise slid from his lap.

Out of the corner of her eye, Faith saw Jonah pick up the newspaper. "What's he angry about?" There was little interest in his voice.

"I don't know." Elise took her place at the table.

"His coach told him he was going to have to move him to the outfield if he doesn't get more practice," Faith responded as she put silverware on the table.

"More practice? Doesn't he practice twice a week?"

"Yes. But he needs to practice on his own time to get better."

Jonah was silent. He had resumed reading his paper.

Faith stopped and put her hands on her hips. "Jonah, are you listening to me?"

"I'm not deaf. Just hungry." He didn't raise his eyes to even look at her.

"No, you're not deaf, and I didn't ask you if you heard me. I asked you if you were listening." She could barely contain her anger at his nonchalance.

There was silence for a moment before Elise asked, "Mommy, what's deaf?"

Faith looked into her daughter's eyes. She could see apprehension and hear their child's earlier words. *I don't like it when you and Daddy are mad.*

Jonah looked up from his paper. "Can we discuss this later?"

A still hush swept over the tension-filled kitchen. Once again the four-year-old tried to break the silence. "Daddy, what's a deaf?" Her eyes moved between her parents.

She shouldn't have used that tone. Faith felt the knife plunge deeper. At the rate she was going, she'd die from internal bleeding by the end of the night.

"Ask Mommy tomorrow when you have playtime." Jonah looked at Elise and smiled, but dismissed her all the same as he refolded his newspaper and resumed reading.

The sound of light steps on the tile in the foyer preceded Eric's entrance into the kitchen. He slid into his chair like he had the weight of the world still on his shoulders and cast a sullen look his father's way.

Faith added the last of the dinner dishes and took her seat. She reached under the table and grabbed Eric's hand. His eyes met hers and she gave his hand a gentle squeeze. She felt bad about promising him a treat and decided she'd still take them for ice cream after dinner.

Unaware that she had sat down, Jonah continued to read. After a moment, Faith cleared her throat. Jonah looked up, let his eyes rest on each of them for a second, like he was doing a head count, and put his paper on the empty chair beside him. They reached for each others' hands, and her husband began to say a well rehearsed grace.

Chapter 2

Faith was not happy, which meant another night with no sex. This was what all married life jokes were about. Here they were, barely married ten years, and he couldn't pay her to let him touch her. When he stepped out of the shower, he caught a glimpse of her perched on the edge of the bed. Attitude with a capital "A". Jonah searched his memory for what he thought might be the source of her sour mood, but he couldn't think of anything. He snatched a towel from the rack and let out a disgusted sigh. It wasn't as if he had to do anything to rouse a funk from her these days.

As he toweled off, Jonah remembered the first time he'd laid eyes on Faith. He'd been working a shift in the emergency room when she'd come in with Eric. The five-month-old was sick, as was his mother, with worry. But even in her distraught state, Jonah was instantly taken by her beauty. Against the perfect shade of brown, she had the most finely chiseled features he'd ever seen on a sister; a thin aristocratic nose, large doe-like eyes, and a body that would get any man's attention. He knew instinctively that if this woman smiled, the entire room would light up.

"I'm Dr. Morgan." He extended his hand, and she took it. "What's going on with this little guy?"

"You're a cardiologist?" Her worried eyes cut from his name badge.

She didn't have a hint of a southern drawl. A northerner. He hoped she wasn't visiting Atlanta, because although he'd only been in her presence for sixty seconds, he was in love.

"I'm not here for my specialty." He gave her a broad smile and opened the thin medical chart. "I'm filling in for a friend who's on his honeymoon."

She relaxed noticeably. "He's been crying and running a high fever since yesterday."

"Let's take a look." He approached the table where her son lay. "Don't worry; we'll get this little guy well in no time, Mrs . . ." He drew it out in a questioning tone.

"Andrews." She hesitated for a moment before saying, "I'm recently widowed."

Jonah thought he heard a bell ringing—ding—ding—ding, over his head. He felt bad about her husband and expressed sincere condolences, because the brother had to be young, but he also couldn't help but think he'd hit the jackpot. She was available, or would be when she stopped grieving. From that night on, he began a carefully crafted campaign to win the former Mrs. Andrews's heart. When he did, he wasted no time making her his wife. But time was kicking the marriage in the proverbial rear end. Happy wives didn't suggest counseling.

Jonah took a deep breath and looked at her. She cut her eyes away from him as she positioned herself higher against the headboard. Hoping to convey the message that he wasn't in the mood for drama, he stared at her a couple of seconds, then took the few steps between the bathroom door and his side of the bed. Angry eyes shot back at him. He wasn't intimidating her tonight. Whatever was on her mind was coming full speed ahead within the next few moments.

Just as he was about to pull back the comforter on his side of the bed, she spoke.

"Jonah, we need to talk."

He sighed again, loud enough to convey his frustration and asked the question he knew she wanted to hear, which would no doubt begin another night of discord. "About what?"

Faith wasted no time answering.

"You promised you would adjust your schedule so you could be home with me and the children more. You're not doing that." She folded her arms in front of her chest.

Jonah slid into bed, pulled the comforter up around his waist, and leaned back on his pillows and closed his eyes.

"Well?" Faith asked.

He could hear the attitude. Jonah sighed, opened his eyes, and turned his head in her direction. "Did you not note the time I got home tonight?"

"Yes, actually, I did. Six P.M., and after dinner you went into your office and didn't come out until way after nine. So tell me how that was spending time with your family?"

"I was home."

"Geographically, you were in the house. The kids asked you to watch a television show, and you told them you were too busy."

Jonah knew she was right, but the first step in the art of war is to know your enemy. If he admitted it now, Faith would have him home every night watching Disney movies.

"I thought you wanted me home," he said resting back on his pillow.

"I *thought* I made myself clear the last time we talked about this. I said I wanted you available." Her tone dripped with sarcasm. He wasn't responding to that.

"We need to talk about something else," she continued.

Faith was making him extremely uncomfortable now. Jonah moved around on his side of the bed, which was starting to feel like a coffin. He opened his eyes and looked at her again. She had uncrossed her arms, but her expression still read mad.

"Go on," Jonah said. "What's next on your list?"

"Eric."

This time, he turned his back to her. He remembered the shushed conversation before dinner. *Eric is mad*, Elise had said.

"Is this about the baseball thing?" He couldn't believe she was going to start this again. Maybe he could tune her out. The last thing he felt like talking about was a silly baseball game.

"The baseball *thing* is important to Eric. He wants to maintain his position on the team, but he needs more practice. He needs you to throw the ball to him."

"It's the new millennium, Faith. Baseball is a coed sport. If you think it's so important, why don't you throw him the ball?"

He heard an exasperated sigh before she said, "All the other fathers on the team work with their kids and attend the games. Besides, you need to do something with him."

He opened his eyes and careened his neck in her direction. "Is this about baseball or me needing to share an activity with Eric?"

"Why can't it be about both?"

There she was, trying to tell him what to do again. This time he sat up. "I don't like baseball." He pointed an angry finger in her direction. "You know that."

"I don't like lots of things in my daily routine, but I do them because they're my responsibility. You think I enjoyed peeling shrimp and chopping onions all afternoon?"

Unbelievable, he thought, shaking his head. The gumbo he'd enjoyed so much was now a sour memory.

Ring! The telephone shrilled.

Faith turned her head to look at it, and then turned back to him. She cleared her throat and said, "I didn't mean to imply I had a problem with making dinner, but there are simpler things I could cook. I chose to make gumbo because I wanted to make you happy."

"Don't go breaking things down to the smallest syllable for me. I'm not stupid," he said.

Ring! Ring!

Faith's eyes widened. She looked over her shoulder at the phone, and then back at him. "Then you understand my point that life isn't always about what we want to do, especially when it comes to kids." She glanced at the phone again.

He was silent, trying to keep his temper in check. They'd had this conversation before and had come to the same impasse.

Ring! Ring! Ring!

Faith nearly jumped out of her skin. Watching her was making him uncomfortable.

"Do you need to get that or what?" he asked.

"No," she whispered, shaking her head. "This is important." She paused for a moment, taking one final look at the phone which was now silent.

"You don't spend any time with the children," she said. "Least of all, Eric. How do you expect to have a relationship with him if you don't spend time with him?"

"I don't need you interfering—"

"No, Eric needs me to interfere. You ignore him, and you know it," she continued. "I'm tired of having this conversation with you." She pounded a fist on the mattress. "I agreed to marry you because—"

Jonah felt like he'd been smacked in the face. "Agreed . . ." he interjected with raised eyebrows. "Did you say agreed to marry me?"

"Yes." Her voice was louder now. "I agreed to marry you because you said you would be his father. You said you would take on the responsibility."

Jonah stared at her for a few seconds. Everything had to be so extreme. They went from talking about the baseball to the scope of the marriage.

"I'm not getting my end of the deal." Her tone couldn't have been nastier.

"Whatever, Faith." He threw the comforter off his legs and stood. "If you think you've gotten such a raw deal in living with me, why don't you explore your other options?"

He walked to the door, pulled it open, and turned back to look at her. "As if with a kid in tow you had so many other viable ones."

Jonah left before he had to see the shock on her face. He went down the stairs to his office and opened his cabinet to get a drink. Last night it had been counseling, now it was baseball. Faith had it all figured out. She could be in this marriage by herself. She really didn't need him, but she had no idea how lucky she was to have him. He was a good man.

If Faith had to settle for the little his mother had to work with, she'd be a little more appreciative of the lifestyle the long hours he put in everyday provided for them. As a child he'd had many a night when they had neck bones, pork 'n beans and hotdogs, or cornbread pancakes. He was sure she'd never had to have a po' man's meal. Her family was always on the better side of a dollar. That had probably been his mistake, marrying a sister who had grown up with more than he had. If he had married someone from the old neighborhood, she would appreciate not having to work, being able to travel, and shop. A girl from his hood wouldn't be picking fights about stupid stuff. Instead of sitting in his office drinking, he'd be having a pleasant evening in his bedroom. But there was no point thinking about what could've been with another woman. He loved Faith. God knows he did. And he hated when they fought, but baseball and counseling? Never.

Jonah took a long sip of his drink and lay back on the sofa. Faith's face flashed through his mind. He thought about her lying upstairs, probably devastated with hurt. The comment about her and Eric had been a low blow, but she deserved it. Maybe next time she'd choose her battles.

Chapter 3

Jonah pulled his Mercedes Benz into his assigned parking space outside of the three story building where he spent his day. Christian Brothers Family Health was the incorporated collaboration of fifteen doctors who provided a wide array of medical services, with the hope that the center would be one stop shopping for patients. All of the doctors in the practice were Christians, hence the name Christian Brothers. Jonah added the specialty of pediatric cardiology to the ranks and was notably the highest paid and most in demand of the group. He had advanced training to perform complex interventional tests and procedures like biopsies and catheterizations necessary for diagnosis and treatment. Pediatric heart problems were more common than most people knew. He saw kids all day who suffered from slight heart murmurs and genetic heart disorders to severe and irreversible congestive heart failure.

He stopped at the reception desk. Mia, a bubbly young woman with an infectious smile greeted him.

"How are you doing this morning, Mia?"

"I'm good." She reached into a slot and handed him a message slip. "I've already sent someone upstairs—a new patient—so they're probably still filling out forms. And your mother called."

Jonah sighed inwardly, but nodded thanks. He took the two flights of stairs that led to his office, walked in, and fell into his chair. He'd been ignoring his mother. The anniversary of his brother's death was looming. Her annual ritual of grieving for Joshua included Jonah's participation whether he wanted to be a part or not. He wasn't ready for it. Not this year. And definitely not this morning.

There was a tap on the door, and then it creaked open.

Tom Cooper, one of the other doctors, peeked in. "Good morning. I don't mean to bother you again, but I really need your numbers."

Jonah groaned against Cooper's annoyance. "You don't have to keep reminding me every day. I'll make my deadline." Jonah crumpled the message slip and tossed it in the trash basket.

Cooper took a few steps into the office. "Are you going to see the Lazarus kid I referred to you last week?"

"Lazarus is my first patient this morning. They're in the waiting room. You just walked past them."

Cooper scratched the side of his face. "Good. Glad you fit him in so fast."

Christian Brothers treated a set number of charity cases on a monthly basis. Each doctor was assigned a minimum of four patients to treat, with the exception of Jonah. His tight schedule didn't permit it because the follow-up on cardiac cases was often extensive. He simply didn't have time to take on so many free patients. He generated his income from billing, and his lifestyle required a lot of billing.

Cooper and several of the doctors in the practice were

furious when he announced he couldn't do as many pro-bono cases. Three of them actually wanted him out of the practice if he weren't going to govern his work by the guiding principle of the organization; in this case, *"Service before profit,"* but he knew they wouldn't be successful in ousting him. Pediatric cardiologists were few in number. Christian Brothers needed him.

Jonah made a pretense of reading something in a medical chart. After a moment, he lifted his head and shot Cooper a hostile glare. "Something else?"

"No, just keep me updated," he said. "On Lazarus and the report." He left the office.

What was that about? Cooper was probably hatching some type of plan to get Jonah's patient load on the meeting agenda again. He didn't know what was wrong with that man. He was seeing the Lazarus child as he requested, but he wasn't satisfied. Cooper wouldn't be happy until Jonah was seeing as many pro-bono cases as he was. He always wanted more. Everyone seemed to these days. At work and at home.

Jonah could hear the voices of his team in the corridor, greeting Cooper just before April Thomas appeared in the doorway.

April, his cardiovascular technologist, was a pretty young woman about twenty-six years of age. She performed all the ultrasound tests on his patients. Accredited in EKG, echocardiology, and even trained to assist with more invasive procedures like cardiac catheterization, April was his right hand.

"Good morning, Dr. Morgan." She approached his desk with a medical record in one hand and a coffee mug in the other.

"Any luck that's for me?"

April seemed to be dragging a little this morning, but

she smiled anyway as she placed the cup in front of him. "I felt like being extra sweet this morning. We're studying servanthood in my Bible Study class."

Jonah reached for the mug, which bore his Alma Mata, Morehouse College of Medicine. "Thanks. I rushed out of the house without my second cup." He took a sip. "So how was your date last night?"

April rolled her eyes. "He was a snoozer. All he did was talk about himself and how great a lawyer he is . . . blah, blah, blah," she replied, waving her hand back and forth. "But you don't have time to hear about that. You're double booked all day, and Lazarus is ready in room one." She handed him the chart. "He's a real cutie. His mother is very nice, but worried to death."

"Hmmm, what else is new? Isn't everyone worried by the time they get to see me?" He opened the thin file, glancing at Dr. Cooper's referral and the nurses' notes. "That's who I am; The Grim Reaper." He looked at her, a chuckle at the end of his words.

"You don't always have bad news." April clutched both elbows across her chest. "I think finding out you have a slight heart murmur is much better than complete heart failure."

"True," he said, standing. "But our patients don't even know the range of conditions the heart can have. Anything irregular is bad news to them." He came around the desk, placed a hand on April's shoulder, and squeezed gently.

"You're the best, and you make the best coffee. Time to get to work."

Amadi Lazarus was a slightly underweight nine-year-old boy with coal black skin that was telling of his African heritage and the darkest eyes Jonah had ever seen. He remembered learning in high school science that no human being actually ever had black eyes. But if ever anyone was close, it was Amadi.

"That's it." Samaria Jacobs, Jonah's registered nurse placed a band aid on the site where she'd drawn blood. "We'll make sure to get you that sticker before you leave, okay?"

Amadi nodded, his hands trembling, and Samaria left the room, closing the door behind her. Amadi's mother stepped closer to the examination table where Amadi sat and reached for her son's hand.

"Tell me why you think you're here today, Amadi." Jonah moved the stethoscope across his chest.

"Something's wr-r-r-rong with my heart," Amadi replied, stuttering. "F-f-f-fat Tommy told me I'm going to have a heart attack and die."

"Who's Fat Tommy?"

"A mean boy who lives in our apartment complex." Amadi's mother, Monifa Lazarus frowned. "With a big mouth."

"Well, Fat Tommy is probably wrong. Kids your age have a very small chance of having a heart attack," Jonah replied.

"But th-th-th-th-they can, if they already have a bad heart, right?"

"They can, but it's rare." Jonah spoke in between listening to heart sounds. "Tell me, Amadi, have you ever been sick before, like sicker than having a cold?"

"I was in the hospital once, in T-T-T-T-Togo. Right, Mama? When I was five."

Monifa Lazarus wrung her hands. "He had an infection. I would know the word if I heard it." Her thick accent broke her speech. "A lot of the kids were sick from the school, and he had to be in the hospital for a few days to get medicine."

"We'll request the medical records. Any preliminary

tests we need can be done here today following my examination."

Mrs. Lazarus's face relaxed some, and for a few seconds, her hands were still.

There was a light tap on the door, and as if she read his mind, April walked in.

"Amadi, this is Miss April. She's going to do a few tests on you. One of them is called an electrocardiogram."

"I had that before." Amadi bobbed his head up and down as he spoke.

"Good, then you know it doesn't hurt." Jonah stepped back a few feet, allowing April space to work.

While her son seemed to be more relaxed than he had been before the exam began, Mrs. Lazarus had gone back to wringing her hands, and the wrinkles in her forehead looked like they were permanently etched there. "What can you tell from this test?" she asked.

"Any irregularity in the heart rhythm can change the heart's electrical activity. We'll get a printout that will show us the rhythm. I'm looking for a certain wave pattern." Jonah placed a hand on Amadi's shoulder. "I'm going to let Miss April do the test, and I'll be back."

Jonah left the exam room, taking the scanty medical record Monifa Lazarus had bought with her. Once in his office, he went directly to his desk and reached into the top drawer for a bottle of Tylenol. He was getting a headache. He swallowed two pills and chased them with the coffee that had gotten cold on the desk. Then he opened Amadi's medical file and began reading.

Not much had been done in the way of diagnosis, but Jonah knew something was there. His heart sounds had murmurs that he suspected would show him an irregular rhythm. After a few minutes, April entered with the EKG tape. Jonah looked at it, noting the gallop pattern he suspected. "Let's do an echo and a chest x-ray."

"Anything in the record?"

"Nothing conclusive. Treating of symptoms. But he's got a bad rhythm—slow too. We'll get to the bottom of it."

"Amadi, go to the waiting room," Mrs. Lazarus instructed, turning his shoulders and pointing him to the door. Although reluctant to leave his mother's side, the boy did as he was told. "Dr. Morgan, I don't know how to thank you for seeing Amadi. I don't have any money or insurance, and you people have been so kind to us."

"Amadi is a great kid. I'm glad to be his doctor," Jonah replied.

"You are a good man," she said. Jonah could tell she still struggled with her English. "Amadi has had a lot of doctors. They don't talk to him sometimes when they see him. They just work like they're handling a piece of meat." She hesitated for a moment. "You'll forgive me if I presume something?"

Jonah acknowledged her with a nod.

"You are a Christian, right? But you aren't like some of the other Christians I know. Saying they love God, but not really loving people."

It occurred to Jonah that this was some big witnessing opportunity, but he was at a loss for words.

"I'm sorry, Doctor, if I'm wrong. I assumed you were a Christian, because of the paperwork I read about the office."

"No, Mrs. Lazarus, I am." He hesitated again, but still didn't respond to her statement. He didn't know what to say.

"I have taken enough of your time. I will talk to you when you have the results." She seemed to sense his discomfort, and Jonah couldn't help but notice she looked a little disappointed. He saw her to the door.

"We'll see you back by the end of the week. By then I should have all the test results."

Mrs. Lazarus nodded and left.

Within seconds, Samaria stuck her head in the door that he had left half open. "Your next patient is ready."

Jonah was still feeling uneasy. *You aren't like all the other Christians.* That troubled him, but it troubled him even more that he hadn't thought to tell her some of the things Pastor Kent talked about, like explaining that all Christians are not at the same maturity level or how some people hadn't been fully changed yet. *What was that he'd preached . . . putting on the new man . . . renewing your mind?* Heck, he didn't know. He was a doctor, not a preacher.

"Dr. Morgan, did you hear me?" Samaria was still standing in the door. "Dr. Gunter asked that you call the National Heart Society back."

Jonah hadn't heard her. He'd received a couple of messages from NHS, but hadn't taken the time to return the calls. Now he was wondering why Gunter was insisting. Although he strongly encouraged continuing education, conferences, and research opportunities, Gunter, the senior partner in the Christian Brothers, didn't often request the doctors do anything outside of patient care. Maybe it was important.

"Their annual benefit is in Atlanta on Friday night," Samaria said. "I heard about it at school."

Jonah nodded absently, thinking he'd try to stop in later and see what was on Gunter's mind. "Did you have a chance to get the blood work ready on the Lazarus kid?"

"It's ready," Samaria replied.

Jonah was thoughtful for a moment, and then made a notation in the chart. "Expedite it, okay? I'd like the results first thing tomorrow."

He noted the confusion on her face. In pro-bono cases, expenses were kept to a minimum. Some of the other doctors had expedited lab work in the past to make diagnosis, but he never had. He'd always followed protocol.

"Okay." Her voice indicated she was looking for a plausible explanation. When he didn't give her one, she put the chart she was holding on his desk and left the office.

Right behind her, April entered, holding the disc of the echogram.

Jonah stood and stuck the pen he'd been writing with in the pocket of his lab coat. He came around the desk just as April stuck the tape in the player.

"How'd it look?" She nodded at the chart on his desk.

"Not much in the record." Silence fell as they watched the film. Jonah used a hand to wipe the frown from his face and stopped the tape. "I'm rushing the blood work. I'm seeing something that may be pretty serious."

They walked out of the office, and Jonah fell into step with April as they walked down the corridor. "Rushed blood work means the Q Labs guy will have to come twice today. That's two times the looking for you ladies."

"What do you know about the Q Labs guy?" April's voice didn't carry the light tone he'd been expecting.

"I hear the break room talk." He leaned closer to her ear, putting a hand on her shoulder. "I know who's being naughty and who's being nice around here."

He heard her intake of breath right before her shoulders stiffened.

"I didn't mean you've been naughty," Jonah attempted to clean up the inference that she'd obviously taken personally.

"No. It's okay, Dr. Morgan. I just have a headache."

"That seems to be going around today, but you've had a lot of those lately. Getting enough sleep?"

She nodded agreeably, but he could still tell he'd jarred her. April had been moody lately. High one minute, low the next.

He returned his hand to her shoulder and began to squeeze gently, hoping to massage tension. "Don't ignore those headaches too long. If they don't get better, let somebody do a CT scan—find out what's going on."

"I will," she said, but her voice was noncommittal.

Jonah knocked on the exam room door, announced himself, and walked into the room, but not before he saw raw hurt glittering in her eyes.

Chapter 4

Finished with her morning appointments, April walked back to the nurse's station and took a seat behind the computer terminal. Samaria was swamped with charting, so she began to type in the codes she needed to change the Lazarus kid's blood work from regular to "stat" for the midday lab pickup.

As the laser jet printer hummed and printed the label and paperwork she needed to attach to the vials of blood, she stared into space. To a passerby it, would seem she was deep in thought. She was not. She had learned the technique of controlling her thoughts from months of therapy. Forcing memories into the recesses of her mind. Thought suppression therapy, her psychiatrist, Dr. Moray, called it.

The printer stopped, and she took the sheet from the bin and turned to the workstation behind her. After pasting the new labels over the old and changing the attached paperwork, she rushed to the ladies room, entered the handicap stall, and sat on the toilet lid. Her heart was banging against her chest, and she had chills. She was having another panic attack. The second one this week.

The images flooded in her head like a million flashes of light. She felt nauseous, and her skin became the home of what felt like a hundred bugs. April rubbed her hands up and down her arms as tears streamed down her face. Someone entered the restroom. She put her hands over her ears to block out the noises they were making. Squeaks, slamming doors—it was all so loud. Her head was going to explode.

Breathe. Just breathe.

After several minutes, April finally caught her breath. The constant rubbing of her hands up and down her arms had quelled the creepy crawlies, but the tears continued to flow. She hated when Dr. Morgan touched her. It wasn't that he was being sexual. She knew when someone was feeling her up. In fact, she knew his intent was to give a fatherly touch, but it didn't matter. After what had happened to her, she didn't want a fatherly touch or any other type of touch from a man. Those days were over for her.

April exited the stall and went to the sink where she splashed handful after handful of cold water on her face. When she was done, she stared in the mirror at her bloodshot eyes. "I used to be beautiful," she cried. Now she was a freak. All her dreams for a husband and children, gone in one night. She'd spend a lifetime covering up the reason she was single by lying to friends and coworkers about dates she hadn't had.

Chapter 5

The telephone call from Bowen and Jefferies Consulting came as a total shock to Faith. She hadn't been expecting anything to come of the resumé she'd submitted online and certainly not within the week. But here she sat in their lobby, dressed to the nines and completely unprepared for the interview they'd summoned her for.

She'd tried to look at some practice questions on the Internet last night, but Jonah had walked into the kitchen and interrupted her. It probably wouldn't have mattered much; even if she had more time to study, she was still nervous about selling her skills after so many years. She'd been a stay at home mom ever since she was pregnant with Elise. Unreasonable workloads, dirty politics, and a nutty boss were stressors she didn't need with the pregnancy. Besides, Jonah was pleading with her to quit, so she did. Sometimes she regretted that decision; mostly because her husband had pushed her to do it.

Faith let out a long breath and let her eyes scan the luxurious décor of the large waiting room. It was an elaborate mix of Art Deco style metals in bronze, copper, and stainless steel. Abstract oil paintings, wall panels, and murals hung in a symmetrical pattern on the walls.

She was way out of her league agreeing to come here. "Why didn't I just tell them I changed my mind when they called?" she asked herself through gritted teeth. Then she pressed her palms on her skirt. Moist palms wouldn't leave a good first impression. Nothing was more annoying than a sweaty handshake, but then she realized she was wearing silk crepe. She didn't want two hand prints on her thighs when she stood.

The waiting ended when a door near the reception desk opened, and a man who looked to be about her age stuck his head out and called her name.

Faith stood, picked up her attaché case, and walked toward him with a smile.

Their right hands met, and Faith gave him a strong, confident shake, belying the tumulus sensation in the pit of her belly where the butterflies danced around.

"Garrison Adams, Director of Special Projects," he said.

She followed him down a long corridor past more opulent art and furniture into the small conference room where two other people sat.

"Faith." Garrison pointed to a chair across from the two people she assumed were other members of the interview panel. "Is it okay if we call you that?"

"Please." She placed her attaché case on the table in front of her.

The interview began with Garrison explaining the special projects department had been formed to bid on request for proposals from state government projects. They had recently won the bid to work on a long-term business process reengineering project with the Department of Human Services' Division of Public Health. Essentially, the person hired would work with a team to go into the public health department, look at their operations and assess efficiency, and make recommendations for change.

"So you understand why we were so interested in speaking with you. Your experience with the department would be invaluable to the team."

Faith shifted in the chair to make herself more comfortable now that she actually felt a little more at ease. No wonder they were so quick to respond to her resume.

The balance of the interview was a discussion about the scope, goals, and timeline of the project. They only asked her a few questions, then Garrison had one of the panel members walk her to the lobby.

"I hope you really want this job," the man said as they approached the door. "Garrison had his mind made up about you half an hour ago. I could see it in his eyes."

Faith pulled into the parking lot of Pegasus, her favorite downtown restaurant. The interview had taken longer than she expected. Yvette was already seated in a booth near the window when she arrived. Cell phone jammed between her ear and shoulder, she held a pen and a small leather notebook in front of her, jotting furiously. Faith placed her handbag in the booth. Yvette gave her a quick smile and raised her finger, signaling for Faith to give her a minute. In turn, Faith pointed toward the ladies room and proceeded in that direction.

As she washed her hands, two women walked in wearing business suits. She noticed they were deeply involved in a conversation about something related to a client and a sale. *Successful*, she thought, or at least they looked the part. But she noticed another thing—they both looked tired and stressed. When they went into their stalls, Faith stared at her own reflection in the mirror. She too was dressed appropriately corporate. Her long hair that normally hung past her shoulders was pinned in a French twist; her makeup, flawlessly natural. She wondered if the high demands of a project like the one Garrison had described would have her looking equally as stressed.

Did she want to do this everyday? Dress up and hit the pavement running like everyone else? Juggle her kids and her household responsibilities? Even if she hired a housekeeper, which she surely would have to do, there was dinner, Eric's homework, and after-school activities. Did she really want the hectic pace that most women had to endure, when in truth, Jonah earned enough money to support three middle-income families? She sighed, the weight of such a decision heavily hampering her soul, and left the restroom.

The waitress approached the table with two glasses of water and a basket of bread just as Faith slid into the booth.

"Hello, ladies. What can I get you to drink?" She removed a small notepad from her apron.

Both women ordered iced tea and rattled off their lunch choices since Yvette had had a chance to peruse the menu and Faith already knew she was having the Jerk Chicken.

"Okay, give me details," Yvette said when the waitress left.

Faith shrugged her shoulders. "I think it was okay. The questions weren't that difficult. Either that or I totally blew it with the simple answers I gave."

Yvette continued to look at her expectantly.

"Actually, it may have gone better than I could've ever anticipated. The project I'd be assigned to is a reorg for public health."

Yvette clapped her hands together. "Girl, I was out of work for six months, had to start my own business to get a job, and here you go sailing right into something with your old employer."

"I know. It really surprised me too."

"They're going to offer you that job."

"It's a strong possibility."

"Are you kidding? More than a strong possibility." Yvette paused. "Did they tell you when they were making a decision?"

"No. I forgot to ask. I don't know. I've been out of this game for so long. I'm starting to wonder if I'm not being foolish for thinking about going back to work."

Yvette was giving her that you've got to be kidding look. "Why would it be foolish? It's only foolish if you don't really want to do it. But if you want a career, you should be able to have one, and it looks like God is opening a door for you. You know we don't believe in coincidences."

"Only divine appointments." Faith finished with Pastor's words on just that Sunday past.

Faith looked at her wedding rings and began twisting them around on her finger. "I keep thinking about how Jonah will react."

"What did he say when you told him about the interview?"

Faith took her straw and popped it into her glass. "I didn't. I figured there was no point in upsetting him when I probably wouldn't get the job anyway."

Yvette's mouth fell open. "Faith Angelica Morgan, no you didn't."

"Yes, I did."

"Now what are you going to do? Tell him they found you at housewives 'r us?"

"I know it looks good, but I'm sure they have other candidates. People who've actually punched a clock recently."

"You need to try talking to him. Tell him what you want in a way that will make him understand. Don't you married women have some kind of whammy you put on 'em when you need them to listen."

Now it was Faith who flashed the *who are you kidding* look.

Yvette giggled a little. "Okay, I'm teasing you. But girl, I've got to tell you to do it God's way. Keeping secrets isn't good."

"Yeah well, the problem is he's adamant, Yvette. Jonah has made it clear in no uncertain terms that he wants me to stay at home." Faith reached into the breadbasket and helped herself to several small pieces of Jamaican bread. "I don't know why he's like this. His mother worked when he was growing up."

"He's probably like that because his mother *did* work." Yvette wrinkled her noise. "He might've had a mean babysitter."

Faith smirked at her friend's silliness. Yvette was always trying to lighten the mood.

The waitress returned with small garden salads and their drink order. They waited for her to leave and picked up the conversation where they'd left off.

"I know men can be a trip, but it would be a bit much for him to assume that just because he makes a lot of money you can't have a career. You had one when you met him."

Faith used the tip of her fingernail to trace the lines in the stripes of the tablecloth as she considered what Yvette was saying.

"Submitting to a husband isn't about giving up who you are. The Bible said Adam and Eve walked in dominion together. It didn't say anything about him walking in front of her or over her, so you keep that in mind, my friend." Yvette's last words took on a serious tone.

Faith sighed deeply. She and Jonah were already on very shaky ground. But then again, would it be her fault if things didn't work out for them just because she refused to follow his every command? And what was he doing to keep her happy? Coming in at odd hours, ignoring the children, ignoring her. And then there were the phone calls.

Faith shook her head in an attempt to clear her thoughts. She mentally scolded herself. *I'm not going to think about this now.* "We are officially moving on from my woes. Tell me about the business," Faith said, picking up her fork.

"Business is good," Yvette began between bites of food. "The two women I hired from the job fair are working out great. I may have to go ahead and interview the third woman I told you about. We're so busy."

Faith nodded. Although she continued to listen to her friend go on about the details of running her fitness clubs, the word *interview* had propelled her back to her own reality, which was an interesting job prospect with a great company and the battle she would have with her uncompromising husband.

Chapter 6

Jonah closed his office door and slid into the chair behind his desk. His mother had paged him. He couldn't keep avoiding her. If he didn't talk to her soon, she'd start calling the house. Then Faith would start asking him questions. The last thing he needed was something else for her to nag about.

Dialing the number from memory, he mused that his mother's phone number had never changed from the time they first got a telephone when he was a child. His mother, ever consistent, could be counted on to do exactly what she always did. That's why he knew the reason for her calls.

He heard the familiar voice on the phone and closed his eyes for a second, briefly reveling in what he could only describe as the voice of an angel. In times past, it had been the only calming, stabilizing force in his life. She had strength, yet gentleness that could make his world rotate correctly on its axis. He'd relied on her most of his life, but in recent years, they'd grown apart, differing in opinion about his relationship with his father. Still, hearing her took him back to a time when he didn't feel this nagging pain in his heart.

"Mama." He attempted to sound upbeat. "How are you?"

"I've called you four times." She stated a fact that he was well aware of. "Why can't I get a call back from you?"

"I'm sorry, Mama. I've been kind of busy."

"Too busy for your mother, too busy for your family, and too busy for your Daddy, I'm sure."

Jonah groaned. "Mama, what did you want to talk to me about? I know it's not my family, and it couldn't be Martin."

"I wish to God you wouldn't refer to your father that way. It's a sin. The Word says to honor thy mother and father. Calling your father by his first name is not honoring him."

"I've been calling him Martin for more than ten years, and that's between the two of us. I'm sure God's too busy to care." He rubbed the creases in his forehead. "Now please, tell me what I can do for you?"

"You know what I want." Silence echoed in the phone. "I need you to take me to the grave on Saturday. I want to put flowers—"

"I-I can't do that," he stuttered.

"You have to. My arthritis is bothering me. I can't drive myself."

"Surely one of the people from the church—"

"No. Most of our members are old or they got little children to see after. It's too far to ask somebody to take me."

"I'll hire a car service."

"No, Jonah Morgan. You'll skip your golf game, get in your fancy car, and take me to the gravesite yo'self."

His mother had no idea how much it bothered him to go to that grave. "I'm busy. I have patients and some things with the kids this Saturday."

"Uh hum. I'm sure it's more work than children," she

groaned. "I'm not taking no for an answer. We won't be there long. You pick the time."

Jonah sighed. He wanted to say he had to work or that he really did have something to do with the kids, but he realized there was no point. *Why fight the inevitable?*

"I don't care how many patients you help, it ain't gonna bring Joshua back."

"Mama—"

"I wish you'd let yourself heal, share your pain with your wife. God knows she wants to know what's eating you. She's been wanting to know for years."

Amadi Lazarus had already assailed his emotions. He didn't need more from his mother, but he respectfully allowed her to continue her speech.

"You've got to tell her sometime. It's going to hurt that you didn't open up to her, and you need to be able to talk to somebody. She don't even know why you so put off with your daddy."

He rolled his eyes upward.

"I know you rolling them eyes. But I'm telling you the truth. You're not being fair."

Jonah looked at his watch, mentally ending the conversation. He'd known what she wanted before he returned the call. He also knew he had no choice but to give in to her. A quick surrender would get him off the phone.

"Mama, if you want me to come on Saturday, fine, I will. But I'm working now, so I'm not going to talk about Joshua or Faith, and I'm certainly not going to talk about Martin."

"Well, son, what exactly do you and me have to talk about if we don't talk about those three things? At my age, all you care about is ya family." She was silent for a moment, and then with her voice trembling said, "I'll see you when you get here. I'll be waiting. Bye, son."

Jonah listened to the dull drone of the dial tone for a

moment before he returned the phone to its cradle. He'd been so preoccupied about getting her off the phone that he hadn't even asked her about her blood pressure.

His heart began an anxious beat. The cemetery, flowers on the grave, mournful reminiscing. She had to make him go there. He swore under his breath and pounded a fist on his desk.

"Mama," he said out loud as if the angst with which he called her name would be felt by her, "why can't you just leave the past in the past?"

"Dr. Morgan do you have time to go over those notes with me?" Samaria stood in his door, a chart in one hand and a soda can in the other. "It's for my cardiac disease class."

Jonah grimaced.

"You already promised," she added. "If I don't get some help, I'm going to fail." She walked in and stood in front of his desk.

Jonah looked at his watch. It was almost noon. He still had six patients to see, charts to update, and those numbers to crunch for the staff meeting on Monday. What had he been thinking when he agreed to help her? *That when you start your own practice, you could use a good Cardiac Nurse Practitioner.*

"I can't do it today. You know my patient load is heavy, and I've got a thing to do with my son. Refresh my memory, exactly what do you need from me?"

Samaria placed the soda can and chart on the desk. "Just an hour of your time to help me get the right framework for clinical diagnosis."

Jonah didn't respond. Even though medicine and nursing were different disciplines, he knew he could help her with this particular problem area. It was the same subject he was lecturing about at Morehouse next week.

Samaria continued. "My professor is awful. Between working, driving to Augusta for classes, and studying, I'm really struggling. I don't know if I'm smart enough for this."

"Don't be ridiculous. You've gotten through what—two semesters? You can do anything you set your mind to."

"I don't know. People who are smart sometimes assume everyone else has the same mental capacity as they do." Samaria sighed. "Maybe I should've just married a doctor."

"Hmmm," Jonah chuckled. "My wife would tell you that's not all it's cracked up to be."

"I'm sure she understands your dedication to your patients."

I'm sure she doesn't.

"Anyway, I could use a tutoring session. It won't take you that long."

"Sam, I'd be glad to help; it's just fitting it in. You can't do Saturday mornings—"

"Actually," she threw up her index finger. "I can do this Saturday. We don't have class."

Jonah let out a sigh. He was trapped. "I'd be giving up golf for you."

"And I'd be eternally grateful."

He laughed. "Okay, just this one time. You need to find a tutor."

Samaria clapped her hands together triumphantly.

"Just an hour," he said, thinking of his mother. "I've got another appointment on Saturday,"

"I'm sure it'll help."

"We'll see."

A moment of silence passed as Jonah pulled a chart from the pile in front of him and opened it.

"You said you had something to do with Eric. Is he still playing baseball?" Samaria asked.

"He is."

"How's the season going?"

Jonah paused briefly. The question caught him off guard. Were they winning or losing? He didn't know. He hadn't even asked. Baseball fields, little league, it all bought back memories he didn't want to revisit. "He's uh . . . doing fine." He stuttered over his words.

Samaria laughed lightly. "You haven't had time to fit that in either."

Jonah just looked at her. Too embarrassed to confirm her suspicions out loud.

"I'm sure your family understands," Samaria said, placing one hand on her hip and twisting a loc of her long hair with the other. "I know I would."

"Yeah," he said, suddenly feeling uncomfortable with the way she was looking at him.

"I'd better go," Samaria said after a moment.

Jonah watched as she exited, trying to recall something he wanted to ask her, but being distracted by the sway of her hips. He had to admit she had a lot of sex appeal and didn't mind flaunting it. Something about her mannerisms, the snugness of her uniforms, the hairstyles and makeup she chose, always seemed to be shouting sex. Many of the doctors had noticed it and commented on how alluring she was. She was pretty, but much too flashy for his taste.

"Not that I'm looking," he let the words roll off his tongue in a song.

Jonah closed the chart he had been working on and found the message from the National Heart Society under it. He had forgotten to call them back. Tomorrow was the annual fundraising benefit. He'd decided not to attend this year. Although he was sure the message was a last attempt by a customer service person to sell another two hundred dollar ticket, he made a mental note to return the call first thing in the morning, particularly since Gunter had asked him to.

Jonah opened another chart and made some notes in it. It was the last one that needed updating. The records manager would be pleased to find them when she arrived in the morning. Jonah was guilty of being over the standard of promptness for completing his records on more than one occasion, but this current pile had been the worst yet.

Jonah stood and faced the window behind the desk. He raised his arms and stretched like a cat that had been in a small cage all day. It was six thirty. If he hurried, he could still make the end of Eric's game. He needed to attend. Faith had been riding him about spending time with the children, and he knew he had been a little neglectful in that department. He picked up his jacket and slid it across his back and inserted both arms. Just as he picked up the charts to deliver to the medical records department, his pager began to beep.

The hospital. Pediatric Intensive Care. He picked up the desk phone and dialed.

"This is Dr. Morgan."

"Henry Morrison was stepped up to PICU, sir. He has a high fever and fluid on the lungs," the nurse said on the other end.

He didn't have time to stop at medical records. He wouldn't make the baseball game. His patient couldn't wait, but everyone else could and would.

Chapter 7

Faith looked at her watch for the fifth time since the baseball game began. She looked over her shoulder hoping to see Jonah's vehicle pulling into the parking lot. The game would be over in forty-five minutes. *Please let him come.*

She'd been begging him to attend a ninety-minute game for a month. Even though she'd spent the better part of the afternoon pitching to him at the batting cage, Eric had missed several balls. He was standing on the base with his head down. He looked so defeated. Eric was super competitive. The more she talked to him about enjoying the game as a form of recreation and exercise, or brought home the concept of teamwork using the cliché, "It's not who wins, but how you play the game," the more Eric wanted to win. One conversation with Jonah would probably make a big difference in his attitude.

She smirked thinking what a hypocrite he would be to give Eric advice when Jonah was pretty much the same way. He was a perfectionist in his work, in his few dealings at the church, and certainly in his play. He was a strong tennis player and had a respectable golf game; he strived to do everything to the best of his ability.

So why was he failing at being in his family?

The answer to that question had to lie in his relationship with his own father. But that was something he just wouldn't share with her. Before they'd gotten married, Faith had read a magazine article that said there were always signs a person is not quite ready for marriage. Often little things dismissed as nothing should be examined a lot more carefully before the exchange of wedding vows, the writer had said.

When they were engaged, planning the list for the invitations, Jonah locked up tight when she asked about his father.

"He's not invited."

"Why?"

"Because he's just not, honey."

"Well, Jonah, we're talking about our wedding. Whatever you and your dad have—"

"Faith, it's not up for discussion. My father and I don't talk. We'll always be that way, and I really don't want to ruin this evening discussing it."

"Another time?" she asked.

"Another time." He kissed her.

That had been her sign. Looking back now, she shouldn't have ignored that situation so easily. His parents were divorced, but still there was more to this story, and now what seemed like a small thing was a big issue that added to the pile that was accumulating between them.

Like this game. A long wind escaped her lungs. Eric only had a few games left, and the thought that he would actually let the season go by and not attend one was making her sick.

Tears began to pool in her eyes. She reached into her

handbag for a tissue. As she did so, she looked around at the people in the bleachers. There were nine men rooting for the twelve boys on the field: fathers. Most of them present and cheering on their boys while her poor son, for all intents and purposes, had no one but her.

Faith was surprised she was able to keep up the front of being "okay" until she put the children to bed because in truth, she was boiling under the surface. How could he do this to her again? How could he do it to Eric?

She pulled Eric's bedroom door closed, took a few steps, and then stopped. Unable to move forward, she leaned sideways against the wall. Her anger and disappointment were mixing together in her spirit like a cocktail of oil and vinegar. Neither dominated, but each equally strong.

"Lord, how much more am I supposed to take?" she spoke into the darkness of the hallway. "How many more times will it be okay for him to break my baby's heart?"

She slid to her knees, squatting now as a bevy of tears poured from her eyes, down her face in a flood. She covered her mouth to keep her moans from escaping. She didn't want to wake the children, but she felt as if she couldn't take another step without having this breakdown.

You want me to forgive him again, she thought. *I don't want to.*

But I've forgiven you.

"How many more times, Lord?"

Her cell phone chirped. Faith rose to her feet and quickly made her way to the bedroom where she looked at the caller I.D. Her mother. She couldn't answer now. Her mom would recognize the pain in her voice and become upset.

Faith waited a minute for the voicemail to finish, and

then she picked up the phone. She heard the familiar tone that indicated a new message, so she dialed the pass code to enter the voicemail system.

Her mother's message implored her to return her call so she could tell her about a funeral at the church. The second call was from one of her neighbors requesting prayer for her brother-in-law who was having prostate surgery the next day. The third message took her completely by surprise. It was the human resources specialist who had originally set up her first interview with Bowen and Jefferies, requesting she contact her about a second interview.

Heart beating wildly, Faith pushed the appropriate button to save the message. *A second interview.* "Wow." She smiled to herself. She'd impressed somebody on the panel.

The sound of the garage door rising killed her buzz and prompted her to get up from her seat. Her face was a mess. Jonah would know she'd been crying, which she didn't want him to see. It wasn't that she wanted to put a strong presence in front of him or that she wanted to keep her pain a secret. It was the fact that he ignored her tears. He behaved like they didn't mean anything and that hurt her more.

Faith turned on the cold water faucet and removed a face cloth from the small wicker basket on the counter. After wetting it, she wiped around her eyes and nose hoping to remove the redness that gave away her secret.

Once downstairs, she found Jonah standing in front of the stove, the microwave turning with a dull hum. He hadn't heard her on the landing. Her shoeless feet and the solid build of the house did not offer the usual creaks and squeaks that would alert him to her presence on the stairs, so she watched him from the back. His broad shoulders, slim waist, handsome height. Jonah was fine. She had to give him that. Visually and professionally, he was every woman's dream; a good-looking doctor. That's what she had fallen in love with. Who he was, maybe on the outside; what he had to offer, this lifestyle. Was she that shallow? And was that now why she was paying? Reaping what she had sown.

"I'm sorry about tonight." He had heard her, because his back was still to her. "I know you're angry, but it was unavoidable."

He turned and faced her. She noted how exhausted he looked. He was burning himself at both ends of the candle.

"You look beat. You're putting in too many hours."

He picked up a glass from the counter. Faith was relieved to see it was cranberry juice and not bourbon, particularly since it seemed to be his drink of choice these days.

He paused before answering. "I work hard because we own this house, and the trappings that go with it."

Faith let her eyes sweep the enormous kitchen. "Then let's sell the house."

He laughed. "Sell the house."

"We can downsize. Lots of people do it. Then you won't have to work so hard." *If that's what you're doing,* she thought.

"Faith, you found the house."

"I didn't know it would tear our marriage apart."

He sighed loudly. "The house isn't tearing our marriage apart."

"Then what is?"

"Our marriage is fine," Jonah said firmly. "You just need to be a little more forgiving of my work schedule."

"Is that it? Is it just me? There's nothing you need to do?"

He turned his back to remove his plate from the microwave, reached into the drawer for silverware, and carried his wares to the table.

She sat down across from him and touched his fingers with the tips of hers own. "Jonah . . ."

His eyes met hers, and then the rich timbre of his voice came from his slightly parted lips. "May I say grace?"

Faith pulled back in her seat.

When he finished saying grace, he began to eat his meal. "Did I tell you I'm lecturing at Morehouse next week?"

"No," she said for the sake of peace, even though he had dismissed her concerns.

"I think I'd like to teach. Probably not there, but somewhere. "

"I thought you liked Morehouse."

"I do. It's a fine school. I'm proud to be an alum. It's the neighborhood. Reminds me too much of my childhood."

"What's wrong with that?"

His chuckle had an undertone of bitterness. "You ask that question because you didn't grow up like I did."

"Maybe not, but to tell you the truth, I have no idea how you really grew up. Remember, you refuse to share," she said bitterly.

"Share?" He looked at her for a second. "Why? So you can misunderstand and try to play amateur psychiatrist?"

Faith could feel the heat of her temper rising. Jonah continued to eat; like he hadn't just thrown a dart at her.

"I asked you a question before you said grace. I asked if there was anything you needed to do to improve our marriage. I'd like the answer to that."

Faith spoke with more confidence than she had. Jonah filled his mouth with two more filled forks before he answered.

"I think we all know that statistically it takes two to mess up a marriage. I'm not perfect, but I am who I am. I'm the same man you married."

"You may very well be. But you are not the man you promised me you would be."

Jonah sat back in his chair. A smug look on his face. "All I remember is saying I would love, honor, and cherish. Did I make any other promises I'm not keeping? I'm faithful to you, though only God knows why. We haven't made love in a month."

Faith flinched. "That's not completely my fault. You might be able to get some sex if you came in at a decent hour," she said. "Or maybe you're getting it where you are."

"If that was the case, would I be complaining about it?" He paused. "Don't make this into something it's not."

Faith took a deep breath, bit her lip, and choked back bringing up the phone calls. She knew her husband. He'd dismiss it as nothing. Besides, it wasn't the most important issue right now. The disappointment on Eric's face as he glanced through the wired fence of the dugout, scanning the crowd for his dad, was fueling her temper.

"You come in and out of this house like it's a hotel, take showers, and eat meals. You could hire a cook and a maid to do what I do."

The expression on his face changed for a fleeting second—from arrogance to something else—and then flickered back. He had regained his controlled composure. But what was that she had seen for that brief moment? She was hoping it was guilt, remorse, recognition of the truth.

He let out a long breath. "I'm just busy right now."

"No, it's not right now. This has been going on a long

time, getting worse by the year, and our marriage is falling apart."

"There's nothing wrong with us that a little less complaining and a little more loving can't fix." His mouth twisted before he added. "You know, the stuff I can't hire a cook or maid to do."

Faith crossed her arms over her chest and counted to ten. He was really getting to her. "I disagree," she said. "You're keeping things from me."

In lightning fast speed, Jonah was on his feet. His fist thundered like a ball of iron as he banged on the tile surface of the table. "I'm tired, and I don't want to hear this crap tonight."

Faith jumped to her feet, making him less of a towering giant. "You missed Eric's game. You promised me you would come."

He ran his hand over his short, cropped hair. "I can't do this."

"You keep breaking promises." It was a struggle to keep from yelling and waking the children.

"I don't want to hear this now," Jonah growled as he mangled the knot on his tie in an attempt to loosen it.

"You never want to hear it, but hear me when I say this; I'm not going to continue to be your little Stepford wife. Sitting around the house making meals for a man who doesn't have the courtesy or respect to even call home and say he isn't coming to eat it."

He picked up his plate and walked to the sink. She followed him.

"I'm not going to continue to raise these kids like a single mother with no man and . . ." she paused for maximum shock appeal. "I'm going back to work."

Jonah dropped the plate into the sink. Chards of glass splintered and flew out like tiny missiles.

Faith flinched, and then steeled herself against his anger. She wasn't backing down; not tonight. "You can break every dish in this house, but things are still going to change around here." She turned her back, left the kitchen, and walked up the stairs trembling with every step.

Chapter 8

Jonah hated days like this. Days when he met a child who was really sick. Some congenital heart diseases were incurable, and it made him feel powerless. That was a feeling he didn't like. Between Amadi Lazarus's discouraging test results, the fight with Faith, and yet another phone message from his mother about picking up flowers on Saturday, this day had gone from bad to worse.

Thinking about all of it made him angry. So angry he wanted to throw something against the wall and listen to it crash. He wanted a drink, one so strong it would burn as it made its way down his throat. But more than anything, he wanted to escape it all, especially the anniversary of his brother's death.

Ten years was a long time in a childhood. Eating meals together, baths, games, and secrets. *Tell me about your childhood.* Faith couldn't possibly understand. She grew up in a middle class neighborhood with both her parents in a house that was one mile from the beach. It literally had a white picket fence around the perimeter. How idyllic was that? Then there was the fact that she was an only child. She had no idea what it was like to even have a sibling, so losing one . . . He shook his head. She'd never begin to understand.

Jonah stood and leaned against the window jam to look out at the spring day. He must have been insane to specialize in cardiology, but he knew what he'd been thinking at the time. If he could just help *somebody*, if he could save somebody's child, he could make it better. He could ease his own pain, and maybe the anger. But it wasn't working. The death of his brother, Joshua, was a pain that tore so deeply into him that he thought he would hemorrhage on the inside. *Cardiac insufficiency.* He hated that word, but it was one he had to use everyday when making diagnoses.

Jonah felt the sting of tears in the corners of his eyes. Nobody cared about poor children in the seventies. No pro-bono care for the black kid from the ghetto with the ignorant father. As much as he tried to suppress the memories, his mind drifted back.

"I'm not going to beg anybody to do anything."

Jonah stood on the screened porch that led to the front door of his family's home.

His mother was crying; sobbing, really. "Lord, Martin, I'm not asking you to beg. He's our son. He's only nine. Please . . . I don't want to lose him."

Jonah's father turned to his mother, his eyebrows knit together in an angry furrow. To Jonah, he looked like a monster standing there with his hands jammed in his pockets. "Some things in life are the way they are, Clarisse. You need to accept that."

"I don't accept it." His mother sniffed loudly.

"Well, then why don't you pray to that Jesus you're always talking about?" His father's tone had an acidic sarcasm that made Jonah's stomach do a nervous flip. They went to church almost every Sunday, but his father

didn't. He said church was a waste of a good Sunday morning.

His mother cried even harder now. "Martin, please," she yelled, grabbing the tail of his T-shirt.

His father yanked his mother's hand away like he wanted to chop it off.

"Call ya' Jesus, Clarisse. It seems now would be a good time for Him to show up."

Jonah reached into his open attaché case under his desk and removed a small silver flask he kept there. He twisted the top off and took a drink. Then he looked back at the pictures of Amadi Lazarus's heart. Amadi was a child he desperately wanted to help. No doubt, based on these test results, the kid's heart had a lot of damage. Cardiomyopathy at age nine. Just like Joshua.

He pressed his thumbs into his temples and rotated them in circles. Life just didn't make sense. More than thirty years had passed, Amadi had state of the art medical care available to him because, pro-bono or not, Jonah would make sure he got the best of care. But if his diagnosis proved to be what he thought, no amount of money or dedication to the case was going to help Amadi. He needed a heart transplant, and with his rare blood type, it was going to take a miracle to get one.

Now would be a good time for Jesus to show up for Amadi. But Jonah didn't count on that. He had prayed long and hard for Joshua, but in the end, Jesus had not shown up because Jesus didn't really care.

Chapter 9

Faith walked into the family life center where the church's administrative offices were located. She couldn't believe she'd forgotten the paperwork she needed after Sunday's service. She'd even asked Jonah and the kids to remind her to pick it up, but as usual, everyone was so anxious to get out of Dodge, that no one remembered. She probably needed to start taping notes on the handle of her purse. But she had always thought that was a sign of old age, and she wasn't going out like that. Not yet.

"Good morning, Sister Morgan." The jubilant greeting from the church receptionist rolled off her tongue like she was already in heaven. "I loved that suit you were wearing on Sunday. I think yellow is your color."

This woman was perfect for her job. She always had a big smile and a kind word for everyone. She even made Faith feel peppier.

"Thank you, I appreciate that. But you know what the showstopper was?"

Amanda Banks began patting her hair, a knowing blush in her cheeks.

"Very stylish cut," Faith said, grinning.

"It was a little extreme, but I decided, heck, I turned forty this year. It's time to be a little daring." She continued to pat her hair as she pulled her top drawer open and removed a compact mirror. "I hadn't snagged a husband with it hanging down to the center of my back in the last twenty years, no point continuing on the same course. A girl needs a new look." She winked.

Everyone thinks they want a husband, Faith thought. Until they get one.

"Are you here for a job interview? I didn't see your name on the list." She returned the mirror to its place.

"No, I'm here to pick up some information Sister Lincoln left me for the women's conference."

"Oh, I just assumed," Sister Banks said.

"What job is Pastor interviewing for?"

"The manager for the women's ministry. It's been advertised for a few months. Pastor has interviewed a ton of people." She had slipped into gossip mode. "He's so picky. I think he has an idea in his head and can't nobody else see it. The ad is right there." She flicked a long, shiny fingernail in the direction of the wall behind Faith.

Faith took a few steps to the church bulletin board and noted the advertisement. Yvette had mentioned it to her before, but she had been preoccupied and hadn't really paid much attention.

WOMEN OF FAITH MINISTRY NEEDS A WOMAN OF FAITH AND VISION.

Faith continued to read the job description. "It doesn't look like he's requiring much. He isn't even looking for a degree of any kind."

"I know," Sister Banks said. "That's why it's such a trip. He's interviewed about thirty women over the last few months and nobody's good enough. You would think he was looking for a co-pastor."

"I guess we should consider ourselves blessed that he's careful about who's in charge."

"I suppose." Sister Banks pulled out a nail file. "I applied for the job, and just like everybody else, he had me out of his office in less than five minutes. I guess I didn't say the magic words."

Faith watched her file her nails for a few seconds. "I'll just go pick up my paperwork," she said, excusing herself.

The phone rang on Sister Banks's desk. Like a little robot, she dropped the nail file into a drawer, picked up the receiver, smiled like she was on a video conferencing phone, and greeted the caller. Faith shook her head. Pastor had Sister Banks exactly where she belonged. Hospitality was definitely her gift.

The offices were just beyond the reception area. Faith opened the door to a room named the "Common Office." Common because it was shared by the different ministry heads when they needed office space for short intervals of time.

She sat down at the desk, reached into the bottom file drawer and removed the red folder Sister Lincoln, one of the more "busy body" planning committee members, had placed in the hanging file marked women's ministry. It included receipts for the hotel and the contact information for the printing service. Sister Lincoln took it upon herself to set up the printing of the church souvenir booklet for the women's conference, and by Faith's estimation, she was paying way too much for what they were getting. Rumor had it the printer was her second cousin. She and Sister Lincoln were going to have a talk about that. Nepotism at the church's expense would never do. Not on her watch.

Faith turned on the computer and waited for it to boot up. Glancing at the clock, she noted she had an hour before Elise needed to be picked up from nursery school.

That wasn't enough time to go by the printer, and it was far too early to sit outside the school in the heat, so she decided to surf the net.

The computer continued to churn and moan as it slowly revealed the desktop. If it took that long for the thing to boot up, what would using the Internet on it be like? Faith clicked the Explorer icon and a search window appeared for Google. She typed in Bowen and Jefferies Consultants, hit enter, and found herself looking at the link for their homepage.

Bowen and Jefferies had one of those grand websites that one could tell cost a fortune. Similar to the office décor, it had a beautiful copper tinted background with various other browns as accent colors for the icons and text she could select. She worked her way through all the links, reading various articles they had posted about their company history, services provided, previous customers, and lastly, employment opportunities.

The job she had applied for wasn't listed. Faith continued to tap on the mouse looking at various other jobs opportunities on the site. She was just killing time and pushing her world out of her mind; the problems with Jonah, particularly the drinking, were getting to her. It seemed the more she prayed the worse he got. Things weren't going in the right direction, and she was tired. She also had to admit she was nervous about the report from the phone company.

Faith stood to her feet and approached a painting that hung on the wall of every office in the church. There was also a twenty foot version of it etched in stained glass behind the pulpit. It was of an African American man, presumably Jesus, pulling and breaking cuffs from His bound hands and feet. Setting Himself free. She raised a hand and touched the brass frame. She wanted the energy, the power of the image to somehow transfer. The inscription

under her fingertips read: *HE came to set the captive free.*
She stepped back, still looking at the painting in awe.
Faith understood why pastor liked it. Everybody—every
living thing in creation wanted to be free. Including her.

Faith shut down the computer and left the church.
Climbing into her vehicle, she continued to think about
the power of the painting. She had to stop being a wimp.
She was going to tell Jonah about the job with Bowen and
Jefferies. Tonight. Jesus had not died on the cross for her
to be a slave to all this confusion.

Chapter 10

The smell of cookies baking greeted Jonah as he entered the family room. He could see that Faith was removing a pan from the oven. The gentle chime that sounded whenever an outer door opened alerted her to his presence, and she responded by looking over her shoulder. She gave him a slight, but promising smile.

She was cooking like she had nowhere to go tonight. He had a bad feeling Samaria hadn't called Faith like he'd asked her to.

Jonah could see Elise peeking from around the island. She stood and leapfrogged down the stairs that led from the kitchen to the sunken family room.

"Daddy!" she squealed, wrapping her arms around his legs.

Jonah scooped her up in his arms and threw her into the air. A cascade of giggles came down with her. His daughter was a beauty, the spitting image of her mother and growing up quickly. In his opinion, they were overdue for adding to their family. But that wasn't a conversation Faith wanted to have these days.

Elise wrapped her arms around his neck and squeezed like she was hanging on for dear life.

"How's my baby girl?"

"Daddy, know what I learned today?"

"No, I don't. I wasn't there," he replied, teasing her.

Elise giggled, playing with the loosened knot in his tie. "Daddy, you're funny. I learned that blood goes to the heart."

Jonah smiled. "Oh yeah? That's impressive," he said, lowering her to the floor.

Faith was coming toward him. She had a pleasant look on her face. Her long, dark brown hair was pulled into a ponytail. Except for a light coat of gloss on her lips, her chestnut brown skin was flawless and without makeup. She was wearing a T-shirt from her alma mater, the University of Georgia, and a pair of blue jeans. Her feet were bare—her delicate toes painted a sexy bronze color that she also wore on her nails. It complemented her skin. Faith was just as beautiful as she was the day he married her. It made him think about what he needed to do to patch things up.

She was calling a truce by kissing him on the cheek. It was something she hadn't done in weeks. He welcomed the small sign of affection, and could only hope it would continue through the evening. She was looking very good, and it was time they ended the standoff in the bedroom.

"You're early," Faith said. "Good. We can eat and get to the field before seven. Maybe you can help Eric warm up. It would mean the world to him."

Jonah dropped his head and whispered a curse. He'd forgotten. "I have to speak at a benefit for the National Heart Society tonight."

Faith's smile disappeared. "What benefit?"

"It's a last minute thing. They asked me this morning.

The surgeon who was scheduled had a death in his family."

She wrapped her arms around herself and spoke through clenched teeth. "You promised."

He wiped a hand over his face.

Her fists went to her hips. "There are only two games left," she said through clenched teeth.

"I'm sorry. I forgot. I was so excited when they called I just—"

"Excited, about what? You give speeches all the time." Faith wasn't going to make this easy for him.

Jonah dropped his eyes and noted Elise was looking at them. Her eyes skittered between their two faces, trying to figure out what was going to happen next. He leaned closer to her and said, "Lesie, go upstairs while I talk to your mom."

Elise began walking slowly. She turned on the stairs, her eyes sad as she gave them one last pleading look that said: *Don't fight.*

Jonah pushed it from his mind and removed his blazer. "I know it's last minute, but speaking at a benefit for the National Heart Society is a big thing for me. I think it would be for any cardiologist."

"But you weren't even attending before they called you, so how could it be so important now?" Faith's mouth formed an angry line.

He struggled to keep his voice even. "I'll make the next game."

"You've been saying that for a month."

"Well, I mean it this time." He was more abrupt than he meant to be. He could tell Faith was unconvinced. "I won't miss the next game," he added, firmly.

She cut her eyes away from him. He could see them wetting with tears. She sniffed and turned back to look at him. "So, you need me to steam your tux?"

"Actually, I need you to go with me."

"What?" Her hands dropped from her hips.

"I called Yvette. She's going to sit with the kids."

"Oh," she guffawed. "So now you have a use for Yvette."

Did this woman ever miss an opportunity to complain? He looked at his watch. "She'll be here by 5:30. We need to leave here by 6:30. It's at the Congress Center."

Faith raised her hand and grabbed her ponytail. "Look at my hair. It would have been nice to have some notice. If they called you this morning, why didn't you call me?"

"I'm sorry—I was busy. I asked one of the girls to do it, but I guess she forgot. It was one of those full moon days, you know."

Faith rolled her eyes. He knew she hated it when he put her on the spot like this.

"You don't take long, babe. You're gorgeous all the time." He raised her chin and kissed her cheek. Once he saw her eyes soften, he released her. Heading for the office he said, "I'm going to go over my speech. I'm tweaking the one I gave at the Southern Association of Pediatric Cardiologists last spring."

She continued to stand with her arms crossed although she nodded her head in agreement that it was appropriate.

"They have a table for Christian Brothers. Some of the staff signed up to attend so we'll be in good company," he said. "Go get more beautiful."

He closed the door behind him.

Chapter 11

The annual benefit for pediatric research for the National Heart Society was held in a different metropolitan city every year. Some years Jonah attended, other years he didn't. It wasn't as important to him as the events held by the American Heart Association or those specifically for African American cardiologists. But the prestige of being the keynote speaker would make the *Atlanta Journal Constitution* tomorrow and every relevant medical journal published in the country within a few months. That's why Gunter had asked him to return the phone call. It was good publicity, and every business needed that.

Jonah looked around at the prestigious gathering of his peers. Cardiologists and surgeons chatted; some local, others not, but he knew most of them from conferences and events he'd attended over the years. He could guess the limited subjects of their conversations. The primary topics were billing, rising cost of malpractice insurance, health maintenance organizations, and golf. Their wives were on to more pleasant conversations like upcoming summer vacations and the rising cost of condo rentals on the Florida coast. When those conversations were spent, they'd move on to interior decorating. It was shallow, but this was his world.

Faith was standing nearby speaking with the wife of a prominent Atlanta pastor. He didn't care where they were, she always seemed to gravitate toward other Christians. It was like she had a radar for finding them or they her. All signs of her earlier anger were now gone, and she looked lovely in the dress she'd chosen. Its knee length hemline showed off the fantastic legs and figure she managed to keep from her morning runs.

"Dr. Morgan."

Jonah turned to find a petite Latino woman behind him.

"I'm Amanda Desoto the coordinator for tonight's event." She presented her hand for him to shake. "I just wanted to come over and personally thank you for agreeing to deliver the speech tonight on such short notice."

"You're welcome. I appreciate the opportunity," Jonah replied.

She hadn't let go of his hand yet, and she was smiling as she continued to look him up and down. "Is that your lovely wife you came in with?"

Jonah gently eased his hand out of her grip. "Yes, it is. I'll introduce you when Reverend Shorter's wife turns her loose."

"Of course." Her eyes darkened, and she smiled devilishly. "I was hoping you'd say it wasn't your wife. I guess it's true all the handsome men in Atlanta are married."

"I'm sure not all." He nodded past her. "Ms. Desoto, do you know my colleague, Tom Cooper?"

"Miss," she corrected, flashing another one of her bright smiles.

"Dr. Cooper is a family practitioner."

"Yes, Christian Brothers." She said the words like they left a nasty aftertaste in her mouth. "What an interesting concept."

"I'll allow Cooper to tell you about it," Jonah said, patting him on the shoulder and walking away. If it was an unfaithful husband she wanted, Cooper was her man.

Jonah pulled out his cell phone just as Faith glanced away from Mrs. Shorter. He pointed to it, and then to the direction of the entrance, letting her know he was stepping out to make a phone call. Once he was away from the noisy crowd, he dialed.

"Kimble Heart Center."

"Hi Evelyn." Jonah recognized the unit clerk's voice.

"Dr. Morgan," she said cheerfully. "How are you this evening?"

"I'm good. I was calling to see if my patient had come in tonight."

"Let me see." He heard her fingers on a computer keyboard. "I'm sure I saw your name earlier, but what's the patient's name?"

"Lazarus is the last name. Amadi"

"Oh yes. He and his family are here. They're actually in with the life specialist right now for pre-testing counseling."

Jonah waved at a couple who walked by. The surgeon was one of his colleagues from Kimble and would probably help with Amadi's case, if he needed an operation.

"Good. I was hoping they were settled in."

"He's got a heavy day tomorrow—MRI—biopsy, he must be a pretty scared little guy."

"I hope not." Jonah reached around to massage the back of his neck with his free hand.

"Will we see you tomorrow?"

"Yes, I'll do the biopsy myself. Tell Amadi hello for me."

"Will do, Doctor. You have a good evening."

"You too."

Jonah returned the phone to his pocket just as Samaria and a young man entered the building. Samaria, clad in a metallic red, skin tight mini-dress, looked like she had just walked off the set of one of those vile, booty shaking, rump rocking music videos. Her feet were strapped into lace up sandals with heels that had to be five inches high. Her hair, a frizzy mess, could have provided a weave for at least three or four other women in the room.

Jonah turned his back, hoping she wouldn't see him. Wishing he hadn't seen her.

"Dr. Morgan." *Too late.* "Is that you?" Then . . ."Malik, come meet my boss."

Jonah turned around.

Malik, a street thug in a surprisingly smart tuxedo, offered one hand to Jonah while rubbing his chin with the other. "Whaz up, Doc?"

Samaria shoved him in the side and cast him a nasty look. "That's Doctor, *Malik*," she said nastily. "Doctor Morgan is the speaker for this evening."

"A'ight, a'ight den, whaz up, Doctor M?" Malik corrected.

This time Samaria stepped in front of her escort. Smiling tightly, she asked, "Are you ready for the big presentation?"

Presentation. Was she kidding? The show was right here in the lobby. The *BET Video* Awards, apparently. He had to force himself to move his eyes from the spectacle. Samaria's breasts, barely concealed in one of those red push-up bras, moved in front of him like dancing globs of Jell-O. Those work scrubs were hiding a lot.

Jonah cleared his throat. "I don't know if I'd use the word excited. You've said one speech, you've said them all. But I'm in my element when I talk about my work, so I'm looking forward to it."

"It must be exciting to be such an important man."
She was flirting.

"It's actually more humbling than exciting." He looked in the main ballroom and noticed several people were now taking their seats. "Look, dinner's about to be served. I'd better find Faith."

"Nice to almost meet ya, Doctor M." Jonah could tell by the assertion in his voice, that Samaria's friend didn't like being pushed aside.

Jonah hated pre-judging anyone, but he hoped the guy wasn't dangerous. The hostile glare he'd given Samaria was a definite sign that he didn't like being disrespected. Didn't she realize she'd only attract one kind of man in a dress like that? A thug. They came in all shapes and sizes. Those in jeans hanging down to the backs of their knees and those in two thousand dollar suits.

Jonah reached for his hand and gave it a firm shake. "Enjoy the evening." He nodded. "Sam."

Walking away, he heard Malik say, "Stay black, brother . . ." and then Samaria let go a string of curse words.

Chapter 12

Faith had to admit she was proud to see Jonah at the podium giving the keynote address for NHS. He was energized with a confidence that she knew was the result of pride. Pride in himself for being chosen, even if he were the second or third choice. There were over a hundred cardiologists in Metro-Atlanta, and quite a few of them were pediatric specialists.

She couldn't help wishing he would bring the same level of enthusiasm to his personal life. Faith knew she shouldn't get in this zone again, but she felt sorry for herself. Jonah had so much potential, but she, hard as she tried, couldn't tap into it—had never really gotten to it—even in the beginning. They went from dating to marriage with no real zeal on his part. She wondered over the years if he actually loved her or just married her because he wanted a trophy wife.

God help my mind. She closed her eyes. She needed to stop obsessing about this.

The speech went well. Within moments of the program ending, Art Dorsey, an associate editor for the *Journal of*

Pediatric Cardiology, approached Jonah for an impromptu interview.

After asking Jonah a series of questions specific to his education at Morehouse and his fellowship at Emory, he began to probe about challenging cases and their outcomes. The technical jargon was giving her a headache. She let her eyes wander the room. The networking was in full swing. The doctors and educators huddled in small groups. Intense conversation, and then the exchange of business cards was the agenda for the evening.

Some of the wives engaged in conversations also, but most sat on the sidelines, nursing a drink and looking bored. Those who were still awake had their eyes peeled in the same direction as Faith's. She had been interested in seeing the face of a woman across the room whose back was to her. A swarm of men surrounded her scantily covered body. Faith had become so curious to see who she was that she'd completely tuned out Jonah and his new seat mate, until a flashlight popped to the left of her. She was temporarily blinded. *People still had cameras that went pop.*

Atlanta Newsweek. She recognized the older reporter that always attended these events for the small paper. He and his antique camera were a team. The camera blinded his subject, and then he got to interrupt the people he'd been shooting, first with an apology for the noisy shutter, and then he usually went ahead and asked his few questions, just as he was doing to Jonah and Art now. She smiled, nodded at him, and he gave her a friendly wave as he walked away. *Mission accomplished,* Faith thought.

She reached for her water goblet and returned her attention back to the interview just in time to hear the editor ask, "Why did you specialize in pediatric cardiology?"

Jonah hesitated for a second. It was a pause that Faith

had seen many times over the years when he was asked that question.

He resumed smiling and gave his standard response. "I knew that cardiology was the specialty for me the first time I held a heart in my hand in medical school, and I love children."

That was a lie if she'd ever heard one. Jonah loved children like she loved dental work. He didn't dislike them. He was just *neutral* about them. Too neutral to really specialize in pediatrics. She turned from the conversation, suddenly becoming uncomfortable with the story she knew couldn't be the truth. She often wondered herself why Jonah specialized in pediatric cardiology, but he would never really say. It was one of those questions she got no answer to.

Faith touched him on the forearm and with an "excuse me," set herself free to find the ladies room. Once inside, she removed her cell phone and dialed home. On the third ring, Yvette answered.

"How's it going?" she asked when Yvette picked up the line.

"All's quiet. They're both in bed."

Faith looked at the face of her diamond watch, a seven-year anniversary present, and noted that it was almost ten o'clock.

"I didn't realize it was so late. I think we'll be out of here soon. Jonah's just doing an interview or two."

"Take your time. I'm getting some paperwork done."

"How was the game?"

"Fun. They won, and Eric caught all of his balls."

Faith smiled. "Good. He's been so nervous about losing his place on first base."

"Well, he won't after his performance tonight," Yvette said.

"Thanks, girl, especially for the last minute call."

"No problem. Look, you know I love my kiddies. If you guys went out more often, I'd get to see them more."

Faith laughed and looked around the room to make sure she was alone. "Yeah well, we'd have to be getting along to get out more."

"Maybe if you had some dates you'd get along better."

"You're probably right, but the man's gotta come home to go back out."

The door to the restroom opened. Faith held a gasp. She couldn't believe her eyes. The woman she had been staring at across the room had just walked in.

"I've got to go, Yvette." She snapped the phone shut and dropped it in her purse.

"Faith." Samaria, Jonah's nurse sashayed across the room. Samaria pulled her into an embrace. Passion, a scent Faith was familiar with, filled her nostrils.

"I was hoping I'd see you before the evening was over. They ran out of room at the Christian Brothers table. I don't think I was supposed to bring a date."

Faith knew she was staring. She couldn't help herself. Samaria's breasts seemed to be yelling *"Look at us!"* She found herself wondering if they were real or fake.

"It's good to see you, Samaria. How's school?" Faith asked, pulling her eyes away.

The woman's entire countenance changed. "Disastrous. I'm not cut out for it, but I'm going to try and stick it out. We're not all married to doctors." Samaria laughed.

Faith held a grunt.

"But I did give my number out a few times tonight, so I'm hopeful," Samaria said, giggling.

No doubt they are too, Faith thought as she watched Samaria pull on the sides of her bra.

Samaria was wasting her time. Those babies weren't getting back in there.

"I'd better go rejoin Jonah. I'm sure he's trying to get out of here," Faith said, thinking she'd had enough of watching Samaria. It was worse than restricted cable after midnight.

Faith had barely taken three steps when Samaria said, "Thanks for letting me borrow him tomorrow." Faith froze in her tracks. Those words had moved through her mind in slow motion. *Borrow my husband???*

"Dr. Morgan is helping me with my cardiology class," Samaria smiled like he was taking her to the prom. "I have a test."

Faith raised her hand to touch the diamond choker around her neck. She saw Samaria's eyes take the necklace in hungrily, like it was a piece of steak. Now who was staring at whose chest? Faith recovered with a casual, "Oh, yes, studying. I'd forgotten. Good luck—on your test." She walked out of the restroom. Her heart slammed against her chest. So he couldn't come home at night and couldn't go to Eric's game, but he has time to study with that . . .

"Faith." Tom Cooper walked toward her. "I was hoping I'd get to say hello."

"Hello, Tom," she said with cheer she didn't feel. "I thought you'd be sitting with us."

"I chose to sit with some other colleagues. No offense, but I see the folks at Christian Brothers all the time." He rocked back on the balls of his feet. "Great speech Jonah gave."

Faith raised her hand to her necklace again. Samaria's face passed through her mind. "Yes, he was impressive."

"How are the kids?"

Faith struggled through the conversation with Tom because she steaming underneath. *Thanks for letting me borrow him.* The nerve of both of them. How could Jonah do this? More importantly, why?

Faith watched Samaria come out of the restroom. The scent of her perfume slammed into her nostrils before the woman even got within ten feet of them. Samaria cast an inappropriate, sexually laced glance Cooper's way and kept going. Cooper had stopped mid sentence and watched as she walked past them, jiggling what either the good Lord or a good plastic surgeon gave her.

Jonah making time for that vixen was all she needed to hear. She'd known they were in trouble earlier this evening, but something told her the lady in red that sauntered across the room was a complication their marriage didn't need.

Chapter 13

Faith waved to Yvette as she backed out of the driveway. Jonah had gone to his office, and Faith climbed the stairs to their bedroom. She checked on both the children. They were sleeping like logs, no doubt from the energy both expended tiring out Yvette.

In her bathroom, Faith looked at her reflection in the mirror. She had pulled herself together surprisingly well with such short lead-time, but it wasn't how she looked that mattered. It was how she felt. Like she was being played for a fool. *You're stupid.* The voice on the telephone had called her. Jonah helping Samaria. Maybe she was.

She showered and climbed into bed, fully exhausted from the events of the day and the banter in the car with Jonah. He said he was only helping her this one time.

What was I supposed to say, Faith? She was begging.

Was he crazy? He apparently didn't know begging when he heard it. *She* had been begging him for years. *Eric* had been begging him to attend one of his games. *His* marriage was begging him to show up.

"I hate him," she muttered in the darkness. He was throwing away everything they'd worked so hard to build. How much more of this debacle of a marriage did he really expect her to hang around for?

Faith rolled over on her side. She thought how badly she needed to pray, but she was so angry, she was liable to explode. Rage was moving the blood through her veins at a rate that couldn't be good for her blood pressure.

Although she was mature enough to believe differently now, as a child her mother taught her that God hears a person best from their knees. She had to admit sometimes when an issue really weighed on her heart she would get on her knees, hoping for an extra blessing.

An extra blessing was what she needed. The way she felt about Jonah and Eric was really disturbing her. Actually, everything about Jonah was bugging her. He never made time for anything that didn't directly affect him. So what was in it for him with Samaria? She hated to think about it, but that dress and those breasts came back to her with agonizing clarity. She closed her eyes and prayed. *Lord, please help me. Tell me what to do God.*

Silence echoed back, and she recognized her words were terse, even with the Lord.

The sound of Jonah's steps on the stairs alerted her that he was on the way up to bed. She was hoping he had just gone in the office to check his email or something, but the twenty minutes since they'd separated in the foyer was an indication that he was more likely having another celebratory drink. He'd already had few at the benefit. This was becoming another area of concern. His drinking was more frequent than it ever had been and certainly more than she cared to live with.

He was holding the jacket to his tuxedo in his hand as he entered. Faith couldn't quite read him in the dim light, but she was guessing he was a little intoxicated.

"Tonight was great," Jonah stated, stopping at the foot of their bed. "And do you want to know what the best part was of all?"

She sat up in the bed, assuring him her full attention without responding in word.

"Coop." Indignation filled his tone. "Coop was green with envy, and I loved every minute of it."

Faith suppressed a sigh. She really expected the man to say the opportunity to be heard, the celebrity of the interviews, pride in being recognized, anything but rubbing it in someone's face.

"Come on. I'm sure Coop wasn't the best part of your evening. What about the interview for the Pediatric Cardiology?"

"I said it was Coop," he snapped. "That smug jerk finally got what he deserved. I'm tired of him thinking he's equal to me." He proceeded to his dressing room where he took off the rest of his tuxedo.

He was drunk.

"He's always trying to control me. All his little comments: Jonah should do this. We need Jonah to do that. Jonah, Jonah, Jonah." He stepped out of the room in his underwear holding a pair of pajama bottoms. "If he spent less time trying to manage my patient load and more time on his own, he'd have a more successful career."

Faith continued to keep her mouth shut. This rivalry between Cooper and Jonah had been going on for years. It was trivial and boring. At some point she'd hoped Jonah would grow spiritually enough to push it into the recesses of his mind, but the growth seemed very slow in coming.

"You allow Cooper to have too much power."

He'd been walking to the bathroom, but paused at her words.

"You know, Faith, if you understood a thing about office politics, you wouldn't be saying that."

She let a silent moment pass, his response adding to the annoyance she already felt. Then she added, "I guess when I go back to work I'll have a better understanding of it all, and then we can swap stories."

"By the time *you* go back to work, I'll probably be out of Christian Brothers and in my own practice." He closed the bathroom door behind him.

Faith started to let him know what she thought. Tell him about her interview with Bowen and Jefferies, but it wasn't the time. Her intentions weren't for it to be a weapon pulled out in a nasty fight, and definitely not when he was half drunk.

She slid down in the bed, gathering the salmon-colored duvet under her chin. Tomorrow. She'd tell him tomorrow.

She rolled over on her right side and looked out the window. The stars sparkled like tiny diamonds against the indigo blue sky. The beauty of it, a gift from God. The gift He'd granted before He even formed man from the earth. If God could make a sky so flawlessly beautiful, He could take away the ugliness she felt in her heart. Faith pulled back her covers and slid to the floor. Tonight God would hear her from her knees.

Chapter 14

Samaria took a last look at herself in the mirror of the ladies restroom. She had tried to look her best without overdoing it on the makeup. She opened her new Prada handbag and removed a bottle of her favorite perfume. Passion. It was sure to lure the man of her dreams to her. One more squirt on the neck. She didn't want him to smell her coming down the hallway, but she did want to arouse his senses. She sniffed the scented air. *Perfect.*

Just as she returned her perfume to the bag, her cell phone rang. Tom Cooper. She recognized the distinct ring tone she'd assigned him.

She pushed the button on her earpiece. "This is the third time you've called me."

"Who was that street hood you were with last night?" Cooper asked. Vexation was evident in the way he growled.

"My date," Samaria answered. "Who was the old bag on your arm?"

"Don't get smart with me, Mair," he said, using the nickname he'd given to her. She hated being called Samaria.

Cooper thought Sam was a guy's name, and as he'd re-marked to her many times, she was all woman. "I thought you were coming with April."

"She cancelled on me. I didn't want to sit alone. Not like I could go with you."

"I didn't give you money for a dress so you could come with your rapper wannabe boyfriend."

"Consider me charity, Coop. Write it off on your taxes. Now I know you couldn't be calling to ask about last night, so what do you want? I'm in the middle of study-ing."

He paused, and then made the statement she knew was coming next. "I want to see you."

Samaria reached into her handbag and pulled out mas-cara. She applied a little more to her eyelashes.

"Mair . . . Mair are you there?"

"Of course I'm here." *He might be more trouble than he's worth,* she thought. "I can't see you tonight. I have a big exam on Tuesday evening, and I have to study all weekend."

"It's been almost two weeks since you've made time for me. What's going on? Are you sleeping with that—"

"I'm not sleeping with anyone, including you, in case you don't remember. We *are* supposed to be friends. Have a few dinners, help each other through our problems. I didn't promise you a permanent spot on my calendar."

"But—"

"But nothing. I've got to go." She ended the call. Samaria knew he'd be fuming. She'd compensate him for his trouble soon enough. Especially since the dress was such a show stopper. Jonah couldn't take his eyes off her, and that's exactly the precursor she wanted for today's meeting.

Cooper was such a sucker. She loved his type. He was spending money, and she hadn't even had to give anything up. Jonah wasn't going to be so easy. Although he wasn't an obvious dog, he was a man. Push the right sensory buttons and they all eventually succumbed. Plus she had an added advantage. She could tell Jonah wasn't happy. He'd come in the office too many mornings looking miserable and stressed. That wasn't work related, not first thing in the morning. It was *"My wife's gonna make me lose my mind, up in here, . . . up in here . . ."* stress.

Samaria was actually feeling a twinge of guilt. Jonah's wife had always been so nice to her. Nicer than most women, and she was pretty in a classic way, but so plain. One couldn't even tell she was married to a successful man; not from the way she dressed. Every time she'd come to the office, she was so casual. Sneakers and sweats. Last night was the first time Samaria had ever seen her dressed up, and she'd chosen an old maid dress.

"Borrrrring," Samaria said, removing a tube of lip gloss from her bag and adding another layer. But she did have to give the sister some credit. That jewelry she was wearing cost mad money. She hadn't missed the diamond necklace or the watch.

Samaria tugged at her tube top, and then pulled down her daisy duke denim shorts. Her body looked great in this outfit. She'd been wearing the same one when she met her last boyfriend, a married lawyer, who she'd been sure was going to leave his wife last summer. Samaria sucked her teeth. Married men were so unpredictable. They complained about their wives, but then she never knew which ones were full of crap and which ones were genuinely looking for someone like her. A woman who would be devoted to satisfying all his needs . . . in between shopping trips, of course.

She put her lip gloss tube away and ran her fingers through her hair. Her watch read 8:25 A.M. Except for one of the accounting people and a medical records technician, the building was empty. Jonah would be there in five minutes. He was always on time.

She fluffed her hair one last time and picked up her backpack. It was time to go get her doctor. Then she could throw away these stupid books forever.

Chapter 15

"Remember, you have to assess risk for complications when considering the interventional tests."

"I think I have it now," Samaria said. "I don't know what I would've done to get ready for that test."

"You would've done fine," Jonah said, tossing the pen he'd been holding on the desk.

"I don't think so. I would have had the patient being referred for unnecessary surgery."

Samaria sat back in the chair and crossed her long legs. Her high shorts revealed every inch of her thighs and most of her hips. She certainly didn't look like she had come to study. But she was single, it was Saturday. He supposed she had a date after this.

"So," Samaria said, smiling and smacking her thigh. "I owe you lunch. I've taken up most of your morning, and you've missed your weekly golf game. The least I can do is buy you a sandwich and fresh cup of coffee." She sat forward, opening her legs a bit and throwing her hair back over her shoulder.

Samaria was all sex appeal. It was oozing from her pores. Jonah was no fool; even if he didn't have to go to the hospital, he wouldn't have lunch with her. "I have to get going to Kimble. Amadi Lazarus."

Samaria took a slight breath and nodded. Silence filled the office again before she said, "I almost forgot you're doing his test today."

"He's already in MRI, I have to do the cath and biopsy in a little more than an hour."

An uncomfortable hush settled over the room.

Jonah swiveled his chair around and stood to his feet, hoping this would clue her that their session was over. Samaria stood. Her heavy perfume seemed to stand with her, another whiff flooded his nostrils. After a few seconds she picked up her bag. They stepped in unison to the door.

Jonah snapped his fingers. "You go ahead. I forgot, I need to make a phone call."

"I guess I'll see you on Monday." Disappointment was obvious in her voice.

Jonah nodded. He didn't know what she was looking for, but he was anxious for her to leave.

"You have a good weekend." She flashed him a smile.

"You, too," he said as he watched her disappear beyond the door. He hadn't realized he'd been holding his breath until he finally released it.

That was the last time he'd carve out space on his calendar to help her study. Samaria was hopeless. She was unfocused and clearly disinterested in learning the material. He couldn't imagine why she wanted to be a cardiac nurse practitioner. He'd tried to keep them on task, but she inevitably would bring up restaurants she wanted to dine at, movies she hadn't seen, traveling she wanted to do, everything but assessment of the disease process, which was what they were supposed to be focusing on.

His pager beeped. It was his mother, no doubt, confirming the time he was coming. Now he really did have a call to make.

Chapter 16

"Stupid!" How had she messed up like that? She knew how dedicated he was to his patients. Of course, he'd be going to Kimble to check on Amadi. She swore under her breath. She wanted, no she *needed*, to have that lunch with him. She pushed the glass doors and stepped into the muggy mid-morning heat. Like a mirage in a sweltering haze, the grill of her late model Honda Civic took on the shape of a mouth and laughed at her. She deserved better. She deserved Jonah's E-Class Mercedes which was sitting a few spaces away. It mocked her too.

Samaria had to start the car twice to get the engine to catch. She knew she needed to get the vehicle serviced, but she hadn't taken time last Saturday after class, and the place she normally used was closed on Sunday. "Stupid car!" she spat, hitting the dashboard. That Faith Morgan was driving around in either the Lexus or the Mercedes SUV.

Overwhelmed by the oppressive heat inside, she put the windows down and stepped back out to put her book bag in the trunk. She wouldn't pull that out until class on

Tuesday. She looked wistfully at the small travel case that sat to her left. It included all the necessities a girl might need should she suddenly find herself in the throws of an impromptu session of loving. She'd brought it along today just in case she got Jonah where she wanted him. A hotel room.

Samaria clucked her teeth. All was not lost. She had to take progress where she could get it. He was obviously interested. She'd seen him looking at her legs a couple of times during the meeting. Samaria knew the shorts would do the trick. She had legs like Tina Turner. No man could resist them.

She pulled out of the parking lot and into ongoing traffic. Progress was good, but she really needed to make her move on Jonah soon because by the end of this semester, she was going to be out of the nurse practitioner's program. She didn't think she was going to pass this class, and last semester her average fell below the minimum C average required for graduate students. The director had given her a final warning about her grades. *Who made the rule that you couldn't have a C average in grad school?* Samaria hissed.

It was a shame she wasn't going to be a nurse practitioner. It would have been quite a bit more money and Lord knows she needed that. With sixty thousand dollars in student loan debt, and another twenty-five on her credit cards, she was in trouble. But that was why a girl always had to have a Plan B. If her mother had taught her anything, it was that. The school thing wasn't working, so it was time to use her other assets to acquire wealth.

"Use what the good Lord gave you. You got a money maker that don't require no formal education." That from the woman who'd paid the bills dancing at strip clubs.

Samaria didn't want to believe all she had was the

money maker between her legs. She wanted to believe her teachers and mentors who told her she was smart, that she could go far with education. But at the end of the day, her mother was right. She was flunking out of grad school. It was time to use her money maker to find her somebody who would appreciate a woman like her. She had to make her move on Jonah and quick. Adding to his stress at home would help.

Samaria reached into her purse and removed the pre-paid cell phone she'd purchased, and dialed.

"Hello," Faith Morgan said on the other end.

"Stupid," Samaria whispered, trying to disguise her voice. "You're stupid." Then she ended the call.

Chapter 17

By early afternoon the temperature had soared into the low eighties. The sun beamed down from the sky and produced a suffocating haze that made it difficult to breathe. In the bright afternoon light, Jonah decided his mother looked old. She also looked tired.

He touched the headstone. A ten-year-old replacement for the original, this more expensive memorial stood out amongst the others in this cemetery. He looked around at the many unmarked graves. *Poverty is a curse that follows a person even into death.*

He imagined the family members struggling to pay to bury their loved ones. Thinking they would pull together the money to purchase a proper grave marker when they could, but most of the graves had been there long before Joshua's. No granite headstones with bronze plaques here; except Joshua's, of course. Jonah had purchased it with money he made working overtime as a senior resident. But looking at it now, he realized it could have been made of gold and he wouldn't feel any better. Dead was dead, and no tombstone made that easier to accept.

Joshua Patrick Morgan "In Our Hearts Forever."

Jonah pushed his fists deep into his pockets. His chest was tight with the burden of almost twenty years of grief and unanswered questions, all beginning with the same word. *Why?* Why had Joshua died so young? Why didn't the doctors try more aggressive treatment? And finally, why had Martin allowed his pride to get in the way of saving his son?

His eyes stung from unshed tears. Bile rose in his throat, and all he could think was, *God, get me out of here before I go crazy.*

"Do you remember how we used to have those summer revivals under the tent in Washington Park?" his mother asked.

Jonah smiled despite his effort not to. "Joshua and I loved those revivals."

"Don't I know it? You would talk about it for weeks before it started. Mama, how many more days until they put the tent up? Mama, what day does it start?" His mother laughed. "Lord, ya'll drove me crazy."

"We liked being under the tent," Jonah said. "There was something, I don't know, free about the tent revivals. It wasn't like having to sit on the pews in church. We could lie on the grass." The memory was so real he felt like he could touch it. Maybe it was the heat. "Mama, remember that red punch? We called it 'the blood of Jesus juice.'" Jonah chuckled. "We could drink the punch that the ladies had on the tables at the back of the tent. We couldn't drink in regular church."

"There was nothing to drink in regular church." His mother laughed.

"Then when the benediction was over, we were free to run and play, because we were already outside. It was cool."

"Jon, when the preacher's finished, I'll race you. Let's count to three," Joshua whispered.

Jonah closed his eyes.

His mother's voice, barely above a whisper, startled him from his trance. He'd been remembering his brother's smile, his voice. "Your brother loved to run. He was probably going to be an athlete. He loved sports from the time he could hold a ball."

Jonah could see her smiling at him in his peripheral vision.

"Your father came home with two of those little foam baseballs when you were almost four years old." She grasped his forearm gently. "You didn't pay much attention to yours after the first evening. But your brother, he threw that ball and threw it, and when he went to bed, he took it with him."

Jonah sighed and closed his eyes. The magic had been broken with talk of his father.

"He was quick and limber with his movements and those—"

"Mama, please." He turned and looked her in the eyes.

She released his arm. "Please what?"

"Please don't talk about Joshua being an athlete."

"Why not? That's the point of coming here, son. To remember—to think about him."

"Mama, he had a heart condition." Jonah's words were firm.

"Why you saying that to me? I know he had a heart condition."

"He had a heart condition that limited his physical activity. He would have never been an athlete."

There was silence between them for a few moments.

"God had a purpose for Joshua's life. Just because he died young, doesn't mean it wasn't fulfilled."

He groaned, reached into his pocket for a handkerchief, and wiped his forehead and neck.

"Life is not always for us to understand. I have had to
accept that. Joshua was my child and—"

"He was my brother," Jonah said, sharper than he
meant. "My twin, my other . . ." He shoved the handkerchief back in his pocket. He took a deep breath and threw
his head back for a few seconds. "I can't do this. I'll wait
in the car."

Jonah turned on his heels and marched on unsteady
legs. He felt sick to his stomach and hot, unbelievably hot.

It was the same thing every year. He hated coming here.
He hated listening to his mother talk about Joshua being
an athlete; Joshua could have been a scientist. Joshua
wrote well. Joshua had so much potential. If Joshua had
so much potential, then why was it all buried in a wooden
box in the ground?

At that very moment he wished he wasn't who he was,
because he hated that too. *Dr. Morgan.* God help him, he
was driven to medicine. There was no other field for him.
When he began medical school he was torn between pediatrics and cardiology. How does one heal a child? How
does one fix the heart? The combination of the two was
brilliant. It seemed the perfect solution. But now that he
was a cardiologist, he knew too much. He knew too much
about the pain his brother suffered, and he knew too
much about the ways he could have been helped and wasn't.
Even in the seventies, doctors had choices. His father had
a choice.

There was a knock on the window to his left. He raised
a hand to push the button to lower the window.

"My feet hurt, but I'm not ready to leave yet. I'm going
to sit down in the park over there for a few minutes."

Jonah nodded as he reached in his jacket pocket for a fresh handkerchief.

He watched his mother move slowly across the narrow one lane path that divided the cemetery from the adjacent park. He could tell by her gait that her knees were bothering her.

He wiped his face, stepped out of the car, and did a quick jog to catch up with her. He took her elbow and assisted her to the bench she'd been ambling to.

They'd been sitting side by side on the park bench in the heat for almost twenty minutes when she spoke. "Your father made a mistake."

"I don't want to talk about Martin."

"You hate what he did, but you're so much like him."

"Ignorant," Jonah spat bitterly.

"No. Stubborn." Her voice was resolute.

His fingers gripped the edge of the bench.

"Your father made a horrible mistake. It cost him a lot. He lost his family. But you're making one too."

"Mama, I don't want to—"

"I know. You don't want to talk about anything."

Jonah was silent. His mother turned her body toward him.

"You don't want to talk about Joshua, you don't want to talk about your daddy, and you don't want to talk about Faith. I repeat what I said. You're just like him. It's a mistake to be like this, and you'll regret it."

Jonah guffawed. "You think he regrets it?"

"Don't be juvenile."

"I don't think he regrets anything. Has he ever told you he was sorry?"

"Your father—"

"Has he ever said 'I'm sorry. I'm sorry I let him die.'?"

She shook her head. Tears began to stream down her cheeks.

"Has he ever said it, Mama?" Jonah fought to keep the tears that stung his eyes in check. He was not going to cry. Not when they were talking about his father.

His mother wiped her own tears before answering. "He's not the type of man to directly apologize. You have to understand—"

"I don't have to understand anything. You want to make peace with Martin, make your own peace. I don't care."

"Why you asking if he apologized if you don't care?"

"I don't care about making peace. But I want him to be sorry. I want him to be sorry the rest of his life."

"Well, no worry about that. I'm sure he will be. Especially since the only child he has left can't find it in his heart to forgive him."

"I'm not going to forgive a man that hasn't asked for forgiveness."

"You know, Jonah, you're not perfect, but Lord knows Jesus forgives you everyday, and you don't ask."

He looked straight ahead. Those were the exact words Pastor Kent had spoken this past Sunday.

"We all make mistakes. Some are easily forgotten and easily forgiven. Others . . . not so simple." She paused. "When your wife finds out you've been lyin' to her, it'll be hard for her to understand."

Jonah pressed his lips together, sniffed to keep his nose from running, and took another swipe at his face with his handkerchief.

"I don't understand why you keepin' this from her. I've tried to respect your choice, because I know you hurt about it." His mother placed a hand on his shoulder. "But it's time to tell her."

Jonah leaned forward, elbows on his knees. He'd lied so long. Faith wouldn't understand.

His mother dropped her hand from his shoulder to his forearm and squeezed. "Tell her, Jonah. Joshua's death already destroyed one marriage. If you're not careful, it will destroy two."

Chapter 18

The New Ladies Fitness Center on Peachtree Street was a bustling hub of activity. Hard working, sweaty women clothed in spandex and fleece moved rhythmically to the sounds of the upbeat contemporary gospel music that blared through the facility.

From the looks of things, business was good. The place was packed. There were actually women waiting for machines. Crowds meant membership, and memberships meant profit.

Faith slid her attendance pass through a slot on the desk to register her visit. She put her handbag and water bottle in one of the small lockers lining the far wall and began stretching. She only worked out once or twice a week depending on her schedule because the downtown Atlanta location was a twenty-five-minute drive from her home. But from time to time she wanted a cardio workout in addition to her normal morning run.

After the prescribed thirty minutes on the interval circuit and another fifteen on the stair-stepper, she removed her things from the locker and went to Yvette's office in the rear of the building.

"Knock, knock," Faith announced herself as she moved through the open doorway. Her friend's head had been intently studying the information displayed on a computer monitor, but she turned when she heard Faith, gave her a radiant smile, and popped out of her chair to walk around the desk.

"Hey, girl." Yvette pulled her into a hug. "You're early."

"I need to get back in time to stop in at Eric's school."

"What for?" Yvette reached into her bottom drawer and pulled out a small handbag.

Faith sighed. "We'll talk about it at lunch. I'm starving. Where do you want to go?"

Yvette shrugged. "Two ladies in workout attire. One still perspiring. I'd say the Underground food court."

Underground Atlanta was exactly as it was called. Shopping, dining, and entertainment venues that were mostly under the ground at Lower Alabama Street in downtown Atlanta.

Faith and Yvette were fortunate to get a table. The food court was packed with other diners.

"So, what's going on with my godson?" Yvette asked.

"He only has a month left of school, but his grades have been sliding." Faith reached for her drink, took a sip, and put the Styrofoam cup down. "I mean really sliding. He usually gets A's and high B's on all his assignments and quizzes. Lately I'm seeing low B's, some C's, and a couple of failing quizzes."

"Maybe it's baseball."

It was a plausible explanation. One that she had considered. "I don't think that's it. Some of it is his attitude about school. It's been getting worse over the past few months."

Yvette nodded.

"I don't know," Faith said. "I'm hoping his teachers can give me some insight about what they think it is."

"What does Eric say?"

Faith shrugged. "Nothing. He just says he doesn't know or it was a hard test."

"What does Jonah say?"

Faith gave her a look. "You know better than that. Jonah doesn't know, and he doesn't care."

"That doesn't mean you stop telling him what's going on."

"Girl, I'm just tired of the rejection." Faith shook her head.

Yvette crossed her arms in front of her on the table.

"I'm a single parent and it's getting old."

"Maybe you two need to get away. Go on a trip. You might be able to talk through some things away from life, you know."

Faith raised an eyebrow and picked up her fork. "Where did that come from?"

"Talk shows, girl. I'm telling you, they got all the answers."

They both laughed, but Faith was thoughtful. She and Jonah hadn't gone away on a romantic trip since their five-year wedding anniversary and she'd gotten pregnant with Elise then.

"Plan it this summer for your anniversary or something. Go to Jamaica. You know it's a balm in Gilead for me."

"So you think some Caribbean sun and Jerk pork can heal what ails us, mon?" Faith said, feigning a Jamaican accent.

They both laughed.

Yvette reached across the table and gave Faith's hand a pat. "Seriously, it's a start. You two are in trouble."

Faith nodded. It was a good idea. Maybe a trip could get them on the right path. Lord knows they needed to try something.

Chapter 19

Jonah turned the black Mercedes onto to Joseph Lowery Boulevard and traveled the short distance from the interstate exit to Morehouse College. Although the name had been changed several years ago, Lowery Boulevard would always be Ashby Street to him. He wondered what made politicians think it was okay to change the names of residential streets. It was as if they thought Ashby meant nothing to the hundreds of people who lived there, made it their home, and had some identity tied to the name. He smirked as he cut his eyes with contempt at the street sign.

What arrogance.

An uneasy heat filled the space in the vehicle. In contrast to his appreciation of the street name, he hated coming back to this neighborhood. Seeing it reminded him of his worst childhood fear: that he would never get out of the ghetto. Jonah decided a long time ago that the only thing worse than being poor was being sick. So sick and poor was the worst possible combination. He learned that painful lesson all too well.

A horn blared behind him and bought him out of the trance he'd slipped into while sitting at the traffic light. Jonah slid his foot from the brake to the gas pedal to move the vehicle forward under the green light. It was then that he saw him. His father.

Martin Josiah Morgan was standing on the corner with three other men, passionately engaged in a conversation. He was clearly the leader in the group, his six foot two frame towering over the others. One hand waved vigorously in the air as he emphasized something. His dad had a talent for entertaining others. A beer being liquid confidence, he could draw anyone into his fantastic exaggerated versions of a story.

Jonah watched him. He looked surprisingly well for someone who drank so much. Martin was lean and sinewy. Jonah boasted a more athletic physique, but their dark chocolate skin and square jaws with dimpled chins were identical. He still had a twin. His father. But Jonah hadn't spoken to him in more than twenty years. Not since his freshman year in college when Martin had come to visit him. Jonah felt the same way then that he felt now. As he'd told his mother on Saturday at the gravesite, it was too late for talking and too late for apologies. The way his father left them at Joshua's funeral was something he could never forgive or forget.

"From ashes to ashes, dust to dust," the minister was saying as the tiny casket disappeared into the dirt. The pallbearers seemed to be struggling with their work which shouldn't be. It was a small casket, almost half the size of the one they'd buried his uncle in last year. But still, they made groaning noises and their shoulders tensed and slumped as they let the padded cords holding the casket slide through their fingers.

Jonah felt his entire body shudder. His mother pulled him into her side where he already had his head pressed into her waist. He supposed it was a natural instinct to try and comfort him or maybe she was holding on to the only thing she had left. Whatever the reason, they clung to each other like it was their last time.

Jonah tilted his head slightly to see her grimaced face covered in tears. She rocked back and forth; tiny grunting noises like muffled cries came from deep inside her. The vibrations of her body sent shock waves through his body, confusing him about whether or not he wanted to be near her because her pain seemed to intensify his own. Just then, from his peripheral vision, he saw his father step forward. He was standing to the right of one of the pallbearers. Jonah had never seen his father stand so still—so straight.

Martin Morgan looked angry, rather than sad. His dry face and piercing eyes were an indicator that his mental state was not like his mother's. She was hurting, while his dad looked simply disgusted. It was the same look he had when one of them left their bike in front of the door or forgot to put the garbage can lid on tight and the neighborhood dogs tore at it. Martin Morgan always looked the same way; like he was sick of life.

Jonah remembered him yelling at his mother the night before. "There ain't no God! That's why we burying our son tomorrow!"

A lone tear slid down Jonah's face. His father was always saying that. He used to think it was just to hurt his mother or to mock them for going to church all the time. But now, as he sat at his brother's funeral, he wondered . . . Was there really a God?

"From the dirt I came. The dirt I return," the preacher added melodiously.

Jonah returned his gaze to the casket, which was now gone from his sight. The pallbearers had stopped working. One was wiping the sweat from his face with a dirty handkerchief. He was an older man with gray hair. He looked tired and worn out. Did it really take all that sweating for four men to bury a ten-year-old child?

Jonah leaned forward to try to get a better angle. He needed to see the casket. He wasn't ready to let go of Joshua yet.

"Martin, Clarisse, and Jonah," the preacher said.

Jonah's head popped up, and he looked into the sad eyes of Reverend Augustus Camp.

"We will be praying for you. We're here for you. Be comforted in knowing that Joshua has gone home with the Lord."

Jonah's mother broke into a sob. Her body lurched forward as she removed her arm from around him and her face fell into her hands. Jonah looked at his father who was still staring straight ahead, though his hand was now stroking the hairs of the goatee on his chin.

Sister Agnes from the church stood to allow Reverend Camp to sit next to his mother. Her sobbing was now gut wrenching and loud. As Reverend Camp put his arm around her shoulder and whispered something in her ear, Jonah saw his father kick the dirt in front of him. With anger blazing, he shot an icy look in their direction and went mumbling back down the center aisle of the small graveside setup.

There was a low hush over the crowd as everyone's eyes were on his father's back; his steps deliberate as his long arms flailed and his long legs charged forth. The last thing Jonah heard before he, too, broke into a full, snot rendering cry, was Martin's angry bellow.

"There ain't no God!"

Jonah shuttered from the memory. He gunned the gas and made the left turn onto Morehouse's campus, parked the car and turned off the engine. *There ain't no God.* He opened the door to his car and stepped out into the blaz-

ing heat. He was beginning to wonder. All his life he had
wanted to believe in something bigger and greater than
himself. Like many, he was comforted to think of an idyllic God in heaven who would ensure that good triumphed
over evil. But when he thought about Joshua and saw kids
like Amadi, he couldn't help but think he was living in a
fantasy land. Conjuring up omnipotence where there was
none. As much as he hated to agree with Martin on anything, he was beginning to wonder if his father was right.

Chapter 20

The visit to Eric's school earlier added to the depression Faith was sliding into. All three of his teachers said they were clueless about Eric's sudden academic turn for the worse. They commented that he wasn't doing horribly, but he just wasn't himself. *Was there anything going on at home?*

She kicked her Gucci slippers under the coffee table and reached for a throw to wrap around her bare arms. A blast from the air conditioning left her cold. Chill bumps were the price she was paying to be sexy in a skimpy, silk nightgown with faux mink straps. She'd taken a long hot bath in a scented gelee that she knew Jonah liked. Her hair hung loose in a cascade of spiral curls. A light application of makeup added a little drama to her eyes.

Talking to him hadn't worked, maybe she needed to pull out the oldest trick in the book and just seduce the man into his right mind. But as the petite grandfather clock on the wall behind her chimed the 11 o'clock hour,

she felt less and less like a seductress and more and more
like a fool, or as her anonymous harasser had so brazenly
called her . . . *stupid.*

Faith remembered Samaria. Those breasts spilling out
of her bra and the way she'd let her know about Saturday . . . and then he was gone *all* day. Claimed he was working, stopped by his mother's, but he could have been . . .

She buried her head in her hands. Letting her imagina-
tion get the better of her wasn't helping. Jonah was a lot
of things, but he was no dog. Her husband, she reasoned,
was on his way home from some hospital; Dekalb Medical, Rockdale, or Emory, the list was longer than it
needed to be, but he was definitely working. She believed
that.

She picked up the remote control and pushed the button to turn off the crooning voice of Anita Baker in the
background and reached for a chocolate covered straw-
berry.

Earlier she'd stopped at a travel agency, explained to an
agent she wanted to go to Jamaica for a long weekend,
and received a half dozen brochures for highly recommended resorts for couples. Those same brochures were
displayed on the coffee table between two champagne
glasses, a chilling bottle of Freixenet, and a burning can-
delabrum. The entire seduction scene was supposed to be
a prelude to asking Jonah to join her on a romantic trip.
Colorful pictures of happy couples were to be an irre-
sistible prop. Brilliant, but simple marketing that beck-
oned them to bring their troubles to Jamaica and *make
everything all right.* But now the plan was ruined. It was
time for bed.

Faith scooped the brochures into a pile and placed
them inside a drawer in the coffee table. She pulled the

throw tighter, and after waiting five more minutes, surrendered to it all being for naught when she leaned forward to blow out the candles. The excitement had waned with the ticking of the clock.

Climbing the stairs to the master bedroom she replayed the question of the day in her mind, *Is anything going on at home?* The conference was tangible evidence that the problems in their marriage were spilling over into the lives of the children.

Faith peeked into both of the kids' bedrooms, and then made her way to her own. The reflection that looked back at her in the bathroom mirror was beautiful, but under close observation, she could see the weariness. The eyes bared the soul.

When had the expectation that he call home *for a night as late as this* been negated? She didn't even remember. His coming home and giving her an hour's notice to get dressed in formal attire was not only unreasonable, but absurd. Simple courtesy and respect were no longer a part of his dealings with her.

She sucked her teeth and scratched her head. "Uhhh," she roared. "Maybe I am stupid."

Her eyes began to well with tears, but she wasn't going to have a pity party for herself. Not tonight. She wasn't even going to get angry. Faith leaned closer to the mirror and stared so deeply into her own eyes she could see a translucent halo around the pupils. *This is a spiritual thing. You are not in a battle with flesh and blood.* But it was a battle. One she was determined to win.

Faith stared at her reflection in the mirror and remembered why she was dressed this way. Her intention was to put the "whammy," as Yvette so eloquently described it, on him and bring him back to his senses. "I'm winning this battle," she murmured to herself and exited the bathroom.

Faith picked up the phone and dialed Jonah's cell number. When he answered she said, "Hello, Mr. Morgan, this is your wife. When can I expect you?"

Chapter 21

"What do you think about us going on a romantic trip together?" Faith draped her arms around his shoulders and rested her chin on top of his head. After last night, she probably thought she could ask him for anything.

"When did you have in mind?"

She came around to the front of his chair, sat on his lap, and wrapped her arms around his neck.

Faith tilted her head playfully. "Hmmm, I don't know. I *was* thinking the last week in this month."

Jonah released the breath he had been holding. She was staring at him intently, waiting for an affirmative response.

Impossible, he thought. "You know I can't do that." He reached for her wrists. She removed her arms and stood with him. "I'm booked into early July."

Avoiding her eyes and hating the seconds of silence, he picked up his coffee mug. "I thought we were taking July 4th week to go to the beach."

"We are, but I'm talking about a little excursion for just you and me."

Jonah shook his head. He didn't want to let her down. "I can't possibly get away at the end of this month."

She pouted for a few seconds, and then exclaimed, "Hold on just a minute!" Excitement had her running to the family room. She returned with the handful of brochures and magazines that she'd obviously picked up at a travel agency.

"Look at these resorts. They're just for couples, you know like the one we went to in Cancun on our fifth anniversary, *five years ago*."

The emphasis on five years wasn't wasted on his guilty conscious. Jonah took one of the brochures from her outstretched hand and dropped into his chair. He tried to focus on the happy people on the cover.

"We could walk on the beach, have some nice dinners, get a couples' massage, act like honeymooners . . ."

"I get the concept, honey."

She slid a chair closer to his and sat down in front of him. Her face beamed with excitement.

Jonah put the brochure down and picked up his mug, again. "It's not a good time at work. I'm extremely busy."

Faith sat back. "I can tell, late nights. The kids haven't seen you in two days."

"I know." Jonah cut her off as he stood again and walked to the counter. He poured another cup of coffee. He could tell from the way her elbows were stuck out on the sides that she was playing with her wedding rings. He needed to offer her something, but the timing . . .

"What about the week before the beach?" he offered.

She popped out of her chair. A pout on the face that had been pleasant. "I have the women's conference."

Keep going, he thought. "The weekend before that."

"I'll be preparing for the conference. Jonah, you know I'm the coordinator."

Actually, he'd forgotten. The church stuff was never-ending. All he did was show up on Sundays and that was more to keep her from complaining about him not going. He looked at his watch. His first appointment was in forty-five minutes. It'd take him that long to get to the office after he stopped for gas. "See, it's like I said. The timing's bad, for both of us."

Faith stood and moved to stand in front of him. She reached for his tie, and then played with one of the buttons on his shirt. He felt his body responding to her.

Big, brown eyes implored before she spoke. "Honey, we could really use this trip."

Jonah took her hand in his and moved it away from his chest. He hated it when she manipulated him this way.

"Going away isn't a magic solution."

"It's a start."

He smiled. "You made a pretty good start last night."

"Oh yeah, you think so?" she said smiling. "Well, take me someplace, and you'll really motivate me."

Jonah let out an exasperated breath. "I shouldn't have to take you some place to motivate you. Married people make love."

Her face took on a serious expression. "Or war," she said. "If it's a one-sided effort."

Jonah stuck a hand in his pocket and looked past her into the family room. He saw a candle stand on the table. A black bottle stuck out of an ice chest. Faith's eyes followed his.

"I had to put in an executive order to get you home last night," she said. "So tell me what you're going to do because I'm tired of being ignored."

He shook his head. "I'm not ignoring you right now." Silence filled the kitchen for a moment. "But I've got to go."

"It's seven A.M." Confusion marred her face.

"Early appointments."

"*Why* are you booked so early?"

"I have a lot of appointments."

"You don't have to see so many patients."

"Yeah I do, actually, so if I had *time* it would be no problem to pay five thousand dollars for a spur of the moment trip to Jamaica." His words were sharper than he'd meant, but he made up for it by kissing her on the forehead before walking out of the kitchen into the office, and then the garage.

With her hands shoved in her back pockets she followed him to his car and watched him get in. He pushed the garage door opener and let down the driver side window.

Her face contorted just before she asked, "Are you cheating on me?"

He turned the key in the ignition. Where had that come from? He didn't answer.

"Are you?"

"No," he barked. "Not yet."

Her eyes widened. "Not yet?"

"You ask a ridiculous question, you get a ridiculous answer."

"I don't think I asked a ridiculous question."

"Look, I said not yet, because before last night, I can't remember the last time we . . . had it going on like that. I'd like to have that kind of enthusiasm a little more often."

Through pursed lips she said, "And I'd like to *want* to be intimate with my husband. But I *can't* do that if I'm unhappy with our family life."

Jonah sighed. "Late August, early September will probably be better. Set something up, and I promise I'll clear my schedule for a long weekend."

"Weekend."

He reached out of the car window. Pulling an arm from the tight pretzel she had them wrapped in, he placed her palm on his cheek, and then kissed it. "Thursday through Monday."

The last thing Jonah saw before he put the car in reverse was a satisfied smile on his wife's face.

Chapter 22

Faith sat in her computer chair, logged onto the Internet, and typed in the web address for the first resort on her pile of brochures. They needed something romantic. She didn't know about her husband, but she needed to be reminded that she was actually in love.

She spent thirty minutes clicking inviting link after inviting link for the resorts she'd been recommended to, and then decided to do a search on a travel website to see what else was available. She came across a resort she had previously seen featured in a television special on the *Travel Network*. The HEART Hotel in Jamaica.

The Heart Hotel was actually a hotel management and culinary training institute. As Faith remembered, it was one of the top picks because of the exceptional detail paid to customers. The service was impeccable because the senior students' evaluations precipitated them being able to acquire good paying jobs in the hotel industry all over the Caribbean. The show's host indicated that it was one of the best kept secrets in the Caribbean.

And the price isn't bad either. Jonah would appreciate

that aspect. He paid more for green fees to play golf. She clapped her hands together in excitement over her find. It was perfect. She couldn't go wrong with a *Travel Network* recommendation, and then there was the name. *Heart*. That was creative for the wife of a cardiologist.

The telephone rang. Faith never thought she'd see the day when her own phone terrorized her, but the calls were coming at least once or twice a day, and the phone company's report hadn't come yet. She glanced at the caller I.D. to makes sure it was someone important enough to interrupt her planning. Yvette.

"Hey, girl."

"Hey to you." Faith leaned way back in the swivel chair and brought a knee up.

"I forgot to tell you yesterday, that Sister Lincoln said she *must* have a preliminary count of the registrants for the women's conference by next Friday."

They laughed in unison.

"Thanks for letting me know my deadline," Faith said.

"You need to check her."

Faith could hear the upbeat sound of Janet Jackson's late eighties music hit "Control" in the background, and she knew that if secular music was playing, Yvette was at the gym.

"I thought you were taking off this morning to go see Doctor Luke," Faith questioned more than actually stated.

"I was, but I had a call out."

"You should have called me. I would have covered the gym while you went to the doctor." Faith tried to keep disappointment out of her tone.

A groan came through the phone, which meant her friend didn't want to talk about how she didn't *want* to go to the doctor.

"Yvette . . . You've got to be a grownup about this. Having all that pain with your period isn't normal." Faith tried not to sound annoyed. Silence hung between them for a few seconds. "You at least have to check it out."

"I know. I know. I don't want to talk about it today. I promise. I'll make another appointment."

"It took you two months to get this one."

"Hold on." Faith heard silence, and then different music as she was put on hold.

After a few seconds, Yvette's voice came back on the phone. "Okay. So whatcha doing today?"

They'd been here before. Faith decided to let it go for now. She couldn't make Yvette go to the doctor, and lecturing her on and on about it wasn't going to change the fact that she'd already missed her appointment this morning. She leaned back in the computer chair, swished the mouse around on the mouse pad to remove the screensaver that had come up, and stared once again at The HEART Hotel.

"Planning a trip for Jonah and me."

"*Oh*, so he said yes," Yvette said, sounding suddenly buoyant.

"He said end of summer," Faith said, not quite sharing her excitement.

"That's better than nothing."

"I suppose. I wanted to leave tomorrow or at least at the end of the month. That's three and half more months. We need to be resuscitated right now."

"You need to pray about it instead of complaining."

Faith frowned. Where had that come from? "So you think I'm not praying?"

"That's not what I said. But I'm being a friend here. Just like you when you tell me to go to the doctor, and I don't want to hear it."

"You're being a friend and telling me what?"

"Stop expecting results overnight."

"*Overnight?* We've been married almost ten years." Faith felt her temper rising.

"But these problems didn't begin ten years ago. You've been dealing with this—a couple years."

Faith raised an eyebrow. "And that's not long enough for you?"

"I'm just echoing Pastor, here. Sometimes you have to wait for your season. We have summer, fall, winter, and spring, and it's not three or four months in God's time. Sometimes fall or winter in your case might last years." Yvette paused and Faith was silent also. "Everything in life is about God's timing, not ours."

Faith sighed. "Just when I thought I was going to get annoyed at my unmarried friend for telling me to endure, you go and say something that makes sense."

"Something biblical."

"The *nerve* of you."

Yvette laughed. "Look, I've got to go. I just needed to give you the Sister Lincoln message while it was still fresh. I wouldn't want you to miss your deadline."

They laughed together. "Say goodbye, silly," Faith said.

"Bye, girl, and hey."

"Yes?"

"Don't be weary in well doing," Yvette's tone was serious.

"Gotcha." Faith returned the phone to the receiver. *What would I do without you?*

The phone rang again and Faith noted it was Yvette calling back.

"What did you forget to tell me now? Sister Lincoln wants to give the opening remarks?"

"No, she'll decide that next week," Yvette said. "I wanted to make sure you knew you'll need a passport to go to Jamaica."

"Oh yeah. Homeland changed the travel laws."

"Right, and you've got to have a passport."

"Well, I have one, and it's current, but I'll have to look at Jonah's. Somehow I think his might not be up to date."

"See, late summer isn't so bad after all," Yvette teased. "Now you have time to handle your business."

Faith scrunched up her face. Yvette was right. They said their goodbyes and ended the call.

Stretching as she stood, she went into Jonah's study. All their important documents were kept in a safe behind a large wedding portrait they'd had commissioned shortly after they moved into the house. She thought it kind of eerie, like something from a haunted mansion in a horror movie to see herself in a four foot painting, but Jonah said he'd always wanted that type of portrait. To him it symbolized affluence, and there was nothing horrifying or scary about that.

Faith pulled the frame, which was on hidden brass hinges away from the wall, and began to turn the combination wheel. Inside she found the passports at the bottom of a pile of documents and extra cash that Jonah kept in the house for emergencies.

Just as she suspected, Jonah's passport had expired in February. She remembered when they were at the airport in Mexico, he'd mentioned needing to renew it, but it was a task she'd forgotten to take care of. She was glad she discovered it because Jonah would be annoyed if he had to travel at the last minute, and his wife had let it expire.

Faith closed the safe, returned the portrait to the wall, and with the passport in hand, went back to her seat at the computer. She did a search for information about passport renewal. It seemed a simple process, but there was one problem. Because the passport was expired and he'd had it issued more than fifteen years ago, he would have to apply in person for a renewal. She also noted that he needed a certified copy of his birth certificate.

"Shoot," Faith said, tapping her fingers on her side. Not as simple as she thought, but certainly not a problem, although she didn't think Jonah's birth certificate was in the safe. Come to think of it, she'd never actually seen his birth certificate.

She returned to the safe, rummaged through the paperwork looking for it. It wasn't there and wouldn't be anywhere else in the house, because he was adamant about keeping important documents locked up.

Faith picked up the telephone on his desk and called her mother-in-law.

"Hi, sweetheart," Mom Morgan said in a voice so genuinely sweet that Faith felt guilty about not taking the time to call more often.

"Hi, Mom."

"Look, I picked it up because I saw your number, but I'm in the middle of a very hot bridge game with my girls. What can I do for you? Are my grandbabies okay?"

"Your grandbabies are fabulous. As a matter of fact, I'll come over Saturday morning if you'd like to see them. I know Jonah's been promising to bring them—"

"Honey, if I waited for my son to bring those children, they'd be in college."

I know that's right, Faith thought. "I was calling because I need to get Jonah's passport renewed, and I realized we don't have a copy of his birth certificate."

There was silence on the other end of the phone. "I gave him the only copy I had. He took it with him when he went off to college."

Faith sighed. "I guess I can go to vital records to get one. He was born in Atlanta so that shouldn't be a problem." She could hear murmurs in the background and knew she'd kept her on the phone too long for her guests.

"I'll let you go, Mom. I can hear your crew."

"Yes, chile, they a rowdy group when I'm winning," Mom Morgan said. "You can just show up Saturday. I'll be here."

They exchanged goodbyes, and Faith hung up the phone.

She returned to her computer. This time to look up the address for Atlanta Vital Records.

Chapter 23

Jonah removed his reading glasses and turned away from the computer monitor. He'd spent the last two hours doing research. He put the pages he'd printed from an online medical journal, in Amadi's medical chart. There was nothing substantial in his findings. Transplantation was the only real option for this disease, especially for children, and the prognosis wasn't even great then.

The medical record had finally arrived by fax from Togo. The Karolyn Kempton Memorial Christian Hospital was a small evangelistic operation that had treated over three hundred children with a nonspecific infection during the summer of 2002. Some fifty children were transferred to a larger hospital in Benin, Nigeria, where twelve died. This was the sickness Amadi spoke of and most likely the infection that weakened his heart. He didn't have much to go on, but based on all the test results and the elimination of another disease, he was left with this. Sometimes medicine was just guesswork.

Jonah reached into his desk for Tylenol. His head was pounding. He wanted a drink, but he'd forgotten to refill the flask in his bag after he'd visited Joshua's grave on Saturday. Faith was right. He could use a vacation away from all of this. If he weren't careful, he'd make himself sick.

After a light rap on his door, Samaria poked her head in. He motioned for her to enter.

"Dr. Morgan." She closed the door behind her. Hands behind her back, she took small cautious steps to the desk. "I'm sorry about Amadi. April told me how upset you were."

He nodded and reached for a water bottle on his desk, took the pills and drank.

"Part of the job. We can't save everybody," Jonah said. He was thinking of Joshua and how they hadn't saved him.

"So is he going to die?"

He looked up at Samaria's frown and saw that his bluntness had jarred her. The despair he'd conveyed was not for Amadi, but for Joshua who hadn't been saved.

"I didn't mean to sound so grim. He'll go on the transplant list, but with that blood type, it's . . ." He didn't want to put a nail in the boy's coffin with his words.

She nodded. "Poor little guy. Odds not in his favor."

"They're not. I mean, a heart could come through, but he needs one soon and . . ." He locked his fingers together on the desk and rotated his thumbs. "It's so important that our people donate blood and organs."

"I see. I mean, I knew we needed to just like everyone else. But I didn't know the specifics about why until I studied it in school last semester."

"Speaking of which, it's 6:00 P.M. I thought you had a test?"

"Class was cancelled. Professor's sick or something." She took a few steps and came closer to his desk. "Can I get something for you? A soda?"

"No, I probably just need to get out of here. I've got some more work to do, but I can do it from home." He moved a hand up to wash over his face and closed his eyes. He tried to push out the image of Amadi's face and the faces of Mrs. Lazarus and Amadi's seven-year-old brother as he gave them the test results. He didn't want the children there, but Monifa Lazarus insisted they stay.

"We are all we have," she'd said. "I'll have to tell them anyway, doctor."

The children were practically in her lap. They were all holding hands—all three petrified and looking to him to offer them hope. He, with all his education and training, had none.

"I am exhausted." He raised his head.

"Just a minute," Samaria said as she began massaging his shoulders. She was rubbing and kneading his muscles with the aptitude of a professional masseuse. His first instinct was to stop her, but then her hands were like magic, relaxing him, releasing the tension. He slowly closed his eyes, again. *Just a few more seconds.* He moaned a little from the pleasure, and then leaned back in his seat to give her better access to work her wonders.

Her hands moved lower. She squeezed and kneaded until she reached his forearms on both sides. He felt her warm breath against his neck when she whispered, "Dr. Morgan, why don't you *really* let me relax you."

Jonah opened his eyes; his mind slowly coming back to clarity. *This wasn't right.*

Samaria let go and he heard rustling behind him. He swiveled his chair around. Samaria had removed her uniform top. A sexy, black bra pushed her breasts up.

She leaned close to him, her perfume adding to the thickness in the air. She mumbled something, and then got down in front of him on her knees and began unbuckling the belt to his slacks, quickly, almost feverishly.

Jonah grabbed her hands and pulled them away from his buckle. "Stop it."

She leaned closer to him, squeezing her torso between his knees.

Jonah pushed his chair back. It hit the desk with a thud and boomeranged in her direction, knocking her over. "I said stop!"

Samaria rocked on her backside and tried to regain her balance. "I just want—"

He stood and walked around to the front of the desk. He reached for the top of his trousers and began to refasten his belt.

She was rising to her feet.

"I don't know what . . . ," he stuttered over his words. "You could be thinking . . ." He lowered his eyes to finish closing his belt.

"Jonah, you've been so tense, so unhappy. I know things couldn't be right between you and Faith."

His head snapped up. "Don't mention my wife's name. You don't know anything about us."

"I'm just saying." Her voice was shaking now, and she was walking toward him. "I'm just saying a man like you deserves a woman who can meet his needs when and where he needs them met."

With each step she took, her huge breasts were closing the space between them. If they could talk, they would be chanting, "Touch us." He forced his eyes away before she got any closer. "Put your top back on," he said, clearing his throat.

"I know it would be good between us, and I can be very discrete."

Jonah took a deep breath and looked her directly in the eye. "Samaria, I told you to *put* your top on!"

He walked to the door, pulled the knob, found it locked

and looked back at her. "When I come back to my office, you had better not be here or you'll be sorry."

Samaria opened her mouth to say something else, but he silenced her with a raised hand. He stepped out into the empty corridor, slammed the door behind him and took a deep breath.

Chapter 24

Samaria stood in the office, stunned at the way things had turned out. She cursed as she walked back behind the desk and picked up her scrub top. She had played him too quickly. What was she going to do now? She had never seen him so angry. How could she make him understand that she loved him, *in her way*, and she was only trying to be there for him? He was the answer to her dreams and her problems.

Samaria slid her shirt on her back and pulled it together in the front. Hands shaking, she fastened the buttons. She raised her finger to her mouth and tapped her bottom lip. *Think, girl, think.* But she couldn't. Tears began to fill her eyes.

There was a light tap on the door, and Samaria heard April's voice. "Dr. Morgan."

Samaria was silent, hoping she would leave, but then she saw the knob turn and April walked in.

"Sam, I'm sorry. I didn't know you were in here."

Samaria wiped her eyes. "It's okay. I was about to leave anyway."

"What's wrong?" April asked, placing the file in her hand on the desk and coming closer.

Samaria raised her hand and waved dismissively. "I'm fine. I just got some bad news . . . you know . . . um . . . about my aunt."

April rubbed her shoulder. "What is it? Is she sick or something?"

"No . . . I mean, yes. She has been having some . . . if you don't mind, I'd prefer to just . . . you know . . . to be alone for a minute."

April nodded and removed her hand from Samaria's shoulder.

"I'll be okay, really." She sobbed loudly for effect.

"Let me know if there's anything I can do for you."

"Thanks." Samaria stood and reached for a tissue from the box on the credenza behind the desk.

April picked up the file and left. She gave Samaria one last sympathetic glance as she closed the door.

Samaria blew her nose and came out from behind the desk. She was going to wait for Jonah. She needed to talk to him before he really got POed. Her best bet was to continue to stroke his ego. She just had to say the right things to get him to see it was his overwhelming sex appeal and masculinity that got the better of her. Samaria sat down in one of the chairs in front of his desk and waited.

Chapter 25

Jonah stood in front of the mirror in the men's room. He'd splashed cold water on his face in hopes of waking himself up from this bad situation, but the truth was he needed a cold shower. He'd made a mistake; he shouldn't have let her begin the back rub. Crap like this always, always escalated to something bigger. He knew better, but she'd caught him off guard.

He had been ignoring the signs of attraction before. A woman doesn't just wake up one day and decide she's going to offer herself to a colleague. He hated to think about what would have happened if he and Faith hadn't made love last night. Sexual need might have gotten the better of him. Samaria was sexy, in a cheap sort of way, but sexy nonetheless.

Jonah splashed more water. He had to get it together. All this thinking about Joshua and Amadi was making him crazy. He wasn't as sharp as he normally would be. He should have seen the entire thing coming with Samaria. They probably wouldn't be able to work together anymore. Seeing her half naked had taken care of that.

The walk back to his office only took a few seconds. He opened the door and was surprised to see Samaria still there standing by the window.

"I'm disappointed," he said. "I asked you to leave."

"Dr. Morgan, I owe you an apology. I'm so sorry." She took a step toward him, but he stopped her with his eyes. "I'm . . . I just . . . you were so upset, and I have to admit . . . I have always found you attractive. I just let that get the better of me."

He didn't say anything.

"I promise, if we can just forget this incident. It won't happen again."

Jonah prided himself on being able to read people. There was a lack of sincerity in what she was saying, and he could feel it. Then there was the matter of the door.

"You turned the lock when you came in the room. How is that letting it get the better of you?"

"I . . ." She looked like a deer caught in headlights.

"You came in here on Saturday half naked, and now you come in here today and get naked. Wasting my time asking for help with a test that you probably don't have."

"I did have a test. My professor . . . is sick."

He washed his hands over his face. "Sam, just leave."

At first she didn't move, but then he gave her another firm look, and she scurried past him like a little mouse.

He willed himself to dismiss the entire episode from his mind. He'd deal with her tomorrow. He walked around the desk and picked up Amadi's file and dropped it back on the desk. He'd deal with this tomorrow too. Faith and the children would be glad to see him. And after today, he'd be glad to see them.

His pager went off. He gritted his teeth as he picked up the phone to place the call. He knew it was about Amadi, because he was the only patient he had at Kimble.

"This is Dr. Morgan."

"Dr. Morgan, we've called a code on Amadi Lazarus."

After putting the file in his bag, he rushed from the office, praying the whole way that traffic wouldn't be bad getting to Kimble, and he wouldn't be too late.

Chapter 26

Faith stood in front of the women's ministry planning committee and watched everyone socialize before they knew she would begin her meeting; on time. Because their congregation was well on its way to being a one hundred percent tithing church, the women's day and the conference events no longer had to be preceded by months of frying chicken and fashion show ticket sales. At Higher Hope Christian, Pastor Kent didn't believe in a lot of fundraising. He preached that the members should pay tithes, and the money for activities comes from a budget.

Faith listened to a group of women on the front pew rehashing the details of Pastor's sermon on Sunday. She loved what she got from Pastor Kent's teaching. The man didn't have to whoop or sweat to bring a message to his people. Just good, biblical teaching with lots of real life examples. It was very effective. She was glad that was his style, because if he had been a "hooper," Jonah assured her they would not be attending his church.

She looked at her notes. Recapping every agenda item

they needed to discuss: the registration process, speakers, workshops, volunteers, and finally, the meal selection. She knew food would get everyone in an uproar. There was nothing like black folks paying for a meal and not feeling they hadn't gotten their money's worth from the venue.

Yvette walked in, greeted women along the way, and approached the podium where she stood. "You do know not having a pork selection is going to put you in a very bad light for next year's planning."

"Please. After that sermon pastor preached about unclean foods, I don't expect to hear one person groan about not having pork."

"They may not say it out loud," Yvette turned and surveyed the room inconspicuously, "but some of these pork eating folks are definitely going to groan."

They laughed.

"As my unofficial co-chair, will you handle finalizing the speakers and their itineraries?" Faith asked, handing her friend a list of names.

"Sure, sure, work a sistah unofficially," Yvette replied, taking it.

"I could make you official if you want."

"No, girl, I don't need you-know-who flattening the tires on my car." Yvette rolled her eyes.

Faith laughed and slapped Yvette playfully on the arm.

"Sister Morgan, it's 7:30, and I know you like starting on time," Sister Arnetta Lincoln stated, taking a seat in the chair closest to the podium.

Yvette's eyes bugged and she whispered, "Speak of the devil." She moved to a chair and sat down.

"Hello," Faith said in a raised voice. She'd gotten the women's attention, and they quieted down within seconds. After she led the group in prayer, they began the

business of discussing the details of the women's conference.

"Does anyone have any questions—pressing issues?"
Faith asked, putting down the pen she had been using to
check things off on her list.

A small fragile woman in the back stood and raised her
hand.

"Sister Carter," Faith stretched her neck to get a better
view of her. "You had a question?"

"Yes, Sister Morgan. I just wanted to say once again we
are so happy to have someone with your planning skills
for this conference. You did an excellent job last year, and
I can tell already this is going to be even better."

Another woman stood. "I agree. Sister Morgan, you
know I have five children that I home school, and because
my husband is the only one working, we don't get to really
take vacations too much. Last year when I was selected
by the scholarship committee to receive a free registration, it was such a blessing. I felt like I had gone to some
fancy resort staying in that hotel. This year I saved a little
money every month to make sure I had enough to pay for
my own registration. I wouldn't miss it for the world, and
I'm glad somebody else will get a scholarship and be
blessed the way I was."

Faith nodded and smiled. She hated being the center of
praise this way, but she had to let the women have their
say.

"Thank you, Sister Hanover. I'm so glad you can make it
again this year. Speaking of the scholarships, I didn't have
it on the agenda for tonight, but do we have a report from
the committee?"

Sister Kennedy, an older retired school teacher, was the
head of the scholarship committee. She stood and gave a
report. "We have notified the recipients, and all have con-

firmed attendance. We also received the money from Girls Gaining Ground Club of America to have the classes for the teenagers. Pastor will announce that on Sunday."

Faith breathed a sigh of relief. Girls Gaining Ground had been putting them off for so long, Faith actually started to believe that the organization wasn't going to fund their abstinence classes. Christian Brothers had graciously provided funding for one hundred T-shirts and goody bags for the girls. She just needed GGG to pay for the speakers and books.

"That's good, good news," Faith said. They went on with the rest of the agenda items, and when they were done, Faith rejoiced inwardly. Another meeting down and only five more to go until the conference. "Well, if there's nothing else, I think we should say a closing prayer until our next assigned meeting date."

Faith couldn't stop thinking about all the wonderful comments the women had this evening. She enjoyed working with the ministry so much. Planning events like this was one of her favorite things to do. She remembered how even as a child, she enjoyed being a part of planning her birthday parties or planning dinner parties' menus with her mom. The best was vacations. It was so nice to grow up in a house where decision making was shared, even with her.

She pulled into the driveway and pushed the button to raise the garage. Jonah still wasn't home. It was almost nine o'clock. She really didn't expect him, not these days, but they needed to talk. She'd gotten a phone call from Bowen and Jefferies telling her that they had a delay in the hiring process. They wanted her to know she was still a strong candidate and they'd be getting back to her. She smiled. She'd needed that boost in her confidence, but it was also problematic because she hadn't decided what she wanted to do.

Faith leaned back, settling into the softness of the leather seat. Resting for what seemed like the first time today. *I'm tired. If I'm this tired and I don't work, what will happen when I do?*

She exhaled long and deep before stepping out of the car. She entered the house and found the children, in their pajamas, lying on the floor with Gaynell, the sitter, watching *American Idol.*

"Mommy, she's going to win," Elise exclaimed, jumping up. "I told you the man wasn't going to beat her."

"The show has *like* three weeks to go." Eric's face reflected the annoyance it always did. He had so little patience with his sister these days, and it showed in almost every word he said to her. "Nobody knows who's gonna win yet."

"Well, I hope the show for this week is ending at nine o'clock, little people, because everybody has to go to bed."

"I want to see Daddy," Elise whined, training huge brown eyes on her mother.

So do I. "Daddy may come in any minute, or he may not till later. You know he has a few children who are very sick right now."

"He always has sick children," Eric added bitterly.

Although Faith understood where Eric was coming from, she didn't respond to the comment. She reached into her purse, removed the money she'd set aside for Gaynell and handed it to the young woman.

"Elise, how about my hug?" Gaynell smiled and opened her arms.

Elise flew from the floor and jumped into Gaynell's arms and squeezed tight.

Gaynell released the child, and she scooted back to her spot next to her brother like she had never moved. "I'll see you next week, Mrs. Morgan. Bye, Eric."

Faith let her out and noticed Jonah's car coming around the corner. Inside, she thanked God. The kids really needed to see him. It had been three nights since they'd laid eyes on him.

She watched Gaynell slip into her car. Faith wiggled her fingers goodbye and waited while Jonah parked his car. She knew his not putting it in the garage only meant one thing.

"Don't tell me you're going back out?" It wasn't a statement, but a protest. She took two steps onto the brick doorstep to meet him.

"I just got a call as I was turning in the subdivision that I have an emergency admission. I'm running in to grab a bite and use the restroom."

"You can't handle it over the phone?"

"I could, but I don't want to, because I also have a child in intensive care. He coded a few hours ago."

She shriveled a little at the thought of that. Poor kid, poor family. "So they're both at Kimble?"

Jonah questioned her with his eyes. They both knew why she asked, and she knew better than to try tell him when he needed to go see a patient. Kimble was a top pediatric cardiac facility. Surely the doctors . . .

Don't go there, her heart whispered. She chose her words carefully. "Emergencies are a part of the job."

Yvette was in her head. *Change doesn't happen overnight.* Fighting with Jonah wasn't going to get her anywhere. "I know you have to go see the sick children, but don't rush too much, the *children* in the house would like to see you."

"I'm sorry." He kissed her lips and held his position there for a moment. "I miss them too. Believe it or not, I had intended to come home early tonight." His tone was weary, his eyes tired. "I really did."

Masking her aggravation with playfulness, Faith poked him in his chest. "You work too much."

"I know," Jonah said. He pushed the remote key to lock his car, gave her one more peck on the lips, and walked through the door.

Seconds later, she heard Elise's shrieks of joy.

Chapter 27

The whoosh of the automatic doors that led to the Pediatric Intensive Care Unit was a welcome sound for Jonah. It gave him the surge of adrenaline that he needed to get him out of the funk he'd been in for the last couple of hours. He wanted a drink, but that would have to wait until he got home. In the meantime, he'd get high from Amadi Lazarus's improved condition.

Last night had been a close call. The now quiet corridor had been filled with a small resuscitation team, residents, nurses, technicians, and respiratory therapists. All with their own part in bringing his critically ill patient back from near death.

Jonah had arrived just after they'd stabilized Amadi. The thrill for the team still apparent in their faces and by chatter he heard at the nurse's station. Like him, they loved when it was over. Stabilizing a critically ill patient was euphoric because there was nothing more precious than bringing a child back from the brink of death. The relief on the parents' faces so raw with emotion, that he was glad to see their vulnerability recede back into the hole from which it bled.

He found the staff physician, Dr. Warwick, a petite blonde and a third year resident. She had been his eyes and ears today as Amadi recovered from the stress of last night's near fatal code.

"How are my patients?"

Dr. Warwick closed the chart she'd been reviewing. "The Collins child is stable, although his oxygen saturations have been slowly, but steadily dropping. I believe Dr. Kite favors turning his heart into a single-pump," she said, referring to the cardiac surgeon that was now a part of the treatment team.

Jonah was disappointed for the patient, but he had to agree with the decision.

Dr. Warwick sighed loud enough to get Jonah's attention. "It's all bad." She pulled another chart from the holder on the desk.

"We're conferencing this afternoon. Will you be sitting in?"

"I wouldn't miss it. Especially the discussion on RCM." She referred to Amadi's condition.

Silence fell while they worked, each previewing notes for the meeting where the medical team assigned to the child's care would explore, discuss, and debate details of the patient's condition until they had come to consensus on what was best.

Jonah looked at the spines of all the notebook charts. When he didn't see what he was looking for he said, "Lazarus."

"I was just making sure all my notes were there. His mother's in with him. I tried to answer her questions, but she prefers you." Dr. Warwick passed the book she had opened to him.

* * *

Amadi was sleeping. Mrs. Lazarus stood near the window, but turned to him when he entered the room. She made silent steps across the room to him.

"I'm so glad you're here. He's been sleeping most of the day, but he asked for you."

"The medication we've been giving him will cause him to sleep. It's best for him to rest."

Jonah gave her an update, explaining that transplantation was a strong option, but the treatment plan was still pending.

"They have so many tubes and things on my baby . . . I just don't know how much more of this I can take." Against her ashen, dark skin, the whites of her eyes were blood red. Unshed tears rested in them. "Tell me, the surgeon, how do you pick him?"

Jonah was glad she'd asked him a question. He had been feeling like a statue standing there with nothing to say. As many years as he'd been doing this, he still had a level of discomfort with parents who were at the end of their rope. He could never seem to find the right words to say unless he was giving a medical update.

"Pediatric cardiology is a really small field. Everybody knows everybody. We all know each others' results, successes."

"Failures . . ." she said, taking the word he wouldn't have said directly from his thoughts.

"I wouldn't say failures. Difficult cases where the odds weren't in our favor." He paused briefly and continued. "When we treat a patient, we, the specialty, know ideally what should happen. And we refer the patient to the best surgeon for the procedure."

Mrs. Lazarus's features relaxed for a moment. She took the hand of her sleeping child and pressed her eyelids together tightly.

She's praying. He remembered her comments about him being a Christian and wondered what religion she practiced.

"I trust you, Dr. Morgan." She opened her eyes and looked directly at him. "I trust you because I know you care."

Jonah gave her a pat on the shoulder. "I'll let you know what's decided after the meeting today."

A nurse came into the room, and before she could speak, Mrs. Lazarus acknowledged her with a nod. Her hourly fifteen minute visit was over.

Jonah stayed behind to review the various tapes coming from the monitors hooked up to Amadi. He knew technology had advanced a great deal over thirty years, but he wondered what it was like when Joshua was in the hospital. Did he have tubes and monitors as well? Amadi slept so still that Jonah had to look twice to make sure he was breathing. Did Joshua have peaceful moments like this, where he slept so heavy that even his disease seemed to take a rest? He shook his head. He didn't know. He couldn't remember what it was like when they visited Joshua in the hospital because unlike Amadi, Joshua was quickly discharged without treatment. No insurance, no help. Unlike Amadi, his brother had been sent home to die.

I know you care.

Jonah took a long sip of the drink he had brought up the stairs with him. Bleary eyed he looked at the clock on wall and noted it was almost two A.M. He had to go to sleep.

Jonah wasn't sure if it were the process or that fact that he'd had about three hours of sleep, but the conference for Amadi Lazarus had irritated him. Although they'd agreed a heart transplant was critical; they weren't sure if he was an appropriate candidate for the transplant registry. The statements and questions in the room seemed to have a tone that didn't feel aggressive.

"He has a rare blood type. What happens if he needs more units of blood than we could get for him?" one doctor asked. *"His pulmonary damage is extensive. We don't want to waste the heart if he needs a lung transplant as well,"* said another.

And then there was administration, commenting on things related to cost. But in the end, everyone agreed on what was best for the patient. Amadi was referred for a heart transplant.

Jonah took another sip from the glass and placed it on the night table. Faith had probably been sleeping for hours. The comforter at her feet and the sheet loosely over her body revealed her perfectly formed silhouette in the light from the moon. She'd be furious if he woke her now. But he wanted her. He needed her warmth.

Jonah rolled her over on her back by gently pushing her left shoulder down. She moaned softly and realigned her body in a semi-fetal position facing him. He kissed her face and her neck.

Still asleep, she mumbled.

He took one hand and moved it over her hips, slowly pulling her silk nightgown up her thighs.

She coughed gently and began to wake from her drowsy state.

He could tell by the stretching of her neck over his head that she was looking back at the clock over her shoulder. Any second now he would hear . . .

"Jonah, it's the middle of the night."

I trust you, Doctor Morgan.

"Come on, baby," he moaned, raising his face from her breasts to kiss her.

She was pushing him away. "You've been drinking."

"I need you." He continued to try to arrest her mouth.

Faith was asking something else, but he ignored her questions continuing to move his hands over her body and kiss her neck and shoulders, trying desperately to push out the faces of Amadi Lazarus and Joshua from his mind. Their faces blurred in his memory like two holographic images being merged under a bright light.

"Jonah." Faith's curt voice lashed at him.

I know you care, was all he could hear.

"I do," he whispered.

"You do?"

"I do," he stated in between kisses.

"What do you mean you do?"

Jonah stopped because she had sat straight up in the bed and began pulling her nightgown back over her hips.

He felt like she had punched him in the gut. "What?"

"I asked you if you had a drinking problem, because it's almost two in the morning and you've just had a drink and you answered 'I do.' What's wrong with you?"

He collapsed back on his set of pillows.

"How could you be drinking at two in the morning?"

Shut up. He wanted to yell it. Why couldn't she just let him make love to her without all this complaining?

"I'm worried. You're scaring me."

Jonah didn't respond. He just kept staring at the ribbon of moon light that cast a shadow on the ceiling.

"You have to talk to me."

He rolled over on his side and stood.

"Jonah."

"Not now, Faith," Jonah said in a hoarse whisper. He moved with heavy steps to the bathroom and turned on the shower. He dropped his body down on the closed toilet seat. Elbows on his knees, he put his head in his hands. She was right. His mother was right. His pain was killing him. He needed to talk to her, but he didn't know how.

Chapter 28

Faith released a grocery bag from her arm onto the counter and dropped car keys. She pulled her ringing cell phone from the pocket of her slacks.

An unfamiliar voice on the other end of her cell phone asked to speak to her.

"This is she."

"Faith, Garrison with Bowen and Jefferies."

She'd been going back to the garage for the last grocery bags and stopped dead in her tracks. "Hello, Mr. Adams."

"I'm calling because I have a very exciting offer for you." After a beat of silence, he continued. "It's not the position you originally interviewed for. We actually think you may have the skills we need for the project coordinator position. One of the other team members has been reassigned to another project."

Faith could hardly believe her ears. He gave her more details about the position and salary, which was more generous than her original request.

"So," Garrison said after a moment of dead silence. "What do you think?"

Faith could hear excitement in his voice. She could feel it in her thudding heart, but she was speechless. She took a deep breath and gathered her thoughts so she could respond. "It sounds like an interesting opportunity and quite a challenge."

"I think you're up to it. Tell me you're interested."

Faith hesitated for a moment, drumming the fingers of her free hand on the counter. "Would it be fair for me to ask for a day or two to consider it? It sounds like a little more than I originally thought I'd be doing."

"Of course. I'll be out of the office until next Tuesday. I'll plan to hear from you when I return." And then she heard the dial tone.

Wow! She had actually done it. Gotten a job offer on the first position she applied for. How incredible was that? Yvette would be so excited for her. She was excited for herself. Jonah would be . . .

Forget him. She wasn't going to let him rain on her parade. Especially after last night. Drinking at two in the morning. He was out of control.

Faith placed the phone on the counter and moved back to the garage to finish getting the groceries. She was going to be the coordinator on a multi-million dollar project. Not only was it a cool job, it was a leadership position. She never dreamed she'd step back into her career and be in charge.

"Hmmm," she mused, dropping more bags on the counter. She was suddenly squeamish. Was she ready for all that?

She'd prayed that God would block the job if it weren't for her, but even so, she wasn't sure if getting it meant God had intervened. Not like God needed instructions.

Faith continued to put the groceries away, thinking to herself how exciting it would be to actually do something like turn public health around, but then she remembered what it was like when she worked for the agency. The culture didn't support change. As a matter of fact, they opposed it. Bureaucracy and politics got in the way of the best of intentions.

With the last of the perishable groceries having been put away, Faith closed the refrigerator. She had to run an errand before she picked up Elise. Grabbing her cell phone from the counter, she sprinted back to the garage. She wasn't sure if she were going to take the job, but she couldn't wait to call Yvette and share that Bowen and Jefferies wanted her.

The City of Atlanta South Vital Statistics Bureau was an aging brick building that Faith thought should be turned into a historical landmark. Vagrants and what appeared to be homeless people sat on the brick wall outside the building in such mass that she almost reconsidered taking her Mercedes SUV home and requesting the birth certificate by mail. Not that she worshipped her truck, but a sista needed a way to get home.

According to the sign on the door, the building included other city of Atlanta business functions such as the tax assessor's office, code enforcement, and public works. She took a deep breath, pushed the heavy glass doors in, and made her way to the one marked Vital Records.

There were customers in various lines waiting to transact business with the individual customer service people. A sign was posted with instructions. Faith obliged by pulling a number from the ticket roster. She picked up a clipboard with the form already on it and made her way to a row of chairs where she sat down. After completing the form, she looked up and noted that the lines were moving quickly. Every five minutes or so, the one customer service person would call a number and serve one of the people who was waiting with her. They were four numbers away from Faith's, so she took the time to make a phone call.

The phone rang, and on the second ring, her mother greeted her.

"Hi, Mom. How are you?" Faith said.

"Missing my family. When are you going to bring my grandbabies to visit?" Her mother's tone was jovial as always. Faith was glad somebody was in a good mood. "Actually, if you don't mind the short notice, I was thinking about Sunday. Eric is out of school on Monday for a teacher workday, and I thought I'd bring them after church and pick them up Monday evening. Jonah and I could use some time together."

"Are you two trying to get romantic, or is there something particular going on?"

"No . . ." she hesitated. "Well, yes. I've been offered a job, and I'm thinking I'm going to take it. If I do, it'll probably begin in two weeks, and I've got to tell Jonah."

"Oh I see." Her mother was silent. "Since when do you make a major decision like this and tell your husband afterward?"

"You know Jonah and I have been talking about this for a long time." Faith rolled her eyes upward.

"Well, honestly, Elise is only four. You don't need the money. Why do you have to work?"

"Because I want to. Working was important to me. I feel like I'm disappearing in that house, inside my marriage. I'm just Mrs. Morgan. My career was important to me."

"You shouldn't need a job to validate you. Who you are in Christ should give you a sense of importance; not a job."

Faith felt a tinge of conviction. She cleared her throat in the silence that followed. "That's not what I mean."

"It is what you mean. Do you know how many mothers out there would kill to trade places with you? To be with their kids when they come home, to make an afternoon snack for them and ask them about their day?"

Faith let out a long breath and rolled her eyes again. "Women work everyday."

"I'm not saying women shouldn't work. I'm saying your husband has asked you not to work for good reason. I think you should respect it."

Her mother paused for a moment, but Faith knew she was only repositioning herself.

"Things are already tense in that house. He's going to be furious that you made this decision behind his back."

Everything in the world had to revolve around Jonah. His schedule and his time. Everything was about Jonah. *Lord, what about me? Don't I matter?*

"Just think about what I'm saying. Give it more time, Faithy. Do some more praying and stop making up your mind and doing what *you* want to do. You've got to trust God."

A few moments passed before she gathered the courage to say, "I do trust God, and I have been praying, but doesn't God give us common sense and free will to make choices?" She looked at the two women sitting next to her, both appeared to be reading magazines, but she would bet they were listening to her end of the conversation.

"God does, but a praying woman doesn't move in her common sense and free will. She moves in God's will."

"Mom," she spoke through clenched teeth. "I said, I *have* been praying."

"So the revelation was to sneak behind his back."

Number seventeen was called over the loud speaker. She looked at the small orange ticket to verify that was her number.

"I've got to go, Mom. We'll talk more, later."

"Okay, but to answer your original question, I'd love to

have my grandbabies. But I'd appreciate you bringing them Saturday night or early Sunday so they can go to church with me. I need to show 'em off sometimes."

Faith stood and walked to the window. "Thanks. I'll call you back."

She snapped the phone shut and approached the window. A short, coffee-skinned woman with tight curls looked at Faith from across the counter. She smiled and asked, "What can I do for you?"

"I'm here to get a copy of my husband's birth certificate." She slid the application across the small counter. "I have my marriage certificate."

"I'll need your photo I.D. too."

Faith removed her driver's license and the cash fee she knew she had to pay.

"Jonas Morgan," the woman stated, staring at the form as she maneuvered her glasses up and down in an effort to see clearly. Then she looked at Faith.

"It's Jon-ah," Faith put emphasis on the second syllable.

The woman squinted. "Oh yes, Jonah." She smiled again. "The eyes aren't so good."

Faith could imagine. She looked to be nearly eighty. God bless her to still be working.

"I need a few minutes. You can have a seat." She turned muttering, "Jonah Morgan, nineteen sixty—" and she walked through a door behind her.

Faith returned to her seat. It was almost eleven, and she needed to pick up Elise at noon. She chose a two-year-old *Jet* magazine amongst the offerings on the table next to her chair and wondered who they thought wanted to read two-year-old news? But she thumbed through it just like everyone else probably did while they waited. It was something to do.

She turned to the wedding pictures in the center and thought that all the smiling couples had probably made the biggest mistake of their lives. Faith had to laugh at herself. She was becoming so cynical. She sounded crazy.

After thumbing through the magazine and picking up another she heard her name spoken softly by the clerk who had her order.

"Mrs. Morgan, that will be ten dollars." The clerk slid paperwork across the counter.

Faith handed her the money and picked up the certificate. A white envelope had been flapped over the top of it, she supposed for her to put the document in when she was finished inspecting it.

"Oh, this is the wrong person." Joshua Morgan was typed in the space. She looked at the birth date. It was Jonah's. Maybe the clerk had spelled the name wrong or it could be another Morgan child born on the same day. Morgan was certainly common enough.

She handed it back to the clerk.

"You said your husband. Is he deceased?"

Faith frowned. "No. He isn't."

The clerk looked confused. "But I have a death certificate attached to the other Morgan child that was born that day."

Faith tried to grin, but this was taking longer than she expected and she needed to get Elise.

The clerk stared at the certificate and shook her head. "I'm certain. But let me double check."

Willing this not to take that long, Faith did not return to her seat. After about three minutes, the clerk returned with a book. She opened it on the table in front of her, but turned it to face Faith. She moved her finger across the line that began with the name Jonah Morgan.

"You see, Jonah Morgan . . ." Her voice trailed off when she saw her mistake. "Oh, you're right. It was his twin that died, not Jonah."

Faith's heart froze. *Twin.* "My husband doesn't have a twin."

The clerk looked at Faith, her eyes uncertain. "Not anymore. Joshua died when he was ten years old." The woman removed her glasses. "You say this is your husband?"

Faith felt as if the air was being sucked from her lungs through her stomach. She looked at the register which was a photocopy of birth records that included all the demographics about the birth. Jonah's clearly stated that his was a twin birth and his parents' names were listed. Joshua's record said the same.

She opened her mouth, but had to make great effort to get the words out. "How did he die?"

The woman turned the register around. She seemed overwhelmed by the confusion.

"May I purchase the birth certificate and the death certificate for Joshua?"

"Well, of course, death certificates are public information. But I can't give you the birth certificate for Joshua. You'd have to be a parent or sibling or spouse."

"That's fine." She opened her purse in search of her wallet so she could pay for it. "I'll take the death certificate."

"I'll also have to still get your husband's. The death certificate is ten dollars," the clerk said.

Faith continued to fumble in her purse for her wallet. Her mind seemed unable to snap back and focus on what she was doing. "How long? I have . . . I have to pick up my daughter."

"I need about ten minutes to do both."

Faith looked at the time. She would be pushing it to get Elise. She opened her cell phone and pushed the menu button for the phonebook. "I'll wait," she responded and dialed the cell number of one of her neighbors.

"Hi, Arlene." She tried to put cheer in her voice, but every muscle in her body was beginning to tense up. "This is Faith. I need a favor. I've gotten tied up downtown, and I was wondering if you could help me out and pick up Elise."

"Sure. I hope you don't mind my having her for an hour or so," Arlene replied. "I promised my daughter a trip to the library today and we're going straight there."

"That's fine," Faith said, glad Elise would be distracted during her absence.

"I'll get them a snack, we'll do the library, and I'll bring her home afterward. We should be about an hour and a half," Arlene assured her.

Faith closed her eyes tightly and struggled to keep her tone even. "Thanks, Arlene. I'll see you then."

Uncontrollable rage began to build inside of her. A twin brother. She could not extract that thought from her mind. What was wrong with him, his mother, these people? Why had they lied to her all these years? She thought Jonah was an only child, just like herself.

Faith removed a tissue from her handbag. She was fighting to keep the tears at bay, but she knew they were coming. She tried to move from the spot where she stood. Maybe she should go to the restroom to pull herself together, but she couldn't move. She stood there, clutching her bag like it was a lifeline that would keep her from drowning in the river of tears that were now making their way down her face, down her chin and dripping like a faucet onto her bright orange blouse. She wanted to raise her hand to wipe her face, but she couldn't do it. She was absolutely paralyzed with anger. How could he not tell her this?

After minutes that felt like hours, the clerk returned with both documents. She looked into Faith's eyes and

came from around the counter. Faith knew she was making a spectacle of herself.

The clerk took her arm and helped her to a nearby
chair. She had no idea how long she'd been standing
there. "Can I do something for you?"

Faith shook her head. She could not speak. She could
not move.

The clerk rose to her feet and went back behind the
counter. Less than a minute later, she came back with a
small paper cup and some napkins. "Baby, drink this
water."

Through blurry vision, Faith looked at her. She realized
why she felt so endeared to the woman when she initially
saw her. She looked like her grandmother, and now she
was treating her with the sort of kindness her grandmother
would offer a stranger.

"I'm . . . okay," she whispered after taking a sip of the
water. "I'm okay."

Faith took the napkins and began to dab at her eyes
and cheeks and chin. Fortunately, she didn't have eye
makeup on or she would have looked like a raccoon by
now.

"I'm okay," she managed to say again. "Just . . . shocked."

The woman nodded knowingly. Faith imagined that issuing death records could be a position where there was
occasionally some drama.

"I'm sure the family had a reason for keeping a secret,"
she said softly. "They always think they do."

Faith finished wiping her face. She patted the woman's
hand and said, "You have been extremely kind." Then she
stood. "I have to get myself together before I pick up my
daughter."

They both walked back to the counter. Faith stood on
her side, and the woman eased around to the side where
she worked.

Faith removed a twenty dollar bill, paid the fees, inspected Jonah's birth certificate, and thanked her. She walked down the hall, embarrassed by the torrent of emotion, near hysteria, that she displayed in the office. She remembered her mother's words spoken often as she grew up. *"You can't truly be shamed in front of strangers."* But she was shamed. She was married to a man for ten years who had a twin brother that died as a child, and he never told her about it.

That was certainly something to be ashamed of.

Chapter 29

Jonah took his pen and slid it into the top pocket of his lab coat. "Are we done here?" Although his anger was simmering underneath, he wore his best poker face in the presence of his enemies.

This doctor's staff meeting had been a bad one. Actually, it had been the continuation of a year long period of nasty meetings. Jonah had just about all he could stand of Cooper's comments about his contribution or lack thereof to the pro-bono work Christian Brothers did.

"Jonah Morgan has a contract just like the rest of us that requires him to comply with the founding principles of this organization. Why do we continue to allow this man so much latitude in performing his duties in line with these obligations?" Cooper had argued vehemently.

Jonah had a rebuttal. "I may only have one patient right now, but I logged seven hours with him in the past two weeks. He's in the hospital and will be there until he has a transplant. I can't take another referral right now."

"I had to refer a patient to another cardiologist last week, because Jonah refused to see him." A vein was visible in Cooper's neck. "What kind of a business are we running?"

"A health care business," Jonah said calmly. "One that requires we all see billable patients."

Cooper tried to continue the discussion, but the response to his attack had been exasperation on the part of the other doctors. Gunter was particularly perturbed. He had recruited and hired Jonah almost five years ago. Cooper just didn't get it. Men like Gunter didn't like anyone questioning their judgment, and by attacking him at every staff meeting, that's exactly what he was doing. He was so set on bringing about Jonah's termination that he didn't realize he was insulting the man who had chosen him for the job. If Cooper wasn't careful, he was going to tear his own pants and find himself looking for another place to work.

"We're done." Gunter stood. Once he was on his feet, business was concluded. "I'll have my secretary send around the vacation calendar for the summer. Don't be too greedy, no more than two weeks at a time unless you can get someone to cover for you."

Jonah joined many of the doctors in rising from their seats. Conversations began around the conference room as he gathered the files and notes in front of him. The quick exodus he so badly wanted had to be delayed because he knew that would signal to Coop that he had unnerved him. He stuck around making small talk with the other doctors as if it had been the average staff meeting and not a trial worthy of the Cochran Firm's defense.

They ate sandwiches, and Gunter congratulated him again for a job well done at the benefit for National Heart Society. Jonah knew he was an asset, and Coop's mouth was becoming a liability. Maybe it was time he started his own campaign to get rid of his enemy. If he put a buzz in the air that he was thinking about starting his own practice, Gunter might silence Tom.

After a sufficient amount of time had been spent socializing, Jonah eased out of the room and headed for his office. He nodded at April as he passed the nurse's desk. She was on the telephone and looking stressed. If he didn't know any better, he'd think she had been crying. Her highs and lows where getting worse. Jonah had been looking for an opportunity to ask her what was going on, but every time he was just about to ask, something came up or someone interrupted.

"Dr. Morgan."

He heard her voice behind him, and with exaggerated frustration, he turned to face Samaria.

"May I have a few moments?" she asked.

Jonah raised his arm and looked at his watch. "This isn't really a good time, Samaria." He emphasized her full name. He hadn't called her that since the first day they'd met more than two years ago. He hoped the tone in which he spoke delivered the message he was thinking, which was get lost.

She cleared her throat. "Actually it would be the best time. I've checked your schedule. You don't have a patient for forty minutes."

She hadn't gotten the message, Jonah thought. He couldn't keep annoyance out of his voice. "You checked my schedule?"

"I only need a minute or two." There was intensity in her lowered voice. She looked from side to side to see if anyone else was watching their exchange.

He extended his hand toward his office and followed her in. She closed the door.

"Make it quick. I have a lot of paperwork," Jonah said.

Samaria took a seat.

"Dr. Morgan, I apologize for coming on to you. I should have used better judgment."

Jonah opened the first of a stack of charts in front of him. "We went through this already. You apologized that day. Get to the point."

"I hate working with Drs. Cooper and Madu," she said.

"I didn't choose your assignment."

"But you did choose to have me reassigned."

"I thought it best under the circumstances."

"There are no circumstances. I'm a professional. My attraction to you has nothing to do with my ability to do my job," Samaria said sharply.

Jonah paused at her tone, and then sat back in his seat. His burning eyes held hers.

He had colleagues who had made that mistake, lost everything over a woman; one, his marriage, and the other, a position at a very prestigious university because his extramarital affair was against the code of personal conduct. A version of his father's advice resonated from his memory: *Never dip your stick where you get your paycheck;* or some colorful play on words that was unique to his father. Good advice stuck.

"It took me almost twelve years to become who I am. If you think I'm stupid enough to throw it all away over a piece of tail, then you underestimate me."

"I'm not underestimating you. I just . . ." She paused, fidgeting with her fingers. Her eyes lowered as if she were ashamed. Then she looked up at him, now their dark brown irises were pleading. "Dr. Morgan, please. I miss my work. Plus this is related to my future career."

He dropped the pen he had been prepared to write with and stroked his chin. What he saw almost made him feel guilty. She was begging him to reconsider. He was thoughtful for a few seconds, wrestling with how badly things had turned out for her. But also sure he had made the right choice. Samaria had crossed the line. Actions had consequences.

"I'm sorry you don't like your assignment. But there's nothing I can do for you. You'll have to talk to Mrs. Pitts." He picked up his pen and returned his attention to the patient charts, dismissing her with the stroke of ink that met the empty space in front of him.

Moments later she popped to her feet and stomped from the office, leaving the scent of her perfume behind.

Chapter 30

Dr. Jonah Morgan was going to pay. Samaria was sick and tired of the way he was treating her. When he saw her coming down the hall, he turned around. If he saw her at the elevator, he took the stairs. It had been pretty bad the first couple of days after the incident. But she'd assumed he was embarrassed and didn't know how to behave around her. But then when he came in on the following Monday and began the same type of treatment, she knew he was snubbing her. And so was the office manager, Lorraine Pitts. By midday, Samaria was paged on the rarely used overhead system. She remembered the entire meeting like it had just happened.

"Samaria Jacobs, please come to the administration office."

She knocked on Lorraine's door. Lorraine nodded and motioned for Samaria to come inside.

"Samaria, please be a dear and close the door behind you." Lorraine grinned at her.

A smile, Samaria immediately knew something was wrong.

"Have a seat."

She rubbed her sweating palms against her purple uniform scrubs and took a seat in front of the woman's small desk. Lorraine shuffled papers around, and then opened a file that Samaria could clearly see was labeled with her name. *Sadist.* She knew the waiting was driving her crazy. Samaria finally asked, "What's going on?"

Lorraine tapped a pile of papers. Smiling again, she said," I have a reassignment for you. Effective immediately, you'll begin to work with Doctors Cooper and Madu."

She couldn't have shocked her more if she'd pulled out a water gun and shot her in the face. Samaria popped out of her seat. "What?"

Lorraine glared at her with fake confusion. Like reassignments happened everyday.

"What do you mean? Why have I been reassigned?"

"I have been looking at work assignments for several weeks. We have to make sure our utilization of all personnel is to the optimum benefit of the facility. Doctors Madu and Cooper could use a nurse with your many years of experience."

"And a cardiologist can't?" Samaria's statement was more of a question.

Lorraine blinked her eyes several times and closed the file. *Liar.* Jonah had told that blabbermouth that he didn't want to work with her anymore.

Samaria had a great deal of respect for Dr. Madu. She was an African gynecologist with a high degree of professionalism and integrity. Her patient load wasn't that heavy. The only real issue was that Samaria had never worked in gynecology. She was sick of looking at women stick their feet in stirrups, spread their legs, and wiggle down to the bottom of the table.

Then on the opposite end of the spectrum was Cooper.

Working with him was a nightmare. Like most family practitioners, he was always seeing new patients. New patients were more work because they required a complete medical history. Cooper also treated sick, contagious adults and some of the children. Running noses and fevers had not been a part of her daily patient load for a long time. It was busy, exhausting work that kept her running all day.

The truth was she had gotten spoiled working with Jonah. He saw lots of patients, but they were easier to deal with. Many of them were sicker than Cooper's patients, but heart disease wasn't contagious. Patients didn't sneeze or cough on her. Children didn't throw up on the floor in the exam rooms. She didn't have to hold them down for the immunizations.

Between the stress of working for the odd couple and the heavier workload, she wanted to pull her hair out.

Jonah had made her life a living hell. She was determined to get back at him. She just had to figure out how.

Chapter 31

Faith avoided making eye contact with anyone at the gym as she made a speedy procession to Yvette's office. As she entered, she found her friend pouring over a bevy of ledgers and books. She had a pen in her hand and a pencil behind her ear. So immersed in what she was doing, Yvette didn't even see Faith standing in the door.

Faith cleared her throat. The music was so loud, Yvette still didn't hear her.

Faith felt terrible about interrupting her. She looked so involved in what she was doing, but if she didn't talk to someone, if someone didn't calm her down, she was packing everything she owned tonight and moving out of that house.

"Oh . . ." Yvette said, looking up and finally seeing her. "I . . . didn't know you were standing there."

Then recognition that something was amiss must have come to her because she sprang from her seat and came around the desk. She took Faith's arm and escorted her to a chair.

"Honey, what's wro—"

Faith began crying and sobbing before Yvette could even get the question out. Yvette closed the office door and sat in the chair next to her.

"What happened?" Yvette reached for Faith's chin and tilted her head to meet her eyes. "You're worrying me. You've got to tell me what happened."

"Jo-Jonah . . ." Faith sniffed, then took a deep breath. She took a tissue from the desk. "Jonah has a—had a twin brother."

Yvette's head snapped back. "What do you mean?"

Faith wiped her eyes and blew her nose. "He died when he was ten."

"How—what happened?"

Faith shook her head and slumped back in the chair. Weariness began to creep into her muscles. "I don't know."

"Why didn't he tell you?"

"Your guess is as good as mine." She spit the words out and let her eyes trace the pattern of stucco on the ceiling. "I feel like I've been living with a stranger. How could he not tell me?"

Yvette shook her head. "How did he die?"

"I'm almost afraid to find out." She sat up and reached into her bag.

"How *did* you find out?"

Faith relayed the story of how she came to be at vital records to Yvette and how the clerk managed to give her the wrong certificate.

"You mean, you found out at the records office?" Yvette exclaimed.

"And I went into shock. I stood there in the middle of the floor, crying like a baby. I'm surprised they didn't call Grady's psych ward to come pick me up."

Faith handed the white envelope with Joshua's death

certificate to Yvette. "I haven't looked at it. I don't know what I'll see. I didn't want to be alone to find out something horrible."

Yvette took the envelope.

"I know it adds to the questions I've had over the years. His relationship with his father, his mother . . . something horrible happened."

Yvette opened the envelope, removed the certificate and read over the details scribed on it. A strange shadow fell over her face as she raised her eyes to meet Faith's.

"What . . . what is it?" Faith asked.

Yvette shook her head and handed the certificate to Faith. "I think it's okay for you to read this yourself. You need to."

Faith's hand trembled as she reached for the paper, but she never removed her eyes from her friend's. Yvette had an odd look, and she couldn't gauge her; didn't know how to prepare for what she would see. She looked down and read the details of the certificate line by line until she came to the end.

Cause of death: Heart failure.

"Oh my God." Faith's breath caught in her throat as she gasped and raised her hand to her chest. It was like someone had seared her fingers. She dropped the paper and watched it float to the floor. "Heart failure," she said. "Jonah's twin brother died from heart disease."

Yvette continued to be silent.

"My God."

"Faith," Yvette began as she touched her hand that was now a balled up fist. "It's obvious that Jonah—"

Faith raised an index finger. ". . . and I don't have very much of a marriage." She chuckled.

"No. I was going to say, it's obvious that he has some real issues from his childhood as a result of this death."

"It's also obvious that something's really wrong with our marriage that he hasn't shared this with me. Who keeps a sibling a secret? A twin?"

Yvette scratched her head. "He's got some issues."

"That, as his wife, I should have known about." Faith collapsed in the chair. "He doesn't trust me."

"Faith, don't do that."

"Don't do what?"

"Turn this into something about you—about your marriage." Yvette stood.

Faith stood also. "This is about our marriage. This is about the trust—the sharing and the intimacy that obviously doesn't exist."

Yvette dropped her head, and then raised it again. "This is about a man in pain who doesn't know how to talk about it."

"No, this is about . . ." Faith lost her words in the emotion. "Yvette, he had a twin. My God, I should know that."

"I agree he should have told you, but—"

"But nothing. I have put up with his moodiness, his obsession with his work, his drinking for years, because he is hurting over the death of his brother." Faith paused. "Jonah is a grown man. He has a responsibility to try to work through his issues so he can be the man he needs to be in this marriage and for this family."

"Now you're spouting textbook psychology."

"No. I'm saying, he's my husband, and I'm nobody to him. Just someone to sleep with, make his meals, and get his passport renewed."

Without listening to another word Yvette had to say, Faith picked up the certificate, rushed out of the office, and back tracked past the many machines. The music blared overhead, but it couldn't drown out her thoughts. Jonah had lied to her from the beginning. How was she supposed to get past this hurt?

Faith pushed the glass doors open. The afternoon heat assailed her like an unwelcome swarm of gnats in her face. She removed her key ring from the pocket of her slacks and pushed the entry key to unlock the vehicle. Once inside, she started it and pulled into traffic so quickly it was only the grace of God that kept her from ramming her truck into the side of another vehicle.

She stopped at a red light and let the window down. She was glad for the light, the reprieve. "Lord, I need you to help me. I don't even know what this is I'm feeling. It's a kind of rejection that I've never felt before in my life."

What was she supposed to do now? Her mother's words reverberated in her mind. "A praying woman doesn't move in her common sense and free will."

Her mother, pain in the neck that she was sometimes, could help her. She wanted to talk to her mother. To climb up on her bed like she did when she was a child and place her head on her chest and listen to her say words that would make it all right. But she couldn't go to her mom now. If she were going to be a woman about this, there was a stop she needed to make.

Faith pulled out her cell phone and found the number she had dialed earlier. "Arlene, how's Elise? After pausing for an answer, Faith absently said, "Good, good." Honestly the woman could have said Elise had grown a third eye, and Faith wouldn't have heard her. "Look, something else has come up. I need until about three. Is that okay?"

Arlene told her to take her time. Faith hung up, satisfied that she didn't have to worry about her daughter. She returned the phone to her purse and drove with determination to her destination. She wasn't going to be guileless. She would get some answers, and she would get them now.

Chapter 32

Faith sat in her vehicle outside 742 Joseph E. Lowery Boulevard, the house where Jonah had grown up. The house equaled the standards of other homes in the modest neighborhood. The yard and flowers well tended. Although community revitalization had come to the area Atlantans called the West End, prospective buyers and developers had not yet found Mom Morgan's street. The structure that bore the numbers 742, in particular, was old and weather beaten; in need of a coat of paint, and repair to the cracked walkway. Faith tried to get a picture in her head of Jonah's life here in a space that was so small— where a death had to be suffocating. In small spaces there was no place to run. No place to hide. Everyone had to grieve together.

Faith took a deep breath and sighed. So many things made sense. His estranged relationship with his father, the fact that he never wanted to talk about his childhood and didn't have any pictures or photo albums. His mother's equal evasiveness. *Secrets and lies. It was all . . .*

The devil.

Faith opened the door, stepped from the vehicle, and looked around. She was once again reminded that her Mercedes didn't belong in every neighborhood, but she shrugged off the thought, locked the doors, and made purposeful steps up the walkway.

Although she was feeling strange about it, Faith knew she had to have this conversation. She didn't want to hurt Jonah's mother and didn't plan to come here accusing her of anything. Faith knew her husband was the one she should be confronting, but if Jonah said one thing—one wrong word—she would leave him. His mother might give her some information that she hoped would make her sympathetic to him. In her soul, she was still fighting for her marriage.

As she raised her hand to knock, it suddenly occurred to her that Mom Morgan might not be at home. The doubt only lasted a second when the door slowly opened.

"Hi, baby," Mom Morgan said, pulling the door open wide. "I've sort of been expecting you."

Faith stepped in the house. Glad to be out of the heat, she stood in the small foyer and waited for Mom to relock the door. The aroma of baked goods greeted her with a gentleness that instantly made her hungry. She realized she hadn't eaten all day. Between the lack of food and the stress of the day, she was running on empty.

"Have a seat," Mom Morgan said, indicating the floral loveseat across from the worn club chair she always sat in when Faith visited. "Can I get you something?"

"No." Although she felt her stomach growl, Faith dismissed the smells that were assailing her senses. Her stomach was in such a knot that she feared anything she ate might come back up.

"Well, I know there's something you want." Mom sat in her chair.

Faith noted she was old for her sixty-three years. Not

like most African American women who looked ten years younger than they were. Mom Morgan looked older. It was the first time Faith had really noticed it, really looked at her as more than Jonah's mother. This was a woman who had endured the pain of losing a ten-year-old child. Suddenly she was ashamed of the anger she'd felt toward her on the drive over here.

"You said you were expecting me." Faith knew that was more of a question than a statement.

"Yes. Ever since you called and said you had to renew Jonah's passport. I knew you would find out about Joshua."

Faith placed her handbag on the empty cushion beside her and steeled her fist against the seat cushions. "Tell me, why the secrecy?"

Mom Morgan paused for a moment, and then shrugged the shoulders of her small frame. "Jonah wanted it that way."

The knot in Faith's stomach got tighter. She clasped her hands together on her lap, then opened them and rubbed both her hands across her knees.

"Are you sure you don't want a cup of tea?" Mom Morgan asked, looking from Faith's hands to her eyes.

Faith shook her head, then relaxed her hands in her lap. "I just want some answers."

Lips in a thin line, Mom Morgan nodded her head and sat back in her chair. "I don't know how to make you understand how Joshua's death tore through this family. It's like when Katrina hit those people in New Orleans. The people knew a storm was coming, but they were unprepared for the devastation of it." She paused. Her expression revealed a struggle with thoughts she had to reach back in time to pull forward. "Although we knew Joshua was sick, we were unprepared for his death. It destroyed us and everything that we were. It took down every tree and tore off the roof of the house. We scattered, and everyone ran to a different corner and hid."

Mom Morgan's face was filled with pain. Faith could feel the agony. "You can imagine that Jonah was devastated. His twin brother—they were so close."

Silence fell. After a moment, Mom Morgan stood to her feet, and without a word, she left the room. She came back seconds later with what appeared to be a photo album or scrapbook. She sat on the cushion next to Faith, pushing the handbag back with a free hand. She handed the album to Faith and put on the eye glasses that were hanging on a string of pearls around her neck.

Faith looked at her, and Mom Morgan motioned her head for her to open the album.

The first picture was of two adorable, identical baby boys. They looked like pieces of chocolate with their sweetness jumping off the page of the photograph. They were dressed the same, positioned sitting back to back, holding trucks in their hands.

"Oh my," Faith responded in surprise. She touched the picture, wanting to draw the reality from it by fingering the children featured.

"Eight months old," Mom Morgan said. "Jonah was the older of the boys. Twelve whole minutes. He took his role as big brother very seriously. He wanted to protect Joshua, as if he were ten years older."

She reached over Faith and turned the next page.

In this picture, the children were dressed identical again and standing with their parents. Each one held a twin's hand. From the black and white photo, Faith could make out pinstripes in their suits. The boys looked about three years old.

"We couldn't afford to take a lot of pictures back then. They were expensive, and we didn't have a camera. But this is Easter Sunday in front of my mother's church the week after my father-in-law died." She sat up straighter and wrung her hands for a moment. "It was the last time Martin went to church."

She reached and turned the page again. "This is the first day of kindergarten. Can you believe they split 'em up in two different sessions? Back then they had half day kindergarten. Jonah went in the morning. Joshua went in the afternoon. They said they looked too much alike to go during the same time."

Faith smiled with Mom Morgan.

They continued to go through the pictures, one by one, with Mom Morgan sharing the memories of her precious twin boys with an enthusiasm that made Faith think she'd been waiting ten years to do it. Finally, she closed the album, placed it on the table, and then made her way back to her seat.

Faith thought the sudden shift in location was almost synonymous with the change in her countenance. She removed her eye glasses and looked directly at Faith like she was ready for the inquisition. The single light bulb was now turned on above her head, and she was willing to answer any and all questions.

"What happened to him? What happened to Jonah and his father? How did it tear you apart?" Faith paused. "What happened to make you grow apart instead of together?"

Mom Morgan closed her eyes and leaned against the back of the chair. Faith didn't know if she was gathering her thoughts or trying to remember, or if the memories themselves were too overwhelming, but whatever the situation, she needed this woman to talk. She needed to leave here with some understanding.

"Joshua was playing in a baseball game. He and his brother. They were just over nine years old then. At the end of the game when the kids were all slapping hands . . .

you know it's high five now, but back in the day, you would just slap five and give some skin." She smiled and Faith cracked a smile to complement it.

"While everyone else was slapping five, Joshua was standing very still. Then he opened his mouth and put his hand to his chest and just collapsed in the grass."

Faith gasped and covered her mouth.

"I thought he was dead right then and there. Martin ran to get him, and we jumped in the car, praying the thing would start, and flew to Grady hospital. My baby was there for five days, getting every needle and test they had in that place. Finally, they came and told us it was his heart. Joshua had a bad aortic valve."

Faith blew out a long breath in the momentary silence. *Did heart disease run in the family?* She thought about her Elise, then pushed worry from her mind. Her daughter was healthy. "Wasn't there something . . ." She didn't want to say the wrong thing. "Was the prognosis fatal?"

Mom Morgan smiled. "No, it wasn't. Joshua needed a surgery. It would repair the valve, but it was expensive, and we didn't have health insurance."

"They wouldn't operate on him anyway?"

"Faith, you're talking about Georgia, 1976 and a little black boy from the ghetto dying. There wasn't a lot of help back then, but there was state medical assistance. You had to be on welfare to get it." Mom Morgan's lips thinned into a line.

"So you weren't eligible for it?"

"Actually, we were. Martin was working construction then, business was slow. We were eligible because he hadn't made hardly any money really for several months. We were scraping by, about to lose this little house because we couldn't pay the $121 mortgage. We were so poor." She shook her head. "We qualified for welfare, and we qualified for food stamps and everything else at the family and children services office. I went and filed the application for the medical insurance. That's all I wanted was the medical. They told me we had to get the cash welfare too, but Martin had to sign the papers." Mom Morgan's mouth turned into an angry knot. "He wouldn't do it."

Faith gasped in horror. "He wouldn't do it? Had the doctors explained to him the need for the surgery?"

"They made it as clear as a bell, but it was the way it was done." Mom Morgan nodded and clenched the arms of the chair. "Martin was a prideful man. A fool, really. I can say that looking back because I've forgiven him. I did that a long time ago. But really, if I had to pinpoint what happened that year, I would say . . . the devil had his way."

Faith shuddered, partly from a cold draft that hit her when the air conditioning kicked on, and partly from Mom Morgan's words.

"The doctor told us to go to the welfare office and get some help. He said it this way: 'They have state help for people like you.' " Mom Morgan was throwing an arm around demonstrating the doctor's body language with contempt. " 'You should go get it. We have a social worker here at the hospital that can help you if you don't read and write.' "

Faith blinked back tears.

"Imagine someone saying that to Martin Morgan." She laughed bitterly.

"I can't do that." Faith shrugged. "I've never met him."

"Okay then, let me help you get a picture of it." Mom Morgan grabbed both arms of the chair and leaned forward. Her eyes filled with sadness. "Imagine someone saying that to your husband, because *Jonah*, God help him, is just like his father." She almost spit the words out; then she sat back and closed her eyes. Her lips clenched so tight, Faith imagined that she had to work harder to breathe through her nostrils.

Faith tried to do what Mom Morgan had suggested. Imagine Jonah. Take the pride, arrogance, and stubbornness she knew her husband possessed and transfer it to that situation, to a man in that situation. Tears streamed down her face. She hated to think of this family, any family, having to endure this type of treatment, this indignation.

"But, Mom," Faith cried. "He wouldn't come around? As time went on you couldn't . . ." Faith was at a loss for words. "He just watched him die?"

"There wasn't time."

"You said he collapsed after their ninth birthday, he died when he was ten."

"Ten years and a couple of months." Mom Morgan was exact. "They stabilized him, then sent him home. We restricted his activity and did all the stuff the doctor said to do. Joshua seemed like a healthy kid. He had gained the weight he lost, so I think it was easy for Martin to overlook the fact that he wasn't well. Joshua was okay for almost eight months. Then he collapsed again. They never revived him."

Faith swallowed a gasp.

"I hated Martin then. Something shut down in me. I couldn't stand the sight of him. The odd, very odd thing was that four months later, he got a job with the city, collecting trash. He'd never gotten anything so stable. He even had health insurance. But it was too late—too late for Joshua."

Faith reached into her purse for a tissue and wiped her eyes.

"He tried to make it up to us. He was making decent money so he would buy things. We got a good used car, but nothing would make up for that one mistake he made. He got sick of trying. He couldn't stand the contempt I felt for him so he stayed out. Drinking and partying and loose women, Lord knows what else he might have been into. I think that may have been when the gambling started. Anyway, I got a job, started making some money, and I asked him to leave our home. I wanted a divorce. He left. A few months later we were divorced, he lost his job, and he's been living hand to mouth doing odd jobs and renting a room in a boarding house ever since."

Faith gave Mom Morgan a chance to catch her breath before saying, "Jonah was a child. Did he really understand the dynamics of what was happening? Why did he blame his father?"

"Because he overheard a conversation between me and his father. He stood on the other side of that screened door," she said, pointing, "and listened to his father tell me he wouldn't go to the welfare office. I cried like a baby. Jonah begged me not to cry. Kept saying Joshua would be all right. I tried to tell him there were things he didn't understand, but he kept saying, 'Daddy will sign the papers.' That's what he really believed. But I knew my husband."

A long silence encapsulated the room. "This is too much." Faith rested her head on the cushion behind her and closed her eyes for a moment. Her mind was racing with a hundred different thoughts. It felt like her life was flashing before her.

Faith opened her eyes, looked up at the ceiling, and then around the room. A picture frame sat on the fireplace mantle. Two twin boys sitting back to back. They were about nine years old. She stood and slowly walked to the picture. She could feel Mom Morgan's eyes on her. Her mouth hung open. She had never seen this before. She had been in this house a hundred times and had never seen this picture. She stood, pointing as she turned to face Mom Morgan who was now standing also.

"I put it away whenever you came to visit." Tears began to flow again, but this time, they came from Mom Mor-

gan's eyes. Faith embraced the woman; she felt the
wracking of her body as she sobbed. "My son asked me to
put it away whenever you or the children were coming to
visit. I felt I owed it to him." She wiped tears with a handkerchief she removed from her house dress. "Faith, I can't
answer some of your questions. There are some things
you are going to have to get from your husband. All I can
tell you is I didn't do what I should have done for Jonah
when Joshua died. I shut down in my grief and left him to
his own. By the time I wanted to talk about Joshua and try
to help him with it all, he was leaving for college. I let him
down, and all these years I've understood why he's the
way he is. I've been talking to him for years about telling
you, but I think the older he gets, the more stubborn he
becomes and the more afraid he is that you won't understand."

Faith turned to face the picture again. Joshua was slightly
chunkier than Jonah, and anyone who knew could tell this
child was not well. You could see it, in both their eyes.

"I'm so sorry. I'm so sorry for everything you endured.
All the pain, losing a child, I can't imagine." She shook her
head. "But I don't understand how he could keep a sibling, a twin from me." Faith could feel the anger coming
back. It was rising from her feet, making a slow but deliberate journey to her heart.

Mom Morgan shook her head. "It's a lot to forgive. But I
know he loves you."

Faith shook her head likewise. "No, he's married to me.
But I don't know that Jonah really loves anyone but himself. It was cruel for him to ask you to put that picture
away. Cruel and selfish." She let out a long sigh, retrieved
her handbag from the sofa and moved to the door. "I've
got to get the kids."

Mom Morgan followed. "Faith, I know my son is a complicated man, but remember, me and his father and our

lack of regard for the Lord made him that way. You're a
good woman. You can use the love of God to unmake
him." She was pleading with her eyes. "He needs you, and
you're wrong, he does love you. Don't give up on him."

Faith touched the woman's soft, freckled hand. She didn't
want to hurt her any more than she had already been hurt.
She was pleading for her son. Jonah was all she had left.

"I'll try." Faith said. She left the house. It was the second time a mother had told her to be a Christian woman
today, but she wasn't just a Christian. She was human.
She had been betrayed, and she was angry.

Faith climbed into her vehicle. She waved one last time
at Mom Morgan, and then watched the woman close the
door. *Secrets and lies.* She shook off an acrid feeling of
foreboding and left the house where the *devil had had his
way.*

Chapter 33

Faith flopped down on the sofa. She was exhausted. The kitchen was clean, the kids were in bed, and she had already taken a long, hot shower. She was glad Jonah was late because she didn't think she would be able to put on a happy face in front of the children. Not tonight.

She picked up the mug she brought in the room with her and took a sip of her chamomile tea. If she weren't saved, she'd be downing a bottle of spirits. In some respects, she could understand how people became addicted to alcohol and drugs. If she weren't a praying woman, she'd have lost it a long time ago; probably when her father died, certainly after her first husband's accident. Life was overwhelming at times. Today was an example of one of those instances, but she had every confidence that God would bring her through it all. He hadn't put any more on her shoulders than she could bear.

Faith put her mug down and reached for the remote control. She flipped through various channels, and when she could find nothing, she chose a gospel music station. The sounds of Israel and New Breed, Yolanda Adams, and

Fred Hammond relaxed her, but it was Bishop Paul Morton's "Your Tears" that moved her in her spirit. When the song ended, she wiped a fresh tear from her cheek.

Faith heard the grandfather clock chime. Nine thirty P.M. She'd been sitting there in the dark for more than twenty minutes, waiting for Jonah to walk through the doors, and still, he wasn't home.

She knew she should be empathetic. She was trying to understand by putting herself in his shoes, losing a sibling. What might that be like? Twins had a unique closeness. She'd read about it, seen reports about it on television. Twins, even if they were raised apart, often liked the same foods, did the same type of work, and married people with similar names. Being a twin wasn't just a physical connection, it was spiritual.

So what happened when that was broken? When one twin died?

Faith sighed. She didn't know. No matter how hard she tried to think of it from Jonah's perspective, she couldn't. She was an only child.

Besides, even if he lost his brother, she and Jonah were also supposed to have a spiritual connection; the husband and wife connection. Something was terribly wrong with their marriage if he couldn't share something like that with her.

The phone rang for the first time this evening. The caller I.D. revealed Yvette's cell phone number. She picked up the handset. "Hey."

"Hi. You okay?" Yvette asked.

"Okay as I can be."

"Have you talked to Jonah yet?"

Faith let her eyes wander to the clock, and noted the time again. "He hasn't gotten home."

"Well, don't be nasty with him, Faith. Make sure you let

him tell you his side of the story. There's got to be some reason why he didn't tell you."

Faith didn't have the energy to disagree about the "don't be nasty" part. Instead she decided to share the rest of it with Yvette. "I talked to his mother today."

There was a momentary pause from Yvette. "You did?"

"I went to see her after I left you."

"What did she say?"

"A whole lot of really sad stuff about Jonah's childhood and her son's death."

"Did she say why the secret?"

"No," Faith said. "She left that story for Jonah to share. I don't even think she really knows what Jonah was thinking."

"It'll be okay, girl. Just don't make it the deal breaker. You know you guys have been under an enormous amount of stress anyway."

Faith let out a long breath. "I'll try."

"Faith," Yvette was pleading.

"Yvette, I said, I'll try. I'll try to listen before I form any judgment. I'll try."

"Okay. Love you."

"Love you too."

Faith ended the call and put the phone on the table. She needed to pray. She knew that's what she should do, but for some reason tonight, she didn't do it. She couldn't make herself do what was right.

The garage door was rising, and within seconds, Jonah walked in.

He flipped the switch to light the family room. He looked surprised to see her. "Why are you sitting in the dark?"

Faith didn't answer at first. She just pushed the button to end the music.

"I don't know, Jonah. I figured being in the dark was probably appropriate for me since I've been in the dark for years."

He raised a single eyebrow. "What's with the melodrama? And the somber face?" He went into the office with his briefcase and the mail. After about thirty seconds, he came back out.

Jonah came to stand directly in front of her, his hands in his pockets. Like he wasn't going to play games with her. She knew that look.

"Faith, is there something you have to say? Otherwise I'm going to get something to eat."

"Help yourself, Dr. Morgan." She opened her hand in the direction of the kitchen. "It's in the warming oven."

He looked at her curiously, but then walked into the kitchen. She sat there, feeling foolish, feeling weak because she didn't confront him right off. But she also had a strange sense of confusion. When the lights came on she saw him—the man who was a little boy—the little boy whose brother died. Now she wondered how she would begin. How she would bring Joshua up. It wasn't like she could say, "By the way, honey, I found out today that you have a dead brother."

"You want to join me in here or should I come in there?" Jonah called from the kitchen.

Faith didn't answer. She continued to sit there not sure how she should explain, and then she realized, she would tell him the truth. After all, that was what she wanted from him.

She went into the kitchen, carrying her empty cup. Her hand trembled as she placed it in the dishwasher. Opening the refrigerator she removed two dessert dishes of pudding. After topping both with whip cream, she grabbed two teaspoons and sat down across from him.

He ate quickly, pausing once to give her a satisfied

smile. Lasagna was one of his favorites. She knew that, and even though her intentions were to blast him for keeping the secret from her, she still made one of his favorites.

"What's going on?" he asked, pulling a pudding toward him. "You look strange. Are the kids okay?"

She played with the lip of the pudding dish. She couldn't eat it. She hadn't really eaten anything since she found out. Her stomach was still in knots.

"I went to vital records today. I needed to get a copy of your birth certificate to renew your passport."

Jonah was silent. She noticed a muscle in his jaw jump.

"The clerk made a mistake." Faith took a deep breath. "She gave me Joshua's birth certificate instead of yours."

Jonah held the teaspoon in midair for about five seconds, then carefully placed it on the table and wiped his mouth with his napkin. He looked directly at her.

Faith's eyelashes fluttered; she raised a hand to cover her mouth. The look in his eyes. He was stunned. "I didn't mean to be so blunt."

Jonah still didn't say anything.

"It was a shock to find out you had a brother."

Jonah cleared his throat and folded his arms on the table. He wasn't looking at her now. He looked down at his arms, at the table; he was looking for anything but her eyes.

The water welling in her eyes blurred her vision. "I can only imagine that it must have been very hard for you losing him that way."

Jonah put both palms down on the table, slid back his chair and pushed himself up. "I can't talk about Joshua tonight."

"Jonah, I am trying hard not to make this about me." She stood and grabbed his hand.

He cast an icy glance down at her. "Then don't." He pulled his hand away.

Faith grabbed his hand again. "Don't walk away from me. Please, Jonah. Not tonight. I need you to talk to me."

"And I need you to give me time," he said.

She watched him walk away from her.

"Ten years hasn't been long enough?" But she did not get an answer. Jonah went into his office. Just as she reached it, he pushed the door closed in her face. He had shut her out again.

Chapter 34

Jonah stood transfixed in a spot in front of the window. He looked at the clock on his desk. He'd been cowering in this office for more than two hours. Now he knew why he'd found Faith sitting in the dark. Something about a secret makes a person want to hide from light.

He reached into the drawer where he kept his bourbon. Something else that had begun as secret: *his drinking.* A real man would have a bar, but he didn't have the courage to do that. He hid his liquor in a drawer as if Faith didn't know it was there. Jonah picked up the bottle and stared at it for a long time. *Liquid courage.* Drinking worked for his dad. He seemed to have no problem letting everyone know exactly how he felt once he had a few beers in him. Jonah shook his head. He really was different from his father. He had a bottle now, and he still couldn't stand up to his wife. Courage was a thing that really came from the inside.

Jonah poured a drink and took a long swig, eradicating the taste of garlic, mozzarella cheese, and chocolate pudding from his mouth. He would hate the headache he'd have in the morning if he had too many, but this drink was the only thing that was going to get him through the night.

Jonah carried the glass and the bottle with him to the sofa and collapsed onto it. The midnight moon was the only light. He peeped through the blinds and illuminated one half of the room. The other half was cast in a shadow. He loved the end of the day, when the sun was down and the moon was high. He wondered what that really said about him, that he preferred it when it was dark.

Faith knew. After all these years, she simply knew. God, how easy would it have been to tell her, but instead, she found out. And now she wanted to talk about it. She wanted him to share his feelings with her. *Women.*

The memory of his brother's death and funeral were a cancer that had been eating him alive for almost thirty years. Images always pushed themselves to the forefront of his mind when he was working with a patient, giving a lecture in a classroom, talking to the children; even when he was playing golf. Always—the memories. They were a part of his soul.

Jonah knew he should have told Faith about Joshua in the beginning. But he'd kept it from her. What was it? Fear that she would see his weakness, he'd be transparent, and she'd begin to psychoanalyze him. No, he knew that wasn't it.

He took another drink. He was ashamed of the fact that Joshua had died because he was poor. He was ashamed that poverty and all of its foot soldiers, ignorance, and pride had taken his brother's life. It was just that simple. He even made his mother an unwilling party in his deception. She had warned him, throwing around that scripture about things done in the dark, coming to the light. In his gut he knew it was a matter of time.

After pouring another glass of bourbon, he removed his shoes and sat back, massaging his toes in the carpet. In the shadows, Jonah could make out the oversized wedding portrait on the wall. Their wedding day; one of the highlights of his life. He had really come up, marrying Faith. Poor boy from a southern ghetto marries an upper middle class girl from up north. Faith was the gold ring on the carousel. She was beautiful, smart, classy, and respectable. Unlike every other woman he'd dated, he had to pursue her, and that was what he wanted; a challenge.

So why are you losing her?

He shook his head and took the final sip that emptied the glass. He was losing her because he was Martin Morgan's son. Jonah poured another drink. As hard as he had fought it over the years, he was losing the battle to not be like his father. He'd have to tell her about all of it. The heartless way his father had been back then. He remembered it like it was yesterday.

Jonah lay on the floor at the top of the stairs listening to his parents toss words back and forth. His father was sitting in his recliner, smoking a cigarette, a mean scowl etched into the deep folds of skin on his face.

He couldn't see his mother, but he knew she was standing where she always stood when she wanted his father's attention, in front of the small black and white television adjacent to his chair in the living room.

"Martin, I need to take your checks to the social worker."

"Woman, I done told you fo' the last time. I ain't going on no welfare."

"It's not welfare. Its state insurance for low income families."

"You sound like that fancy social worker. State insurance for low income families." His tone menacing in its mimic of her. "It's welfare. Tax payer money."

"If we don't' get this insurance for Joshua . . ."

"I told you I'm gonna get on with the city soon. My in-

surance be turned on the job right after I start. The boy be all right 'til then."

"The doctor said he don't have the—"

"Medicaid is welfare, and I ain't goin' on no welfare!" his father said, cutting her off. He was out of his chair and moving to the door. Jonah heard the sound of the screen door snapping shut.

The sound of the door opening to his right pulled him from his childhood memory to the present. His wife, wrapped in a satin robe, stood in the doorway. She would have been appealing in the sexy nightwear if it hadn't been for the look on her face. She was displeased that he was drinking.

"I thought you were asleep," he said, placing the glass on the coffee table.

"I hoped you weren't drinking."

He leaned forward to sit up. Faith raised one hand signaling him to stop.

"Don't bother. I don't want to talk to you when you've been drinking. You can just sleep down here with your bottle."

Before he could respond, the door slammed close.

A bizarre and overwhelming urge to cry came over him. Instead he cursed and took another long sip of his drink to suppress it. Jonah had the sense that his life was spiraling into an abyss. His career was going well, but somehow he felt things were out of control, like something was about to happen. Maybe the politics with Cooper were wearing on him, or it could be the Lazarus case. Waiting for a heart always made him feel powerless.

He took the final sip that finished his drink, reached for the bottle he'd placed on the coffee table, and poured another. The muscles in his face contorted, and he again had to fight the tears that welled in his eyes. Sitting back on the sofa, he clutched the glass to his chest. He was in so much pain. It was like the bourbon in front of him. *Bottled up.*

A lone tear slowly slid down his cheek.

Jonah stretched out on the sofa and closed his eyes. He *would* sleep here tonight, away from Faith's questions—away from her disapproving eyes. It didn't matter that the sofa was narrow and he had a king size bed upstairs. It didn't matter that it was lumpy—when his mattress was smooth. It didn't matter that he would be uncomfortable, because no matter where he was, comfort would not find him tonight.

Chapter 35

April yawned as she pushed the door open for the ladies room. The lack of sleep had finally gotten the better of her. Jonah had her running all day from room to room, performing every cardiac test they had on all his patients like he was afraid he was going to miss something. It was a very weird day.

The truth was she couldn't blame her exhaustion on the job. She'd been tired when she came in. She'd had another one of the nightmares last night. She woke at three A.M. and watched television until it was time to get dressed for work. The dream was the one she hated the most. She lay on a dirty floor, half naked, surrounded by creatures that looked like demons. They held her down, chopped at her hair and hit her repeatedly. One even stuck a hot poker on her belly. It was horrible.

It was her own stupidity for not refilling the medication her doctor had prescribed to help her sleep. Subconsciously she knew the omission was an attempt to see if she were better. Every night when she emptied one of the small white pills into her hand, she prayed for the return of sleep on its own without the drugs that induced the comatose state she slipped into every night. But the insomnia and night-mares had won. The pharmacy would be her first stop on the way home.

Nightmares weren't her only problem. She had visions during the day that were almost as bad. Her senses awak-ened to the panoramic flashes of imagery cascading through her mind. The smell of sweat mixed with beer, the grimy scrape of sawdust against her arms and breasts, the re-volting grunts each time he . . .

April shook the image from her head. She turned on the water and wet a few paper towels and began patting it against her forehead and neck to give her temporary relief from the perspiring. Even though the air conditioning was running at full blast, she had wet rings under her arms. She was nervous as a cat tied to a pole in a dog house. She wasn't going to be able to hide her problems much longer.

April leaned in toward the mirror. "You could carry clothing in those bags," she said, pulling down on the skin just below her eyes and willing the dark circles to go back into hiding.

No wonder everyone was asking her if she were okay. She looked horrible.

Her cell phone rang, shocking her heart into such rapid palpations that a cardiac arrest should have followed. Her hands shook as she pulled it from her lab coat pocket. She hoped it wasn't her father. Her dad was worried about her too. But now it had gotten to the point where he was nag-ging her everyday with the same questions. "Are you being careful? You aren't going out at night. You're not taking anymore of those anxiety drugs, are you?"

She knew he cared, but he was driving her crazier than . . . well, crazier than she was making herself.

April noted the number was an unknown one and de-cided to avoid the call for now. If it were important, they'd leave a message. She returned the phone to her pocket and pulled the door open to leave the ladies room. She saw Samaria and Dr. Morgan passing each other in the hall. Even though Dr. Morgan had his back to her, April could tell he hadn't even acknowledged Samaria, and Samaria, facing her, rolled her eyes once Dr. Morgan was farther down the hall. As she'd suspected, there was more to the reassignment story than she'd thought. Lorraine Pitts might be the office manger, but the doctors got to pick and choose the nurses they worked with; especially, a specialist like Dr. Morgan. Something bad had happened between them. April knew she had been hallucinating these days, but she hadn't imagined what she'd just seen.

Chapter 36

Samaria entered the break room, exhausted from another afternoon of hard labor. She was thirsty and needed a shot of caffeinated soda to help her make it through the rest of her charting so she could finish her work and go home. She opened the refrigerator, removed a can of cola, and dropped fifty cents into a small basket on the counter next to the refrigerator where employees paid on the honor system for the supply. Just as the tab cracked the aluminum opening to the can, she heard someone push the door in and join her in the room.

She turned to find April. Eyes red and slightly swollen, it looked like she'd been crying.

"What's going on with you, girl?" Samaria asked, easing into a spot next to the chair April had slid into.

April shoved a tissue she'd been using to wipe her face into her jacket pocket.

"I get allergies bad this time of year."

"Hmm," Samaria groaned. "I don't remember you having any allergies this time last year."

April avoided her eyes. "They're worse this year than they usually are."

Samaria was silent for a moment. She didn't know who she was trying to kid. Something was seriously wrong with this chick. Samaria watched her file echocardiogram pictures in patient medical charts.

"How is Amadi Lazarus?" It was one of the charts April had put to the side after she put files in it.

"He's on the transplant list. The walls of his heart are badly damaged."

"From what?"

"He's not sure."

"Jonah the Great is unsure of something?" Samaria knew she sounded snide.

"Doctor." April was firm. "Dr. Morgan doesn't have much of a medical history to work with, and you know Amadi's only been in the U.S. for two years."

"You certainly are defensive about *Doctor* Morgan." Samaria opened Amadi's chart. "You need to be careful. He may not deserve your loyalty."

April looked totally confused, like Samaria had just poured water on her and told her it was raining. "What do you mean?"

April's cell phone rang. Samaria noticed that April looked like she was nearly going to jump out of her skin from the sound. She pulled the phone from her pocket and sucked her teeth. Sighing, she pushed the talk button to take the call.

"Hello . . . oh . . . Dr. Moray."

Samaria's ears perked up and she made a mental note of the doctor's name.

April bought her free hand up and grabbed the back of her neck. Samaria could tell she was nervous. Samaria listened to a series of "yes—I know—I will—I am" on April's end of the conversation, along with excuses about being busy with school and work.

April wasn't in school. She specifically remembered April telling her she'd taken this semester off. Who was she lying to and why?

They talked a minute longer, with April insisting she couldn't come today and her schedule for the next few weeks being uncertain—more nodding—some grimacing, and a very thoughtful goodbye.

Samaria didn't say anything about the fact that April had fresh tears, especially since she'd been pretending to read Amadi's chart. "It says here that he was sick in the hospital in Togo. What for?"

April dabbed the corners of her eyes with a tissue. "What do you mean? Dr. Morgan doesn't deserve my loyalty?"

Samaria closed the chart and laid it back in the pile. Dr. Moray had rattled her. It was also clear that Dr. Moray wanted to see April, but the feeling wasn't mutual.

Samaria sighed. "Why do you think I've been reassigned?"

"I don't know. Mrs. Pitts moved you, or maybe you and Dr. Morgan had a disagreement, or something."

"You didn't ask him?"

April looked at her like she had used a four-letter word. "No. I didn't ask him. I'm busy. I have other things on my mind."

"Yeah—I'm sure. Like what's causing those allergies, right?"

Samaria stood and walked away, leaving April curious. She knew she wouldn't ask Jonah anything. The girl was a wimp. She didn't have the nerve. But she would wonder, and that's what Samaria wanted her to do.

Samaria went into the medical records department and

knocked on the counter. "Hey in there. It's me, Sam." She leaned against the desk while she waited for one of the clerks to come.

"Hi. What can I get for you, Sam?"

"Actually, I was wondering if I could get back there and borrow a computer for about sixty seconds. I need to get on the Internet."

The clerk hesitated for a moment.

"It's work related, and it'll only take me a minute. You can stand over my shoulder to make sure I'm not looking at porn," Samaria said, feigning irritation.

The clerk relaxed. "Okay. I guess if it's only a minute and you aren't shopping or anything."

"I'm telling you—stand over my shoulder. I just have to look something up."

The clerk unlocked the latch to the waist high swing door and let Samaria in.

"Use that one there." She pointed to a computer near the window.

Samaria sat down and pulled up Google. She typed in the name, Dr. Moray and the word, Atlanta and did a search.

Two Dr. Moray's came up for the metro area. One was a podiatrist and the other a psychiatrist. This was obviously not about feet, so she clicked on the link for the psychiatrist.

"I knew she was crazy," Samaria whispered under her breath.

Dr. Moray was a general psychologist. She treated anxiety, depression, marriage, and family issues.

"That didn't help much, but at least she knew April was having some kind of psychological problem.

"You done?" The medical records clerk was standing over her monitor peering down like the Gestapo.

"Lord, chile, I'm finished. They sure got you scared in here."

"I'm the only one here today, and I don't want anything blamed on me that I didn't do, if you know what I mean. They check the histories on these computers all the time."

"No sweat. As you can see, I was getting information about a doctor." Samaria grabbed a nearby sheet of paper and pen and wrote down the telephone number and address for Dr. Moray, folded it, and put it in her pocket.

"Thanks, girl," she said, clearing the screen and sliding from behind the desk.

The clerk let her out the door, and once she was in the hall, she pulled out the sheet of paper she'd written on. With any luck, this blank requisition for medical records would be just the thing she needed to get April's file from Dr. Moray, so she could find out what was really going on.

Chapter 37

They had a hiccup in the women's day conference planning. Faith called a special meeting of the committee.

"Reverend Mason is leaving for Afghanistan on June 13th. She has firm orders," the committee chairperson said.

Faith's heart dropped, because in addition to this, the hotel had a mix up, so the rooms they'd been assigned for classes had to be switched around to accommodate smaller groups.

"So we've got two problems," Faith said, "a speaker and now, the registrations. Anything else?" She looked at her ten-person planning group, but all eyes were on her.

"We only have a little more than a month before the conference," Sister Lincoln said, breaking the silence in the room. "I've called all the alternate people on the list, and everyone is booked with other engagements. What are we going to do?"

Faith pressed her lips together into a thin smile. Okay, *future project coordinator, coordinate,* she chided herself.

"We need to think of someone else. There is someone out there who would be perfect to give the keynote address."

The women looked at each other, but no one suggested anyone.

"Who was that woman that spoke at Megafest last year?" Faith asked.

"Darlene Bishop—Susie Owens?" Yvette threw out.

"Both booked," Sister Lincoln said before Yvette could get both names off her tongue.

"Reverend Jackie McCullough—Dr. Cynthia Hale?" said another woman.

"I called them both. They're booked." Sister Lincoln had a smirk on her face. Faith wondered if she was pleased with herself for having already made the calls, or actually glad Faith had this blip in the agenda. She didn't know, but decided it didn't matter. Sister Lincoln was complex, and Faith didn't have time to analyze another soul. She had that waiting at home.

Faith sighed. They tossed the names around of every female preacher and speaker on the ministry circuit, and Sister Lincoln said she had called them all. She was waiting to hear back from a couple of people, but as of right now, no one was available.

The women had gotten riled up now. With every unavailable name they explored, they were chatting gloom and doom over the conference events. Faith was tired of the exercise. It was time to take control of the drama.

"Look ladies, let's calm down and refocus. This is a matter that we'll just have to pray about," Faith said. "God intends to bless the lives of women with this conference. Not having a speaker is really something we can't worry about. We just to have to pray, trust God, and the right person will be available at the time."

The women moved around in their seats, noticeably uncomfortable with the idea of waiting for God's divine intervention. *Church folk.* If they had the faith of a mustard seed.

Yvette winked at her.

"Let's move on to the second agenda item," Faith said. "We have a couple of smaller rooms than what we were originally promised by the hotel, so we need to decide how we're going to handle that."

Faith and the women spent the next hour restructuring the conference schedule. Stress levels were high, and opinions were varied, but in the end they'd done a good job of rearranging the space. She concluded the meeting with a prayer and waited until all the women left the room before she made a dramatic presentation of collapsing into a chair.

Yvette laughed. "You're great with them. I don't know how you do it."

Faith wiped her hand over her face. "I don't know why I do it."

Yvette laughed again and stood. "Girl, this is your ministry. You need to stop looking for jobs all over town and apply for that position pastor has posted."

Faith shook her head. "I don't think so. They just wore me out."

"It's no different than working with a team in a corporate environment. Where there are people, there are challenges," Yvette said. "Speaking of which, I have to go fight some more. It's time for choir rehearsal, and everyone wants to sing a solo." She left the room.

Faith thought about the job pastor was trying to fill, and then the project coordinator position at Bowen and Jefferies. Her mind was telling her she wasn't up for either. How could she lead without faith? She'd said the right words to the women, but the idea of waiting on a speaker made her *just* as nervous.

Faith walked out of the small conference room and exited the church. The sounds of piano music and drums from the music ministry followed her to the parking lot. She waved at choir members as they walked from their cars into the building. Once in her car, she pulled out her cell phone.

"Hi, Mommy." Elise's cheerful voice came through the phone.

"Hey, baby. What are you doing?"

"Waiting for you to come home. Daddy is boring. He's busy."

"Busy? What's he doing?" Faith asked, although she wasn't surprised.

"He's in his office, on his computer."

"Well, I'm sorry Daddy's busy. I'll be home soon, but I need to do one more thing." She paused. "I have to stop by the store. Tell Daddy for me."

"Okay, Mommy."

"Don't forget."

"I won't," Elise replied. "I'm gonna go tell him now."

"Okay."

"Bye, Mommy." Elise hung up the phone.

Faith smiled and pulled out of the parking lot. She'd pick up a few things for the kids to snack on at her mother's house, pack their clothes, and drive down to Zebulon before it became too late. Without the kids in the house, she was going to insist that Jonah talk to her about Joshua. He owed her an explanation about why he'd lied to her all these years, and she was tired of waiting for it.

Chapter 38

Amadi wasn't doing well. If the boy didn't get a heart soon, he was going to be dead. His name was at the top of the transplant list because he was one of few people waiting with his blood type. He just needed a donor. Someone somewhere had to die, in order for Amadi to live.

Jonah felt bad about it, wanting someone to die, but the reality was, people died every day, every minute of the day, but too many of them took their internal organs with them to the grave. Somebody was dying right now with the heart that could save Amadi's life, but he would not get it because people just didn't part with their organs. Lack of education about the need for organs—religious beliefs—the reasons were many. But the end result was more people waited, than organs became available.

Jonah turned off the computer monitor and raised the half empty glass in front of him to take another drink. He lowered it when he saw Elise standing in the door, holding a doll.

"Daddy, Mommy called. She went to the store."

Jonah shook his head. Faith had Monday through Friday to go to the store, but she had to wait until Saturday evening. And she was complaining about him being out of order? She had some nerve.

Elise took small cautious steps to his desk, and then came to put her hand on his knee. "Do you want to watch a movie with me?"

Jonah removed his reading glasses. For a moment her face blurred. He wasn't sure if it was the adjustment to his eyes or that he'd had too much bourbon. Big brown eyes stared at him, but he couldn't turn them from anxious to happy. He didn't have it in him today. "No, honey, I'm busy."

"But you turned off the computer." Elise pointed at the monitor.

Jonah fingered the glass in front of him. "That doesn't mean I'm not working, Lesie." He could hear his words coming out slurred.

"You're always busy, Daddy," she responded in a whiney tone. She reached for his discarded reading glasses and tried to put them on her face.

Jonah sighed. "I'm not always busy, Elise." His tone was firmer than it should have been. "But I am busy now."

She pouted, twisting the frames of his glasses. "Why can't you watch a movie with me?"

"Where's your mother?" he asked, taking them from her and putting them farther back on his desk

"Remember, she was going to the store."

"Yeah, that was a long time ago." Jonah pushed the button to turn the monitor back on. He clicked the computer mouse to move to the next screen of the medical journal he'd put on the task bar before he went rooting around on the transplant registry.

"Not that long, Daddy. I only watched one show since she called."

He glanced at her again. "Yeah, well you probably watch too much TV."

"Is a movie the same as TV, Daddy?"

"Yeah. Of course. It's on the television. It's watching TV."

The screen flickered. Was it the monitor or his eyes? Where were his glasses?

Elise was getting on his nerves.

"Is your working like watching TV?"

Jonah was distracted by something he saw in the journal article. He didn't answer.

Elise continued. "Daddy, is it?"

"No. Of course not. Why do you ask that?"

"Because it's shaped just like a TV." She reached over her doll to point at the monitor, and when she pulled her hand back, she knocked over Jonah's glass.

"Elise!" He jumped up and tried to save his papers, but they were covered with liquor. He swore under his breath. "Get your stuff, and go play in your room."

"But, Daddy, I didn't—"

"Go! I told you I'm working!"

Her eyes filled with tears, and she tore from the room.

Jonah pulled several tissues from the holder on the corner of his desk and began blotting the paperwork that had become drenched. He hadn't meant to yell at her, but couldn't anyone in this house understand how much he had to do? He did his best to dry the documents, but they were ruined. Now he'd have to start over again. He reached for the mouse, but not before he heard Eric's voice.

"Dad, can you play catch with me?" Eric was standing in the door of his office with a baseball glove in his hand and anticipation on his face. Jonah's vision blurred. When he looked again he was looking at his brother. Joshua was wearing his baseball uniform. Jonah shook his head. When he opened his eyes again, Eric was standing there.

"Dad," Eric said. "Can you practice with me?"

Where was Faith, Jonah thought. He needed her to come deal with the kids. "Your mother isn't back?" he asked.

"No. But she can't catch anyway. I need you to help me."

Jonah sighed. "Not now."

"Tomorrow?"

Jonah looked at the glove in Eric's hand. He didn't think he hated anything more than baseball. He shook his head before saying. "No. I've got a lot to do this weekend."

Eric continued to stand in the door. His lips and eyes were angry slits. In contrast to his sister, he was not about to run out of the room crying.

"Where's your sister?" Jonah asked, feeling somewhat guilty about how he had yelled. His head was beginning to pound. He'd had too much to drink.

Eric didn't respond. He just kept pounding his ball into his glove the same way Joshua did.

"I asked you a question? Where's your sister?"

Eric mumbled under his breath—something that sounded like, "See for yourself." And walked out of the room.

"Eric!" His tone a clap of thunder. "Get back here!" He waited a moment, and Eric returned. "What did you say?"

Eric was silent.

Through clenched teeth he said, "Come here."

Eric didn't move.

The sound of the garage door rising could be heard in the background. Jonah noticed Eric look back over his shoulder toward the door.

"I'm not repeating myself."

Eric moved toward him. The boy was trying to keep up

a front of not being intimidated, but his eyes were filling with tears and his light beige skin had turned a red color.

"You don't talk back to me! I'm sick of both of you mouthing off at me. I'm sick of you and the stupid baseball. Don't ask me again."

Eric's eyes filled with tears.

"If you hadn't been playing that stupid game, you wouldn't have gotten sick." He was screaming at the top of his lungs at Joshua. No, it was Eric, and he was silent and angry.

Jonah grabbed his arm and began to shake him. "Answer me!"

Eric's facial expression changed to one of pure terror and pain. Tears fell from his eyes as he screamed and pulled his arm from Jonah's vice-like grip. Jonah reached for him again, but his arm slipped from his grasp. Eric fell to the floor. "Dad," he cried.

"Jonah, stop it!" Faith threw her body between them. "What are you doing?"

He stepped back, suddenly jolted from his rage.

"Oh God. You're drunk."

Faith ushered Eric out of the room. No, it was Joshua. He picked up the baseball glove at his feet. He stepped back, falling into his chair. He looked at the glove. Eric's name was written inside of it. This wasn't Joshua's mitt. What had happened? What had he almost done?

Chapter 39

The ride to Zebulon was completed in a car filled with silence. Elise had fallen asleep, and Eric stared out the window the entire hour and a half it took to reach her mother's house. Faith tried to talk to him, but he was so upset and hurt about what his father had done, that she'd grown tired of the one syllable responses.

Her mother greeted them with warm hugs and fervent kisses. Elise had opened her eyes for a few minutes to smile at her grandmother, but fallen back to sleep. Faith tucked Elise into the bed in the room the two of them would share and kissed her on the forehead before leaving.

Outside the door, she leaned on it, her heart heavy, hoping this reprieve would help her clear her mind and make the right decision for her family. Jonah had gone too far. They had reached the end. He'd almost hurt her child. She had no choices now.

When Faith entered the kitchen, she found her mother and Eric playing UNO. Signs of the earlier damage done

by his father, whisked away by the overabundance of love
his grandmother had showered on him.

Love does cover a multitude of faults, she thought. But
could she make it cover her husband's? She didn't believe
it could anymore.

Faith joined them in several hands of cards, but when
Eric started yawning, she sent him to bed.

"Sometimes I wish we had never left New Jersey," Faith
said, letting a breath she'd been holding escape her lungs.

Her mother stood and walked to the stove for the tea
kettle that had just started whistling. "Faithy, if you never
left Jersey, you wouldn't have your children. You can't go
wishing away things that affect other things."

Faith nodded. "The truth is . . . I miss Daddy."

Her mother nodded. Faith knew she did too, but her
mother changed the subject.

"So tell me. What does Jonah think about this new job?"
she asked, pouring hot water into two mugs that held
herbal tea bags.

Faith reached mid table for the sugar jar, and after
putting two teaspoons in her mug, she responded, "I
haven't told him."

Her mother stopped cold and gave her a penetrating
gaze. "You still haven't told him? That was almost three
days ago. What are you waiting for?"

"Mom, spare me the lecture that's coming. You're about
to get an earful about what's been going on in my house,
and I need your support, not your judgment."

Her mother slipped into the chair opposite her at the
table. The sun, having gone down over an hour ago, left the
moon hanging high in the night sky. Moonlight bounced
off the windows in the small kitchen and seemed to com-
pete with the fluorescence from the overhead fixture in
the room. The lighting produced a golden haze that filled

the kitchen with what felt like sunshine. It contrasted with the darkness that was quickly filling her heart.

Faith blew on the hot liquid steaming in her cup. She took a small sip and burned her lip. Grimacing, she put down the cup and looked up to catch her mother's eye.

"You always touched things that were hot. Hot drinks, hot stove, hot iron." Her mother laughed weakly.

"I don't remember being so hardheaded. You make me out to be a terror."

"You were just spoiled. Spoiled by your daddy."

Faith felt tears welling in her eyes. "I need Daddy. If he were here, I'd be able to talk to him about some of the stuff I'm going through with Jonah and Eric."

"He would be able to help," her mother volunteered softly.

"It seems like I lost him right when I needed him. Girls need their fathers, not just when they're children, but when they're adults." Faith played with the pattern on the lace tablecloth.

Tears rolled down her face unchecked. "Sometimes I feel *so* confused."

"God is not the author of confusion." Her mother's words moved through her. She could feel the Spirit of God trying to pull her back from the hurt, but she was afraid to let go of her pain. Afraid to trust what she was feeling in her soul. *Forgiveness.* I can't, she almost said it audibly, but then she looked at her mother.

"No, God is not the author of confusion. But God is also not the one controlling my husband," Faith said firmly, standing and walking to look out the large picture window over the kitchen sink. In the twinkling starlight, she could see her mother's expansive garden. Both her parents loved to garden. They had hobbies together, things they shared. She didn't have any of that. How had her life gone so horribly wrong? She shook her head.

"How's the new greenhouse?" Faith turned away from the window to face her mother once again.

"I should have tomatoes soon. With the greenhouse I get to plant early so they should be coming up." There was no enthusiasm or excitement in her mother's voice. Faith knew she didn't want to talk about her garden. Her mother wanted to know what was going on with her family.

Faith raised her mug again. Seeing the steam had receded she put it back to her lips. "Jonah hit Eric."

Her mother's lips turned into a thin line. Silence hung between them for a few seconds.

"Not a spanking type of hit." Faith's words were slow and deliberate. "He was drunk. I went to a church meeting. I came into the house and heard Jonah screaming at Eric. I walked into the office and he was shaking him. He threw him down on the floor."

Her mother whistled low and hard.

"He would never have done that if he weren't drunk." Faith continued to shock her mother with her discovery about Joshua, the conversation with Mom Morgan and Jonah's ensuing silence ever since. "I can't live with him anymore. It's not just about him being a lousy husband or a lousy father."

"Yeah, 'cause in that respect, he ain't no worse then any other man."

Faith bit her lip, and after first avoiding her mother's stern gaze, looked her in the eye. "You don't think so? What was Daddy, an enigma? He was the best."

Her mother shook her head. "The best Daddy. He was a bear of a husband, especially in the early years," she said. "All men have quirks. All of them are full of something, honey. At least Jonah's a decent man, loves you and the kids, and provides well. So he's stubborn, and he drinks a little."

"He drinks a lot, and he drinks because he's over-worked. He's overworked probably because he's in some kind of personal battle against pediatric heart disease. He won't talk to me about that, so it's a cycle that I don't have a chance of breaking." Faith felt like every bit of energy was being drained from her body. She let out a deep breath. "This can only work if he stops working all the time."

"In his mind, maybe by working, he's being a good hus-band and father. That might be his way."

"Well, I can't live with his way. There's got to be some compromise. It can't all be about what I'm willing to do for the marriage. Jonah has to be willing to do something to make it work too."

"You have to pray and wait on the Lord. God is faithful. Wait on Him to fix your marriage. Stop talking about what Jonah has to do."

Faith tried to swallow, but her lips were pinched to-gether from annoyance. Her mother never sided with her. "What about Eric? Don't you care how this affects your grandson?"

Her mother looked at her like she was stupid. "Of course I care. I'd have to be made of stone not to care."

"And the drinking? What kind of example is he setting?"

Her mother threw up her hands, and then brought them down in fists onto her thighs. Shaking her head she said, "Faith, I named you that for a reason." She sighed heavily, weariness in her voice. "Without faith, it is impossible to please God."

Faith put a hand on her hip and dropped her head. "This is not about me or my faith."

"It's always about you and your faith, honey." Her mother stood and took both of Faith's hands in hers. "I under-stand that you're hurting. You have a right to be angry about how he handled Eric. He had no right getting drunk and shaking him. But God hates divorce and so do children. You have to work this thing out."

Faith pulled her hands from her mother's grip.

"Do you believe God is sovereign? That He's big enough to fix anything?"

Faith was silent. She'd heard this before, from Yvette, and Pastor's messages. She walked back to the table and slipped into her chair. "Mom, I don't have the tenacity to keep enduring what you're asking me to endure, and now that he's almost hurt my child because he was drunk. How can I trust him?"

"You need to trust the love. The love of Christ, your love for Jonah, your love for Eric. Love covers a multitude of faults."

Faith took a long sip from her now cool cup of tea. She couldn't believe her mother had just used that scripture.

"There's love all over this situation, so in the end, love will fix it. In God's time."

Faith put her cup down. "My mind's made up. It's my job to protect the kids. I'm going home tomorrow, and I'm asking him to move out of the house. If he doesn't leave, I'll pack and move. I'm not going to give him a second chance at my son."

Her mother shook her head. She picked up a worn Bible that lay on the end of the table, stood from her chair, and walked out of the kitchen. "I'm going to pray," she said. "Somebody has to." Then she disappeared into the darkened hallway.

Chapter 40

Jonah was almost finished getting dressed when his mute wife, who'd been gone all weekend, finally spoke.

"I want you to leave," Faith said.

Jonah hesitated for a second, and then pulled his tie methodically through the last loop, pressed it down over his chest and twisted the knot into its perfect place. He hunched his shoulders forward, stuck his hands in his pockets, and turned to look at her. He really wasn't sure what she meant. At least he hoped he wasn't. Moments passed as he stared into her eyes. She was stoic and unwavering. "What do you mean you want me to leave?"

Faith cleared her throat. "I want a separation."

Jonah felt like someone had kicked him in the stomach. He was certain the blood was rushing from every vein and artery in his body to collide in one massive knot in his heart. *What the . . .*

"I've been thinking about this for a while."

Jonah thought about the way he'd treated Eric. He thought about Joshua. The baseball issue and Joshua collapsing. He hadn't been able to think about anything else since she took the kids and got in her car Saturday. But a separation?

"It was wrong of me to be drinking and watching the kids. I owe Eric an apology."

Faith crossed her arms together in front of her chest and looked away.

"I'll apologize when you bring him home." He walked to the door of his closet and slid his feet into his shoes. "I'm also going to cut the drinking. I know it's been a problem, but I'm going to—"

"Just stop," she said. Her tone commanded attention, and he gave it to her. Cool eyes met his. "That's not the way it's going to go. You're not going to apologize and throw me a bunch of empty promises and make it all right."

"Come on, Faith. We've been married for almost ten years. I make one little mistake and you want me to move out of the house? "

"I can't make myself believe this is going to work anymore. I'm too tired."

"Tired?"

She was angry, but he could see the tears forming in her eyes. "You just don't get it." She laughed a dry, humorless laugh. "You're so clueless." Her voice became louder with each word. "I'm sick of this. I'm sick of you." Her lip trembled violently, and she snatched her hand through her hair. Faith took a deep breath. "Your craziness, your work schedule, the drinking, your secrets." Tears spilled from her eyes. "I want you to move out!"

He was running late for Amadi's procedure. He removed his blazer from the valet. "I have to go. We'll talk about this later."

"No, I need to know if you're going to move out."

He leaned close to her face. He was starting to feel a fury of his own. "What happens after I move out?"

She wiped her eyes and took a step back. "I don't know."

"What, no master plan from Mrs. Perfect?"

"We go to counseling." She said the words, but they were weak.

He shook his head and a grunt escaped his throat. "You do what you want, Faith. I'm not going anywhere, least of all to a counselor."

"It's not a threat this time," she said to his back as he walked out of the room.

He waved his hand and continued down the stairs. The last thing he had time for today was an argument with his wife. They both knew Faith Morgan wasn't going anywhere.

Chapter 41

Faith sat up in the bed. She'd thought she needed to rest for a few minutes, but she had fallen asleep. It was almost noon. She had to get back to Zebulon.

Her head hurt, her muscles ached, and her heart was broken. She held the letter she'd written for Jonah in her hand. Clenching it now made her feel physically ill. The pain in her heart invaded every corner of her soul. But she'd had enough. The disappointment, anger, and frustration had to end. Everybody had a breaking point.

If Jonah wasn't going to leave, she would have to, but separated they would be.

She looked at the carefully written letter in her hand and read over it for the third time. She had to make sure it conveyed the words she needed him to understand. He had choices. She had given them to him. This move would either propel him to make the right ones, or the separation would be the first step toward the divorce. At this point, she didn't care anymore. Jonah needed help he was unwilling to get. Work-a-holism, alcoholism, unresolved childhoodisms ... It was a miracle they had lasted this long.

Her cell phone rang; she saw Yvette's work number on the screen. She knew her friend was worried because they hadn't talked since Saturday, and Faith hadn't attended church yesterday, deciding instead to stay in Zebulon.

Yvette would be sympathetic, but she wasn't up to sharing her decision right now. She might be in agreement with her mother, and Faith didn't want to hear that. Not from another soul. Her feelings were already a crazy mix of emotions. But one feeling was dominant, and it permeated the chambers of her heart. *Betrayal.* He had betrayed her with his drinking and working and secrets. Mostly she felt that Jonah had become a stranger.

She'd tried everything she knew to hold this family together. Jonah had pinned her into this difficult spot. She was left with no choice but to choose her son or her husband.

Faith stood, eyes now dry, and went to the closet for the luggage.

Chapter 42

April's head was pounding. She shut off the echocardiogram machine and closed the door to the lab. She massaged her temples as she walked. She was unable to escape the visions that kept popping into her head. Ever since she'd seen the congressman's son on television with him last night, bragging about how he'd graduated from law school with honors, she had been positively sick.

"He's a dog," she spat at the television before turning it off. He was a dog and so were his friends. If he were so great, why couldn't he get a woman in bed without forcing her?

April grabbed a clump of her hair and pulled until it hurt. She wanted to pull it out by the roots. She wanted some pain that was worse than the one in her soul.

She should have gone to see Dr. Moray. She should have picked up her medication. Why was she trying to do this alone? She was losing her mind.

April went to Dr. Morgan's office. He was engrossed in films and records from a large medical chart. He looked up and saw her, and then back at the record.

"Amadi Lazarus," he said. "There's an experimental drug therapy they're using in Africa that might . . ."

April had already tuned him out. She tried to appear interested. Normally she would be, but not today. Today, she should have called in sick.

Dr. Morgan had said something about a drug. There was enthusiasm in his voice. But she was feeling dizzy.

"Is that going to help you treat him?" she asked, rubbing her temple.

"Yes." He stood triumphantly. "He still needs a heart, but I've been concerned about the fact that his heart could fail him at any time."

Dr. Morgan was saying something else, but she hadn't heard a word. The room was spinning, her head was pounding.

"I have to go," she whispered.

Dr. Morgan walked around the desk. Before she could stop him he had his hands all over her. He was saying something—asking her something—but he wouldn't stop touching her. He was just like them. All men were just like them.

April heard herself scream, and then she ran out of the office and down the hall. She was crying and rubbing her arms, trying to remove his touch. She kept running until she made it to the parking lot where she saw Samaria walking toward her car.

"Help me! Help me!"

Samaria turned around.

"Hey, what's wrong?" Samaria grabbed April's arms and kept her from falling into a heap on the asphalt.

"I can't . . . I . . . he . . . please . . . I can't stand it. He touched me. I don't want him to touch me!"

"April, come on. Let's get in the car."

April felt better with Samaria. She wasn't alone this time.

"Don't worry. I'll take care of you," Samaria said. "Everything is going to be okay."

April closed her eyes. No one would hurt her now.

Chapter 43

Jonah couldn't believe what he was hearing. He knew this wouldn't be pleasant. Dr. Gunter calling him for an impromptu meeting that involved Ben Lewiston, the attorney for Christian Brothers, never did. He'd had them before, but they usually meant malpractice, not this.

The terms sexual harassment had hit him like a boxer's uppercut. He shook his head feeling the need to regain his balance even though he was seated. Then he looked at Gunter and tried to focus on the words that were coming out of his mouth.

"I don't expect anything will come of the investigation, however, as an organization, we *are* required to investigate; to protect our employees."

"*All the* employees," Lewiston added tersely. He wasn't making eye contact.

Jonah had never liked Ben Lewiston. He was a weasel if he had ever known one. As a long time friend of Gunter's, he got to hang around and intimidate them all in the name of protecting the business's legal interests. You could never get a straight answer out of him. He was always on the fence about everything.

Jonah clenched his teeth and put so much pressure on the pen he was holding that he had to stop himself from breaking it and spraying ink all over the desk. Never in all his life had he had to deal with an allegation of misconduct. *Sexual Harassment.* This could *not* be happening.

"Dr. Morgan." Lewiston finally looked up from his legal pad. "Do you ever remember an incident with Ms. Jacobs that might have been misinterpreted? Something you may have said that was a little . . . what shall we say . . . careless?" Lewiston paused. "It's the slights that lead to these things."

Jonah took a deep breath. "Do you mean anything like her coming on to me a couple of weeks ago, all but pulling her uniform over her head and lying on my desk and me rejecting her? Is that the careless slight you might be talking about?"

Lewiston removed a small micro cassette recorder from his pocket. "You don't mind if I record my notes."

"Sure, go ahead, turn it on," he responded with acidy sarcasm. "I mean, it's only my career."

Lewiston proceeded as if Jonah had said nothing. "This approach Ms. Jacobs made a few weeks ago. Tell us about it."

"She came on to me. Told me she was interested in a relationship with me. She said she could tell I wasn't happy at home."

"Is that true?" Lewiston interrupted abruptly.

"Is what true?"

"Are you unhappy at home?"

"What does that have to do with anything?"

"It's a simple question that could be relevant. You work with attractive nurses. You would agree Ms. Jacobs is certainly very attractive. If you aren't happy at home, well . . . it could be a reason to be interested in Ms. Jacobs."

"But I'm not interested in Ms. Jacobs. I *did not* make a pass at her."

"Okay, let's move past this. Go on with your version of the story."

His version of the story. Jonah's heart began to thud.

"What was the exact date of the incident?" Lewiston asked.

Jonah looked at his calendar. Lewiston stood and came around the desk. He nodded when Jonah pointed, identifying the date and went back to his seat across the desk.

Lewiston was saying something into the cassette recorder, but Jonah was trying to get his mind around this entire situation. He couldn't get over the statement. *Your version.* As if there were other accepted versions of the story. Versions that might be considered.

"Dr. Morgan," Lewiston said. "Go on."

Jonah cleared his throat and pulled at his tie knot. "As I was saying, she told me I wasn't happy, and I needed a real woman or something like that. I rebuffed her. I reminded her I was married."

"Was that a *I need to be discreet because I'm married*?"

"No, it wasn't like that. I mean, I think she may have mentioned my wife."

"Humph." The muscle over Lewiston's left eye twitched visibly as he jotted a note on the legal pad on his lap.

Jonah pulled back in his chair, took a deep breath and let it out slowly. "What does humph mean?"

Gunter and Lewiston didn't respond, but Gunter's expression was somber, almost grave. They made him uncomfortable, and Jonah knew it showed in the way he chuckled nervously before he spoke again. "Look, I'm sorry she misunderstood, I don't even see how she could have. I think this is more a case of rejection getting the better of her. I wasn't interested. Then I had her reassigned, and she became angry."

Lewiston and Gunter were stoic.

"Jonah," Gunter's flat, unspeaking eyes prolonged the seconds before he asked, "why didn't you tell Mrs. Pitts *why* you wanted another nurse?"

Jonah took a deep breath and reached for his tie knot again. He loosened it just a little and then proceeded to roll up the sleeves of his dress shirt. He looked into Gunter's eyes. The man who'd always had more confidence in him than he'd had in himself was questioning his judgment, because of Samaria, and it made him sick.

"I . . . didn't want to get her in trouble," he said. "Nurses want doctors, heck, all women do for that matter. She's a decent nurse. I just didn't think we could work together anymore."

Gunter nodded, but Jonah couldn't read him.He stood and raked his hands over his face. "Come on, guys, one person's statement couldn't possibly carry that much weight. I mean, it's got to be her word against mine."

"You're correct, Jonah. Ordinarily it would be, her word against yours," Lewiston said. "But you see the problem is she's not the only one alleging you harassed her."

Jonah didn't know how long it had been since Gunter and Lewiston had left his office. Sexual harassment. He couldn't believe this crap. He'd worked hard his entire life and shown the utmost integrity in dealing with his colleagues and patients. Now despite his efforts he was standing accused, not just by a conniving witch like Samaria, but by April, someone he trusted.

He'd racked his brain trying to come up with a reason why April would let Samaria pull her into this mess, but he couldn't think of anything that he'd done that would precipitate this. He gathered his things and locked the door to his office as he was leaving. It was the first time he'd ever felt compelled to do so. He knew he had nothing to hide, but people could take nothing and make it into something. That was pretty obvious from his current situation.

Jonah realized he had enemies now, and he didn't know how far the drama was going to reach, so he had to be careful. And he'd thought Cooper was a problem.

As usual he was the last person to leave the office. He took the stairs down to the first floor, waved at the evening security guard as he exited the building and made a quick jog to his vehicle. For the first time in months he couldn't wait to get home. Then he realized, home—*Faith*—what was she going to say about this whole mess? Things had been so tenuous between them, she might really lose it. Especially since it seemed like she was looking for something to be pissed off about these days. And then there was that study session with Samaria. His behind was really in a sling.

Once inside the car he took out his phone, searching until he found the telephone number for his personal attorney, Les Parker. He needed advice. The office was closed as he expected, so he left a message on the voicemail for Les to call him first thing tomorrow on his cell phone only. Just that moment, he'd decided he wasn't going to tell Faith yet. This entire thing could blow over without her ever having to know about the allegations.

Jonah started his car and drove out of the parking lot. It was almost seven thirty, so most rush hour traffic was over, and he didn't face the mob that he would have if he'd left an hour ago. It was remarkably empty on the I-20. So empty Jonah began to wonder about the sudden peace he had been granted to get his thoughts together. Then his mind started to ponder the situation.

April had accused him of sexually harassing her. The one woman other than his wife and mother that he'd trusted for any extended period of time had completely let him down. He knew she was having personal problems. That breakdown she'd had in the office was a sure sign something deep was going on, but for her to join in a campaign against him was incredulous. Jonah was tempted to call her and demand she explain herself, but Lewiston had forbid him to have any contact with the women outside of normal work in the office. They were also bringing in another technician from a temporary service to replace April during the investigation. This was, of course, to make it easier on the women, who at this point, were afraid of him. More lies.

He'd missed Samaria's attraction to him, but now it was obvious he missed something about April too. He was slipping. Working too hard. His wife and mother had warned him. What was the world coming to when an honest, hardworking, married man couldn't even say no to an extramarital affair? This was crazy.

Jonah let out a string of expletives and hit the gas to move around a slow cruising vehicle in front of him. He wanted to ram into something, mostly Samaria's face. That conniving tramp. He knew she was bitter about that night in the office, and then when he wouldn't take her back as his assigned nurse, but he'd never seen this coming—not in a million years. He expected her to continue to be annoyed until she either got her attitude together or found another job. He didn't expect to be blindsided.

He banged a fist on the steering wheel and pushed even harder on the gas. A thin shadowy veil began to form over his eyes. He was actually seeing red. And then he heard a noise behind him—a siren. There was more red, right behind him; a police car.

Jonah let out another expletive, looked at his speed gauge and pulled the car over to the shoulder of the road.

Could this day get any worse?

After waiting what he considered an unreasonable amount of time, Jonah finally saw the police officer get out of his cruiser. He made his way to Jonah's side window.

Jonah pressed the button for the power window to come down, letting the muggy heat into the vehicle. "Is there something I can do for you, officer?"

The policeman removed a pair of mirrored sunglasses and tucked them into the breast pocket of his uniform. "You can hand me your driver's license, sir."

Jonah reached into the inside pocket of his blazer.

"Slowly." The officer placed his hand on his gun holster. Jonah noticed the snap had already been undone, probably as he approached the vehicle. What did he think he was going to do, pull out a gun and shoot him? *Was his entire world one big drama?*

The officer looked at the identifying information on Jonah's license.

"Dr. Morgan, are you aware that you were driving fourteen miles over the posted speed limit?"

Jonah groaned inwardly. He hadn't really been aware he'd picked up that much speed while he was driving. Anger had fueled adrenaline, and his adrenaline, the lead foot on the gas pedal.

"Actually, I wasn't. I've had a rough day, bad situation with a patient, and I think I was a little caught up in my thoughts."

"Sir, are you aware that more than fourteen miles over the limit is considered reckless driving?"

Jonah sighed, stretching his arms out as he moved his

tightened hands over his thighs. "Yes, officer. I am aware of the rules of the road. As I was saying, I was distracted, and I'll make sure not to let it happen again."

"If you had been driving another two miles over the limit, I would have to charge you with reckless driving."

Jonah snapped. "Look, officer, it's been a bear of a day, in more ways than I can describe, and I'm tired. Either you're going to give me the ticket or a warning. Either way, can we commence with it so I can get home to my family?"

Jonah could see annoyance flicker across the hard features of the police officer's face. "I guess it's a ticket, then. I'll go write it up." He strolled back to his police car.

Jonah put up the driver's side window, wishing he had a drink.

Chapter 44

The absence of Faith's car from the driveway was a
clear message that she was still angry with him. It was
just before eight, and she was usually dealing with the
dinner dishes and sending the kids to take baths. Or did
Eric have a game tonight? He didn't remember her men-
tioning it. But then she wouldn't have. The conversation
this morning was much heavier than a discussion about a
baseball.

As Jonah entered the kitchen, he could see that there
weren't any pots on the stove. The entire room somehow
seemed bare. Faith was a fastidious housekeeper, but it
was cleaner than usual, shining even. He pulled open the
oven warmer and looked for a plate Faith may have left
for him. *Nothing.* She hadn't cooked anything. That wasn't
like her.

Disappointed and groaning about it, he pulled the refrigerator door open looking for something quick he
could have. He removed an individually wrapped block of
cheese from the cold cut bin. He reasoned that this had to

be the type of thing Faith put in Eric's lunch box; it was too small for anything else.

Dissatisfied with his choices, he decided he could move on to a drink. He opened the cabinet, removed a small juice glass, and went into his office. Flipping the ticket from the pocket of his blazer where he'd placed it, he looked on the corkboard to the left of his desk for a note from Faith. *Nothing.* He laid the ticket down and picked up the home phone to dial her cell. It went directly to the voicemail.

Jonah replaced the phone in the cradle roughly and sat down behind his desk. Today of all days was the day he needed to see the faces of his family, the comfort of his home. Even if she were still angry, at this point, seeing her would be a relief. If nothing else he needed dinner.

Opening the door to the cabinet that housed the mini tower for his computer, he removed the bottle of bourbon he kept there. He was already breaking his promise to Faith that he'd stop drinking, but this day had begun and ended disastrously. He needed a drink to smooth out the rough edges and relieve the stress.

Faith was clear in her opinion that drinking was not the way Christians handled their problems. He shook his head. That woman had a list of rules that could fill a book. Or maybe she'd gotten them from a book. He glanced over at the large Bible on the corner of his desk. Praying hands adorned the leather cover. Yes, that was his wife's source.

The Bible and prayer. Not his cup of tea. The notion that prayer changes anything, as his mother had told him many times, was ludicrous. Prayer had never changed anything for him, and he didn't know how his mother could continue to contend that it worked for her when prayer had failed to help save her son.

Jonah raised his glass to the Bible. "If it's all the same to

you, God, I'll leave the praying to Faith. She's better at it."
He finished the drink quickly and poured another.

Stomach growling, he decided to change clothes and
run to the Chinese takeout place just outside of the subdivision for something to eat. As he climbed the stairs to the
bedroom, his thoughts returned to Samaria, April, Lewiston, the police officer, even at his wife this morning. All
had contributed to the demise of a perfectly good day.
Heck, a perfectly good life for that matter. Faith probably
hadn't made it back from Zebulon, but at this point she
was in the lot with everyone else. *To heck with all of
them.*

He entered the bedroom and went directly to his closet.
After changing into a Morehouse T-shirt and a pair of
shorts, he slid his feet into a pair of warn leather mules
and headed for the bathroom.

Jonah didn't notice the object taped to the mirror when
he first came in. It was only after he used the toilet and
went to the sink that he saw an envelope with his name
written on it, taped to the mirror. He washed his hands,
dried them, curiously pulled down the envelope and removed the note inside. He scanned the words, taking in
the ones that jumped out at him.

Jonah,

    *I've expressed to you many times my disappoint-
ment . . . your refusal to work on our marital problems . . . can't fix things by myself . . . won't continue
to live with . . . your refusal to care . . . my happi-
ness . . . my children . . . first priority . . . .not coming back to the house until you're gone . . . your
choice . . . children in a hotel.*
Sincerely,
Faith

Jonah let the letter drop into the wet sink underneath it. He put both his fists on the counter and leaned forward, seeing that thin red veil again. He opened the toiletry cabinet on her side of the bathroom mirror. It was empty. Rushing out of the bathroom, he pulled her closet open. It was easy to see that her things had been seriously disturbed. Although he knew what he would find, he went to the children's bedrooms anyway and found the same for their closets and bathrooms.

What was going on? Was this some type of conspiracy? Had all the women in his life gone completely insane?

Jonah reentered his bedroom, went to the bedside table and picked up the phone. He dialed Faith's cell and got her voicemail again. He cursed and flung the phone with such force it splintered into pieces as it bounced off the wall. Faith had left him.

Chapter 45

Faith pulled into the driveway of her house with one prayer on her lips, and that was for Jonah to be gone.

Even though it didn't feel quite right to be praying about his moving out, if a separation was going to happen, she wanted it to go smoothly. She opened the garage, glad to see his car missing, and breathed a sigh of relief.

She entered the house, noted the few dishes in the sink, and went to his office. A bottle of bourbon rested on the desk with an accompanying glass. The screensaver from his computer flashed pictures of golfers. Faith looked at his things, and before she could get sentimental or regret the choice she'd made, she pulled the door closed tight and ventured up the stairs.

The bed had been slept in and the shower recently used. She took tentative steps to his closet, frightened of what she would find, but was relieved when she saw most of his suits, shoes and shirts—gone.

Faith let out the breath she'd been holding and collapsed onto her unmade side of the bed. Different emotions mixed in her spirit that gave her the sense that once the shock wore off, she was going to be very depressed. But for the moment, the feeling that overwhelmed her was the mocking notion of failure. Nearly ten years of marriage had come to an end in an instant. After all her praying and waiting she still had the same result.

Her cell phone vibrated in the pocket of her slacks. She sat up and removed it, noting it was Yvette.

"What's going on?" Yvette asked.

"He's gone."

"For work, or gone from the house?"

Faith sighed and bit her lip. "Gone from the house." She barely recognized her own hoarse voice when she spoke again. "Yvette, I'm scared."

"I know, but it's going to be okay. You guys will get back together. Separation doesn't mean divorce."

Faith shut her eyes against the tears that had been forming. "I wasn't expecting him to really go. I mean . . . I wanted him to leave me the house, but I just . . . I thought he would put up more of a fight."

"He's being decent. Don't question it, just appreciate it. A hotel is no place for you and the kids, although I would have rung your neck if you guys didn't come here."

Faith sucked in a big gulp of air. She was drowning in a pool of her own salty tears. "I didn't want him blaming you," she said. "It doesn't matter. He's gone now."

"Do you want me to come over?" Yvette asked.

"No. You have a business to run. I'm going to take a hot bath and a nap before I pick up Elise. I've got to figure out what I'm going to tell the kids."

"You've also got to give Jonah the courtesy of returning his phone calls. If you don't, you might find yourself looking at him on the other side of your door tonight, and I know you aren't ready for that."

"I'll call him. I promise—before I get Elise."

She'd dropped both kids at school, feeling horribly that

they'd had to ride in the car all the way back from Zebulon before reaching their perspective schools, but it was the only way to make sure they didn't miss without taking the risk of running into Jonah last night.

"Let me know if I can do anything. I mean anything, okay?"

"I will. You're the best."

"I keep pretty good company too." Her voice smiled through the phone.

They ended the call, and Faith lay back on the pillows once again. She was so tired, but she needed to make that phone call to Jonah before she took a nap. She owed him that much. Faith sat up and reached for the phone that sat on her night table. It wasn't there. It was then that she noticed the large gash on the wall across from her and some small pieces of broken plastic. She stood and walked to the spot. As soon she retrieved the pieces from the floor she recognized the smooth material as the outer shell for the cordless phone.

So he'd gotten a *little* angry last night. To be expected. Putting a hole in the wall and breaking the phone, not really Jonah's style. But then neither was climbing into bed drunk at two in the morning or shaking Eric in a rage. Her husband had changed. That was something she was going to have to accept. It was the reason they weren't together at this very moment.

Faith reached into her pocket and removed her cell phone. She steeled herself against the words he would say when he picked up the call, but instead she got voicemail. For the second time today, she had to thank God for keeping her distance from her husband.

After the beep, she left a message. "Jonah, thanks for making this easy on the kids. I know it wasn't an easy thing for you to do. I'm home now. I'd prefer if you'd give us a couple of days to get settled without you. Email me

later to let me know where you're staying ... I ..." She
started to say I love you. "I ... have to go now. I'll talk to
you later. Have a good day."

Jonah was really going to love that request, she
thought, placing the phone on the night table. Then she
stood and walked into the bathroom.

A hot soak in a jetted tub was just what the doctor ordered, but afterward, Faith found that she could not go to
sleep. After an hour of tossing and turning, she realized
her highly desired nap escaped her, so she dressed and
went down to the kitchen for a cup of tea. Her stomach
growled, but she honestly thought with the state her
nerves were in, that if she ate anything she would be sick
within moments. She needed to relax.

She reminded herself that this is what she wanted. It
was the only solution to the problem. *Short of murder.*
But she was reminded of words her father often said:
"The solution to a problem sometimes creates another
problem."

"You were so right, Daddy." Standing and putting her
weight against the sink, she stared out the large bay window. The sun was high in the sky, promising heat in the
low eighties. It was days like this that she missed New
Jersey. This kind of heat in May was something she'd
never gotten used to. She longed for the days of her childhood when the seasons actually transitioned from winter
to spring and spring to summer and fall. Not like Atlanta
where you had the heater on one day, air conditioning the
next. Summers held her prisoner to the inside, daring not
to go out lest she melt.

The kettle whistled, reminding her of the last time she
held a kettle in her hand. Saturday night as her mother re-
lentlessly fought the good fight of faith to insist she save
her marriage. She hated that she and her mother were so

at odds. She needed all the folks in her corner she could gather to help her make it through this difficult time.

Yvette was supportive of any decision she made, and Faith was glad to have her, but her mother's word's haunted her as she left that morning and still continued to intermittently replay in her mind. "This doesn't give God glory. You would have done better to touch the hem of His garment."

Faith was puzzled. She knew those words had to relate to a verse of scripture. Her mother's advice seldom didn't. But she couldn't quite pull it from her subconscious memory, and she was too embarrassed to ask her mother. Carrying her tea cup, she walked to her desk, sat, and pulled her Bible to her. Opening the concordance, she searched for garment and hem. She didn't find anything that related to what her mother said, but she had a nagging feeling that those words were from a very familiar story. She'd have to remember to ask Yvette about it later.

Faith pushed the power button to boot up her computer. Once open, she went straight for her email. She had several pieces of junk mail, but two things stood out. One from Bowen and Jefferies and a second from Jonah advising her where he was staying. The *Panola Corporate Suites* was not too far from the house. She'd passed the place a thousand times. It was an upscale extended stay hotel that included a full kitchen and living room. It was perfect for a cast out husband, because it included most of the conveniences of home, save for the wife-slave to bang the pots around. She noted the telephone and room number, jotting them on a Post-it note so she'd have it handy should she need to give him a ring.

She wasn't going to dwell on Jonah. She didn't need to add to the anxiety she was already feeling. She opened the email from Bowen and Jefferies just as she remembered . . . she'd promised Garrison Adams a decision

today about the job. With everything that happened over
the weekend, she hadn't even given the offer any thought.

Faith sank back in her chair, indecision adding to the
depression that was settling over her like a cloud in the
rain. It almost didn't make sense for her to make any
more changes in her life, but she also didn't want to pass
up on the perfect job opportunity. She ran her fingers
through her hair, leaving her hand to rest on her neck
when she reached the end of her tresses. What was she
going to do?

She was tempted to call Yvette, but she knew what
Yvette would say. "Do what you think is right for you."
Well, she didn't know what that was at this very moment,
so Yvette's advice wasn't going to get her anywhere.

She sucked her teeth and dropped her hands in her lap.
My life needs to be simpler, she thought. But the simpler
she tried to make it, the more complicated it seemed to
become. She'd wanted a job, thought it was the solution
to the ineptness she was feeling about being a stay home
mom, but now that the solution to that problem had arrived, she was plagued with the problem of actually
choosing the solution. *I'm making myself crazy*, she
thought. Solutions did sometimes create more problems.
She raised her tea mug. "Here's to you, Daddy. Right
again."

Chapter 46

Jonah clenched the arms of his chair and turned to look out his office window. "I need to find a way to tell Faith," he said. He spun his chair around, but still avoided looking at his attorney.

Les Parker and Jonah had been roommates at Morehouse during their junior and senior years of undergrad. Having both grown up on Atlanta's southwest side, affectionately known as the S.W.A.T.S., they shared a common background and desire to move beyond their humble beginnings, which had cemented their friendship over the years. Les, a two time winner of the Atlanta Association of Black Lawyers "Man of the Year," had proven himself to be an exceptional attorney in the Atlanta legal community.

"Look," Les removed his glasses from the bridge of his nose and slid them into the inside pocket of his two thousand dollar custom made suit, "I'm not a marriage counselor. As you well know, I'm looking for my second wife. What I can advise you to do is tell her quickly. Information has a way of finding its way to the ears of those you don't want to have it."

Jonah shifted uncomfortably in his seat. He knew what he was about to say would further complicate things and embarrass him at the same time. "The problem is," he began, and then paused to start again, "we're not together right now."

Les glared at him with a tell-me-more look on his face.

"She asked me to leave."

Les squinted. "When?"

"A week ago. The same day I found out about this mess. I came home, and she was gone. I mean, she's back at the house now. I didn't see any point in uprooting the kids, but I've moved into a motel."

"You'd better make sure no one here finds that out," Les whispered like the room was bugged. "A separation won't look good."

Jonah nodded.

"Anything you want to talk about?" Les had changed from his lawyer voice to the friend tone.

Jonah slumped in his chair and waved his hand. "Typical man works too many hours, woman feels neglected stuff. We can work that out, but not with *this* hanging over my head."

Les pushed a stream of air through his lips. "That complicates this legal issue. If it goes past mediation, it'll appear your wife doesn't believe you, and we can't have that. A judge or jury could see it as a credibility issue."

"Jury?" Jonah sat straight up, his heart thumping.

Les put both hands out in front of him. "I doubt if it would ever get there, but if it happened to, mediation records would be available for the judge and/or jury to review and her attorney to disclose in civil court."

Jonah closed his eyes and shook his head.

"It may even speak to your need to make a pass at Miss

Jacobs. You know, because the wife is gone. The old *if you can't have the one you love . . .*"

There was no humor in Jonah's chuckle. ". . . love the one you're with."

"You know it, brother." Les stood and clapped a hand over Jonah's shoulder. "You'll work it out, my friend. Just tell her. Soon."

Jonah nodded.

Les made his way to the door, and just as he was about to open it, he turned and said, "If the motel gets old, you're welcome at my place."

"I appreciate it, but the motel's halfway between here and the house. It's as convenient as being put out can be. That Cascade Castle of yours is too far."

Les smiled and pulled his jacket together. "If you were really clocking some dollars, you'd move where the real rich black folks live."

"Um, hump. Atlanta's *old* money. You perpetrating big time. I know where you came from."

"Yeah, well, now I'm chillin' like a villain, so it don't really matter." Les held a pointed finger in Jonah's direction.

Jonah waved and smiled for the first time in days.

"Offer's open." Les turned the knob and exited the office, closing the door behind him.

Jonah sat in silence for several minutes. He couldn't believe his life.

"All the way from Ashby Street for this." Jonah barely recognized his own voice. On heavy legs, he stood and walked around his desk to the windows. His view, mostly parking lot, did offer a fair amount of greenery and trees that he enjoyed looking at when he made time.

He noted a family of four climbing out a of small, late model sedan. After removing the children from what had to be two car seats, the couple grabbed one child each, and then took each others hands. The man kissed the woman on the forehead, and Jonah noticed as they began walking, that she was pregnant. These people already had two children and an older car. But they were still clearly in love. What was wrong with him and Faith? They had all the money they needed, a beautiful home, three luxury cars between them, and yet he couldn't for the life of him remember the last time he and his wife held hands and walked anywhere. Everything was a mess between them, and now he had more mess to pile on top of the fact that they were separated.

Jonah walked to his desk and looked at the patient roster. He didn't have anyone for forty-five minutes. He walked to the door, opened it, and after turning the lock behind him, went to the main desk where his new nurse, a man named Rick, was writing in a medical chart.

"I'm running out for about thirty minutes," Jonah told him.

Rick barely raised his eyes to acknowledge Jonah was there and nodded.

They couldn't trust him with a woman. He hated having to put up with temps from nursing services. They didn't care about his patients, and he had to take the time to train them on everything. Things flowed so well when he worked with Samaria and April, but Samaria had gone and spoiled it all.

Jonah took the stairs, and as he got to the bottom, he saw the young family talking to the receptionist and getting instructions for the elevator. The man had his hand in the small of the wife's back. They had pleasant looks on their faces. Whatever they were here for, it was a good day.

What would it take for him to have a good day, to get his wife back, to work past these allegations?

Bury the past. That caution from his mother was always in the back of his mind. But he didn't know how. He didn't know how to reach inside himself and pull out his organs and guts. Because in truth, that's what he imagined in his mind that he would feel if he ever started talking about Joshua. It was just too painful for him to be cut open that way.

He clicked the remote for the alarm and the door locks for his car and climbed in. He lowered the windows to let out the stifling heat with one hand and loosened the knot on his tie with the other.

Jonah had no idea where he was going. He rarely left the office in the middle of the day. Then he thought of the park he passed most days on his route to and from work. He pulled out of the parking lot and headed in that direction. *I need some peace,* was the thought that reverberated in his mind. A park would be quiet and serene. Maybe he could think.

Once the car was moving, he could feel the coolness of the air conditioning begin to fill the interior of the vehicle. He pushed the button again; this time to put up the windows and pushed the button for the radio.

I give you all the glory, Lord. You are my God.

He recognized it as a song Yvette led during the worship part of church service. He looked at the radio. This wasn't even a Christian station. Maybe he wasn't the only one feeling out of sorts today.

Jehovah Jireh you are my provider.

I don't want for anything, when I'm in your will.

Jonah pushed the button to turn off the radio. He wasn't in the mood for music, really, and the idea that God was sovereign wasn't sitting right. Not when he was going through so much. He needed to work some things out, and as usual, God was nowhere to be found.

He thought of all the issues in his life right now. Faith and the children... Faith possibly going to work...

Samaria and April conspiring against him . . . Amadi dying, and he asked himself what it was going to take for him to have some peace. For him to get his life back.

He pulled into a parking space in front of the lake that was the center of the small park. The cool air in the vehicle did nothing to make him feel comfortable. He needed to crawl out of his skin. This uneasiness was unfamiliar and uncomfortable. He hadn't felt this way since . . . the day of Joshua's funeral. He squeezed his eyes tight. *Don't go there*. Instead he had to focus on the present. Les was right. He did need to tell Faith, and soon. For all he knew, one of those conniving women would call his house. He couldn't trust anyone, but he needed to trust his wife.

He unclipped the holster and removed his cell phone from his belt. After pushing the appropriate speed dial number, he waited until he heard the connection on the other end.

"Hey, it's me." He tried to sound cheerful.

Silence rang out like white noise in the phone.

"What's wrong?" Faith asked above the clanging of pots in a rhythm in the background.

"I can't call my wife in the middle of the day just to say hello?"

"You haven't done that in . . . let's see . . . three years. So yes, I'm thinking something's wrong."

Three years. She had to be exaggerating. "Faith, I think that's stretching the truth just a little bit."

"Actually, it's not." Her tone was snappy. "The last time you called home in the middle of the day, Elise was about eleven months old. She'd fallen on the steps the day before, and you called to check on her."

He breathed in deeply and rolled his eyes upward. "Must you always point out my shortcomings?"

"Must you always come up short?"

Jonah looked at the phone for a second, and then put it

back to his ear. "Faith, what in the heck is wrong with you? We aren't going to be able to work this out if you won't stop checking off marks on the scoreboard." Silence fell again. "Are you there?"

"Do you think you can call me in the middle of the day after almost four years and I should be excited about it?"

He gritted his teeth to keep from cursing. She was impossible.

"Let me tell you what you need to do, Mr. Morgan. Take a good, long, hard look at yourself instead of my attitude, and try to figure out what happened to the woman you married. What might you have done to change her into a bitter, score keeping—"

Jonah pressed END on the phone. Calling had been a mistake. He banged his fist on the steering wheel over and over again. His life was totally out of control, and he hadn't the ingenuity or creativity to figure out how to fix any of it. He couldn't even talk to Faith without pissing her off.

He rested his head on the wheel. *Had it really been three years?* God, he needed her. If he ever needed anyone in his life before, he needed her. He wanted to bury his face in her waist like a little boy. Just as before, when his life was spinning out of control, he needed to feel the comfort of the woman who loved him.

Chapter 47

"No he didn't just hang up the phone on me." He was wrong for that, even if they were separated. Admittedly, she had been a little rude, but how dare he call her like it was something he did all the time. She could be home sick, or the kids could be sick, and that man would not make the time to call and check on his family. He wanted credit for calling in the middle of the day? *What a joke.*

She slammed the phone down on the counter and continued to search for the extra long baking pan she needed for the peach cobbler she was making for the Bible Study meeting. Higher Hope was such a large church that Bible Study was done in small groups that they called cell groups. Pastor met with each cell at least quarterly, and when he did, they added food to the fellowship. Her grandmother's cobbler recipe was a favorite amongst the members. It was one of those desserts the group never got tired of. She'd tried bringing other things and was promptly told by the head usher, "Please don't try to fix what ain't broke. We could eat that cobbler until Jesus comes back."

Faith smiled thinking about it. *At least somebody appreciates my efforts.*

And then she had an attack of conscience. Jonah did faithfully compliment her on the cobbler every time she prepared it. But that didn't make up for all the other things he did. All the other slights and times when he didn't show he cared.

What had he wanted to talk about anyway? It was almost too early for him to be trying to make nice so he could come home.

The doorbell rang, and she rushed to get it.

Yvette came in huffing and puffing. Faith could feel the heat on her body as she removed a grocery bag from her overburdened arms.

"It's a hundred degrees outside," Yvette said, dropping her handbag on the foyer table. "For some reason, the air conditioning vent in my car is blowing hot air."

Faith frowned. "No wonder you look like you're melting."

"I have an appointment to have it looked at in the morning."

Faith waved her into the kitchen. "Come on. Let me get you some lemonade."

They put both grocery bags on the kitchen island. Faith removed an oversized pitcher from the refrigerator. She poured, and Yvette drank.

"Bless you," Yvette said after she finished. Then she went to the powder room to wash her hands. When she came back, she began to take her salad ingredients out the bag. "I hate to miss the meeting, but I've got to wait for the guy to come and look at that treadmill tonight."

"We'll be glad to have your salad. They'll need it before

they dig into this fattening cobbler," Faith said, sifting flour. "I read if you cut the sugar in half in a recipe it wouldn't affect the taste, just calories."

"Girl, please." Yvette looked at her like she had lost her mind. "Those folks will tear the place apart if that cobbler ain't right." She helped herself to another glass of lemonade.

Faith noticed she was looking around, and then she listened like she was trying to hear upstairs. "Where's Elise?"

"The library. It's become a weekly thing with our neighbor."

"Speaking of the kids, how's it going?" Yvette took another sip and parked on one of the stools in front of the island.

"Not as bad as I was expecting. I thought there'd be weeping and gnashing of teeth."

Yvette almost choked. "Don't tell me the kids don't miss him?"

"No, they miss him. I mean, Elise cries every night for thirty minutes. 'I want to see my Daddy, I want my Daddy.' And every night, I keep thinking, you didn't see him when he was living here."

Yvette shot her a stern look. "No you didn't just say that."

"Yes, I did." Faith widened her eyes and rolled them.

They both laughed.

"Anyway, it ain't hardly funny. She's real tore up and so is Eric. He just does a better job hiding it."

They worked in silence for a moment as Faith measured and stirred and Yvette peeled and chopped.

"And how are *you* doing?" Yvette raised her eyes to meet Faith's.

Faith put her hands on her hips and cocked her head to the side. "I don't miss him."

Now it was time for Yvette's eyes to get wide.

"I mean it's been less than a week, and I'm adjusting."

"Okay," Yvette drew out the word, and then let out a low whistle.

Faith had to admit, she didn't like being in bed alone all night, but she really didn't miss Jonah. Not yet.

"I'm wondering if the day is going to come that I do miss him, or is it too late for us."

Yvette stuck a grape tomato in her mouth. "You're questioning God's sovereignty. He is your God. He makes all things new," she said between chews. "Revelations, chapter 21, verse 1 through 3."

"That's some new Bible," Faith said, smiling.

"No, it's old Bible, newly found scripture. I read it in my devotion this morning." Yvette went to the sink and began washing lettuce. When she returned to the counter, she asked, "What did you read in yours?"

"My what?" Faith wiped her forehead. When her friend didn't answer, she looked up from her work.

Yvette raised an eyebrow. "Your morning devotion, your Bible study, your daily prayer."

Faith didn't answer.

"I don't think it's a very good time for you to be slacking on your time with the Lord."

Faith went to the refrigerator for the milk. "Is it ever?"

"Aren't you a little flippant today?" Yvette said, grimacing.

Faith took a deep breath and let it out. "I know. I'm a crab. I'm disappointed in myself. I turned down the job with Bowen and Jefferies this morning."

"Ouch," Yvette grimaced like she was in pain.

"I had to think about the kids. It's not the right time. If I hadn't gotten separated, maybe, but now, definitely no."

"What'd they say?"

"Gee, thanks for wasting our time." Faith grunted and shook her head.

"Did they?"

"In more words or less." Faith bit down on her lip. "I felt so unprofessional."

"Well, if it's any consolation, I think you did the right thing. Timing is important." Yvette sighed, and then eyed her curiously. "Is that it?"

Faith threw her hands up. "You know me too well." She shook her head. "No, that's not the only thing bugging me. I finally got the report from the phone company. The person, who by the way is no longer calling, was harassing me from a pre-paid cell phone."

"No longer calling?" Yvette asked. "When did they stop?"

Faith thought about it. "You know it's been more than a week, maybe two." She pulled a drawer open and removed her rolling pin. "They just stopped as suddenly as they started."

"See, I told you it was kids," Yvette said.

Faith shook her head. "No. I'm thinking kids aren't spending money on a prepaid cell phone. Those minutes are expensive."

"They might have found the phone," Yvette said.

"And instead of calling their friends, they called me?" Faith shook her head again. "I'm not buying that. Something is going on . . . was going on. Someone was trying to tell me something."

Yvette took a deep breath, and Faith could tell her friend agreed with her.

Faith stopped rolling out her crust and crossed her arms over her chest. Tears filled her eyes. "It's so hard to accept that after ten years of marriage it's come to this."

"Separated is not done."

"Well, if it's not done, it certainly feels that way. I don't think we have potential, not if he won't go to counseling, and not if he's cheating, Yvette."

Yvette didn't say anything. The weight of Faith's words hung heavy in the room. They worked in silence.

I am your God, *I* make all things new.

Faith didn't want to deal with *that* thought right now. Her internal battle was wearing her out and hanging heavy on her spirit. She sighed and went to the pantry for the peaches. Cobbler. That was something she could get right.

Chapter 48

"Mommy, Daddy's home," Elise yelled with exuberant excitement. Faith came out of the powder room to find Jonah standing in the door.

"Hey, pumpkin." He scooped her up into his arms and kissed her. "How's my angel?"

"I miss you, Daddy. When are you coming back to live with us?"

Avoiding Jonah's eyes, Faith looked at her shoes. She crossed her arms and waited for his answer.

"I don't know, baby. Soon, I hope." Continuing to carry Elise, he removed a small shopping bag from the doorknob. He pulled out two DVD cases with gift bows attached and handed them to Elise.

"Dora," she shrieked and grabbed him around his neck. "Thank you!"

Jonah placed her on her feet. "Where's your brother?"

"Baseball," Elise said, taking the other DVD.

"Practice or a game?" he asked, looking at Faith.

She cut her eyes. "Don't." Was the only word she could manage.

He took in a deep breath that caused his chest to rise high. He returned his attention to his daughter.

"What's this one?" Elise asked.

"The new *Masters of Magic*," Jonah replied proudly.

Elsie shook her head. "Mommy doesn't let Eric look at magic."

"Sweetie, take your movie upstairs, and then pick up your things in your room, so we can have dinner when Eric comes in," Faith said.

"But, Mommy."

"No, buts," Faith said, turning her by the top of her head toward the stairs.

"Daddy, will you watch the movie with me?" Elise was climbing the stairs.

He looked at Faith and she shook her head. "I have to go out tonight."

"Let me talk to Mommy first, baby."

Elise nodded and continued to go up the stairs.

Faith kept her arms crossed as he closed the distance between them. "Do we need to talk about drop-in visits?"

Jonah closed his eyes and sighed. He looked like he had aged five years. "No, I'm sorry. I needed to talk to you, and I wanted to see the kids."

"You were talking to me before you hung up the phone earlier."

He threw up both hands in surrender. "I apologize for that. It was . . . you were—"

"In a foul mood. I'll own that." She dropped her arms and lowered her eyes.

Jonah reached to her chin and raised it so she was looking at him again.

"I miss you. I miss the kids."

"Jonah . . ." She rolled her eyes upward.

"Please hear me out. I'll do better with Eric. The message you've been trying to send me. I got it. I need to spend more time with him."

"Jonah, it's not just Eric, it's everything. We can't even talk anymore and the drinking."

He wiped a hand over his face.

"I want to go back to work."

His jaw tightened visibly.

"I actually had a great job offer with a very prestigious firm. I just turned it down today."

Jonah released a breath. "What . . . when did you have time for that?"

"It's been in the works a few weeks."

He stuck his hands in his pocket. "So you were job hunting behind my back?"

"It's a long story, but yes. I interviewed without telling you."

"And you think that's okay."

Faith put her hands on her hips. "I know you aren't trying to check me about keeping a secret."

After a few moments of silence he said, "You *did* turn the job down."

She lowered her hands. "This one, yes, because of the timing, but maybe not the next one. Can you handle that?"

He shook his head and mumbled. "Not today."

"I'm sure not tomorrow either. Your dinner won't be on the table at 6 P.M. sharp. You may have to pick Elise up from the daycare center or help with homework."

"Enough, Faith," he said sharply. "I mean, what do you want from me? I am who I am. I've been this way since we got married. So I don't think my wife should work while the children are young, and no, I don't want to stand in a checkout line at the Food Depot. I'm a busy doctor. Does that make me someone you can't live with?"

"No, but it does make you someone I don't want to live with."

"And those things are reasons enough to throw away ten years of marriage?"

She paused briefly. "I don't see any point in throwing good time after bad."

A nerve twitched under his left eye. Faith could tell by the look that flashed across his face that she had hurt him, and she felt guilty.

"I'm sorry. I don't mean to be so nasty. It's just you were unwilling to talk to me before about anything, and now that we're separated, you want to talk everyday. I feel like it's too little, too late."

They just stared at each other for a few seconds. Jonah took steps to close the space between them. "Too late? Are you planning to file for a divorce?"

"I don't know anything right now." She shook her head. "I'm trying to think. I'm trying to decide what's best."

"What's *best* is our family. The commitment you made to me in front of God and two hundred people." His voice was firm, but then softened. "I love you. I'm not perfect, but I do love you, and contrary to what you may think, I love Eric too."

Faith turned from his pleading eyes. "I need more time."

She heard his sharp intake of breath. "I hope it's not too long. I'm coming unglued without you and the kids. And then there's this mess," his voice trembled, "at work."

Faith turned around. "What mess at work?"

Jonah paused for a moment. "Can we sit?" He pointed to the family room.

Faith walked ahead of him. She felt her stomach turn to knots. Something was wrong. *Really wrong.*

She sat on the sofa, and Jonah claimed a club chair adjacent to her. "Don't beat around the bush." She rested her elbows on her knees.

He dropped his head in his hands and then looked up. "Samaria came on to me a few weeks ago."

Faith's sense that something was wrong heightened the rush of adrenaline that already had the blood rushing through her veins. With her eyes she told him to go on.

"I rejected her, but she got angry, and now she's filed a sexual harassment complaint with human resources."

Faith blinked a few times and stood.

"I absolutely told her I wasn't interested. In fact, I had her reassigned to work with another doctor. About a week ago she came to me and begged to have the reassignment undone. I told her no, she had ruined any chance of us working together professionally."

Jonah continued to fill in the details. Faith struggled to hear him because all she could see was Samaria in that sleazy dress at the benefit. She shook her head. "This doesn't make sense."

"I agree, but she's determined to punish me."

"For not sleeping with her?"

"No, I think the real issue is the reassignment."

Hands on her hips, Faith paced the room. "That makes even less sense. Why would she go through so much trouble?"

Jonah stood. "It's no trouble for her. I mean nothing more than lying."

Faith stopped moving and began rubbing her neck. A knot of tension settled at the base. "What's next, what are they going to—"

"There's more."

She noticed Jonah's face had become stiff.

Her heart pounded so wildly she could barely say the word. "More." He reached for her hands and she pulled away. "Tell me."

Jonah cleared his throat. "Somehow she's managed to

get . . . I don't know how to even say this . . . but I need you to trust me."

The doorbell rang.

"I'll get it," he said so hastily. Faith knew he was looking to escape.

He's in trouble.

Faith listened as Eric and Jonah exchanged some words. From his tone, she could tell Eric was glad to see him.

"Hi, Mom." Eric removed his cleats.

"Hi, baby." Her eyes caught Jonah's. A knot of fear was lodged in her throat. She tried to keep her voice from cracking so she could talk to her son. "How was practice?"

Eric tilted his head to the side. "What's wrong with you?"

Faith and Jonah's eyes met again. She shook her head. "Your dad and I are just talking." She placed a hand on his shoulder and kissed the top of his head. "Go clean up for dinner."

"Okay," Eric said. He cast his father a warning glance and went up the stairs.

Once he was out of sight she said, "Go on before we're interrupted again."

Jonah swallowed and twisted his lip, but he didn't delay. "Somehow, she's gotten April to file a complaint also. They're both saying I've harassed them."

Faith felt the wind escape her chest so quickly she thought she would faint. Instead, she dropped into a nearby chair. She bit her lip and tried to breathe normally, but her mouth would not allow an intake of air.

She blinked against tears and stood. "You expect me to believe that?"

"I—"

"You expect me to believe both of them are out to get you? Samaria came on to you, but somehow, April is bitter about that too."

"I honestly don't know what's going on with April. Lewiston won't let me talk to her."

Faith shook her head. "The kids are going to be down in a few minutes. I don't want . . ." She threw her head back and groaned. "I don't want them to see me upset."

Jonah touched her arm. "I need you to believe me."

She snatched her arm back. "Believe . . . that ridiculous story?"

He cast his eyes to the open hallway above, and she let hers follow. The children were nowhere to be seen. His voice was a hoarse whisper. "I'm asking you to not jump to any conclusions."

Faith's mind was racing even faster than her heart was pounding. She wanted to claw at him, but instead of inflicting bodily pain, she said the words that would do equal damage to a physical beating. "You're a liar."

Jonah flinched.

"Two women." There was no humor in her chuckle. "Accusing you of sexual harassment." She walked into the kitchen. She could feel him on her heels.

"Faith wait—"

"You said you would be cheating soon, I just didn't expect you to be so aggressive. Using force—"

"That's not what happened." Jonah raised his voice. "And you know that's not me. I'm a lot of things, but that isn't one of them."

Faith took a deep breath and considered his words. Hadn't she just said them to herself a few weeks ago, when an affair had crossed her mind? But then there were the phone calls. Was she being naïve? Faith wanted to continue to boil, to put him out, but something in her told her she knew her husband wouldn't do what he was accused of. Cheating was hard enough for her to wrap her mind around, but sexual harassment . . .

Then she thought about Joshua, and her heart froze. *I don't know him.*

Her voice was weaker this time, the sarcasm gone. "One could be questionable, but not two."

"I'm telling you, they made it up. Samaria I'm not so surprised about anymore, but April . . . I don't understand. She's like a daughter to me."

Faith felt her defenses weakening. He was clearly disappointed, hurt, and confused. But so was she. "I don't know what to believe. You kept Joshua from me for ten years . . ." She shook her head. "I don't trust you anymore. I don't know who you are, or what I mean to you."

"Faith—"

"I can't talk to you right now. I need you to leave."

Jonah's head hung for a moment. "I'll say goodbye to the kids."

Faith followed him into the foyer and watched him climb the stairs. At the top, he turned, and holding the end of the banister, looked at her once before he went in the direction of the children's bedrooms. Once he walked away, she realized she'd seen something that she never in a million years thought she would see.

Jonah was scared.

Faith took a deep breath, closed her eyes for a moment, and looked back at the empty stairwell. *What was he afraid of, the truth or a lie?*

Chapter 49

Faith stood back from the crowd and watched the members devour the peach cobbler. She felt guilty that she'd made it and Jonah wouldn't have a piece. It was his favorite dessert, and he'd probably smelled it when he stood near the kitchen this evening. She wondered how he was faring with meals. He hated takeout so much. But then she was reminded that he brought this on himself. His missing her, his family life, even missing her cooking was a part of the process. If he didn't go through what he was going through now, he would never change.

Faith pushed out the voice in her head that was telling her not to repay evil for evil, that love covers a multitude of faults. She didn't want to think about the scriptures that kept flooding her brain. She was tired of waiting for God to change Jonah. That drunk tyrant that almost attacked Eric was not the man God intended for her to live with. That she knew for certain. So she had to take some responsibility for her part. It was her job to do the human things and depend on God for the impossible. If she were going to get different behavior from her husband, she was going to have to try to manage things a different way. After all, insanity was doing the same thing and expecting different results. Harsh as it might seem, she had to be this way with him. Tough love had to be tough.

But now she wondered what marriage she was trying to save. The allegations against him were humiliating and disgusting. Two witnesses against his statement that both were lying. She shook her head. And then there was still the fact that someone had been calling the house. She hadn't even confronted him about that yet.

"Sister Morgan, your cobbler is the hit of the evening as always." Pastor Kent had walked up, fork in hand and finished the last of his dessert and tossed the paper plate in a nearby trash can.

"Thank you, Pastor," she said, embarrassed that he had caught her by surprise.

"I got a message that you wanted to speak with me. Is now a good time?"

Faith tugged and pulled at the strap to her handbag, nervously wringing it so that she was twisting the leather.

"Did you want to go to my office?"

"No, Pastor. What I have to say will only take a few minutes."

Pastor Kent pointed to two seats in a private corner of the room. Faith sat, and he did the same across from her.

"You look troubled. I have to say, you've been looking troubled for some time now."

"Pastor." She paused, ashamed of the words that were about to come from her mouth. "I'm separated from my husband."

Pastor Kent's face registered some surprise, but he recovered with amazing speed. "I'm sorry to hear that."

"I guess I should have talked to you before. I just

thought if I prayed and waited that things would get better, but they aren't, and I just felt separation was for the best." She had to fight to keep tears from welling.

"I see."

"My husband isn't going to change."

Pastor Kent chuckled lightly. "Well, let's not say that. Remember there isn't anything too hard for God."

Two points for you, Mom, she thought as she reached up and scratched her shoulder.

"To work it out, both parties have to be willing." Her lip was trembling. Tears were forming in her eyes. Now she wished she had asked for privacy.

Pastor Kent had to sense it. He took her arm and escorted her out of the room with such efficiency that she didn't think the other members who were still eating even noticed their hasty exit. Once in the hall, he led her to a private office around the corner.

"Is Brother Morgan not interested in reconciling?" He handed her a tissue from the holder on the desk.

"He wants to come home, but he doesn't want to work on our problems." Faith sniffed sharply. "And now he's gotten himself in trouble at work."

Pastor Kent's eyes softened.

"He's been accused of harassing a woman—actually, two women that he worked with. He denies it. Says that they're conspiring against him. I don't know why they would do that, both of them. His side of the story doesn't make sense."

"And theirs does?"

"I guess it would be easier to trust him if we hadn't just gone through a huge trust issue in the last few weeks. I don't know what I need to do."

"That means you probably don't need to do anything," Pastor Kent said gently. "Sister Morgan, I don't know

Brother Morgan very well, so I can't say what I think he would or would not do. You have to search your heart for that answer. What do you feel in your heart?" He was pointing at his own chest.

Faith pressed her eyes closed against his question. *What was her heart saying?* She didn't know. "I'm . . . confused," she whispered.

"God is not the author of confusion."

Her mother's words again.

"I know that, and I'm still confused. I want to believe him. I do so badly, but our marriage has been just unbearable for a long time. He's been hard to live with, and I've been praying for God to either change him or release me."

"Have you tried counseling?"

"He won't do it," she cried.

Pastor Kent shook his head. He'd probably heard that statement from many a person married to a reluctant spouse.

"Okay, if Brother Morgan won't come in, how about you?"

"What do you think is wrong with me?" she asked, wiping her eyes.

"For starters, you're under a tremendous amount of stress. A troubled marriage, the harassment allegation, the women's ministry. You have a lot to handle right now. Talking to someone may help."

Faith nodded. She had never considered talking to anyone except her mother and Yvette.

"Besides, I'm of the belief that if a marriage is broken, getting one half of it better is better than two broken parts. There are some things that may improve just from you getting help with dealing with your husband."

Faith nodded. "Okay, that makes sense." She smiled. "That's only part of the reason I wanted to talk to you."

"Something else?"

"The reason I asked to see you was to resign from my position as women's ministry leader."

Pastor Kent's eyebrows came together. "Why is that?"

"I don't think anyone knows about this yet, because it's so recent, but I didn't want people questioning my ability to lead the women with my husband and I being separated."

Pastor sat back in his seat for a moment, and then leaned forward. "That is a legitimate concern, and yes, people will question that, but have you prayed about this decision, Sister Morgan?"

"Well, no, I just assumed—"

"Sister Morgan. You do great work with the women's ministry. We need you, honestly . . . at least until I fill the job I have posted. Just because you're having some marital issues doesn't mean you can't continue with the ministry."

Faith felt an overwhelming sense of relief. She hadn't really wanted to step down, but she thought it was the right thing to do.

"Why don't we let the Lord be the judge? We'll both pray and give it some time. If the Lord leads you to give up the ministry or things become too emotionally demanding, let me know, and we'll talk about it then. In the meantime, the women are counting on you for the conference. You do an awesome job every year."

Faith wiped her eyes for the last time as she continued to nod happily. They stood. As they exited the room, he turned off the lights and closed the door behind them. They both looked down the long hallway where the other group members were still congregating as they always did after their session.

Faith paused for a moment, trying to think of the right words to express how she was feeling in her spirit. She was overcome with relief. She didn't want to give up her work at the church. It was her only chance to be someone other than a wife and mother. She needed that so badly.

"I really appreciate you having so much faith in me," Faith said.

"When God called me to start this church, I prayed about my choices for leadership. I don't believe now, a few years later, that the Lord is saying, 'We made a mistake.' We all have problems. I wish you and Brother Morgan could work them out together, but I also realize that's not always the way people choose to do things, and it's certainly not the only way."

Faith wiped tears away.

"I'm confident that you and Brother Morgan will work this out. Don't hesitate to call me if you need something." He used his right hand to pat her shoulder. "And do set up an appointment in the counseling center."

Faith let out a long breath and nodded as he walked away and began greeting other members of the group. For the first time in weeks she felt peace come over her. Maybe there was hope for them. She retrieved her empty cobbler dishes and exited the church.

Chapter 50

Faith set a cup of tea on the night table and reached for her new bedside telephone. She had missed a call from Jonah on the way home from church, so she dialed his hotel room, and when prompted, pushed his room number for the extension.

She glanced at the alarm clock and saw it was after eleven and could tell he had been sleeping when he answered.

"I'm sorry I woke you. I got your message," she said, feeling awkward.

Faith could tell he was sitting up by the noises in the background, bed creaking, and a louder breath from him. "Where have you been?"

"Remember I told you I was going out. Cell group Bible Study. It's the first Friday of the month."

"Oh," he said in mock recognition. "It's eleven."

"I came home and took a bath. I think I stayed in longer than I expected," she said, supposing he had a right to question her whereabouts.

Jonah grunted.

"Was there something you wanted?"

"To make sure you were okay."

Faith was silent for a moment. The peace she felt after speaking with Pastor Kent evaporated when she climbed into her empty bed. She was *not* okay, but she wasn't going to say so. "You didn't get a chance to tell me how they're handling things at work."

Jonah was silent. So silent she wondered if he were still on the phone. Then he spoke. "I haven't heard or been told anything. I'm not working with them anymore."

Silence again.

"You've talked to Les?" Faith asked, knowing he would have, but attempting to move the conversation.

"We're waiting for a response to a letter he sent." Jonah paused. "It's kind of a formal threat suggesting they retract their statements alleging slander, libel, and defamation of character. Kind of an 'I can sue you too' type of thing."

"That seems like a waste of time. Why would they do that?"

"Because they're lying." He finally sounded awake.

"That would be a fact only known between you and them, wouldn't it?"

"I wish it were one known by my wife."

Now it was her turn to be quiet.

After a few seconds, Jonah added, "Les says it's part of the process."

His voice sounded so far away. Like he was calling her from the moon. Faith looked at Jonah's empty side of the bed and shifted. She was feeling lonely tonight and understood if he felt the same. "I um . . . guess there's nothing else to say." She suspected there was something Jonah wanted, but she wasn't quite getting it out of him. When silence continued to crackle through the phone, she said, "I think you should take the children to visit your mother soon. Have you told her about work and about us?"

"No. I didn't want to upset her, especially when I told her we were working things out after you found out about Joshua."

Faith felt herself getting angry. They hadn't even talked about Joshua. Had he lied to his mother or was that his perception? Maybe Jonah just didn't see things the way they were. Maybe he'd done something inappropriate to Samaria and April. Maybe he'd given some woman the impression that he was interested in her and that woman had been calling the house. After all, perception was everything.

"I'm sorry you don't trust me. But I need you, baby," he said, desperation in his tone.

Faith let out a frustrated breath and crossed her ankles. She felt her hand tightening on the phone receiver before she said, "There's something else." The words tumbled out of her mouth demanding silence between them. "Someone's been calling the house . . . had been calling and hanging up. A few times they called me stupid."

"What?" Jonah's voice carried an incredulous tone. "What do you mean? When?"

"It's been or had been happening for a few weeks. I called the phone company—"

"Wait a minute," he interrupted. "Someone had been harassing you on the telephone for weeks, and you call the phone company, and don't tell me?"

Faith swallowed. "I had the phone company trace the calls, and they were made from a prepaid cell phone."

Jonah didn't say anything.

"Jonah," she said, questioning his silence.

"Who owns the phone?" He asked.

"They don't know. There's nothing they can tell when it's a prepaid phone like that. No one registered a name."

"So it could be anyone?"

"Yes," she said.

"Any psycho in Atlanta could be calling the house."

Suddenly Faith felt exposed. She used her free hand to pull the comforter up around her.

"Why didn't you tell me about this?"

"I assumed it was your girlfriend," Faith snapped, digging for an emotional response.

Jonah laughed sarcastically. "My girlfriend. Interesting assumption," he said. "It never occurred to you that someone could actually be stalking you, and that by you not telling me, you gave me no power to protect my wife and my children."

Faith felt her breath coming quicker. All the indignation had left her. "The calls have stopped," she stuttered. "They stopped last week."

"And you accuse me of not communicating."

No he didn't, she thought. "Maybe you're reaping what you've sown in your home." Renewed anger fueled the words.

Jonah sighed and Faith didn't say anything else.

"Maybe you're right."He sounded defeated.

Faith could see him, sitting on the side of the hotel room bed; his body slumped, washing his face with his hand like he always did when he was frustrated.

"I want to come by in the morning. I'll take the kids to Mom's, but I have to talk to you first. It's related to this work thing," he paused. "I . . . I need something."

"Okay." Her anger was cooled by the desperation in his voice.

"I'll be there at eleven."

"You promise you won't change your mind, no matter what goes down between you and me? I don't want to promise them, and then you decide you'd prefer to play golf."

Faith heard a harsh sigh on the other end of the phone before he said, "I promise."

"Okay, well, I guess we can say goodnight."

"I love you."

Faith paused, but before she could say anything she heard a click and realized Jonah had hung up the phone.

Still reeling from the emotion his words stirred, she didn't comprehend that Elise was standing in front of her.

"Mommy, can I sleep with you?"

She nodded and Elise climbed over her and flopped down on the pillows behind her. "Can I sleep in here every night now that Daddy's gone?"

"Are you thinking your dad will never come back?"

"The daddies don't come back when the mommies get a divorce."

"Divorce. That's a big word," Faith said, tickling Elise into a frenzy.

When the child recovered from her giggles, Faith propped up some pillows so Elise could lay back.

"Tell me what you know about divorce," Faith asked her daughter.

"The mommies and daddies don't live together anymore because they hate each other," Elise said, playing with the tassels that trimmed the pillow sham. "And sometimes they hate the kids."

"Hate. I don't know if parents hate each other."

"Lindsey West says her mommy hates her daddy. She heard her telling her grandma on the phone."

Sister West was in the women's ministry. She made a mental note to tell her to be careful about her phone conversations. Then she thought Lindsey, Sister West, Elise would tell Lindsey her parents were separated. Lindsey would tell her mother and then the entire women's ministry would know.

What would Pastor think if he knew everyone knew about her separation? Would he still want her to continue leading the ministry if everyone knew about her separation? Faith shook off the thought. Pastor Kent had more than assured her that she could continue leading the ministry. He had confidence in her. Why couldn't she get that from her own husband? For that matter, why didn't she have it in herself?

"Mommy, what do you think?"

"I'm sorry, baby. What did you say?"

"I said Lindsey says all the mommies and daddies that get divorced live in two houses first, like you and Daddy. Are you and Daddy divorced?"

Faith looked into Elise's huge brown eyes. All at once, she saw fear, sadness, and exhaustion in them.

"Elise, only God knows the future. But I promise Daddy and I will try really, really hard to fix things between us. Okay?"

Elise nodded as she yawned.

"And you remember to pray for Jesus to help us make it better," Faith said.

Elise nodded again and finally Faith was rewarded with a weak smile. She kissed her daughter on the forehead and helped the child climb under the comforter. She was fast asleep before Faith turned off the overhead light seconds later.

Faith lay down on her side of the bed and closed her eyes. She needed to get back to her exercise routine. She missed running in the morning, but it was the price she had to pay for Jonah not being here.

"Lord, please help me do what's right. I don't know what's right anymore." She knew she should pray. She needed to get on her knees and pray for her husband and their marriage and her children and for the women's ministry and even for Samaria and April. She needed to pray for so many things. But just like the night before, she didn't get up. She just lay there staring at the darkened ceiling, looking for a miracle to drop through the plaster.

Faith yawned, and then remembered her tea on the nightstand. She leaned over, reached for the cup, and took a sip. Dissatisfied with the temperature of the drink, she pushed it away from her. *Lukewarm, just like me,* were her last thoughts as she closed her eyes for the night.

Chapter 51

At 10 o'clock A.M. Jonah pulled his car in the driveway of the house and climbed out. He knew he was early, and Faith might pitch a fit about it, but he was sick of the hotel. He just couldn't sleep any later or continue to stare at the plain gray walls any longer.

He stood in front of the door trying to predict how she would respond to what he had to say. "God, please just let her understand," he mumbled under his breath.

Jonah wasn't sure that he really expected God to hear him or do anything for him, but really, what could it hurt? He'd found himself doing that these days. Funny how desperation could get even the most obstinate person praying. Plus he had to have some points for going to church a few times a month, even if it were to satisfy his wife.

Jonah rang the doorbell, and after what seemed an interminable wait, Faith pulled the door open. She was wearing a bathrobe and her hair was still wet from her morning shower. He could smell the fragrance of the floral scented shampoo she used. She was barefoot, her lightly freckled face clean and shiny. She looked so beautiful and young he wanted to kiss her. He wanted to put his nose in her hair and smell scent for the rest of the day. God, he missed her.

"You're early," Faith pointed out.

"I know."

Faith walked into the kitchen with him following. She removed two juice glasses from the cabinet, and after placing them on the counter, she opened the refrigerator.

"You surprised me ringing the bell. I thought you'd use your key like yesterday." She poured and handed him one.

"I'm respecting the boundaries." He accepted the glass. "I don't live here right now."

Faith took a sip. "Glad I didn't have to tell you."

Jonah nodded and changed the subject. "Are you running these days?"

"Nobody to stay with the kids in the morning."

"You'll miss it."

"I've been going to the gym after I drop Elise off."

"You could let me come home." He finished his glass and placed it on the counter.

She cocked her head to the side. "I know that's not why you wanted to talk to me. We had that conversation yesterday."

"Can we sit?" Jonah said pointing to the family room.

Faith gave him an exasperated look, but then quickly walked into the family room where she took a seat on the sofa. Jonah sat on the other end.

He didn't waste any time. "I've got to move back into the house."

She popped up from her seat like he had startled her. "I told you I needed—"

"Hear me out. There are some issues we need to talk about." He had rehearsed this speech over and over again, but seeing her look so determined not to have him come home rattled him so that he stuttered over his words. "I could . . . stay . . . in the guest bedroom. We can live here as roommates if that's what you want, but you need me, the kids don't need to see us like this."

"And separate bedrooms would make it better?"

"It wouldn't be me gone from the house."

She shook her head. A firm "no" resonating from her silence.

"Why can't we work this out together?"

"Because nothing would be different," she shouted.

Jonah kept his tone even and stood. "What do you mean nothing would be different? What happened with Eric was an accident."

"How do I know it won't happen again?"

"It won't. I would never—"

"I thought you would never in the first place."

He shook his head.

"You're still drinking, so how do I know—"

"Because, I swear to you, it won't." He paused. "Look, if you let me come home, all the liquor goes in the trash. I'll never take another drink."

Faith rolled her eyes. "It's not just Eric, or the drinking. It's the secret you kept for ten years and now this thing at work."

Jonah hung his head, then raised it. "Samaria is lying." He sighed.

"Seems a stretch that she would be willing to risk her job to get back at you."

"Well, you can either believe that or believe she's just crazy. I don't care, as long as you believe me."

Faith folded her arms at her waist. "I don't feel like . . . I know who you are anymore." Her eyes bore into him. "The drinking, the secret—I've been unhappy for so long, I feel like maybe we—"

He stepped to her and put his hands on her forearms. The scent of her hair was strong in his nostrils. "We'll be fine. I know not telling you about Joshua caused this rift, but Faith, harassment? I didn't do it. I swear. You're the only woman I've wanted for ten years."

She stepped back and jerked her arms free of him and pointed an index finger. "Don't manipulate me."

"I'm not trying to manipulate you. I'm trying to talk to you." He shook his head. "I've made some mistakes here at home. I . . . maybe . . . I . . ." he paused. "Maybe I've worked too hard.

"And the kids . . . I've been a single parent."

"Rome wasn't built in a day. I'm trying."

Fire flashed in her eyes. "You must think I'm stupid."

He jerked his head back. "Why would you say that?"

"Because the man I live with is not this accommodating. You're so desperate to get back in this house that you'd say anything."

"That's not true. I'm admitting I've been wrong, that's what I thought you wanted."

She shook her head. "What's really going on here, Jonah? I want you to be honest with me."

There was a voice in his head saying, *Trust her.*

He relented. "I do want to work out these issues we're having, but the truth is, I need to come home." Faith didn't say anything. "Les told me our being separated could be bad for me."

She shook her head and turned her back.

"Honey, I'm in trouble." He turned her back around to face him. "You're my wife. I need your support. If you don't want to believe me, that hurts, but now I'm telling you . . ." Jonah heard his own voice trembling and tried to stop it by taking a breath. "I need to live in this house. I need you to put up a front—for anyone that's looking—that things are okay."

Faith rolled her eyes and clenched her fist.

"Les says in sexual harassment cases, the spouse's support is critical. If you and I are separated, it looks like you don't even believe me. How can I get a judge or jury to believe me if I don't have the support of my wife?"

"Judge or jury? What are you talking about?"

"The potential for civil court action—Samaria could take this that far."

"What about April?"

"April will end this at some point."

"What makes you so sure?"

"Because she's not a liar," he said softly. "Samaria, she's a different type of woman. But April's a decent person, and I haven't done anything to her. For the life of me I can't figure out how Samaria got her involved in this. That's what bugs me the most. April hasn't been herself. She hasn't been for a long time, really, and I kept ignoring it, passing it off as moodiness or stress. I didn't get to the bottom of it, and I should have."

Faith turned her head. He could just imagine the thoughts running through her head. He had ignored her cries for help, why should she hear his?

"Do you understand? This is not just about us. It's my entire career—our financial future. Faith, I need you to let me come home."

Chapter 52

Faith rarely ran in the middle of the day. She preferred the morning mist and dew to the heat that emanated from the robust afternoon sun. It threatened to suffocate her as she made her way up a steep incline of grassy mountain and granite terrain. Their subdivision had great running trails, but they didn't compare to the hills and valleys that she paced on her infrequent trips to the park. This challenged her and made her push herself.

At first the fresh air had helped her to clear her mind, but she'd spent at least ten minutes agonizing over her problems. The run had been an attempt to shut out the pleading voice of her husband, but Faith had been unsuccessful at silencing Jonah.

She'd asked him for a few days to think about it, and he'd stared at her incredulously before saying, "A couple of days?"

Even as she thought about it, she could feel the blood rushing through her veins.

"Did you come here expecting me to just say, oh yeah, honey, go back to the hotel and get your stuff?"

"Actually I did. I mean the gravity of the situation—"

"The gravity of the situation *for me* is that I feel like I don't know you anymore." She'd moved out of his grasp. "I am sick and tired of living my life around your needs, your job, your issues."

He hadn't said anything and that was good. It would've made things worse.

"It's my turn to be heard." She'd tried to calm her voice, but the words had come out in a high pitched squeal. "I've got something to bargain with, and I'm going to use it. It's time you know what it feels like to need the one person you shouldn't have to beg."

Tail between his legs, he'd taken the children and left for his mother's house.

Faith slowed her pace as she came to a narrow creek. There was a bridge that led to the other side of the small waterway made from natural limestone that had been hollowed out by the parks association to give walkers and runners more access to the most intensively sloped region of the park. This was her favorite part of the run because the natural landscape was so beautiful. All God's awesome splendor showed in the trees, bushes, the mountainous formations, and crystal clear waters.

Faith thought about the scripture in Romans, "... *that we have evidence of God by what we see, by creation itself.*" We should be able to recognize His existence by the trees and birds and insects. Evidence was certainly here. She couldn't think of anything more beautiful than the sight she was looking at right this minute.

Her breath came in rapid gasps as she climbed a steep slope. Sweat trickled down from every pore in her body. The only sound was her footfalls as they snapped twigs and crunched dry leaves. She took a deep breath, inhaling the scent of trees and leaves.

She'd been trying to talk to Jonah for years. Just when

she might be making some headway with the separation, he really needed her. Timing. The timing stunk.

She was trying to accept his explanation for the allegations, but it didn't make sense to her. How did she accept or believe that he didn't do anything to Samaria and April? Why would someone he trusted implicitly do this to him unless he had actually done something inappropriate?

Jonah could be so oblivious sometimes. Oblivious to her, the kids, his family . . . maybe he had done something or said something and not realized how serious it was to the women. She'd said as much and Jonah became angry.

"Being oblivious and being a liar are two different things. I did not grab her breasts, and rip her scrub top and force my mouth over hers."

Faith cringed thinking about it even now.

"That's what she said in the complaint. Samaria has accused me of attempting to rape her in my office, so we're not talking about a misunderstanding here. We're not talking about me not paying attention to something little, or misinterpreting how I made someone feel when I said something. I'm an idiot at times, but I'm a decent idiot."

Jonah had stepped to her and put his hands on her forearms. "You've shut down on me. I know why. God knows, I've given you reason to. But I need you to come back around and be the woman I married."

He was so humble. Faith had never seen him like that. She wanted to hold on to her master plan, but his words would not leave her mind.

"I married you because I knew you had what it took to stand by my side for better or worse. I can't get through this without you. I'll give you a couple of days. But please think about what's being said, and think about who I am."

Those words cut her.

A sharp stitch in her side made her stop cold on the trail. She massaged the muscle as she continued to move, hoping to walk it off quickly so she could resume her run. She threw her head back and brightness of the sun hit her in the eyes.

Think about who I am.

She hadn't agonized for months about putting him out so he could come home unchanged in a week. That was insane. But if Les was right and Jonah was telling the truth about April and Samaria, he deserved her help.

Faith thought about what Pastor Kent had granted her. Even in the midst of turmoil, he was committed to believing in her. She thought about the Bible parable of the unmerciful debtor. Those he owed had forgiven him his debt, but then he didn't pass on the same mercy to the people who owed him. Was she being like that debtor, not passing mercy on to Jonah?

She was feeling confused.

God is not the author of confusion.

The stitch in her side gone, Faith picked up her pace. She knew where she would get some clarity. If she couldn't trust herself, it was time for her to start trusting others.

Chapter 53

Jonah entered his mother's house with his key when she didn't answer after he'd knocked several times. He knew she was home because her car, usually kept in the small garage, was on the curb. Although she didn't drive much, she often took her car out just to keep the battery charged and the engine oiled as he'd told her she needed to do.

"Grandma," Elise yelled, running ahead of him to the kitchen. "She's back here, Daddy. In the garden." She pushed the screen door open and disappeared outside.

Eric followed her with more enthusiasm than he had shown the entire morning. Eric loved her like she was his natural grandmother, and she loved him likewise. Jonah hung back for a moment. He'd been a fool.

Somewhere in the Bible it said, *A fool and what's of value to him is soon parted.* No wonder Faith put him out.

He looked at the picture of Joshua and himself that now sat on the fireplace mantle, proudly displayed at all times for his family to see, now that the secret had been unearthed.

"Would I be this foolish if I had a brother to talk to? I wish you were here," he whispered.

It was hard being all alone in the world.

You are not alone. I said I would never leave you or forsake you.

That voice had been getting louder and louder these days, and he'd been arguing with it just like he was about to now. And he did feel alone. He'd felt alone since the day Joshua died.

Jonah sat in his mother's club chair and closed his eyes. This house offered him no peace. Too many bad memories. "Where were you, God, when Joshua got sick and died?" Silence echoed back to him.

"Son," he heard his mother say before she came to stand next to him.

Dressed in old blue jeans and a long sleeve T-shirt, she wore gardening gloves, an Atlanta Braves sun visor, and a worn pair of sneakers.

"I wish you'd sell this house, and let me put you somewhere decent."

"This is my home. There's nothing indecent about it."

"It's a bad neighborhood, Mama. The house is old; you don't even have a dishwasher."

Her voice held a trace of laughter. "I prefer to wash my own dishes. I'm used to the neighborhood. We all take care of each other here."

"You deserve better."

"I deserve better, or you deserve better?" His mother frowned. "Selling this house isn't going to change what happened here. That's in our hearts."

"It doesn't have to keep smacking me in the face. Every time I come here, I feel like a weight is on my shoulders."

"That's because when you come here, you're reminded of your father. The real weight is the burden of unforgiveness; that's what you're feeling."

Jonah decided it was time to change the subject. "What are the kids doing?"

"Pulling weeds. I told them I'd give whoever got the most a dollar."

He smiled remembering the childhood game she used with him and Joshua. "As I recall, it was a quarter when I was pulling weeds."

"That was some thirty years ago. Everything's gone up. Besides, a quarter was all I could spare back then."

"You couldn't spare that, Mama, but you always tried to do things for us." He choked back emotion. "It was Martin. Martin was determined to make sure everyone around him was just as miserable as he was. I hated that about him."

"We all have faults. I remember your wife describing you in almost the same way here recently."

Jonah was silent. He looked at his mother. She was tired, he could see it in her face, sense it in her movements, but he had to talk to her. He needed somebody on his side. He wasn't sure about Faith. He took a deep breath and let it out.

"I'm in trouble, Mama," he said. The expression in her eyes told him to go on. "Some women I work with have accused me of sexual harassment. There's an investigation. I may have to go to court."

His mother was silent for a moment. He assumed she was processing what he'd said. "It's going to work out fine, son."

"Faith put me out."

"Because of this?"

"No. It was an incident with Eric."

"What happened? What did you do?"

He was ashamed to say, so he skirted around it. "There's been a lot going on. I didn't hurt him physically. I just yelled, and I was drinking. It was ugly. I've been under a lot of pressure. It was shortly after she found out about Joshua."

"You didn't hurt him physically." His mother's lips were in a tight line. "Jonah, you of all people should know what emotional cruelty can do. I don't much remember your father hitting you."

He threw his body back against the sofa cushions and shook his head. She was right.

"Where you staying?" she asked.

"In a motel not too far from the house." He met his mother's sympathetic eyes, and the embarrassment and guilt he felt went away. "Les told me it looks bad in this particular type of investigation to be separated from your spouse. I asked Faith to let me come home. She's thinking about."

"She'll come around."

"How can you be so sure?"

"Because I have faith, Jonah, and you should too."

He let out a dry chuckle. "Mama, the only faith I need right now is my wife. I'm not in the mood to hear about faith in God."

"Yes you are. That's why you came here to talk to me, because you know I ain't got nothing else to say."

"Where was Jesus when the mess happened? Where was Jesus when my wife put me out?" His voice broke. "Where was Jesus when my brother died?"

"Jesus was right there all along, son, weeping with and for you and helping you keep your mind from slipping away when it was happening."

"I don't need a spectator."

She shook her head. "Jonah, being a Christian doesn't mean that only good things will happen to you. At some point in our lives many of us will face the trials of Job."

He raised an eyebrow.

"You do remember Job, don't you, from vacation Bible school?"

"He was the man that God allowed the devil to take all his children and money."

"Right, Job was a righteous man, but he was tested and tried in the worst possible way. And do you know what he said when his wife told him to curse God and die?"

Jonah shifted uncomfortably in his seat.

"He asked her if we should only receive good from God? The Lord giveth and the Lord taketh away, blessed be the name of the Lord." She closed her eyes for a moment, and then opened them. "I'm sorry you lost your brother. I'm sorry I lost my son, but we can't blame God for that. We have to accept life as it is and celebrate Joshua, not despise the day he was ever born." His mother's eyes filled with tears. "Joshua is in heaven, Jonah. In heaven with God. If you ever want to see your brother again, you'd better figure out how to let go of that bitterness in your heart."

Jonah was jolted when the kids rushed into the house, both yelling as they made their way to the living room. He had been transfixed on his mother's words. *See Joshua again?*

"I won, Grandma," Eric said proudly.

"It's not fair. He's older than me," Elise pouted.

"She only has to get half of what I find because she's half my age, and I still won. It doesn't have anything to do with me being older."

Elise pouted as she moved to stand in front of her father. "Daddy, it's not fair."

Jonah pulled her into his lap and looked into Eric's eyes. He could tell the boy was waiting to hear how he would respond.

He looked at Elise. A younger version of her mother, pouting in the exact same way his wife would at times. "It may not seem fair, but Grandma's given you all the credit for age she can give. Your brother won, fair and square. You have to be a good loser."

Eric smiled and nodded his head victoriously. "I told you. It's just like when we lose baseball games. Coach tells us it's not always about winning. Losers are the people who never get in the game. Right, Dad?"

"That's right. Now what do you say we go for a ride. I've got a surprise for you."

The kids both shrieked with excitement.

"Wash you hands." Jonah was laughing at their response. "You too, Mama. It's time you had some fun."

Rome wasn't built in a day, but he had attempted to do it. Jonah glanced at the children sleeping in the back of his car. They were exhausted. He'd surprised them with a visit to the annual Renaissance Festival held on a two-hundred acre site about twenty minutes south of Atlanta. His mother was tickled by the recreation of a 16th-Century European Country Fair, where they played, shopped, and ate until their hearts were content. The kids made candles and blew glass, took pictures with court jesters and rode every contraption on site at least twice.

His mother was worn out, but the kids were hyped and ready for more. Probably the victims of a cotton candy induced sugar high. They didn't want to go home, so he'd dropped his mother at her house, and he and the kids continued the fun at the movie theater. Now it was nearly ten P.M., almost twelve hours since he'd picked them up.

Jonah pushed the garage door opener, and within moments, Faith came outside. It was the second time he'd found her in a robe today, but this one wasn't terrycloth, it was a silky, flowing fabric that made him wish he hadn't been so foolish as to have gotten himself kicked out of his house and her bed.

He put Elise over his shoulder and used his free arm to steady Eric as he stumbled into the house. Faith didn't say anything, but he could tell she was impressed by his endurance. It was the little things she'd asked for. Why did it take all of this heartache for him to realize it?

A fool and what's of value is soon parted.

That's all he could hear reverberate in his mind as he walked past her.

When he came back downstairs she handed him a small plastic container. A smile threatened to part her lips.

"What's this?" he asked, fiddling with the top.

"I'm not telling. Wait 'til you're in your room, then open it." She kissed him on the cheek. "Thank you for taking the children today."

"They're my kids. I should have been doing what I did today a long time ago."

She nodded and walked him to the door.

As he left he saw Faith's silhouette in his rearview mirror. She stood in the garage the same way she'd been standing when he pulled in with the kids. Tonight she had looked at him with a tenderness he hadn't seen in months. *I can't lose her.* He sighed and pulled out of the subdivision onto the main road.

His mother's words had haunted him for the rest of the day. *"Let go of the bitterness."* Every time he caught her eye while they were at the festival he could still see them beckoning him. He was making her beg, just like his father had. She looked so tired today. It was time for her to have some peace from the begging.

The Panola Road Corporate Suites' perimeter had soft exterior lights that were supposed to be soothing, but try as they might to make it inviting, Jonah felt like he was suffocating inside its elegant walls. He looked at the plastic container on the seat and decided to open it. Peach cobbler. His favorite. He closed the plastic lid, stepped out of the car, and stopped in front of the door to his room. The cobbler should have made him feel better, but it didn't. It just reminded him of everything he was missing at home. Maybe his mother was right. Maybe it *was* time for him to let go of the bitterness. Look where it had gotten him.

Chapter 54

It was the second Monday in a row that Faith found herself pulling in front of the small, neat country house that her mother called home. Behind the red door of the white two story wood frame waited the wisdom that Faith knew she needed to cement her choice. She'd already made up her mind, but she knew it was more about feeling sorry for Jonah than about what was biblically sound. Her mother would put the meat on the bones of her decision.

Faith stepped out of the car and slid on her sunglasses. The morning sun was high in the sky. The temperature had cooled by almost ten degrees. Glad for the reprieve from the heat, Faith strode toward the house wishing this weather could last forever.

"Good morning." Her mother's voice came from behind her. Faith turned to find her coming from the side of the porch railing. A large straw hat sat on her head, and she wore a yellow sundress that looked like it was more suitable for church than gardening.

Faith walked back down the steps and joined her mother, who had her hands behind her back.

"Look at my tomatoes," she said, bringing them forth. She was like a kid who'd just found two candy bars. "They're not ripe, but if I put them in the window they'll be good for eating in a few days."

Faith smiled.

They went into the greenhouse. Her mother showed her all her vegetables.

"I even have some Bibb Lettuce growing hydroponically," her mother said as if whispering a secret. "I learned to do that in my 'Gardening for the Future' class. It's all organic."

"It's beautiful," Faith said, taking in a last look at the green beans, carrots, tomatoes, and various other plants her mother had. "It's a lot. What are you going to do with it all?"

Her mother shrugged and led the way to the back door of the house. Faith could hear the kettle whistling as they entered.

"I take a bunch to the senior citizen center for the cooking class. I give some to your cousins, and I donate some to the church. The church mostly sells them at the summer fundraiser. I give some to my neighbors, and I eat the rest," she said. "How do you think I maintain this tight skin?" She removed her hat and patted her face on both sides. "You'd best get you a garden going. From the look of them bags under your eyes, you're going to need it." She turned off the burner on the stove.

Faith pursed her lips and joined her mother in the kitchen.

"Tea?" her mother asked, washing the tomatoes and then her hands.

"Yes." Faith removed two tea cups from the cabinet and a teaspoon from the silverware drawer.

Her mother placed the kettle on a trivet on the table and slid into a chair opposite Faith. "How are my grand-babies?" She smiled, removing two tea bags from their holder on the table and placing one in each cup.

"They're good, actually. Jonah came and picked them up on Saturday. He spent the entire day with them. They went to a festival and the movies. He even took his mother."

Her mother nodded.

"I tell you," Faith said, picking up the kettle and pour-ing hot water into both cups, "he's a new man now that he's out."

"Maybe he was always this man, just had his priorities in the wrong order."

They stirred their tea in silence.

"I made a dessert for my grandbabies," her mother, said jumping up and going to the counter. She returned with two layers of cake that had been cooling on wire racks near the stove, and then retrieved a small bowl with a spatula sticking out of it from the counter.

Homemade frosting. Faith recognized that smell in-stantly.

Mom began smoothing it on the cake. Faith watched in-tently as she drank her tea. She could remember her mother doing this every Saturday evening in the house in New Jersey where she grew up. It was a much larger kitchen, but it still welcomed the occupants with the same cozy warmth of this farmhouse style cottage her mother now owned. Her father had a sweet tooth, and Sunday dinner's cake went into his lunch box everyday until piece by piece it was gone, and it was time to bake another. Faith could only imagine how much her mother had to miss her father because she was starting to miss

Jonah. He'd come to visit the kids again last night, and when he got into his car, she felt the same longing she'd felt Saturday night when he pulled out of the driveway. Marriage truly did make a couple one flesh in soul and spirit. In good times and in bad.

Faith put her empty cup down and looked at her mother's abandoned cup. "Your tea is getting cool."

"When you get to be my age, you drink things room temperature. It's better for the body," her mother said, smiling. "I can feel the difference in my stomach and bowels when I drink stuff too hot or cold."

Faith turned up her lip. "That was too much information, Mother."

"Chile, I'm teaching you something. You aren't gonna be young all your life. If you live long enough, you'll be figuring out ways to preserve what you have left too."

Faith supposed that was true. If she didn't get some of this stress off of her, being old would come sooner, not later.

"What's on your mind?" her mother asked, pausing. "You didn't drive all the way back down here for nothing."

"Jonah is having a legal problem at work. It's pretty serious."

Her mother stopped and placed her hands on her hips. "Go on with it."

Faith relayed the story about the sexual harassment allegations, Les's recommendation and Jonah's plea to come home. "I just don't know, Mom," she said. "On one hand it makes sense for me to let him come home, but on the other hand it doesn't."

Her mother grunted, and went back to frosting the cake.

"I didn't put him out to let him back in a week." Faith stood and walked to the sink where she put her weight against the counter. "It's like that saying . . . you never put somebody out for one reason and take them back for another, because the reason you put them out is still there."

Mom grunted again.

"I have to think long term. If I let him come home, am I going to really get the change I want?"

Mom didn't bother to grunt this time, just gave her a disapproving glance.

"I would hate to let him come home, then he slides back into his old ways, and I'm right back where I started."

Her mother's face was implacable. "Sit down."

Faith sulked over to the chair and took a seat.

"You know for the last few minutes, you have begun every sentence with one word, and the word has been *I*. I would hate, I want, I didn't, I . . . I . . . I . . . You sound like a broken record. Do you know why I named you Faith?"

"Yes, you've told me a hundred times, including last week."

"I've told you, but you have not heard. You keep saying, I can't, I can't. What you don't understand is two things." Her mother was looking her in the eyes squarely now. "Last week I told you that you should have touched the hem of His garment."

Faith rolled her eyes up. "With everything that was going on, I forgot to look it up."

"It's a story. You know it, about the woman with the issue of blood."

"Oh yeah; she pushed through the crowd and touched Jesus and was healed."

"Yes." Her mother smiled. "Glad to know Vacation Bible School wasn't a waste."

Faith smirked. "My pastor taught on her during a healing series he did last fall."

"Ah ha," Her mother paused for a moment to put the final swirl on the cake. She then laid the knife down, pushed the plate to the far end of the table, and sat directly across from her. "You've been taught, but you still haven't learned."

Faith shook her head. "What does a sick woman being healed have to do with me?"

"She has everything to do with you. She has everything to do with all of us. We're all sick in some way or another. Maybe not physically, but some are sick in our spirits, our relationships, it could be finances. We all have issues that cause us to reach for Jesus."

Faith blinked sharply. She felt a chill across her body.

"I remember when you were a child, about six years old. You wanted to go to Patty Singer's birthday party at the community center in the Village."

Faith twisted her face trying to recall, and when she did, she nodded her head.

"Your father said you couldn't go. He didn't like the neighborhood—there were drugs and all kinds of bad things in that area. You were a child, you didn't understand." She stopped and smiled as she remembered. "You came and told us if you didn't get to go you wouldn't eat any of your peas. Your father and I laughed, but then you became angry because we laughed at you and said 'If you don't let me go, I'll runaway.' Do you remember that?"

Faith smiled and nodded her head again.

"I wanted to spank you for that remark, but your father, God rest his soul, couldn't bear to see you cry, so he told me not to." She paused again, a smile touched her lips. "You continued to do it over and over again when you were growing up . . . tell us if we don't . . . I'll this . . . and your father always let you get away with it, even as a teenager."

Faith smiled thinking of her father. He *had* indulged her.

"Well, it seems I was right. I should have spanked you, because maybe you wouldn't be issuing ultimatums today."

Her mother stood and walked to the pantry where she removed a plastic cake carrier from the top shelf and bought it to the table.

"You think you'll strong-arm that man into changing." She clucked her tongue against her teeth. "That's not the way it works. Change won't happen until God makes it happen."

Tears welled in Faith's eyes. By the time her mother transferred the cake from the plate to the carrier, they were streaming down her cheeks.

"The woman with the issue of blood waited twelve years for Jesus to walk through that crowd and heal her, but you can reach out to Him anytime. All you have to do is get on your knees and pray."

Faith took a napkin from the holder on the table and began wiping her eyes. "I have prayed," she protested.

"Faith, you're my child and I know you. You pray, and then you doubt. You have to learn to make war in the spirit realm where the true battle exists. Your husband is wrestling with demons and devils from the past and present."

Faith blew her nose and reached for another napkin. Her mother's words were tearing her in two.

"You know he's about as saved as a stick of gum, but you put him out on his own. That's not love, baby. Why can't you see this crucible in his life may be the very thing God will use to bring him to his knees?"

Tears continued to stream down her face. Her mother's words were so true, so true. *God forgive me*, she said in her spirit because she could not mouth the words. *God forgive me.*

"Do you have a prayer partner?" Her mother opened the Bible. "Matthew 18:19-20 says that *if two of you shall agree on earth as touching anything that they shall asked, it shall be done before them of our Father which is in heaven. For where two or three are gathered together in my name, there am I in the midst of them."* She paused for a moment, and then asked. "Do you and Yvette pray together?"

"No, we just talk."

"Talk will get you nowhere. You must pray together. Then again, Yvette may not be the right person. You need to pray with someone who's been where you are. Someone with some wisdom and experience.

Faith sniffed and reached across the table for her mother's hand. She was silent, digesting the weight of her mother's words. She sniffed one more time and said, "Someone like you."

Tears came to her mother's eyes. She squeezed Faith's hand tightly. "Yes, someone like me."

As if on cue, she and her mother stood at the same time. Faith reached out to her, put her arms around her petite frame, squeezed, and hugged her until the last tears of the day poured from the depth of her soul.

Chapter 55

Faith pulled her SUV into the parking space marked *The Doctor's Wife*. Dr. Gunter believed they should always honor the women who served the doctors. Faith knew on the tire guard at the head of the space was an engraved plate that read "Servants at Heart."

Faith reflected on the words, *Servants at Heart*. She had never thought of herself that way, but now God's words were all around her. Her mother had shared scriptures with her that she'd never seen in the Bible. She was supposed to serve Jonah, spiritually. It was amazing how free she felt with this new revelation of her purpose.

The Lord had been trying to get her here for a long time, but she'd been so caught up in her "I's" that she couldn't see the big picture.

She climbed down from the tall vehicle, closed the door, and made a steady pace to the building. When she entered, she exchanged a greeting with the receptionist, then she stepped into the elevator and pushed the button for Jonah's floor. As the doors closed and the elevator began to ascend, she closed her eyes and said a brief prayer for the right words to say to her husband.

The doors opened and Faith could see the bustling staff and patients in the main corridor. At the far end of the hall she saw Samaria standing close to Dr. Cooper and talking with him. Her body language in itself seemed to suggest the woman was speaking to him in a flirtatious manner.

How could she ever have doubted Jonah when she knew what type of woman Samaria was?

She shook her head and walked around to the front of the desk. She was surprised to see April sitting there instead of the medical assistant.

From the "caught" look on April's face, it was clear that she was startled by her presence as well.

"Mrs. Morgan," April stuttered. "How are you . . . today?"

"I'm good, April. How are you?"

"I'm okay. I guess."

"Do you happen to know if Dr. Morgan is in with a patient?"

"No." April turned her eyes away. Faith knew that April wasn't working with Jonah anymore. She had merely been fishing for an emotional response when she asked.

"I just saw him go into his office," a voice said from behind Faith. She recognized it as Tom Cooper's. She turned around to see him and Samaria.

Samaria walked around the desk, her stride confident and sure. Faith tried to pinpoint the image in her mind that always fleeted in and out when she saw Samaria. Then a scripture came to her mind. *". . . roaring lion, seeking whom he may devour."*

"Hmmm," she said with a small grin. A tri-archy of trouble: Samaria, April, and Cooper. For a moment she glanced between the three of them. April lowered her head and looked away.

How could I have left Jonah to contend with this? Her mother was right. She had left him alone with the devil, and he had nothing to fight with, but his flesh.

"It's good to see you, Faith." Cooper's eyes followed Samaria down the hall.

Faith cleared her throat to get his attention. "How is Karen?" she asked, reminding him of his wife.

Cooper pulled his eyes away from Samaria's switching derriere. "She's well. Busy with the children and such."

"I'm glad to hear that," she said. "If you'll excuse me, I need to talk to my husband."

As she walked away, she imagined herself moving through the crowd, reaching for Jesus' hem.

"You're the last person I was expecting to see today," Jonah stated, standing from behind his desk. "I certainly hope you aren't coming to ask me for a divorce or anything final like that."

Faith pointed to the seat in front of her. "May I?"

Jonah nodded and sat in unison with her. "How were the kids this morning?" he asked, his voice coming across with a baritone inflection that Faith realized she missed hearing around the house.

"They miss you at breakfast." She put her purse in the seat next to her.

He smiled proudly, and then his smile dissipated. "Do they really miss me, or do they just miss me being around?"

"Isn't that the same thing?"

"You know it's not." He leaned forward, chin on one fist. "I know it's not."

Faith sat back in her seat. She had come here prepared to tell Jonah to come home as he was, and she'd live with him. But now he was confessing that she had been right. Was this an opportunity for her to be heard? *Lord should I talk to him?*

The voice in her spirit answered, **"Do what God said do."**

"I came here to tell you to come home," Faith said.

Surprised registered on his face.

"I've had an opportunity to think about some things. I shouldn't have muscled you the way I did."

"You were right about Eric."

"I still didn't have the right to pack up the kids and force you to move out."

He acknowledged her apology with a smile. "I love you, Faith. I just . . ." He stood. "I need to learn balance or something."

Faith stood and walked around his desk to him. He wrapped his arms around her waist and kissed her on top of her head gently several times until she raised her face to his. After he planted several light kisses along her face from her forehead to her jaw line, his lips found hers and they touched. His kiss was gentle at first and then harder and much more passionate. Faith felt tingling all over her body and a familiar flutter in her stomach. She closed her eyes for a moment, absorbing his presence.

Jonah's hands moved across her back in a circular motion. He lowered one to her backside and stopped suddenly when a knock sounded at the door.

The two jumped apart and laughed at each other like high school kids.

"You'd better get that door." She straightened her blouse and smoothed her hair.

As he passed her to move toward the door, he swatted her once across her bottom and said, "Boy, do I miss you."

Another knock sounded. Jonah turned the knob and opened it to Lorraine Pitts. She looked into the room, and when she saw Faith, said, "Hello, Mrs. Morgan, good to see you."

Faith smiled and gave her a little two finger wave.

"I don't mean to disturb you, but Mr. Lewiston said he needed to see you before you left for the day."

Jonah nodded and Lorraine left.

When he turned back to face Faith, worry lines had etched into his forehead. His eyes avoided hers, and then he looked at her directly. "I'm . . ." he paused, ". . . sorry this whole thing with Samaria and April hasn't been re-solved."

She walked to him and took his hands in hers. "No, I'm sorry. I'm sorry I haven't been here for you."

His shoulders dropped. "I don't know what to do at this point. I've told them my side of the story until I'm blue in the face."

"You can tell me over dinner." She picked up her purse and pulled it onto her shoulder. "I've been tied up all day so you won't have a home cooked meal. I hope you don't mind pizza and a salad."

"Any meal with you will be gourmet." His smile erased the worry lines. "I'll just run by the motel and get my things."

She curled her lip into a seductive smile. "Don't be long, Dr. Morgan. I think I'm in the mood to play nurse."

The smile in his eyes contained a sensuous flame. "I'll make sure to hurry," he said. She walked out the door.

Passing the nurse's station she caught one more glance of April working on the computer. The woman raised her eyes and locked them with hers just as Faith walked by. Faith recognized the look she saw on April's face. It was the same one she'd seen reflected in her own mirror.

Confusion.

Whatever was on *this* young woman's mind, God had not authored it.

Chapter 56

Hand in hand, Jonah and Faith walked into the lobby of the New Treasures Family Life Center and looked for a wall map. New Treasures was one of the largest churches in Metropolitan Atlanta. Because of its close proximity to Christian Brothers, Gunter had arranged for mediation to be held in one of their meeting rooms.

Jonah had been relieved last week when Lewiston advised him both women had agreed to mediation. He was anxious to put the entire matter behind him. They walked past the empty receptionist desk and found the meeting room without incident. Through beveled glass that lined the outside of the large wood door, they could see from peeking in that the room was empty.

"We're early," Faith said. "I guess we should wait out here for Les." Jonah thought she had to sense his anxiety because she added, "This is going to be over before you know it."

"I'm trying to believe that," he said. "I'm so glad you're here. I hate not knowing how this is going to turnout. I don't want it dragging on and going to court."

She covered one of his hands with both hers. "You need to have some faith, honey."

He smiled, pulled his hand free, wrapped his arms around her and squeezed tight. "I've got the *Faith* I need right next to me, and believe me, I'm thanking God for it."

She smiled easily and stepped out of his embrace. "You've got to depend on someone other than yourself and me. We have to put our trust in the Lord."

Jonah wasn't sure he agreed, but he swallowed his protest.

She tilted her head. "Let me ask you a question. Why do you go to church?"

Jonah shook his head. "Not the time for this discussion."

"You need to be distracted. I can't think of a better conversation we can have to take your mind off your troubles."

He hesitated. "Why do I go to church?" He shrugged. "Because people go to church, it's Sunday, you want me to go, any number of reasons."

"Those are really the reasons you go to church?"

"That and I respect God. I'm not an atheist." He could see the concern flash in her eyes.

"What do you believe about Jesus?"

Jonah sighed again. "Now it's getting hairier."

Faith's frown deepened.

Jonah swallowed and took a deep breath. He felt like he was trapped on a game show without the right answers to the million dollar question. "I don't know, Faith. He's the one who's supposed to be walking with us or helping us, interceding for the Father, or whatever it says in the Bible."

"Jonah, if you don't believe that Jesus is your Savior, then you're not saved."

"Saved." He guffawed. "Saved from what and saved for what?"

"Saved so that when you die your soul doesn't go to hell. Saved so that while you live you have the gift of the Holy Spirit to lead and guide you in your choices. Saved so that you can live your life as witness to the good news of Christ's resurrection and evangelize to those who are not saved. Saved so the kingdom of heaven—"

He cut her off. "Sweetheart, I don't mean any harm. But I'm telling you right now, you can have all that saved talk. I am not feeding into that again. I did it once, and it was a waste of time."

"You're talking about Joshua's death?"

"I'm talking about his sickness, his death, and everything that happened after his death."

Just then, Les came rushing down the hall.

"See, I distracted you." Faith fixed the knot of his tie and smiled.

Les kissed her on the cheek and squeezed her hand. "Faith, marvelous to see you. Let's go on in and sit down, we need to talk about a couple of things before this begins. Ms. Jacobs is asking for monetary damages. That was added to the complaint yesterday."

Jonah had been trying to keep it together, but now he wanted to scream.

"The good news is Ms. Jacobs needs Ms. Thomas to corroborate her claim, but I found out something very interesting about April Thomas that's going to impact the outcome of this entire thing."

"My name is Deborah Othneil. I'm a mediator with East Atlanta Center for Mediation and Reconciliation Services." She paused, reached into a large suitcase type briefcase on her side, and removed several pamphlets and passed them to members on each side of the table. She qualified herself by advising them that she was an attorney and explained in painful detail how the mediation process would work.

Jonah let a long wind escape his lungs. He hadn't realized he'd been holding his breath until Faith squeezed his hand.

"The reason we are here today is to mediate between Dr. Jonah Morgan and plaintiffs, Samaria Jacobs and April Thomas, on behalf of Christian Brothers Medical Center, LLC."

She stopped and took what Jonah decided was a well deserved sip of water.

"As you know, allegations of sexual harassment in the workplace have been filed against you, Dr. Morgan, by two of your subordinate female employees, the first being Ms. Samaria Jacobs who is present here today. The reason your employer has selected mediation as a method of handling this allegation is because your statements are markedly different, and the legal representative for Christian Brothers is unable to move forward in this matter. It is your statement, Dr. Morgan, that you did not harass, or in any way do anything inappropriate to Ms. Jacobs. It is further your statement that this is retaliation because she wanted to enter into a relationship with you and you refused and had her reassigned to work with another doctor."

Les nodded and Jonah said, "That is correct."

"Ms. Jacobs, it is your statement that Dr. Morgan has been aggressive in a sexual nature for many months, beginning in February. That on May 12th his behavior became physical as he attempted to remove your clothing and kiss you in his office."

"Yes, ma'am." Samaria batted her eyelashes and reached into her handbag for a tissue. Dressed like a church mouse, a large cross hung from a chain around her neck. She wore very little makeup, and her hair was pinned in a conservative bun.

Jonah could hear Faith's intake of breath. She removed her hand from his and began to twist her wedding rings back and forth on her finger.

Samaria sniffed loudly and asked her attorney for a glass of water.

The drama had begun.

Les held the door open for Jonah and Faith as they walked into the Ruby Tuesday's Restaurant on Panola Road.

"Sorry I don't have time to take you to the Pegasus," Jonah said. "I have patients arriving in an hour."

"I know. We'll go to the Pegasus for our celebration dinner when this is all over," Faith said, looking around the half empty dining room. It was only 11:15; most of the lunch crowd had not piled in yet. "I'm going to the ladies room."

Faith looked around for the sign indicating restrooms and followed the arrow to her destination. Once inside, she closed the toilet seat and sat down. She felt hot tears begin to fill her eyes as she tore a long piece of toilet paper from the roll next to her.

Samaria had been allowed to speak first. She had painted Jonah to be a sex crazed maniac who couldn't keep his hands off of her, or any of the other women in the office. Her statements were so graphic and detailed that Faith had no choice but to believe either she was an absolute sociopathic liar or she was emphatically telling the truth.

They have to be lies.

Faith wiped her nose and patted beneath her eyes to keep from creating a raccoon look from her eyeliner.

"I believe my husband," she spoke aloud as she looked up at the fluorescent lights as if they were the resting place of her Heavenly Father. "He *did not* do those things."

She cried. She cried for her marriage, she cried for Jonah's reputation, she cried because she was insulted and humiliated.

Someone entered the ladies room, and she put her hands over her mouth to muffle the noise. It was uncontrollable now. A dam had broken inside her soul, and the waters could not be contained. She knew Jonah was telling her the truth. She had to believe him, or their marriage would be over. But what concerned her more was the fact that even in this dark situation, Jonah would not turn to Jesus as his source of help.

God, what's wrong with him? What's it going to take to get him saved?

He's like his patients. His issue is his heart.

She waited until the other occupant exited the ladies room then stood up and opened the door to the stall. She ran cold water and used more of the tissue she had rolled off to pat her eyes. Thankful that she had the forethought to put eye drops in her purse, she removed them and leaned her head back to let the contents of the tiny bottle splash into each eye. The redness was instantly gone. She patted her hair, smoothed her dress, and wished the stain on her soul was as easily washed away.

Chapter 57

Jonah pulled into the mass of traffic on I-20. It was 7 P.M. and cars were still jammed bumper to bumper. He wanted to make it home before 7:30, but at this rate, it wasn't going to happen. He pulled out his cell phone to call Faith.

"I'm sitting in traffic," he said, trying to look around him to see what might be the hold up.

"A traffic update just came on the TV. There was a car accident a few minutes ago at Wesley Chapel. You may be stuck for a minute," she said.

"I promised the kids I'd get home in time to watch that Disney Cruise special. Will you record it for me? We can do it tomorrow."

He could hear her smiling through the phone. "I already put the recorder on."

It was him who smiled now. "I swear you remember everything."

"My job," she said. "How was Amadi?"

Jonah's mind instantly went back to the picture he had been trying to forget about for the last fifteen minutes.

Amadi's dropping heart rate. His mother's desperate prayers to her God.

"How much longer do we have to wait, Doctor?" Her eyes were crimson from her tears.

Jonah cleared his throat before giving his wife his full attention again. "We've done everything we can, but the diuretics aren't draining enough fluid. Pretty soon, his lungs are going to be so compromised that he won't be a good candidate for a transplant. He'll have to come off the list. He won't last much longer."

He heard Faith moan. "I'm so sorry. I know how much this kid means to you."

Jonah felt tears burning the back of his eyes. "Occupational hazard. Look, I'm going to hang up. Traffic seems to have picked up a little."

"See you soon."

Jonah felt bad about the lie. Traffic hadn't picked up. He just didn't want to talk anymore. He was frustrated about Amadi, angry about Amadi, and scared for Amadi.

"God, I've got no one else to turn to. I know my mother and wife would be ashamed that I was praying this way, like you were the last resort instead of the best option, but I told Mrs. Lazarus that I would pray for her son." Jonah barely recognized his own guttural tone. He cleared his throat. "So I'm praying. Please don't let Amadi die. He's a good kid, he's smart, he has his whole life in front of him and . . . so Lord . . . God . . . please let him get a heart before it's too late." A lone tear fell down Jonah's face. He struggled with the wave of emotions that overtook him. "I . . . guess this prayer isn't really just about Amadi. I can't stop thinking about what my mother said."

If you want to see your brother again, you'd better get right with God.

"If there's a chance that I could see Joshua again, then I need to try and do better about believing you care." He stopped and looked out his window. The guy next to him was staring. Jonah put his hands on the steering wheel and pushed the gas to move his car ahead and out of his neighbor's sight. That was embarrassing. Maybe he should save his prayers for the privacy of his office or bedroom.

After about five minutes, he came to the accident scene that had the road tied up. As he passed, he noticed a woman running back and forth in a desperate panic. There was only one ambulance on the scene, but there were three vehicles. One turned upside down. *This is bad.*

He could hear a helicopter overhead, probably an air dispatched paramedic, but it was in the distance. He wouldn't normally get involved, but these people needed help. He pulled his car over to the side of the road and jumped out.

"My son is bleeding," the woman yelled, grabbing Jonah's hand as he got closer. He could tell she was African. He recognized some of the Swahili words she intermixed with English as she yelled in a fitful cry at the EMT.

"I'm a doctor," Jonah said, rolling up his sleeves as he approached the EMT. "What can I do?"

Panicky eyes above a sweat drenched nose looked back at him. "Put pressure on this abdominal wound. The bleeding's pretty heavy." He jumped up and handed Jonah gloves and a fresh wad of gauze. "I'll go check on her son."

Jonah put on the gloves, got on his knees and applied pressure to a large gash just above the older gentleman's groin. He was conscious, but badly shaken. Police sirens wailed, bringing traffic to a complete stop. Jonah felt a strong wind and looked up. The helicopter had touched down on the highway. Within seconds, four EMT's, mega duffel bags and a stretcher in tow, were charging toward them.

"He needs to get to the hospital. I've applied pressure, and the bleeding won't stop," Jonah said, moving out of the way.

He searched for the woman who had been crying for her son. She was being pushed back by two of the EMT's while the third leaned into the upside down vehicle. Jonah realized her son had to be trapped in the car. He removed the bloody gloves from his hand, rolled his shirt sleeves up higher and walked down into the grassy ditch.

"My son, please help my son," the woman was crying. "He's only sixteen years old, please help him!" Jonah noticed she had blood on her arm and shoulder.

He got on his knees next to the EMT whose name tag read Tim.

"How's the abdominal wound?" Tim asked.

"Still bleeding. He's being taken to the hospital," Jonah responded, trying to look into the vehicle Tim was squatting near. "Is it bad?"

"Head injury. He's unresponsive." Tim wiped the sweat off his forehead with his arm. "It's bad."

Jonah heard the loud wail of a fire truck arriving on the scene. He stood and stepped out of the way so the fireman carrying the "Jaws of Life" could reach the vehicle. He watched as they cut away at metal and rubber with deft swiftness. Within minutes, they had him on a stretcher.

Nearby, his mother was sobbing. One of the people who had gotten out of their cars was trying to calm her down.

What a horrible way to see your child, Jonah thought. He pulled one of his business cards from his wallet and stuck it in Tim's shirt pocket.

"Just in case you need it." He stepped back as they carried the teen boy to the waiting helicopter.

Jonah looked around at the rest of the scene. Everything seemed to be under control. He jogged back to his car. Once inside, he opened his glove compartment and reached for a handkerchief to wipe his hands and face. He was sweating, partly from the heat and partly from the adrenaline.

He turned the air conditioner on full blast and pulled out his cell phone to call Faith when his pager went off. *Kimble.* Fear clenched his heart as he dialed the number.

Jonah pulled out ahead of the other cars waiting and flagged down a police officer.

He took out his identification. "I need to get out of here. I have a medical emergency."

The officer gave him instructions on how to get around the accident. Once he had cleared the ambulance, he moved through the space and used the shoulder of the road to get to the next exit. Amadi was crashing.

Chapter 58

"We have a heart," Dr. Warrick said. Her normally pale complexion was bright red from excitement.

Jonah couldn't have been more shocked if she'd hit him.

"Trauma at Grady. A sixteen-year-old in a car accident, died a few minutes ago. They asked the mother to donate, and she did. Amadi's at the top of the list." Warrick was practically bouncing with glee.

Jonah merely stared, tongue tied. He couldn't even take a breath. His excitement was sobered by the fact that it was probably the kid from the accident scene. The woman had lost her son.

For some reason the scripture from Job that his mother had quoted came to his mind. *"The Lord giveth and the Lord taketh away."*

"It should be here soon. I've already called Dr. Zorbani. He's waiting for the compatibility test to be done before he comes in."

Warwick was on his heels as he entered Amadi's room.

A nurse's aide was cleaning up the discarded supplies the resuscitation team had left behind. Amadi was on a ventilator, and they had inserted a ventricular assist device to keep his heart beating. His mother was sitting in a corner in a chair. *Another sobbing mother*, he thought. Pain was everywhere. He wasn't the only one who had experienced loss.

Mrs. Lazarus stood. "He's dead," she said, grabbing Jonah's hands. "The only thing pumping my baby's heart is that machine."

"Mrs. Lazarus, I have to discuss something with you. Let's talk outside." They left Dr. Warwick with Amadi and went across the hall to a small waiting room. Jonah handed her a box of tissues from the end table nearest him, and she blew her nose and wiped her eyes.

"I thought God would make a miracle," she cried.

Jonah heard noise in the hallway, turned and watched several of the staff walk past the door. One of the social workers stopped and gave him a thumbs up. Jonah nodded, and she disappeared from the door. He closed his eyes for a second. *Lord, please let it be compatible.*

"What's going on, Dr. Morgan?" Mrs. Lazarus asked, looking over his shoulder into the hallway. "Is it Amadi again?"

"Mrs. Lazarus, we have a heart."

"Oh God," she yelled. Her body lurched forward like she had a severe belly ache. She reached for the chair she'd been sitting in to steady herself. "Oh God . . . Oh God!"

A new river of tears began to flow down her face. "I knew God wasn't going to take my baby," she said, wiping her eyes. "I knew . . . Oh thank you, God," she exclaimed.

"Mrs. Lazarus, you remember the things we discussed about heart transplantation, that there are risks. There's a chance that the new heart will be rejected, infection . . ."

Monifa Lazarus took Jonah's hands, her bloodshot eyes leaked with tears. "Dr. Morgan, God *did not* allow someone else to die today for my child not to live."

Hiccupping she said, "I have to call my mother. I have to call my sister and tell them. Amadi was dead and God has bought him back to life."

Jonah stood and watched her leave the room. He could still hear the commotion at the end of the hall. A transplant surgery was exciting, even the simple test for tissue compatibility got the staff charged. The heart would probably be there in another hour or so. Then Dr. Warwick would be calling Dr. Zorbani in for the surgery. The pediatric anesthesiologists would arrive as would all the other specialists who assisted in the four- to six-hour procedure. At the end of it all, God willing, Amadi would have his life back.

The Lord giveth and the Lord taketh away.

"Blessed be the name of the Lord," Jonah said as he walked out of the room.

Chapter 59

Jonah's pager vibrated, and he noted the number was home with a 911 at the end. He rushed to the front desk and dialed the phone.

"Jonah, thank God you answered. You have to hurry to Grady. Your mother's neighbor called. They took her to the hospital."

His stomach dropped. He'd just seen her. He felt a sharp pain as every muscle in his chest tightened. His mother . . . the hospital.

His voice caught in his throat and silenced him for a few seconds. "Is she . . . okay?"

"The neighbor, Mrs. Jones, only said they took her by ambulance. She was talking a little, enough to give them our number. I've got Yvette coming to sit with the kids. I'll leave as soon as she gets here."

Jonah squeezed his eyes shut for a moment and tried to block the thoughts rushing to his mind, the dread filling his soul. "I'm still at Kimble, I'll meet you there."

"Honey, don't panic. She'll be okay."

He nodded his head in agreement as if she were standing there. "I know," Jonah said, but he wasn't sure. He thought of the accident—cars rolled over in the ditch— smoking—with badly injured occupants. Then there was the heart that was on the way here for Amadi.

Things happen.

He returned the phone to its cradle and went to find Dr. Warwick. She was standing outside Amadi's room typing into the computerized medical chart.

"I have to leave. My mother has been taken to the hospital," he said. Just saying the words made him feel vulnerable.

"Oh," Dr. Warwick responded, blinking several times. "Is it serious?"

"I don't have any of the details."

Warwick nodded sympathetically. "I'll tell the rest of the team."

"Call me if you need anything. Please tell Mrs. Lazarus I had to go."

Jonah took one more look in Amadi's room and was reminded of the words he was trying to forget.

The Lord giveth, the Lord taketh away.

Life was a cycle of births and deaths, healings and mortal illnesses. He had seen that cycle over his career in medicine, and he was a part of it tonight from the stop on the road, to the life saving operation that would commence in the next few hours. The Lord did give and take away. Amadi had been given his life back, but would God take his mother's?

Jonah paced the floor of the small corridor in the emergency room. His nerves were a crazy mixture of hope and fear. The sensation in his stomach made him think he was going to lose its contents at any second. He had that disturbing thought, again. *What if Mom dies?*

Panic like he'd never known before welled in his throat, and he was praying . . . again. "God, please don't take my mother away from me."

The charge nurse he'd inquired with earlier was coming in his direction.

"Mrs. Morgan?" His statement was a question the nurse fully understood.

"She's still on her way from X-ray."

She'd been coming from X-ray for twenty minutes. Hospitals. Sluggish institutions that had too much waste in their processes. Nobody knew that better than a doctor. He hated this waiting.

"Jonah." He turned to see Faith. "How is she?"

He grabbed her outstretched hand. "Coming from x-ray." He looked at his watch. "She should be here any minute. We won't really know anything until all the tests are done."

He'd called on the way over and was told it was probably a mild stroke, but he didn't trust anyone's assessment. He needed to see her for himself.

They heard the squeak of the old gurney before it rounded the corner. His mother lay flat. She had an oxygen mask on her face.

Jonah rushed to her side and grabbed her hand. She looked exhausted, but was moving her eyes and trying to speak.

"Don't talk, Mama," he told her.

One of the attendants looked at the chart that lay at her feet. "Room B. This is it."

Jonah let go of his mother's hand. He and Faith backed up against the wall to allow room for the attendants to turn the bed at a slant, and then they followed them in.

A nurse walked into the room. "I'm Kathy." She looked directly at his mother, and then between him and Faith. "I'm your nurse until they send you to the floor." Kathy nodded and the two attendants left the room. Then she took a pulse and blood pressure and jotted notes. "Are you comfortable, Mrs. Morgan?"

His mother nodded her head.

"She's worn out," Kathy said, making more notations in the chart. "All the tests they did. She really needs her rest."

Neither Jonah or Faith said anything. His mother reached up to remove her mask.

"No no, Mrs. Morgan. We need you to stay on that oxygen for a while. I know it's not the most comfortable thing, but you need it."

His mother's eyes were questioning Jonah. "Please listen to the staff, Mom," he said. "You need the oxygen to keep the blood going to your brain."

Kathy looked up from her writing. "You in the medical field?"

"Cardiologist," Jonah responded.

Kathy seemed to be unfazed, but he knew his being a doctor meant one thing to all hospital staff. *Handle this one with kid gloves.*

"Her attending is Dr. Yarborough. He's down the hall if you want to talk to him. We already started her on TPA to dissolve the clot, and he's ordered some other medications," she said to him. Then she turned to his mother. "You're on a liquid diet, Mrs. Morgan."

Jonah squeezed his mother's hand. "Mom, are you in pain?"

She shook her head.

"Anything feel numb?" he asked.

She returned the same no, but with less certainty.

Jonah nodded and looked at Faith. "She's going to be okay." His voice cracked. He could feel himself breaking down. Tears formed in his eyes, and he felt wobbly on his feet.

Faith wrapped her arms around him. "You said yourself she's going to be okay. Trust your judgment."

He looked at his mother who was resting with her eyes closed. He moved near her bed and whispered, "Don't ever leave me. I still need you."

Jonah pulled a handkerchief from his jacket pocket and wiped his face. He had to pull himself together so he could talk to the doctors and find out what they knew about the diagnosis and prognosis.

Chapter 60

"Go home, honey." Faith blinked and felt the gentle nudge of Jonah's hand. She had nodded off. She shifted in her seat to get more comfortable, and then looked at the wall clock. It was almost ten thirty.

"Go before you really get sleepy," he implored.

She looked at Mom Morgan. The oxygen mask was still on her face, and she was sleeping like a baby.

"Yvette will wait," she whispered.

Jonah motioned for her to join him in the hallway.

"We're just waiting for a room on a regular floor. I called a nursing service. Someone will be here at midnight. As soon as she arrives, I'll leave." He looked at his watch. "I need to go back to Kimble."

"How much longer will Amadi be in surgery?"

"It should be over in a few hours. I want to be there until he's in recovery."

"Are you sure you don't want me to wait for the nurse and you go on to Kimble?"

Jonah shook his head. "I want you safe at home." They walked farther down the hall. "That accident I saw tonight . . ." He shook his head. "It was awful. Really shook me up. I . . . I just want you safe in our home." He rubbed a hand up and down her arm. "I'm tempted to drive you myself."

Her heart swelled. "I'll be fine."

"Let me walk you to the car."

Before they stepped into the elevator, Jonah stopped at the nurse's station to let Kathy know he would be back shortly. Once the doors closed, he leaned against the wall, tilted his head back, and closed his eyes. When he opened them he spoke just above a whisper. "Something incredible happened tonight."

Faith watched him intently, waiting for him to tell her what he wanted to share. They hadn't talked in so long. It was a foreign thing to her. She found herself holding her breath.

"You remember that accident that had traffic backed up?" Jonah asked her.

She nodded.

The elevator pinged at street level, the doors opened, and they stepped out.

Jonah wrinkled his brow. He had a confused look on his face, but at the same time she saw something else. He seemed to be awestruck.

"A miracle happened," he said. "I've been trying for hours to title it . . . quantify it . . . explain it." He let out a long breath. "I just have to accept it for what it is."

Faith took his hand. "What happened?"

"A sixteen-year-old African boy died. I tried to help at the scene," he said.

Faith felt herself blink a few times.

"He died here at Grady." Jonah sighed. "Amadi has a rare blood type. He would almost certainly need a heart from a person of African descent. This kid was a match."

She touched his arm. She could tell he was overcome with emotion.

"I . . . prayed for him," Jonah said, shaking his head. His white teeth gleamed through a nervous smile. "I've never prayed for a patient."

Faith squeezed his hand tight. Closing her eyes for a second, she let out the breath she'd been holding. Then she remembered her mother's words. *This crucible in his life may be the very thing God will use to bring him to his knees.* She blinked against tears.

"How did it feel?"

Jonah shook his head. "I don't know." She could feel him struggling with his emotions. "It felt like . . . there was hope."

She nodded and smiled. "That's what a good prayer feels like. Hope."

"But I was scared," he said. "When you called about my mom, I felt like . . . like God had given me something, but I had to lose something too."

Faith shook her head. "It doesn't work like that. God is a giving, loving God."

Jonah let out a long breath. "But things happen. Bad things happen to good people."

Faith's heart was breaking for him. She waited a few seconds, and then said, "Like Joshua."

Jonah's words came out in a whisper. "Yeah. Like Joshua." He looked down at his shoes. "I just . . . it was so . . . unfair. I mean, we were twins."

Faith could see unshed tears in his eyes.

"I was healthy," he said. "I've always been healthy." He shook his head. "Why Joshua and not me?"

Faith reached for him and wrapped her arms around his neck. She kissed his forehead and whispered, "I don't know, Jonah, but it's okay for you to be alive. You're special too."

Jonah nodded and looked so deeply into her eyes she felt like he was inside her soul.

"Talk to me, baby. I love you. Just tell me what you're feeling," Faith said.

He sighed and tightened his grip on her hands. He closed his eyes for a second, and then opened them. "I was so ashamed," he said. "My family, my dad . . . us being poor. I hated it. I hated being poor so much." He let go of her wrist and turned his head. She took a hand and redirected his eyes to hers. She wasn't going to lose him now.

"I feel . . . I felt like poverty and ignorance killed my brother. My father didn't have a decent job." He shrugged his shoulders. "We didn't have insurance."

Faith could see him struggling not to cry. "It's okay. It's okay to feel that way." She reached up and stroked the side of his face.

Jonah straightened his back and regained his composure.

They stood there in the quiet of the parking garage, holding hands and staring into each others eyes.

Jonah was the first to speak. "That wasn't so bad."

Faith smiled.

"I guess I'll never really know why my brother died."

Faith shook her head. "Not on this side of heaven. But you know what?"

"What?"

"You can know why you didn't die," she said. "You can focus on your purpose. Think about all the children you've made better. Look at Amadi. You cared enough to treat a poor little African child with no insurance. He might have died without you, Jonah. God needed you to save Amadi and who knows what that young boy will grow up to be."

"He's a great kid."

"God used you to save that great kid. That's an honor.

Focus on what you can continue to do in your brother's memory. What would make Joshua proud?"

Jonah kissed her gently on the lips. "I love you," he said. "I always knew I was lucky to have you."

Faith gave him another squeeze. She hated to let him go.

He opened the car door, she climbed in, and he pushed it closed.

"Drive carefully," he said. "I've got a lot to make up to you and the kids."

Faith's heart melted. She started the car and pulled away. In her rear view mirror she could see Jonah step back into the elevator. They'd both left the pain of the past behind them.

Faith pulled into the garage and climbed out of the car. When she entered the kitchen, she found Yvette sitting at the kitchen table with a pile of paperwork.

Faith fell into a chair. After a few seconds she then leaned forward and removed her shoes. "I do *not* need a job. My life is wearing me out."

Yvette laughed and pushed down the lid to her laptop. "How's his mom?"

"She's going to be okay. It was a stroke. She has mild paralysis on her right side, but if she begins rehab right away, it should get better."

"What caused it?"

"Blood clot from sky high blood pressure. She admitted she was breaking her pills in half because she didn't like the way they made her feel. Plus she'd been eating a few too many barbeque pork sandwiches from a little rib shack near the church."

Yvette nodded. "Hypertension. Black folks disease."

"You got it," Faith shot a finger in Yvette's direction. "How's Jonah?"

"He's good." She pulled a foot onto her thigh, kneading it with her palm. "He hired a nurse to sit with Mom overnight. He should be on his way back to Kimble."

"Again?" Yvette frowned.

"He had a child that was on the transplant list. They got a heart. He's in surgery."

The frown dropped from Yvette's face.

"The entire team of doctors is involved in this type of thing. It's a really important case for Jonah. Reminds him of his brother," Faith said.

Yvette leaned back, surprised. "He told you that."

"And more," Faith said. "He talked to me about Joshua. About feeling guilty to be the one alive." She shook her head. "It's sad the way he's been carrying that around."

Yvette inhaled. "Pretty deep."

"I mean, we knew it was deep, but I guess I just didn't think it was that deep." Faith let go of her foot and lay back. The women were silent for a few moments, digesting the heaviness of Jonah's confession. The grandfather clock struck midnight in a rhythm of dings and dongs.

Yvette stood, stretched like a cat, and reached for her purse on the table. "I'm going, girlfriend. Gotta open at the crack of dawn."

Faith stood, walked her friend to the door, and watched as Yvette climbed into her car and pulled away. The night air was seductive. It was a perfect, sixty-eight degree evening. Instead of going back into the house, Faith sat on one of the chairs in the small alcove she liked to think of as her porch. She took a deep breath and looked up at the million stars that twinkled in the sky like diamonds. She remembered a night just like this not so long ago when she had fled to Zebulon with her children. Running from the stranger her husband had become.

She smiled thinking of one of her father's favorite sayings: *What a difference a day makes.* Her dad always told her God had a way of working things out—of turning things around in an instant.

Faith thought of her father, his wisdom, and tears careened down her face. She sat on the stoop for a long time, praying for Mom Morgan, Amadi, the mediation session tomorrow, her children, her husband, and her marriage. Her knees weren't necessary tonight. She met God with a heart that was open and running over with repentance, gratitude, and hope. When she was done, she stood and blew a kiss into the midnight sky.

"Thank you, Lord, for being so good to me."

Faith walked into the house. She pulled a tissue from the holder on the foyer table and wiped her eyes.

Finally, tears of joy.

Chapter 61

Jonah fought to suppress a yawn. He had only had three hours of sleep. He felt like he had during his medical residency, except the big difference thirteen years of age made. What a cup of coffee would bounce him back from, only a bed could fix now.

Faith bumped his knee with hers. He looked into her eyes. They were tired also. Although she had gone home, knowing her, she probably hadn't slept a wink. Faith was a natural born worrier, and he knew she'd spent half the night thinking about him and his mother. His wife was always concerned about other people. He felt guilty for accusing her of being selfish. It just wasn't true.

Debra Othniel completed her summary of April's complaint and Jonah let out a loud yawn. All eyes, except Faith's, rested on him. She was probably too embarrassed to look his way.

"Are we keeping you awake, Dr. Morgan?" Ms. Othniel asked.

"Please, excuse me."

"My client's mother had a stroke last night, and he had a

patient who had surgery that ended at 2 A.M.," Les inter-jected.

Ms. Othniel's brow wrinkled considerably. "My sympathies for your mother's illness. We certainly could have cancelled today's session."

Jonah coughed and shook his head. "No. It's okay. I really prefer to proceed." He cast a glance April's way. She was nervous as a cat and looking like she hadn't had much more sleep than he had.

"Then we'll move forward." Ms. Othniel nodded to Les.

"Miss Thomas, tell us about your working relationship with Dr. Morgan," Les began.

"I used to work with Dr. Morgan as a cardiology technician. I performed tests on patients as ordered by him," April answered.

"How long had you worked with Dr. Morgan?"

"Two years."

"How did you enjoy your working relationship?"

April paused for a moment, confusion marring her face. "What do you mean?"

"Did you get along? Was he a good boss? Did he evaluate you fairly?"

April began wringing her hands. Jonah stared at her intently, but she refused to look in his direction. She cut her eyes between Les and the mediator. "He wasn't really my direct supervisor. . . . I was assigned to work with him."

"But he did evaluate you?"

"Yes. He had input, but the nursing manager did my evaluations."

"You worked almost exclusively with Dr. Morgan for two years, at least eight hours a day, so would you say the content of your evaluations were heavily weighed by what Dr. Morgan had to say about your performance?" Les asked.

"Well, yes," April said. She looked in Jonah's direction for just a moment, but then looked away.

"Let me ask you another question, Miss Thomas. As a cardiology technologist, are you in high demand in the work force?"

April twisted in her seat. "I don't know. I haven't had to look for a job in a while."

Les pulled out several copies of a sheet of paper, handing one to April and her attorney and one to Debra Othneil. "I did some research. You're a cardiac sonographer. Am I correct?"

April pulled the sheet of paper closer to her.

"You're registered with the American Registry of Diagnostic Medical Sonographers and Cardiovascular Credentialing International for the maximum number of credentials in your field. The report I ascertained from the American Society of Echocardiography describes the job market as robust for cardiac sonographers, particularly those of your caliber. At this point there is no higher designation you can achieve in your field."

"The point of all this?" Derrick Hill, the attorney Christian Brothers had hired to assist both women leaned forward in his seat and interrupted.

"I'll get to the point," Les said, looking in Hill's direction. "Miss Thomas is currently enrolled in a pediatric nurse practitioner program at Georgia State. Upon graduation she plans or planned to go to Boston University for a year where she would do post graduate work in cardiology in order to become a cardiac nurse practitioner. Is that correct, Miss Thomas?"

April nodded, seeming to be confused.

"What I am saying here is you have a career in a robust job market, you have the highest levels of certification that are in your field. Dr. Morgan has been instrumental in

helping you plan your future career goals and has assured
you that he will help you get into the program at Boston
University where one of his college friends is the director
of the program. He's been a mentor to you, but it's a . . .
hostile work environment." With the last statement Les
raised his fingers and made a quotation marks gesture.

April sighed and rolled her eyes upward. "I never said
Dr. Morgan was a bad boss."

"But he threatened you physically, sexually . . . isn't
that the worst kind of boss?"

April reached for the glass of water in front her, took
two sips, and returned it to the coaster with a clank.

"Is there a question on the table for my client?" Hill
asked.

"No. That was an attempt to get the facts of Dr. Morgan
and Miss Thomas's relationship as Dr. Morgan sees it and
has demonstrated it, on the table. I do have a question for
Miss Thomas."

"Let's hear it." Hill was looking at his fingernails now,
like he wanted to file them.

"Have you ever made an allegation of sexual harassment or any other sexually based situation in the past?"
Les's question flew from his mouth like a dagger of ice,
and April froze. Her eyes locked with Jonah's.

"Why are you asking that question?" Hill opened a file
folder in front of him and began flipping through it.

"Because I think it's relevant to these proceedings
whether or not Miss Thomas has made such an allegation
before," Les said.

"It is not relevant, and I move to strike that question
from the record."

"This is not a trial." Les was stoned faced. "It's a fact
finding session and an attempt to get the facts on the table
so all parties can consider them in coming to a decision."

A look of terror transformed April's face. Her honey-colored skin was turning white right before their eyes. She looked at her attorney, then Ms. Othniel.

"I'd like Miss Thomas to answer my question," Les pressed.

"Miss Thomas," Ms. Othniel said firmly. "Please answer the question so we may move forward."

April closed her eyes and shook her head.

"Perhaps, I can answer the question for Miss Thomas, or at least refresh her memory," Les said. "On November 21 of last year, she accused four men at a party of sexual assault and sexual battery, and a fifth man with assault and robbery."

Jonah sat up and clasped his hands together. He felt badly about what he knew was coming.

"Then she dropped the charges," Les said leaning back in his chair and poking his chest out like he had just won a prize fight.

"Please respond to this, Miss Thomas," Ms. Othniel said.

April's eyes met Jonah's. He didn't know if she were hurt that he'd allowed this questioning, or embarrassed that everyone at the table knew. She paused for a few moments, and then in words they could barely discern, she whispered, "I . . . can't."

Demonstrating his inability to hear her, Les pulled down on his ear lobe. "You can't what?"

"I can't . . ." She began crying. "I can't talk about that."

"You can't talk about how you did the same thing last year. Can we expect you to drop *these* charges in a few days?"

"Sexual assault and sexual battery are different crimes and cannot in anyway be compared as Mr. Parker is attempting to—" Hill began.

Les cut him off. "They can be compared. They are crimes of a sexual nature of which Miss Thomas has had a prior—"

"We are not talking about assault in Miss Thomas's case. The charge is a hostile work environment."

Deborah Othniel raised her hand to silence the two men like they were children at a breakfast table. "They're both crimes of a sexual nature, Mr. Hill, and all the facts regarding a prior allegation need to be disclosed because this is a criminal matter. In addition to the criminal case, there is the potential for a civil suit. Ms. Jacobs has made a request for monetary damages."

Jonah cleared his throat. "Could we take a break? Perhaps give Miss Thomas a chance to pull herself together." To his left, Jonah heard Les groan. On his right, Faith released a long breath. Jonah looked straight ahead because today was the first time in weeks that April had looked into his eyes. Wordlessly, she said thank you and he nodded.

"I know you're sympathetic to this woman, but you need to let me do my job," Les said, firmly.

Jonah waved him off. "It's just a recess."

"No. I was about to break her, and now you've given her a chance to regroup. She might even call Ms. Jacobs for reinforcement."

"It'll be okay, Les."

"It'll be okay? We're talking about your career, your reputation, and your money. We've *got* to play hard ball, and you've got to let me do this my way."

"We cannot destroy her in the process." Jonah's voice trembled as he spoke.

April had come from around the corner and stood shocked, staring at the three of them as if she had been caught with her hand in a cookie jar.

Jonah spoke as he looked into her bloodshot eyes. "I never did anything inappropriate to Miss Thomas. I've treated her like a daughter. She'll stop this on her own." He broke contact with April's eyes and turned to face Les. "She'll drop the charges on her own."

Jonah could hear the clicking of April's heels move farther and farther away on the tile behind him.

"That was good," Les said. "I just hope it works. I've got to return a phone call. Faith, talk to him." He walked down the hall in the direction of the lobby.

Faith positioned herself in front of Jonah and smoothed the lapels of his suit. "Honey, do what Les says."

"She was attacked, and I remember when it happened. Les didn't even have to tell me the date. April was out sick for two weeks with the flu, and when she came back she was a different person."

"I know she's been through a lot."

"And Samaria is using her. She's got things all mixed up in that kid's head. Just so she can get back at me. Or better yet, this used to be about getting back at me, now there's a potential payday involved."

"You hired Les because you trust him."

"I should've been there for her. I knew something was wrong, but I didn't really push it. I was too busy with work to take the time."

Faith put her arms around his neck and gave him a tight squeeze.

"Always too busy with work." He clenched his fist.

Faith released him, and they took seats on a bench against the wall. She took his hand.

"It's like the only people who can get my attention are patients. You had to leave our home to get me to spend time with you and the kids. April has to charge me with sexual harassment for me to try to find out what's wrong with her, and now my mom. My mom had to have a stroke."

Faith rubbed his hand.

"What's wrong with me? Why am I like this?" he asked.

"I'm not a psychiatrist, so I'm not going to try to analyze you." She was smiling. "But I discovered something about myself recently, and I think the same thing is wrong with you that's wrong with me. " She paused again. He could tell she was searching for the right words. "There's something wrong with your heart."

Jonah pinned her with his gaze, but he was silent.

"Your heart is full of things that keep you from having peace. Unforgiveness, an unwillingness to let go of pain, anger, guilt. Although you're a good person," she squeezed his hand, "and you care about people, you don't love freely because the love that would flow from your heart is stopped by . . ." Faith paused and then smiled, saying, "clogged arteries."

Jonah swallowed. He wanted to smile at her joke, but he couldn't. He knew that even though the metaphor was cute, it was hitting home.

"You've already begun to settle some things in your mind about Joshua, but even that won't free you if you don't do the one thing that God requires you do in order to really have peace."

He knew what was coming before she said it. His mother had told him a thousand times.

"The time has come for you to forgive your father."

Derrick Hill entered the meeting where Jonah, Faith and Les had been waiting for more than fifteen minutes. "I haven't been able to locate Miss Thomas. She's not answering her cell phone, and her car is no longer in the parking lot."

Debra Othniel looked at her watch for the fourth time. "Mr. Hill, we have no choice but to dismiss these proceedings. We can't continue without your client."

"I'm aware of that. Perhaps we can reschedule. She must have been overwhelmed by the questions this morning."

Everyone in the room stood to their feet.

"Get in contact with your client this evening, Mr. Hill, and let me know how she wants to proceed." Debra Othniel left the room.

"She'll withdraw her complaint," Les said, confidently.

"We'll see you tomorrow," Hill stated, putting a file in his briefcase and leaving the room.

Les turned to Faith and Jonah. "Samaria Jacobs has nothing without April Thomas."

Jonah nodded. He knew he should be happy, but he couldn't help being concerned about April.

"I told you to trust me," Les said. "Everyone has skeletons. We just have to find the closet they're buried in."

The three of them left the building. Les promised to call them first thing in the morning to let them know if they needed to be back in session with the mediator.

Faith kissed Jonah, then climbed into her car. He had to go to the office, and she was going to see his mother. He watched his wife pull off before getting into his own vehicle. Sitting behind the wheel, he noticed the sleepiness he'd been feeling earlier had disappeared completely. *Forgive your father.* Faith's words, his mother's words, God's words were rolling around in his head.

"I can't," he said, putting the key in the ignition. "Why should I?"

Because I've forgiven you.

Jonah knew that he wasn't perfect. He'd made mistakes, and Faith had forgiven him. His mother had made mistakes, and he'd forgiven her. He turned the key over and let the windows down. But forgive Martin? He'd let his brother die. Jonah wasn't sure if he could reach that deep. It was going to take a move of God for him to forgive his father.

Chapter 62

Jonah leaned across the thin plastic railing that separated him from his mother. From a chair in the corner of the room, he'd been watching her sleep, but he'd gotten an overwhelming urge to be closer to her. He leaned and kissed her forehead.

"I'm so sorry I didn't make time for you. I'm sorry I didn't listen to you." Jonah felt a hot tear fall from his eyes and watched it splash on her arm. "You'll get better. You have the best doctors in Atlanta, and they'll take good care of you."

His mother coughed and opened her eyes. "Son—"

"Don't try to talk, Mama; just rest." He wiped the moisture from under his eyes.

"No," she stated, firmly. "I've been waiting to talk to you."

"What do you mean, waiting?"

"I thought about you all night, son. I thought about you when they strapped me down and put me in the ambulance." She coughed again and Jonah reached for her water cup and held it for her. After a few sips, she shoved it away. She cleared her throat and reached up to feel the oxygen tube in her nose. "When am I going to be rid of this?"

Jonah sighed. "When you don't need it anymore."

"Humph," she grunted. "As I was saying—"

"Mama, please don't try to talk."

Annoyance was etched deeply in her face, and she waved a hand. "I gots to talk, because I have something to say." She paused for a moment and pushed the button on her bed to raise her head. When she was done, she locked her eyes with his. "I appreciate the fact that you think I have the best doctors in Atlanta. But I'm not counting on being healed by a doctor," she said. "If'in I make it out of this horrible place alive, it'll be because of Jesus."

Jonah swallowed his protest.

"If I don't make it out of here, I don't want to die knowing you aren't reconciled with the Lord."

"You're not going to die."

"Then why you looking like you want to cry?"

"Because I don't like to think of you in pain."

"Son, pain is a part of life. I been trying to tell you that for years. Y'all can give me all the medication in this hospital, but the only thing that's gonna make me feel better is knowing my only child was living in a right relationship with Jesus."

Jonah felt uneasy. *Jesus* had been making him uneasy for weeks.

"You were saved as a child. Nothing can separate you from the Savior. Only you can do that." She paused for a moment, catching her breath. "You've blamed God for things you don't understand, and you *cannot* do that."

"I've been thinking about the past. I realize I've made some mistakes."

"But now it's time to move past realizing mistakes and

make the move to change your life." She coughed weakly. "Get my Bible."

He reached for the worn Bible she'd insisted he go to the house and pick up for her. He remembered his mother carrying it to church when he was a child. "I'm amazed it hasn't fallen apart. It's almost 40 years old."

"The truth in it is older than that. Open it to the page with the bookmark."

Jonah pulled the chair near the bed closer and opened to the book of Hebrews, chapter three as he was instructed.

"Read the part I marked." She closed her eyes.

Jonah cleared his throat and looked at verses seven and eight. It'd been a long time since he'd read from the Bible. *"Wherefore as the Holy Ghost saith, Today if ye will hear his voice, harden not your hearts."*

Instantly Faith's words flooded to his mind. *You have issues in your heart.*

He chuckled uncomfortably. "So you and Faith are talking."

His mother shook her head. "No, I didn't talk to Faith. But we both been talking to our God. God has been trying to reach you, but you keep hardening your heart. You've got to reconcile to Christ."

He could feel his eyes stinging. "I don't know how. It's been so long."

"Just speak to Him, son. Tell Him you're sorry. Tell Him you didn't mean to fall away. Tell Him you love Him."

Talk to Jesus. Was it really that simple? Would it change anything? Jonah thought.

His mother closed her eyes. She mumbled some words for a few seconds, and then fell asleep.

After a few minutes, Jonah stood and walked to the window that overlooked a park across the street. He squinted, not because he couldn't see, but because he couldn't believe what he was seeing. A tent, set up with about fifty people sitting in folding chairs underneath. The banner hanging across the front had two phrases penned in red:

New Birth Reconciliation Ministry. Coming Home to Jesus.

A tent revival. Hadn't he and his mother just talked about those times under the tent with Joshua?

God, what are you doing to me? He squeezed his eyes shut, and when he opened them, he looked at his mother. *First, I pray about Amadi, and he gets a heart. Faith has forgiven me. The harassment complaint is probably dropped, and now it looks like Mama is going to be okay.*

Jonah clenched and unclenched his fist. "What do you want me to do?" he whispered.

Come home to Jesus.

The words tugged at his heart. No. This was stronger than a tug. They pulled at his heart.

Jonah returned his attention to the assembly outside. This time his focus was on the man behind the pulpit. He was speaking with such enthusiasm and energy that Jonah wished the windows would open just so he could hear what was being said.

He looked at his sleeping mother, and then at his watch. Faith would arrive in a few minutes. But the desire to revisit the familiar memory from his childhood got the best of him. He stepped into the hall and went to the bank of elevators. He didn't know why, but his stomach was in knots. He felt anxious, afraid even, but he was compelled to move forward. Jonah had to hear what the young preacher with the microphone was saying, because according to the banner, he was inviting lost souls to come home.

Chapter 63

Faith saw Jonah going down the hall as she stepped out of the ladies room. She called to him, but he was too far. He kept going. Thinking he must be stepping out for air, she went ahead and entered Mom Morgan's room. Soft breath sounds escaped Mom Morgan's lungs as she slept, and Faith thought she looked more peaceful than she had even earlier today.

She noticed Mom Morgan's Bible was open on the window ledge and curiously walked to it. She read the highlighted words and noted Jonah's name scribbled next to the text. She closed the Bible and put it back on the bedside table where Mom Morgan kept it.

She reached for the woman's hand and lightly stroked it, "God is speaking to both of us." After a few minutes she looked at her watch. *Where was Jonah?* He would have called her if he were leaving the hospital.

Faith walked back to the window, and this time noticed the tent revival set up across the street. Just as she was about to turn, she saw a man stand from a seat in the back of the gathering.

It was Jonah.

"What is he . . . doing down there?" she asked herself the question, expecting the silence to continue.

"He's coming home," Mom Morgan whispered.

Faith turned to look at the woman who now lay with her eyes open.

"I dreamt it, just as clear as clear can be." Tears burst from her eyes as she sobbed the words. "My son is coming home to Jesus."

Faith took the stairs two at a time, moving as fast as her runner's legs would carry her. Pushing the metal door that served to enter and exit the stairwell, she rushed out and practically sprinted through the lobby of the hospital and out the glass doors to the street.

She could hear the preacher saying, "The doors of the church are open. Come be reconciled to Jesus—all who are weary—if you want to find peace—come be reconciled to Jesus."

Faith crossed the street. She saw Jonah still standing in the same spot he was in when she'd seen him from the window.

She stopped, watched, and prayed. *Lord, please move his heart.*

Chapter 64

"*Come to Jesus, come to Jesus, come to Jesus, just now . . .*" the choir sang.

Jonah was frozen in the spot where he stood, but he could feel himself melting as the preacher's plea pulled him . . . moved him.

"There are some of you who think, 'it's too late for me. I've been out here on my own trying to make it without God for too long. God doesn't even want me anymore.' That's what Satan is telling you."

Jonah's heart was pounding in his chest at such a rapid rate; he thought it would leap out if he opened his mouth.

"Some of you have been angry with God, things have happened, people have left you, somebody close to you died. God is saying come home, be comforted in His arms. He will give you peace."

Those are my thoughts, Jonah admitted to himself.

"*Come to Jesus, come to Jesus, come to Jesus just now . . .*"

Jonah closed his eyes. People were staring at him. He

wanted to cry like he had thirty years ago when Joshua died.

"Some of you have been angry with your brothers, your father, your mother. They let you down. God is telling you to forgive."

Jonah wanted to move, but forgiving Martin . . .

I have forgiven you.

He choked back a loud sob. *God has forgiven me.* The words of the song, *Come to Jesus*, propelled him forward in his spirit, but still his feet would not move.

There were ten people standing at the makeshift altar. From the short distance of about fifty feet, Jonah could see the preacher staring directly into his eyes.

"Sir, back there." The preacher waved his hand toward Jonah. "God has a message for you. His Word says in Hebrews, third chapter, '*Today, if you hear my voice, do not harden your heart.*' It's time to get your heart fixed, brother. It's time to come to Jesus."

Jonah felt a hand on his back, he turned his head, and through eyes that threatened to erupt tears, he saw his wife's face. She nodded in the direction of the altar, took his hand, and they walked up the aisle together.

Chapter 65

"I felt like my heart was going to burst wide open," Jonah said. "It was the most confusing, but liberating experience I've ever had."

"Confusing?" Faith asked, thinking how glad she was that Yvette had dropped her off and borrowed the car while the air conditioning was being fixed in hers. Otherwise she would have to ride separately from Jonah. She didn't want to miss a second of the peace that was radiating from her husband's face. "What was confusing?"

"The fact that I felt compelled to go out to that tent. I couldn't just walk away from the whole thing. As badly as I wanted to, in my heart I couldn't." He shook his head. "It was like . . . God was calling me."

Faith was silent. She was almost afraid that if she said something, the blessing of this evening might disappear.

"All these years, I've been angry and rejecting God, and the truth is, you can't reject God. He's always there," Jonah said. His cell phone rang, and he reached into his jacket pocket. "It's Les."

"Hey, Les," he said. "Let me put you on speaker. Faith and I are in the car."

Faith took the phone, pushed the speaker button, and held the small device between them so they could listen.

"Good news. April Thomas's case is finished."

Jonah let out a breath. "What happened?"

"She hasn't been reached. Even her attorney can't get her on the phone, so he had no choice but to drop it. Even if she files a motion in court, with the previous sexual assault thing in her history, there's no way her word against yours is going to work. Ms. Jacobs can kiss her case goodbye as well."

"I'm glad to hear it's just about over," Jonah said.

"What's the next step, Les?" Faith interjected squeezing Jonah's knee.

"I'll go back to mediation with Ms. Jacobs. You don't even need to come. In fact, you not showing will actually help the case because at this point, the mediator will just do some hard reality testing with her," Les said. "That's where we get her to think things like—if I go to court with this, what is my chance of winning? Do I have witnesses? Do I have evidence? Is there really a case?" Les paused for a moment. Chatter with another party could be heard coming through the speaker before Les returned and said, "Sorry about that. I was ordering dinner. Anyway, without Miss Thomas or some other witness, it's her word against yours. Christian Brothers will close the investigation and simply tell her she has to accept the reassignment. Either she'll stay or leave, but it'll be over."

Jonah took both hands off the steering wheel and shook his fists in victory. "That's what I wanted to hear." He put one hand back on the wheel and slid the other into Faith's waiting hand. She winked at him before he turned his attention back to the road.

"I'll call you tomorrow after I talk to Lewiston. You two

get some sleep. And plan that celebratory dinner at Pega-sus."

"Will do," Jonah chuckled. "I'll talk to you tomorrow."

Faith pushed the end button on the call.

"I'm glad that's over." Jonah took a deep breath and let it out slowly.

Faith raised his hand to her lips and kissed it. They rode in silence for a few minutes, and then Jonah spoke. "I want to go to April's apartment."

"But weren't you told we couldn't go near her?"

"I need to apologize to her. I want to do it tonight."

Faith was quiet for a moment, and then she said, "Apologize?"

Jonah turned and caught her eye for a moment again. "Yes, but not for what you think."

He sighed and said, "Les said something that cut me to the core today. He said that April and I worked together every day for eight hours a day for two years. I should have known, Faith. I should have known something was wrong."

Faith released a long breath. He could tell she was relieved.

"It's not just the apology. Something doesn't feel right. The way she left today, the allegation, you know. I want to check on her."

He could see Faith nodding her head in his peripheral vision. "Let's go."

After plugging the street address into the vehicle's navigation system, Jonah pulled the car into the parking lot for the street April lived on. It was a small townhouse subdivision with about thirty homes. They knew the street she lived on, but neither one was sure of the number.

"There aren't many of them. I remember it's a yellow house," Faith said, thinking of the one time Jonah and she had attended the housewarming when April had purchased it. "Maybe her car will be in front too."

"It's there." Jonah pointed. Even in the shadow of light from dusk, he could see the little red Mazda she'd purchased last summer.

"Good. She's home," Faith added. "Now all we have to do is get in."

They both exited the vehicle and walked to the front door.

Faith halted him with a hand on his arm. "Are you sure you don't want to wait until you hear from Lewiston?"

"No. I have a feeling she needs someone."

Jonah could see new concern etched on his wife's face. He needed to reassure her that everything was going to be okay. "I having a feeling . . . I don't know how to describe it . . . it's like something is telling me to come here." He raised a hand to knock, but when he did, he saw that the door was slightly separated from its frame. "It's not really closed," he said, looking at Faith.

He knocked anyway, but all that did was cause it to open wider.

Chapter 66

April sensed a presence in the room that made her uncomfortable. The darkness was cloaked in heaviness; the air thick and musty.

Had demons come to take her to hell? If they had, she deserved it. She had nobody to blame but herself. Like all the other decisions in her life, taking the pills had probably been a mistake. But even though she knew it was wrong, she couldn't push out the voice in her head that kept telling her she should have done it a long time ago. The voice that kept telling her she was no one.

A strong cramp hit her stomach and she squeezed her eyes shut. It wouldn't be long now. No more nightmares, no more memories, no more pain.

April looked at the Bible on her nightstand. Some people thought suicide was an unforgivable sin. But what did she believe? Was suicide like murder? She released the empty bottle from her hand and began to cry. It was a little too late to ask those questions. She had taken all her sleeping pills.

God would forgive her. God understood her pain.

Her eyelids were so heavy. She was slipping away now. No more filthy men. No more doctors, and no more lies.

She felt a sharp pain in her stomach and then a rush of nausea. She should have eaten before she took the pills. The pain came again and she doubled over in the bed. Vomit rose in her throat and she began to gag.

"No," she screamed in her mind. *If I throw up, I won't die.*

You have to make things right.

Make things right? The lies . . . not just her rapist's, but Samaria's lie and her lie. Jonah hadn't hurt her. He'd been her friend, a mentor, a father. And she'd stabbed him in the back. Sitting up on the side of the bed wasn't helping. She clutched her stomach as another sharp pain ripped through her abdomen.

Make things right.

"I have to do the right thing," she whispered.

April stood. The room began to spin, and then she fell back down on the bed.

"It's too late," was the last thing she muttered before the blackness closed in around her.

Chapter 67

"April, hang on," Jonah yelled.

Faith could hear sirens outside. She ran to the bedroom window and looked out to see two police cars followed by an ambulance whipping into the parking lot. They pulled right behind their car, and within seconds, she was in the hallway. Just as the front door flew open, she yelled, "We're up here! Hurry, please!"

Jonah moved out of the way as the paramedics scrambled to do their work, checking her vitals and her breath sounds.

"Her pulse is weak," Jonah said. The paramedic paused for a second to look at him. "I'm a doctor." He picked up the empty bottle on the bedside table. "I think she took these."

They strapped April on a gurney and carried her out of the room and down the stairs with Jonah, Faith, and the police officers in a line right behind them.

"We'll need a statement," one of the officers said once they reached the bottom floor. "Are you family?"

"No. I work with her," Jonah said.

"Anybody riding?" one of the paramedics called out after they put April in the ambulance. Jonah looked at Faith.

The unresolved issues around the allegations popped in his mind, and he gave her a knowing glance.

"I'll go. You talk to the police," Faith said.

"Panola Medical?" Jonah asked looking at the paramedic.

The man nodded and Faith climbed in.

Jonah stared at April. She looked like a teenager—so young and innocent. Despite all her pain, she appeared to be sleeping peacefully.

God, thank you for saving her. He dropped his head in his hands. *Thank you for saving me.*

The door opened, and Faith walked in. Jonah noted how completely exhausted she looked. "We should go home; you look tired."

"We're both tired. You had three hours of sleep last night. We're in this together." She sat in the chair next to him and put a hand on his knee. "Do you want something to eat?"

Jonah looked at his watch. "Yes, I'm starving."

Faith stood. "I'll see what I can find. Worse case scenario, there's always a Snickers bar."

"Got me through college." Jonah winked.

She left the room.

Jonah sat back and closed his eyes. The strain of the day was slowly creeping into every muscle in his body. It had been an exhausting twenty-seven hours since he'd gotten out of his car at the accident scene. Events had not stopped unfolding ever since.

"I'm sorry."

Jonah opened his eyes and blinked the sleep away. He

looked in April's direction and found her looking at him. He hadn't imagined he'd heard a voice. She was awake.

He stood to his feet and was at the bedside in an instant.

She coughed and lifted a hand to her throat.

Jonah reached for her water cup and handed it to her.

"What happened?" Her weak voice was barely audible in the quiet room.

"You took sleeping pills."

"I remember that. What happened afterward? Why aren't I dead?" She coughed.

"When you walked out today, it worried me. I wanted to make sure you were okay. So, Faith and I came to check on you."

April grimaced. "After what I did to you?" She began to cry. "I'm so sorry, Dr. Morgan."

Jonah was careful not to touch her, but he did lean closer. "No, I'm the one who should be sorry."

April stopped sobbing. "Other than for the day you ever met me, why are you sorry?"

Jonah reached for a handful of tissues from the bedside table and handed them to her. "We work together every day. I should have known something was wrong. I mean, I saw a difference in you, but I didn't take the time to find out what it was."

"There was no way for you to know."

"I never asked you. Not once," he said. "I'm sorry about that."

"The cafeteria is closed," Faith stated. The door swung closed behind her. "April, you're awake."

"Hi, Mrs. Morgan."

Faith approached the bed. "You sure do know how to scare some folks."

"In more ways than one." April shifted her body on the bed and sat up a little. "I feel like I've been hit by a truck."

"You need to rest. Let me buzz the nurse." Jonah picked up the remote near her bed.

"No," April coughed. "Not yet, I have to explain."

Jonah caught Faith's eye, and then looked back at April. "You need to rest. We can talk tomorrow," he said.

"No, I owe you." She looked pointedly at Jonah, and then turned to Faith. "And you, an explanation right now."

Jonah released the nurse call controller and let it hang over the bedrail.

"I let Sam manipulate me," April confessed. "She told me that you had attacked her, and I had to help her get rid of you or you'd do it to me."

Jonah and Faith exchanged a glance.

"I was raped in November," April choked out the words. "Five of them at a party."

Jonah took in a deep breath, and Faith's hand went to her chest.

"I did go to counseling. I have a therapist, but I stopped taking my anti-anxiety medicine. I wanted to fight my demons myself." She wiped her eyes again. "It didn't work. I've been depressed and confused."

Jonah could see how much pain she was in. "It's okay. It really is. You can make everything right. But first, you have to get better."

"Jonah always knew Samaria manipulated you," Faith added. "We forgive you. But you've got to forgive yourself. Suicide isn't the answer."

The door opened and a nurse walked in. "My patient is awake," she bristled.

Jonah and Faith moved back from the bed to allow the nurse to do her work, checking April's vitals and charting them.

"I've got to strap you down, hon. It's procedure. The only reason we didn't do it before was because Dr. Morgan was here." The nurse looked at Jonah. "But I know he's leaving now so you can rest. Hint, hint." She smiled at Faith, and then turned her attention back to April. "Did you want to use the restroom?"

April shook her head.

"If you don't mind, we'd like to pray with her first," Faith said.

The nurse nodded. "Just let me know when you're done."

Jonah and Faith joined one hand across the bed, and with the other, both grabbed April's hands. They all closed their eyes and Faith began to pray.

Chapter 68

Samaria screamed and threw her cell phone across the room. She couldn't believe it. Things were coming together so well, and then that weak little April had to have a breakdown.

"That was *so* very inconvenient of you, April," she murmured, letting the thought that she should feel bad that the girl had almost killed herself slip from her mind. *Women.* You couldn't count on them, and the worst thing about it was that not only wasn't she going to get any money, she wasn't going to have a job. No way was she hanging around Christian Brothers. That Lorraine Pitts would have her cleaning toilets after this.

So Jonah had won. He and his perfect little wife would go back to their perfect little world and continue to be perfect together . . . or miserable.

Maybe he hadn't been quite as miserable as I thought he'd been. After all, he hadn't slept with me, she thought, looking at her reflection in the mirror. She closed her eyes and reopened them. For a moment she remembered the teasing from her childhood. The teasing that told her she had bucked teeth and nappy hair. The teasing that came before she got braces and a perm. No, she didn't see that girl anymore. The Samaria that looked back in this mirror was fine. Jonah was just one of those enigmas in life: a faithful man.

Samaria heard the faint chirp of her cell phone. She couldn't believe the thing was still working after the way she'd flung it. She rushed over to it and pushed the talk button before she lost the caller. Maybe it was the lawyer. Maybe there'd been a mistake, but she immediately regretted saying hello when she heard the voice of the dean on the other end telling her she was out of the program. She cursed, and this time she made sure the energy she expended throwing the phone shattered it into pieces that would never ring in bad news again.

Samaria paced back and forth, throwing her hands up at her stupidity. She had no Plan B. If there was one thing her conniving, scheming mother had always told her was to have a Plan B.

Wait, she thought. "Girl, why are you tripping? Plan B is another man." She went to her closet and rifled through it until she found the item she was looking for. She pulled out a sexy little tennis outfit she'd bought on sale at the end of the season last year and walked back to the mirror. She held the skimpy jersey material against her body and smiled. She was no loser. It was just time to get back into the game. Men with money either played tennis or golf, and the country club down the street had a new man with her name written all over his wallet. She just had to find him.

Chapter 69

Jonah held a stethoscope to his mother's chest and listened. "That ticker sounds great to me." He removed it from around his neck and returned it to inside of his jacket pocket.

"I'm going home tomorrow."

"I don't know about that." Jonah picked up the clipboard that hung at the bottom of her bed.

"Don't you never mind 'bout knowing," his mother grumbled. "I had a talk with Jesus last night, and *He* assured me I was gettin' out of here. Besides, I feel good as new. Hospitals are for sick people."

"I'm not questioning your conversation with the Lord, but I'm pretty sure a short stay in rehab is the next step," Jonah replied, returning the chart to the footboard.

"They said they'll send a nurse to check on me and somebody to do my physical therapy." His mother picked up the television remote and busied herself changing the channels. "That's good enough."

Jonah caught Faith's eye. Faith smiled and continued to add water to the flower arrangements in the room. When she finished with the plant that was just to the right of his mother's head she said, "When you're ready to go home, I hope you'll come stay with us for a little while."

"I don't know about that either." His mother's tone was stubborn.

Jonah shook his head. "You know, Mama, I think it's only fair you help us out. Someone would have to check on you everyday. Faith and I've got enough going on right now, without worrying about you."

His mother pushed the button to turn off the television. "Aren't we being firm?"

"I'm firm when it's necessary," he replied. "Besides, work is a little crazy right now. I don't need to be worrying about you."

"I thought that Jacobs woman quit, and all the harassment stuff was dropped?"

"That's right, but I have a backload of rescheduled appointments due to the mediation meetings, and I need to make those up," he said. "Plus I'm determined to get home at a decent hour, so I can spend time with my family."

He caught Faith's eye again. This time he winked.

"Okay, okay," his mother agreed, positioning her body higher on the bed. "You sound just like your daddy, bossing me around."

"Well, if it works, I almost wish he were here so I could thank him for the gift of being able to intimidate when necessary."

Jonah's pager began to beep. It hadn't gone off all day. "Just when I thought I might need to check the battery," he said, looking at it. "I'll be right back."

He walked out to the nurse's desk to use the phone. It was good news. Amadi was doing so well he was being transferred from PICU. Jonah gave Dr. Warwick some instructions and told her he'd be there first thing in the morning. He returned the phone to the cradle and looked down the hall in the direction of his mother's room. Jonah couldn't believe his eyes. His father was standing there. He held a small bouquet of flowers in his hand. He could tell by the way he was twisting and turning that he was having a hard time deciding whether or not to go in.

Jonah took a deep breath. Martin was literally standing between him and the two women he loved.

It's time to forgive your father. Faith's words, his mother's words echoed in his mind. He had forgiven April without hesitation, and Faith had forgiven him. And he didn't believe in coincidences. Martin was here. He was here. Maybe it was time.

Jonah sighed and reluctantly moved forward.

Jonah raised the coffee cup to his lips and let the hot liquid burn as he sipped it down. He let his eyes scan the empty hospital cafeteria. He couldn't believe he was sitting here, sitting anywhere with his father.

"Your wife is beautiful," Martin said, pulling Jonah from his trance. Martin made an okay sign with his right hand. "Real good looking, son. Ya' mother showed me pictures of her before, but she's something else in person."

Jonah nodded. "She's a really good woman. I don't know what I would do without her."

"I remember saying that about ya' mother." His hands shook as he lowered the cup.

Alcoholism. Those shakes were a sure sign he was still a heavy drinker. Jonah winced and thought about his own drinking. He didn't want to end up like that.

He took in his father's appearance. Martin was clean shaven, dressed in a new polo shirt and a pair of khakis. He'd obviously dressed up for the occasion of visiting his mother.

"You done real good for yourself, son, being a doctor and all. I tell people that. and they never believe me."

"Dad."

"Son."

Both men spoke at the same time.

"Let me go first. I'm older, and I been waiting to say what I want to say for a long time." Martin's eyes were watery, his skin leathery in texture. He was in his early sixties, but like his mother, his appearance was far older than his years.

"I made a mistake with your mother. I made a mistake with you and Joshua. I should have known that being a man was about doing what needed to be done, not what I wanted to do."

Jonah took in a deep breath and sat back.

Martin couldn't control the spasmodic trembling of his hands. He clasped them together and hid them under the table.

"I cost your brother his life—maybe, probably. I should have handled things different." He had been looking down as he spoke, and now he raised his eyes to meet Jonah's. "I'm sorry. I been wanting to say that for more than twenty years. I'm sorry, son."

Jonah's heart seemed to melt instantly. Raw emotion ran unchecked through his veins like a wildfire. This apology was timely. It couldn't have been delivered a week before. It would have been rejected. He had forgiven his father when he walked down that aisle at the tent meeting earlier this week. It was incredible; the thing he thought would be so hard was so easy.

"Dad." He let the word settle in the air for a moment. He hadn't said it in more than twenty years, not to his father anyway. "I have let the anger over Joshua's death almost

destroy my life—my marriage—my family. I let the bitterness make me into the kind of man I never wanted to be."

"I'm sure you let it make you into the only example you
had," his father said, raising his eyes to meet Jonah's.
Jonah saw pain and weariness. Martin drove his fist into
the palm of his hand. "Don't be like me. Find a way to forgive me and God. If you ever listen to anything your old
man has to say, listen to this. Live your life. Joshua would
have wanted all of us to live *our* lives."

Jonah raised his coffee cup and sipped the liquid con-
tentedly. His father did the same until both their cups
were empty. Then he reached into his pocket and removed his wallet. He pulled out pictures, and one by one
placed them in front of his father. "This is my family.
Elise, my four-year-old and my adopted son, Eric. Faith's
first husband died."

His father took the pictures from him and stared at
them. Once again, his eyes filled with tears.

"They'd really like to meet their grandfather. My wife's
father is deceased and so are Eric's father's parents, so
you're the only one they have."

His father raised his eyes to meet his. The beginning of
a smile tipped the corners of his mouth. Jonah felt a
strange surge of affection that would have frightened him,
if it had not been for the peace that came with it.

. . . **the Lord giveth.**

Chapter 70

Through the slightly opened shutters, the morning sun shone, lighting up the floors of the bedroom and filling the room and her heart with its natural warmth. Faith rolled over on her side to face the windows as she continued to draw energy from the light that within seconds seemed to fill every corner of the bedroom.

Jonah slept bare-chested and his arms lay across her waist. She noted the time was almost seven A.M. She wanted to run, but she knew if she disturbed his arm, he would awaken. The man needed every minute of sleep he could get after the last few weeks' events.

"I'm already awake," he mumbled, surprising her.

"Oh," she replied, running her hands over his head, stroking his scalp like she knew he liked.

He opened his eyes and pulled his arm from around her. "I can feel that brain of yours churning. Do you run or do you stay?"

She smiled. "You're right."

He sat up and leaned against the headboard. "Of course,

you could stay right here and get your morning exercise. I'd be more than happy to help you burn some calories." He leaned forward and kissed her on the back of her neck.

Faith slid from under the covers. "That is not exercise, Dr. Morgan."

"I think it'll be a good workout for me."

"That's because you're out of shape." She slapped his foot and went into the bathroom.

She was halfway through her morning routine when Jonah tapped on the door and entered.

"Are you sure you want to run?" he asked, wrapping his arms around her waist and kissing her neck again.

"Actually, the only thing I'm *sure* of is that I don't ever want you to let me go," she said passionately. "You've got about two minutes, and then I expect you to join me in the bed."

She moved out of his grasp, hit him on the buttocks and left the bathroom. Running could wait.

"Are we going to see Grandma today?" Elise shoved a spoonful of breakfast cereal in her mouth.

"Actually, your grandmother is being released from the rehab center this morning, and your Dad is going to bring her here to the house to live with us for awhile." Faith put an apple in front of Elise.

"Really?" The excitement was audible in her tone.

"She needs someone to keep an eye on her for a few weeks, and I don't think anyone can do that better than us," Faith replied. "What do you think?"

"I think it's a good idea to have Grandma here. She likes to play Go Fish."

"Always searching for someone to beat at Go Fish," Jonah said, walking out of his office.

He kissed Elise on her forehead and took the seat next

to her. "We've got to be careful not to wear Grandma out with too many card games."

Faith placed a cup of coffee and a bowl of oatmeal in front of him.

"Thanks, babe." Jonah said grace and then asked Elise, "Where's your brother?"

"He's slower than me," Elise said, shrugging her shoulders and giggling after Jonah reached in to tickle her.

Jonah sat the child back, stood and walked to the intercom system on the wall. He raised a finger, hesitated, and then walked into the hallway.

"Eric, come down for breakfast," he yelled and then returned to the table.

Eric could be heard bolting down the stairs, and then appeared in the doorway of the two rooms.

"Morning," he mumbled as he slid into his seat at the table and began to pour himself some of the breakfast cereal that sat opened on the table.

"Good morning," Faith said, taking the milk out of the refrigerator. "Glad to have you."

Eric nodded.

"Don't you have some news to share with us?" Faith sat next to him.

Eric caught his father's eye, then he looked back down. After a few moments he said, "Our team made the championships."

"Yes, congratulations. Coach told me you have a game on Monday night," Jonah replied.

Eric popped his head back up. "You talked to Coach?"

"I stopped by his house yesterday on the way home. Not only did he tell me about the championships, but he told me about a really good baseball camp that begins two weeks after you get out of school."

Eric was still dumbstruck over the first statement. "You stopped by Coach's house?"

"I'm sorry, really sorry, I didn't make time for your games before, but I promise you, I won't miss any of the championship games. As a matter of fact, after we go get Grandma, I was thinking we could go to the batting cage. Get some practice in, so you'll be at your best Monday night."

Eric's smile was brighter than the sunlight that streamed in through the breakfast room window.

As they had many times before, Faith found her eyes filling with tears. Tears of joy.

Chapter 71

"Church, before I bring the message this week, I have a few comments and announcements to make." Pastor Kent stood in front of the congregation on what Faith thought had to be the most beautiful Sunday morning she'd ever seen in her life.

She looked down the pew to her right to see her children and Mom Morgan. She was recovering wonderfully, able to function at almost the same level she could before the stroke. She was selling the old house on Lowery Street, and although she refused to come live with them, she had agreed to move to a small, albeit upscale, adult assisted living community that was only ten minutes from the house. She had her own apartment, but there were nurses available if needed. Jonah was very happy about that.

Mom Morgan winked at Faith, and Faith winked back and raised her hand in a thumbs-up. Her prayer partners had been many. She had not gotten to this Sunday morning alone.

She sat back on the pew again, listening to pastor make announcements about awards for the upcoming graduates. Jonah, looking straight ahead, squeezed her hand and she turned her head slightly to look at him. His face held an expression of contentment that she honestly had never seen in all the years of their marriage. He had finally buried Joshua and made peace with his father. Just thinking about it set her heart to fluttering with joy.

Pastor Kent's words pulled her from her musing. "I know that all the women are looking forward to the conference in a few weeks. I have an exciting announcement to share with you." He walked from behind the pulpit to the front of the stage. "As you know, we have had a part-time management position advertised for the women's ministry. I'm pleased to announce that Sister Faith Morgan has accepted the position." A rousing round of applause and even a partial standing ovation filled the sanctuary.

She felt Jonah squeeze her hand. "Don't you just love a win-win," he whispered, poking his chest out like it had been *his* idea.

Faith smiled at his profile. She knew that feeling like she was unimportant without a job was just a symptom of what was going on with her marriage. When she talked to Pastor Kent about it, he convinced her that the same skills and talents she would be using at Bowen and Jefferies could be used in the church. And it was part-time, so she'd still have time to be there for her family.

"Sister Morgan, we look forward to seeing you in the office in a couple of weeks."

Everyone returned to their seats and Pastor Kent walked back to the pulpit and opened his Bible. "I'm excited this morning about the Word the Lord has given me. Today, I'm going to preach a message that I pray will challenge you to search your hearts and your lives. Go with me to Psalm 44, and we'll begin at verse 17. After a brief pause and the hurried rustling of Bible pages, Pastor Kent began to read. When he reached the 21st verse he repeated it with emphasis, ". . . *would not God have discovered it, since he knows the secrets of the heart?*" Then he continued. "Saints, so many Christians go through life with issues in their hearts. Some of us are so bitter and angry with people and circumstances that we never come to a place where we trust God enough to release these feelings to Him. We try to control things. We get in His way with our own agenda, and we make a mess of it all."

A chorus of "amens and preach pastor" rang out from the pews.

"We try to fix things that are broken, because the truth is in our heart, we don't trust God. He's not moving fast enough for us, so we make our own plan." Pastor said, "Some of us don't even come up with a plan. We just give up on God, because we think He doesn't really understand, or we blame Him. We come to church every Sunday, but in our hearts, we are not submitted to Him or His Word. And the truth is, you might as well let it go and give all your issues to Him. He knows how you feel. He knows that you're hurt, and most importantly, He knows the thoughts you want to hide from Him. '*Would not God have discovered it, since he knows the secrets of the heart?*' That's a powerful scripture."

Faith's own heart skipped a beat. She felt like he was talking directly to her row. But she knew the Lord spoke to all of His children. There were others struggling with the same things that Jonah and she had dealt with.

"After the choir renders a selection, I will begin teaching on the '*Issues of Heart*'."

She felt Jonah's eyes on her. "Looks like God's going to break it all the way down and make it a little plainer for me." He closed his Bible and placed it on the space next to him. "I'm all ears."

"No," Faith raised a hand to stroke his chin. "You, Dr. Morgan, are all heart."

Jonah stretched his arm across the back of the pew, and Faith laid her head on his shoulder. She closed her eyes and listened to the choir sing.

Sexual Harassment Disclaimer

Dear Readers:

Sexual harassment is a form of sex discrimination that violates Title VII of the Civil Rights Act of 1964. Unwelcome sexual advances, requests for sexual favors, and other verbal or physical conduct of a sexual nature constitutes sexual harassment when submission to or rejection of this conduct explicitly or implicitly affects an individual's employment, unreasonably interferes with an individual's work performance or creates an intimidating, hostile or offensive work environment.

Sexual harassment is a very real and serious problem in the U.S. workforce. In Fiscal Year 2007, EEOC received 12,510 charges of sexual harassment. 16.0% of those charges were filed by males. EEOC resolved 11,592 sexual harassment charges in FY 2007 and recovered $49.9 million in monetary benefits for charging parties and other aggrieved individuals (not including monetary benefits obtained through litigation).

The false allegation of sexual harassment in this book was not intended to diminish the very real problem many people face everyday when harassment occurs.

Respectfully,

Rhonda McKnight

Source
U.S. Equal Opportunity Commission Homepage at
 www.eeoc.gov/types/sexual_harassment.html

Reading Guide Questions

1. Faith feels pressure to do what she thinks a godly woman should do. Some of this is internal and some external. Do you feel the same thing, and do you think it comes from the Holy Spirit or our own minds? How do you feel when you hear sermons preached about the Proverbs 31 woman?

2. Throughout the book, Jonah is angry with God for the death of his brother. In Chapter 46 he is further distressed about his marital separation and the sexual harassment lawsuit. His mother talks to him about bad things happening to good people. How do you minister to people who are suffering from loss or trials in their lives?

3. Faith decides to keep a secret from Jonah because she believes he won't understand her decision. She is also angry about the fact that he has not given all he should to the marriage. One of the greatest hindrances to a comfortable walk with God as a Christian is the tendency to give into our emotions. What are your thoughts about this? What are some tools you use to control your emotions?

4. Jonah's mother chastises him about his estrangement from his father and the fact that he refers to his father by his first name. The Bible says in Exodus 20:12 *"Honour thy father and thy mother: that thy days may be long upon the land which The Lord thy God giveth thee"* (KJV). Do you think that Jonah has

a lack of honor for his father? Is it right to ever be estranged from a parent the way Jonah was from his father?

5. In Chapter 7, Faith remembers a magazine article where she read "there are always signs a person is not ready for marriage, often little things we dismiss as nothing should be examined a lot more carefully before the exchange of vows." Do you believe this is true? What about the idea that God brings people together? How does the idea of God's divine plan contrast with the notion of choosing your spouse based on perceived readiness and/or a set of qualities you determine to be godly?

6. Faith lies in bed thinking she should get on her knees and pray. What do you think about how, when, and where prayer should be done?

7. Faith's mother insists that Faith honors Jonah's wishes and not return to the workforce. Consider the principle in scripture that places the man as the authority over his family. Do you think a spouse should have that much control over what another wants to do? How should these disagreements be handled in a marriage?

8. Jonah is concerned about Amadi's prognosis. He grieves over the fact that people die every day and take their internal organs with them. Passages such as 1 Corinthians 6:19-20 are used to defend the idea that organs should not be harvested from a person's body. Are you an organ donor? Why or why not? If not, do you think Amadi's story has had any impact on the way you think about organ donation?

9. After years of marital strife, Faith decides leaving Jonah is the only way to get him to change. Do you think the Bible makes a provision for separation based on anything other than an extramarital affair?

10. In Chapter 49, Faith thinks she should resign from the women's ministry because she and Jonah are separated, but Pastor Kent encourages her to continue. Do you agree with his position on why she should stay in leadership?

11. Faith's mother warns her about talking to Yvette about her marriage. She tells her to talk to someone who's been married that's older and wiser than her. Do you agree with this position? Why or why not?

12. Jonah begins to pray to God over several chapters of the book before he's reconciled to Christ. Do a study of the following scriptures: Exodus 2:23-25, Exodus 3:9-10, Exodus 22:22-23, Numbers 20:15-16, Psalm 9:12, Isaiah 30:19 and Isaiah 30:1-3; 9-11. What do you think about the prayers of the backslidden and/or unsaved?

13. April has decided to end her life. Some people believe suicide is an unforgivable sin because the dead do not have an opportunity to confess their sins and repent. What is your opinion about that? If a Christian commits suicide is he/she still forgiven?

14. God's leadership and direction take many forms. God leads though His written Word, through wisdom, through godly counsel, through circumstance, and by direct communication from His Holy Spirit. What are some examples of this in the book?

About the Author

Rhonda McKnight is the Vice President of *Faith Based Fiction Writers*, in Atlanta. A natural born orator, she looks forward to reaching out to readers and aspiring writers through book club meetings and writing workshops. A native of Asbury Park, New Jersey, she is a graduate of the infamous *Fashion Institute of Technology*, and the prestigious *Mercer University*. Rhonda has built a career in human services as a regional program specialist for a federal food and nutrition program, but considers the ministry of writing to be her true calling. She resides in Atlanta, Georgia with her family.

UC His Glory Book Club members pledge to:

- Follow the guidelines of *UC His Glory Book Club.*
- Provide input, opinions, and reviews that build up, rather than tear down.
- Commit to purchasing, reading and discussing featured book(s) of the month.
- Respect the Christian beliefs of *UC His Glory Book Club.*
- Believe that Jesus is the Christ, Son of the Living God

We look forward to the online fellowship.

Many Blessings to You!

Shelia E Lipsey
President
UC His Glory Book Club

**Visit the official Urban Christian Book Club website at *www.uchisglorybookclub.net*

Urban Christian His Glory Book Club!

Established January 2007, **UC His Glory Book Club** is another way by which to introduce to the literary world, Urban Book's much-anticipated new imprint, **Urban Christian** and its authors. We are an online book club supporting Urban Christian authors by purchasing, reading and providing written reviews of the authors' books that are read. *UC His Glory* welcomes both men and women of the literary world who have a passion for reading Christian based fiction.

UC His Glory Book Club is the brainchild of Joylynn Jossel, Author and Executive Editor of Urban Christian and Kendra Norman-Bellamy, Copy Editor for Urban Christian. The book club will provide support, positive feedback, encouragement and a forum whereby members can openly discuss and review the literary works of Urban Christian authors. In the future, we anticipate broadening our spectrum of services to include: online author chats, author spotlights, interviews with your favorite Urban Christian author(s), special online groups for *UC His Glory Book Club* members, ability to post reviews on the website and amazon.com, membership ID cards, *UC His Glory* Yahoo Group and much more.

Even though there will be no membership fees attached to becoming a member of *UC His Glory Book Club*, we do expect our members to be active, committed and to follow the guidelines of the Book Club.